A Rebellious Oak

by Margaret Callow

Published in 2012 by the Running Hare Press

Margaret Callow asserts her moral right to be identified as the author of this work.

ISBN 978-0-9555478-36

A CIP Catalogue record for this book is available from the British Library.

This book is a work of fiction. Many historical events and characters appear. The author has as far as possible tried to keep to the truth where these events and people are concerned. If the story includes any errors or omissions the author and publisher apologize.

Cover illustration by Valery Larson © 2012, www.zhibit.org/crosseyeddog
Book design by Graham Land Creative Limited, Wymondham, 01953 603200
Printed in Norwich U.K. by Page Brothers

We pray your grace...that from henceforth no man shall enclose anymore...We pray your grace...that all men may enjoy their commons with all profits...We pray that all bond men may be made free, for God made all free with his precious blood shedding...'

Extracts from twenty nine statements contained in the "Requests and Demands" petition sent by Robert Kett to the King in the enclosure-related rebellion in Norfolk in 1549.

Wikipedia: Kett's Rebellion.

– Characters –

REBELS

Robert Kett, – tanner, yeoman farmer, leader of the rebellion
William Kett, – mercer, grazier, brother to Robert

Peasants.
Council of Wymondham.
Thom Barwick
John Moulder
Will Medler
Richard Mayhew
Matthew Mayhew
Giles son of Rupert
Edmund
Arthur

Others
Francis Smith, – serf to John Flowerdew
Elias of Attleborough, – cousin of Will Medler
Martha Barwick, – wife of Thom
Sible Moulder, – wife of John
Alice Kett, – wife of Robert
Mary-Ann, – wife of Arthur
Jack & Humfrey Moore
William Fulke, – butcher, responsible for the death of Lord Sheffield in
    Norwich
John Flotman, – leader of a group of Norwich rebels
Edgerly, – servant of Roger Woodhouse

ESTABLISHMENT

Hampton Court Palace
King Edward V1
Edward Seymour, – The Duke of Somerset, Lord Protector – uncle to the
    King.
Thomas Seymour, Baron Sudely, – brother to Edward
William Parr 1st Marquis of Northampton 1st Earl of Essex
John Dudley 1st Duke of Northumberland Earl of Warwick

Philip de Montfort, – private secretary to Edward Seymour (changed allegiance)
William Page
Charles Tyler
George Shelbourne
Edmund, Lord Sheffield
Captain Bury, – Aide to Earl of Warwick
York Herald, – an officer of the College of Arms
Pursiuvant Groves, – ranking one below a herald at the College of Arms.
Charles Dethick, – King's Herald
General Harry Sutton, – King's Envoy

Norfolk Administration
Thomas Codde, – Mayor of Norwich
Augustine Steward, – Deputy Mayor of Norwich
Sir Edmund Wyndham, – High Sheriff of Norwich
Thomas Aldrich, – senior Alderman
Nicholas Brownlow, – Mayor of Great Yarmouth

Notables
John Flowerdew, – wealthy landowner and lawyer
Squire Green of Wylby nr Attleborough
Squire Hobart of Hingham
Edmund Pynchyn, – city gentleman
Robert Watson, – preacher from Norwich
Sir Thomas Gawdy, – Recorder & MP for Kings Lynn
Sir David Melloe, – affluent builder
Robert Chase, – banker & Under Lord Treasurer of the Privy Coffers
The Appleyard Brothers, – wool merchants & brothers-in-law to Robert Kett.
Roger Woodhouse, – banker & landowner

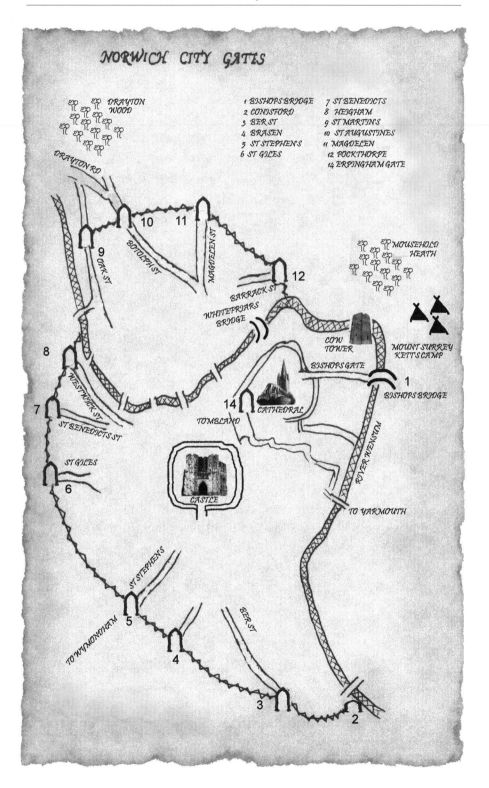

NORWICH CITY GATES

1 BISHOPS BRIDGE   7 ST BENEDICTS
2 CONISFORD   8 HEIGHAM
3 BER ST   9 ST MARTINS
4 BRASEN   10 ST AUGUSTINES
5 ST STEPHEN'S   11 MAGDELEN
6 ST GILES   12 POCKTHORPE
   14 ERPINGHAM GATE

Wymondham
Winter 1549

Loud and troubled, the squeal of a distressed animal reverberated through the trees and across the hollows then stopped abruptly. In a small farmyard a woman shielded her eyes and looked into the distance. The scenery still crisp from the last snowfall showed her nothing unusual.

No matter what the time of year the changing landscape in the Tiffey Valley drew the gaze. Large spreads of dense woodland carried a melancholy air. Passive slopes and gentle rises of rough pasture softened the view. Ignored by the beasts put to graze, great tufts of coarse grass mouldered in peace amongst meadow land whilst on dark rich soil, grain ripened in wide ochre swathes.

Nourished by the easy flow of the river, green ditches thrived. It seeped precious moisture to feed water meadows, colour washed by wild flowers in the summer and when autumn tired of shedding leaves of gold, reds and browns, it allowed winter to supply a white mantle to hold fast until spring arrived.

The woman moved quietly about her chores. Like all of her status Martha Barwick didn't shirk her share of hard work nor disrespect the land which permitted a meagre existence for the peasants in Norfolk. Those who tilled the soil paid no attention to words in political places nor would many of them grasp the significance of them. Yet changes would be made as surely as the seasons turned on the land which succoured them.

When Martha entered the barn she inhaled its aroma with deep satisfaction. The mix of hay, straw and livestock gave off a comfortable smell. An atmosphere she felt safe in. At the sight of her a thin cockerel collected his ladies and strutted his way towards her. None of the hens carried much weight since their grain was rationed and the earth offered little nourishment until spring arrived. With heads tipped and button-bright eyes fixed on her the birds gathered round her feet and she spoiled them as she always did.

"I shall only give you a little. If Thom was here, he'd say something. Now let me be. I've vegetables to find and not many of them left by the look of it," she said.

A handful of grain tossed onto the floor, she picked her way between the fowl to reach the storage rack. Bending over she sorted through the turnips and heard nothing over the sound of the chickens. When suddenly she was robbed of light she turned to see the cause.

The men startled her and fearful, she backed against the bales. Lances of straw pricked through her skirt, but she ignored the discomfort. Their appearance alone frightened her. Coarse-featured with close-set eyes and unkempt ginger hair they bore a familial resemblance to one another. Dressed in filthy clothes they both gave off an unpleasant smell which managed to overwhelm the gentle air of the barn.

"Good day, Mistress Barwick," the older of the two said his smile marred by rotten teeth.

"Who are you and what do you want?" Martha said. "If it's my husband you've come to see, he'll be home very soon."

Her courage sought and found she walked towards them and hoped they would move. Neither shifted a step. The older man shook his head.

"I don't think so. We saw him. After a deer he was on the top pastures. He didn't seem in a hurry did he, boy?"

The youth snorted and nodded in agreement. He might have been considered handsome had he not the loose mouth and the vacant stare of one who was slightly witless.

"When are we going to do it, Uncle?" He slid his hand to his chin to wipe away the dribble.

"You hold your patience. Where are your manners? Tell the lady your name."

"Thank you, it doesn't matter. Please let me pass. Whatever it is you want you must wait for Thom," Martha said firmly her hands clenched so they shouldn't see them tremble.

They stepped forward, but the doorway was still out of reach and she felt the terror rise inside her. Their faces were clear to her once they moved and she thought she'd seen the older man at work on neighbouring land.

"Moses," the youth spluttered through a fatuous giggle.

"And I'm Francis, tenant of Squire Flowerdew, but I also carry out business for him," Francis said, his skinny chest thrust out with self-importance. "That's why we're here."

"I still don't see how I can help you," Martha said her smile polite despite her trepidation. "What business the Squire has with my husband is nothing to do with me."

For a moment she thought she heard footfall, but her silent prayer went unanswered when Thom didn't appear. She took deep breaths to calm herself and edged forward. About to dive through the small gap to escape the barn, she saw Francis stoop and pick up one of her hens.

"Get it, Uncle, get it," Moses shrieked. Enthusiasm made the flush-faced youth bounce up and down. His ripped jerkin flapped against his oddly bent legs when he moved, a noise which sent the hens into a huddle of alarm.

Anger replaced Martha's unease. "Give me that bird and get out of here," she snapped, her hand outstretched to take it.

Francis reached into his pocket and the dull glint of metal surprised her. For a moment she puzzled over what it might be. By then it was too late. The chicken's throat gaped and spurted a scarlet stream of blood. She felt the warm droplets on her skin whilst more trailed across the front of her body. Her hand over her mouth Martha recoiled in horror. She was no stranger to the culling of animals, but under these circumstances it was heinous. Her cry of distress went unheard over the hysterical laughter from Moses.

Dropped on the earth the hen jigged for a second, its plumage spoilt by blood and dust until the body finally stilled.

"Squire Flowerdew says to tell you, the first one is for the number of times your animals have spoilt his crops," Francis said with the toe of his boot directed at the dead bird.

"No, no. You must stop. By the Almighty, I don't understand." Martha said.

Tears mingled with the blood on her face so when they dropped they tinged her apron pink. Her confusion clearly amused Francis and he smirked. Another hen in his arms he said.

"The Squire said you wouldn't understand that's what he said, so this is so you do proper- like. Do something useful, boy, hold her still."

Fear clawed her throat and agitated her heartbeat, but her eyes were fixed on the pitchfork which rested on the wall nearby. She was about to reach for it, but Moses moved fast to hold her arms. His sweat- ridden palms on her flesh made her flinch and she thought she might faint. With the strength of youth in his body she was pinioned close to him and could feel his hot breath on her neck. All she could do was pray for some sort of end to the nightmare.

"Can I do one, Uncle?" Moses called over her shoulder, his body a squirm of excitement.

Francis debated and then nodded.

"Just the one, mind," he warned, and passed over the knife.

Martha closed her eyes her gut knotted with nausea. When she heard the youth's elated shriek and felt herself prisoner again she knew it was over. One after the other, Francis dispatched the rest of the hens. He muttered throughout and Martha caught words like patience, fair, oxen and neighbour: And always the same name, Flowerdew. Martha realised it was some sort of punishment ordered by their neighbour. The cockerel was last. She heard its strident complaint turn into a gurgled rasp followed by another demented cry from Moses.

When she looked, the gruesome sight left her stunned. Her precious birds strewn across the floor reduced to piles of feathers and gore. Francis panted and sweat ran from his brow and clustered on the mass of straggly hair on his cheeks and chin. He wiped the knife blade down his stained breeches and said.

"This is a warning, Mistress Barwick. Tell that husband of yours next time it might be you. Squire Flowerdew doesn't care for those who break the law. His land is his. Best not let anything of yours stray on there again."

She thought they were about to leave. Her energy drained, her feeble efforts to get free of Moses were useless. Francis was already by the door.

"Tell him to let me go," her words clung to the roof of her mouth and she was forced to whisper.

"You heard the pretty lady, Moses. Time we were going," he said.

The arms round her didn't slacken. Instead she felt a hand on her shoulder and damp fingers started to grope down the front of her gown.

"But, Uncle," he slobbered, his drool warm on her flesh.

"No, boy, you behave yourself. We've done what we came to do," Francis said with an impatient hiss of breath.

For a moment she was too horrified to move. When the fingers tightened on her breast strength flooded through her veins and gave her the will she needed. Moses wasn't prepared for her sudden wrench as she hurled herself away from him. Unconcerned Francis leant against the side of the door. At the sound of material torn apart he laughed and louder still when Moses lunged at Martha and missed.

"That'll teach you, boy. Now, come on. We should have been gone a long while ago."

His nephew's expression changed to a sulky look as he straightened his clothes and swept his lank hair away from his face.

"Sorry about that, Mistress," Francis murmured. "He's just a boy, one of those things..."

He cuffed Moses with a playful hand and pushed him into the yard. As the crunch of their feet on the frozen ground faded, Martha sank to the floor too weak to weep.

A grin creased the weathered skin of Thom Barwick's face as he anticipated Martha's smile. He pulled out the arrow and examined it for damage. Satisfied there was none he wiped its tip on the hoar-crusted grass. No longer lush the green blades bent easily with the weight of bright blood and wisps of the rabbit's entrails. The arrow returned to his quiver he leant against the twisted trunk of an ancient elm. Now a meal was assured he could afford a few moments to rest. The deer had led him in a vigorous chase when, about to take aim, he lost sight of it. Only by chance did he notice a rabbit nibbling on a turnip top.

Although past his prime as he approached forty, hard work kept Thom lean and well muscled. On a well worn path he covered the miles with an easy lope, yew bow on his shoulder and a rabbit hanging at his side. The thought of his good wife's cooking skills speeded his step towards home. With a handful of vegetables, fresh-gathered wild herbs and rabbit flesh she would create a stew exquisite in flavour.

A weak afternoon sun was about to slip out of sight. Its meagre warmth touched his back through his coarse linen shirt as he threw open the flimsy timbered door.

"Martha…" Puzzled by her absence, he called again. "Martha, are you there?"

There was no comfort in the silence which greeted him. Instead he felt disturbed. Tossing the rabbit on the step, he saw the common room was as neat as usual. It smelt of fresh straw, tallow and newly baked bread. His wife knew how to keep a good home. He expected no less.

To look in the barn was for him more out of habit, he did not expect to find his wife there. Made of the same mud plastered branches, ox hair and dung as his two roomed home it was only a little larger and wouldn't take long to check. It housed bales of straw, a few vegetables and odd tools. When he halted in the doorway it took him a moment to steady himself. Martha looked up at him her coif dislodged from her head. She sat among wood shavings and shreds of straw. Her forehead was smeared with blood, more stained her white apron red. When he looked further ruby stains splattered the earth floor in all directions.

"Blood?" he said. "In God's name, wife, what's happened? Have you fallen?"

"It's not mine," she whispered and spread her hands wide, a futile gesture of explanation. Then he saw, brown, white, black, mottled, her chickens lying nearby, each with its throat cut.

"They killed them all," she said dully.

"Who?"

"They said to tell you it's a warning. Next time, it will be me." Her words tailed off, overcome by sobs.

On his haunches he pulled her toward him. His broad hand offered awkward comfort as he stroked her dishevelled hair. The rough wool of her dress grazed his cheek when she sank against him. His hand dropped to her shoulder. Startled by the sudden feel of her flesh he cast his eyes down and saw the start of a jagged rent exposing the pale skin of her upper arm. To look more closely he held her away from him. The tear continued its journey stopping just above her breast but instead of pallor the exposed skin was the colour of crushed elderberries.

"How did that happen?" His words ended in a barely disguised sound of pain.

"I stumbled," she said.

He saw her avert her eyes and knew she lied. Anger made his movement rough and she winced when he forced her chin up so their gaze met.

"I'm sorry," he whispered, appalled at his clumsiness. "Martha, we have no secrets between us. Who did this? Was it them? Was it the men who slaughtered the birds?"

Silence hung between them, an awkward moment of uncertainty. Then he saw a single tear hover before it trickled down her face. His thumb looked large against her frail cheekbone as he sought to dry her skin.

"Forgive me, Thom..."

Without warning his stomach heaved and he almost choked. He swallowed hard. "Did they...?"

The shake of her head was emphatic. "It was only one of them, the other stopped him. I swear by the Almighty nothing happened."

"You have to tell me, who?"

He could see Martha was in such shock it took her every effort to focus her thoughts. He in turn fought with his rage. As he waited for her to speak he vowed whoever was responsible would not go unpunished.

"Two of John Flowerdew's men came. The older one said John had run out of patience. He's warned you many times to keep the cattle off his fields. Today they were found taking his turnip crop. As a good neighbour, he has tried to overlook this but will do so longer."

"Good neighbour, good neighbour? What sort of good neighbour sends his men to ravish another man's wife? By God Almighty, he'll pay for this."

"No, Thom, I beg you. Enough blood has been spilt, I was spared and we can replace the birds."

"Replace them, how woman? We have scarce enough coppers as it is. The bean harvest was poor and winter grips us hard. Besides this is no time to talk of such things. Not after this."

A sudden gust of wind raced through the building. Over the window slits, cobwebs draped like veils shivered and the listless plumage of dead birds fluttered. Martha trembled and clung closer to Thom.

"Go back to the cottage. I'll finish off here," he said with a curt nod at the carnage.

He helped her to her feet and spat on the corner of his kerchief to gently wipe her forehead. He waited until he saw her disappear then collected up the chickens in a skep. His face screwed into a scowl he ran his hand over the breast of one. His fingers found little meat, but a mouthful from each would make a meal.

He put the skep in a corner until later. In the half-light their pale, scaly legs stuck out of the heap of feathers at grotesque angles. The sight of them only served to increase his fury.

"A curse on you and your spawn, John Flowerdew, may you rot in Hell," he swore as he mixed scraps with mash for the swine and fetched them fresh water from the stream. Next he checked a beast soon to calve and counted the geese before he shut them away.

The jobs were routine which allowed his anger to fester as he completed them. As he worked ugly images of filthy hands at work on his wife's body threatened to overwhelm his reason. He needed to stop and breathe deeply whilst he struggled to control his temper. His mood was no better as he wrenched off his boots and untied the pieces of cloth bound round his bare legs. Leaving both by the door he followed the smell of cooking coming from the common room.

Martha stood stirring the iron pot. Her dress and apron had been replaced by clean ones and her russet-coloured hair was brushed and coiled neatly. For a moment his calm returned at the sight of her. He brushed his lips on the exposed skin at the nape of her neck and she flinched at the feel of his unruly beard. When she turned to reprove him he saw her eyes were still reddened from tears, but her pale face was composed and her mouth curved into a weak smile.

"The rabbit was young, it won't take long," she said.

Deftly she cleared the table of fur, entrails and vegetable parings. He took her hand and touched her fingers. "How quick you are. These work miracles, do you know that? Skinned and gutted, you have that rabbit in the pot in no time. I'm a lucky man and I love you, Mistress Barwick," he said soft pink flushing the brown of his weather-worn cheeks.

Her giggle at his obvious embarrassment made more warmth rush to his cheeks. He found it hard to express his feelings and knew some thought him a hard man. A harsh existence toughened them all and Thom more than some wore his trials like a coat of armour. Even the timbre of his voice could intimidate although he tried to moderate it.

When she tilted her head he looked into her rich brown eyes. They told of her love for him and it was all he needed to know. He put his hand on her arm and hoped it confirmed his reply. Her husky laugh told him it had.

He watched her and admired her shape still slim and nubile as when she agreed to be his wife. Yet how they'd both prayed that one day her stomach would swell and hold the child they longed for. When it didn't happen and with the passage of the years both began to doubt it ever would.

He stocked the open hearth with logs and sat beside the fire on a stool.

At first smoke curled from the green wood in a surly swirl, but then as draughts forced it out of a hole in the roof it drew straight and burned well. Contentment eluded him despite the quiet domesticity. It usually pleased him to see Martha about her work, her quiet footfall and capable hands instilling peace in him. But it was not so today. Today he felt upset and angry as his gaze followed her about the room.

Pain pulsed across his temple and he held a hand to it as if to push away his dark thoughts about his neighbour. Local squire and lawyer John Flowerdew was an unpopular man. A loud- mouthed, blustering sort of fellow who deemed his wealth and social position put him above the law and civility to those who crossed his path. Thom's animals frequently strayed onto John's land and were the cause of many heated arguments between them. But it had never been more than that. Martha's ordeal and the loss of their stock changed things and were not something he could forgive.

The pastures of the Tiffey Valley were good ground. Each joined the next in a seamless green coverlet. Handed down through the family Thom's smallholding was about thirty acres give or take. Without fencing the boundaries were no more than a gentlemen's agreement, a handshake and a good- natured nod. To graze animals and grow food was free to all. A means of existence for centuries, but this was a time when the wealthy grew more greedy at the expense of the poor. Now land tenure was the cause of much unrest throughout the land and when Thom heard talk of it he felt fearful. His sigh was loud and his hand heavy when he mopped up meat juices on his platter with the last of the dumpling. Puffball light he savoured the taste, but it felt no more than solid dough in his mouth.

"You look displeased, Thom. Is the food not to your liking?" Martha's voice wavered and her concern showed.

"A fine meal, wife," he said trying to keep lightness in his tone. She smiled her gratitude and set to washing the dishes in a bucket of water drawn from the well.

It allowed Thom to think about his revenge without disturbance.

Wood, thatch and size distinguished John Flowerdew's manorial abode from those of lesser means in the village. Beside the manor house an established kitchen garden and well cared for lawn marked the start of his extensive acreage. Although it was mid-evening the frame of the house dozed in the unexpected warmth of the February day. It would soon change as a blood-red sky told of another frosty night.

At the sound of horses outside the window, John stirred himself from the comfort of his armchair. Overheated he loosened the neck of his shirt and frowned at the bank of logs ablaze on the fire. His wife complained of the cold whatever the time of year which exasperated him.

Agnes snored on in the chair opposite. Dressed in purple satin, a colour which only served to highlight her unattractive looks, her rapid breaths fluttered her lace collar with each exhalation. As he passed, his fingers loitered over her thick wool shawl. She didn't stir as he plucked a vestige of food from the yarn and flicked it into the fireplace. He left the room closing the door noisily behind him and went to see who was calling at this hour.

Before he opened the front door he reached for his silk handkerchief and dabbed his face. Whenever he perspired sweat collected in knotted scar tissue which laced the top of his cheek. Not only did it irritate his flesh, but embarrassed him too and the damage did nothing to enhance his thin, dour features. Comfortable again, he reached for the door knob.

The two men he'd sent to the Barwick's cottage stood by the step. They held their shaggy cobs steady so as not to disturb the raked stones of the drive. Raising a candle stick high to illuminate their faces, John nodded. Satisfied with their identity, he beckoned them nearer to the door and said.

"Is it done, Francis?"

A weasel-faced straggle-bearded fellow nodded and stepped closer. Henry sniffed and moved back a pace. Downwind, Francis smelt far from flavoursome.

"Aye, 'tis indeed, Master. He'll think twice before he lets his beasts stray again."

Gratified, John smiled, but the twist of his lips made it a sneer. Francis' younger companion sniggered as he rocked back and forth on his heels.

"I did well, didn't I, Uncle?" he said, tugging at the edge of the other's buff-jerkin for approval.

"Yes, boy, you did very well," his uncle replied. "Killed a chicken..."

"God's truth man, surely you didn't allow him near with a knife. The boy isn't right in the head."

"No, just the one, for his learning," his uncle interrupted anxious to reassure.

"What about the woman Uncle? Tell him about the woman." The lad grew agitated and slobber dripped from his flaccid lips and dangled above his chin.

John frowned. "What does the boy mean?"

Francis touched his temple with a dirty, nail-bitten finger and rolled his eyes.

"Take no notice, Master the boy is feeble minded, his mind wanders, he can't help it. If you could see your way to settling with me we'll be gone from here."

The candle flame faded and then flared in the evening breeze. John put it back on the massive oak side table and felt in his pocket. From its depths a money bag made a reluctant appearance. His bony fingers probed the leather and made the coins clink as he sorted them.

"How much did we say?" he murmured.

"Two groats and a weeks' fishing in your river," Francis said.

"Was it not one groat and two days?"

Defiant, Francis stood his ground. "You said a week, Master."

"Three days at most," John countered.

Enjoying the haggle over reward his nephew's face wore an inane grin as he looked first at one and then the other. Francis sighed heavily.

"Three days it is then and what of the groats?"

"I'll give you one groat, take it or not," John shrugged.

Suddenly the peeved voice of Agnes filtered into the hallway. "John, John, is the door open? I can feel a fierce draught."

In haste the coin exchanged hands and John started to close the door. At the last moment he called out.

"I need you tomorrow. I'm thinking about making some changes to the land. Come a little after dawn and don't bring your nephew."

He watched as the couple seated themselves on their horses. Francis raised a stick to acknowledge the request and they cantered down the drive.

"The boy's nothing but a fool," John uttered with contempt.

Mist hung like pale smoke above the river when John took his first walk of the day. A drape of it smothered the alder trees. Here and there the occasional bare branch protruded like stick arms that begged release. Eager to make sure he'd selected the right arable land to enclose he moved quickly. His feet crunched on frosted grass and the vapours of his breath hung around him in the cold air. As he paced the perimeters of the pastures he'd chosen, he ignored Thom Barwick's oxen grazing nearby and both his bean field and the last of the onion crop. He included common land in his calculations. As long as they favoured him their ownership was of no consequence.

Once he had enough for his purpose he could set Francis to work on the hedges. He'd give him a small meadow to start with until he was satisfied with the work. With the fields properly enclosed, he would then be able to start his new and very profitable venture. Idle chatter he'd overheard in the Cattle Market in Norwich set him thinking about buying sheep. The demand for wool had seen prices soar, so the farmers said as they waited for the sales to begin. Since then, anticipating further wealth, he thought of little else.

He was aware that taking common land was illegal, but when it suited, he and the law were one and in his opinion the Government dallied on such matters. His actions would have a profound effect on those with common rights but he thought them too unworthy for him to waste breath on.

Satisfied with his deliberations he turned for home. His jaunty step and smug smile were the mark of a man in good spirits. He wondered if Francis had remembered to call early and indeed he saw him as he emerged through the gate from the apple orchard.

Uneasy in the company of such a shifty- eyed and unsavoury looking person Agnes left him on the step. John understood perfectly. He was barely able to mask the expression of distaste which registered on his face when he looked at the other's clothing. The front of the serf's tunic from the neck to the knee was crusted with spilt food, his trousers no better and the ill-fitting sheepskin waistcoat had clearly not been cured. It gave off the odour of decomposition and John fought the urge to retch. He fumbled urgently to find his kerchief and blew his nose several times.

"Good morning, Master, not ill I hope," Francis said his scrawny arms hugged against his body for warmth.

"Nothing but a case of nose dribble, it's the chill air," John replied, keeping the cloth close to his face.

"So, Master, yesterday you talked of your land. What is it you want?"

"I have work for you if you're interested. Likely you'll need help though, I want no delays."

John waved at Francis to join him.

"What sort of work would that be?" Francis said as he increased his stride to catch up.

"Follow me and I'll show you."

The two of them walked the meadows. John's arms flailed in the air as he indicated where the fences should go. If he was surprised at the idea Francis kept silent. Face expressionless he merely nodded every so often. Relieved the serf offered no interruption, John continued.

"Hedges here perhaps? Use plenty of brush, I need them high," he said, his stick jabbed in the direction of Thom Barwick's vegetable plots and the meadow beyond it.

It was then Francis found his voice.

"Surely not there Master? Barwick plants that land and his father afore him. It's common land. Always has been. Over there belongs to John Moulder. It's his swine which run there."

John tightened his lips "Once, I grant you but not anymore. I intend to keep sheep and that's fine looking turf."

Privately he congratulated himself on clever timing. Coming so soon after the chickens he doubted Barwick would find the courage to protest about the fences now he'd seen what power could achieve. A good job, a very good job, he'd taught him a lesson, he thought.

Francis wasn't sure whether the cold or anger accounted for the sudden high colour in John's cheeks. Not anxious to find out, he said no more. His mind was at work though. He knew all the common land was evenly distributed amongst the villagers. The squire's sudden claim on it would cause trouble and more beside when they found out.

It wasn't he particularly cared what happened to the land. As long as he paid his rent on time his smallholding wasn't affected. What bothered him was his own safety when the likes of Thom Barwick found out who'd put up the squire's hedges.

Since his idiotic nephew put his hands on the woman he'd kept well away from the Barwick's home and advised his nephew to do the same. For a moment he wondered if he really wanted the work. On the way back, John strode ahead and Francis debated. He knew he had little choice, his thin wife and six undernourished children were powerful images in his conflict. Besides his status as a serf, demanded he repay his squire on demand. Through the fog of his thoughts he heard John say.

"So when can you start?"

The decision made for him, Francis said. "We haven't discussed favours yet."

"I shall need to work out the costs. It will be the usual arrangement. You may gather dead-wood for your fire, apples when the fruits are ripe, nuts too provided there is a good crop. Will you be working on your own? Time is important. The animals will arrive in less than a week, a thousand of them."

Francis sucked air in through the gaps in his teeth, a habit of his when he pondered on things. His master was not known to be a patient man and his irritation showed.

"Well, will you or won't you need help?" John asked his voice terse.

Francis pushed aside his worn felt hat and scratched his head.

"My nephew is a willing boy, I could ask him."

"Your nephew is a simpleton," John retorted rudely. "I doubt he would know one end of a thorn hedge from another."

Far from being offended, Francis laughed. "He's slow witted right enough, but helpful."

"Suit yourself but I shan't pay the boy," John said when they reached the front door. "We'll say tomorrow then. Wood poles, hazel sticks, willow, thorn branches, whatever you can find. Use what you want but the fences must be stout mind. I don't want my stock to wander. Is that clear?"

"Yes, Master." Francis was uneasy, still concerned about payment. "And will there be any other rewards?"

"You demand too much, Francis. Perhaps you may take a fish or two in return for digging out some ditches when the fences are done." John said quickly, anxious to rid himself of Francis's company

But Francis hadn't finished. "Then there's my vittles," he persisted. "I shall need a little something to keep me going. Its hard work is fencing."

With a flash of red and tawny brown, a pair of pheasants came in low across the meadow. John narrowed his eyes and watched them thoughtfully until they dropped out of sight.

"I daresay Mistress Flowerdew can find you a pheasant carcase to gnaw on," he said over his shoulder as he stepped into the house.

Francis groaned inwardly. All was not going well. Firewood apart, it was still only February. He would wait a long time for his dues to be paid. "But..."

The links of the metal bell pull quivered as the door closed with a bang. Francis waited in hope the door might reopen. Then he might get another chance to plead his case. He bent to the urn of bulbs beside the step. A few spikes of green thrust themselves out of the soil. He thought quickly. Mistress Flowerdew was protective of her blooms. If she watched she'd likely reward him for his care so he pulled out a few imaginary weeds.

The door flew open. "Just what are you doing?"

"I begs your pardon, Master." Francis whined, a servile smirk on his face.

"You're nothing but a wretch. Get going before I set the dogs on you. And make sure you start work immediately."

John didn't shut the door again. Instead he peered through a narrow gap until he was sure Francis had reached the end of the drive.

Melancholy sounds made by his three oxen first alerted Thom that something was wrong. Bereft of anything to graze they stood bewildered amongst the shrivelled bean pods. Their plaintive calls persisted as he left the barn where he'd been repairing a broken axe. In fear of some dreadful accident he didn't bother to put on his jerkin. Outside the cottage door Martha was stuffing fresh straw into their pallets. As he ran towards the field she threw down her armful and followed him.

"Thom, what is it? Wait for me."

He stopped and chided himself for leaving her. Since events in the barn he made sure she was rarely left alone. In his present frame of mind he trusted no one.

Despite the turn of the year cold still prevailed and the crisp air blew puffs of their breath into hazy shapes and suffused their cheeks with bright colour. Together they slowed to scramble up the slope to a vantage point that overlooked the meadows. Thom got to the top first.

"They're alright," he called. "They've got themselves into the bean field, that's all."

Relaxed by the relief in his voice, Martha stopped to catch her breath. His sudden change of tone alarmed her.

"Wait a minute, what this?"

He pointed and her eyes followed his finger. "It looks like a hedge, some sort of fence," she said. "No, it can't be. Who would put up such a thing?"

They both strained to see better through a landscape dulled grey by the low clouds.

"That's why the beasts complain. I checked them first thing this morning. Somebody's moved them," he said, his brow ridged in annoyance.

"Isn't that another hedge round our onion patch," she said, concentrating on the fields below them. The sudden hiss of Thom's breath was impossible to miss.

"Look hard, wife. All we have for grazing is where the oxen are standing. There's one there and another. The bastard has fenced us out," he snarled.

He knew immediately who was responsible and had John Flowerdew stood before him at that moment, he would likely have killed him. He felt her hand on his sleeve to calm him.

"Who would do this Thom?"

"Who do you think? Who is it who lays claim to all the land around here?"

"You believe its Flowerdew? Perhaps that explains why I saw his serf, Francis, with a cartload of brushwood only yesterday," she said. "He passed at the end of the track but I thought nothing of it."

"Now we know why," Thom said, with a wild wave of his hand. "Do you see the sheep in the corner? There are hundreds of them by the look of it, well we'll see about that."

Rage sucked the colour from his face and tightened his mouth. He started down the slope and heard her running behind him. He knew she'd be frightened, she always was when she saw him angered. Her hand clung to his arm as she tried to slow him.

"What will you do?"

He shook her off roughly.

"Give me peace, wife. I have to think."

Martha tried her best to make the stew wholesome. Without meat the flavour was thin and the bean pods tough and stringy. They'd kept them back as unfit to sell and would have fed the animals. She was glad to see the last of them. Thom made no comment and spooned in the grey liquid without complaint. She could see he was preoccupied with thought rather than taste. Occasionally a piece of bean fell off the spoon and tumbled back into his dish but he didn't seem to notice the splashes on the table and his linen shirt.

Had the atmosphere been lighter she might have remarked on it. Tonight the look on his face told her to keep her tongue still. Instead she left the table to replace the rushes which burnt low for want of fresh oil. When she returned, he'd laced his boots.

"Are you going out?" she asked.

"Aye," he muttered, reluctant to meet her eyes.

"Is it the animals?"

He nodded and shrugged on his jerkin followed by a thick woollen jacket. Just before it covered his chest, she caught a glimpse of the sullen steel of a knife hilt wedged firmly in his waistband. She knew then this was no ordinary inspection of their livestock.

"Will you take a lamp? It's fearful dark," she said, anxious for him.

He turned at the door.

"There is no need, plenty of stars up there," he said, eyes rolled upward.

She took his hand. "And what of the knife, why do you carry it?"

"Boar," he said, sharp with her.

His look warned her not to ask any more questions but she waited by the door until the crunch of his steps faded. The water she'd set to boil over the fire burbled loudly to attract her attention. She washed the few pots and replenished the logs so as he should have warmth when he returned. Even the few moments the door was open made her shiver as the frozen air forced its way in.

Just standing in the doorway of the small inner room where they slept, the cold nipped her bones despite Thom's effort to stuff the window slits with rags and ox hair. She dragged their pallets one after the other and laid them close to the fire. She hoped Thom would appreciate her thoughtfulness. In the past in such bitter weather he'd brought in an ox to warm them. Its massive bulk gave off a sweaty heat but the rank odour of the beast turned her stomach.

Comforted by the thought of being spared from his suggestion she slipped her night tunic over her dress and sitting cross-legged on her bed, picked up her comb. Thom took days to carve the teeth from a bone and to smooth an edge with which to hold it. This and a fragment of glass that reflected an image were precious possessions. He'd found the odd shaped glass relic when he was turning the ground over to plant turnips. They'd mused for days as to where it might have come from. She smiled at the memory as she peered through the discoloured surface.

Less pleased, she noticed fine as a cobweb, streaks of silver laced through her dark hair. When she braided it for the night she turned the glass so only the rough red glaze on the back showed. Signs of ageing gave her no joy.

Each time she heard a sound she lifted her head from her pillow and listened intently for Thom's return. Disappointingly, it was always the crackle of the wood on the fire.

Cat-like, Thom's eyes adjusted to the ebony darkness. Above him benign stars offered him a thousand candles to light his way, but he had no need of them. Every inch of the land for miles around was known to him. The smell of sheep, carried on a crisp winter wind, was unmistakable. Sure footed, purposeful, Thom found his way to the first of the fences. He rested a hand on the top branches with a tentative touch and gave a derisive snort. The easy sway told him of the poor workmanship and the next section was even weaker. Dry branches of thorn tree and all manner of dead sticks layered loosely one upon another snapped and tumbled when he pushed it.

Any tough bits he severed with his knife until the length of it sprawled on the grass. An artisan would have laboured several days to make a sturdy fence. This was a poor effort and built by someone in a hurry. He'd no doubt who'd fashioned it. What he didn't understand was why.

His expression morose, he kicked the heap of scrub with impatience.

On impact with his heavy boot it scattered across the hoar-frosted grass. When the debris landed, the ground shimmered as the silver tipped blades were disturbed.

First Martha and now this, both matters he needed to settle. Until then, Francis and Flowerdew were like ticks on the back of an ox. Best cut out and destroyed but this was not the time. It must wait until opportunity appeared, he thought, tonight he'd other work to do.

He wondered if he might need to herd the sheep through the space but they didn't wait for encouragement. They sensed the change of grass and when the first of them trotted through the whole flock surged forward.

More idle than the rest the tup was slow to pass him. It was a giant of a ram, horns coiled in massive spirals. On a moment of impulse, he grabbed the beast and wrestled it to the ground. With a quick move he held his knife to its throat. As the blade severed its windpipe its outraged cry ended in a gurgle of wasted air.

His only concern was the noise the rest of the flock made. Sporadic bleats changed to a cacophony of calls which drowned out all other night noises. Praying the animals would quieten before long, Thom retreated, dragging the dead sheep with him. He waited behind a shield of holly bushes, shuffling his feet to restore the circulation.

When he thought it long enough and no one appeared, he hitched his woollen jacket closer to his body to ward off the cold and hoisted the carcase on his shoulder. All his strength was needed to carry the weight of it. Satisfied the rest of the sheep were well scattered, he made his way to John Flowerdew's house.

Martha knew he was back. She smelt the cold and the odour of animals on him but kept her eyes shut. If she looked at him she would want to ask where he'd been. Good sense told her to feign sleep.

Livened by the chill which worked its relentless way under her sheepskin cover, she awoke early. Thom's mattress was empty. A glance at the fire forced her to get up. Only a weak coil of thin smoke and a single burnt log remained in the hearth. She blew on it, encouraged a spark of orange and with a few twigs and careful attention coaxed it into activity again.

When the porridge was thick and the room neatened, she went in search of Thom. Barely light the rosy-blue glow in the sky promised another cold day and her feet snapped the frozen puddles as she trod on them. She didn't have to look far. His voice joined by another drew her to the barn. Inside she found him squatted on a bale as he listened to the irate rant of John Moulder, one of their neighbours, who shared the common land for a living.

"I'd gladly take his genitals and...Why, Mistress Barwick, I didn't see you there. Please pardon my speech," he said his cheeks bright with a blush of embarrassment.

"Good morning, John. What brings you here so early?"

"It's sheep, Mistress Barwick, all over my pasture and a hedge to hold them in. I've made enquiries and it seems Squire Flowerdew and others like him are laying claim to all the common land for their own needs."

Thom stood up and stretched stiff limbs from sitting awkwardly.

"If this continues we shall be beggars before long and no one to care about it," Thom said a bitter edge to his voice. "And it's all because the rich hunger for more."

"He's taken the land where I ran my swine," John continued. "That's not all. My cousin tells me Master Kett has put up hedges too. It seems soon all our land will be taken."

"We need to talk about what's to be done but first my belly complains. Is breakfast ready, wife?" Thom said.

Huddled into her woollen tunic to rebuff the cold, Martha said.

"The porridge should be cooked. We can stretch to a bowl for you, John, if you'd care to stay."

"That's most kind of you, Mistress Barwick," John said as he followed them out of the barn.

Walking side by side, Martha stole a sideways glance at her husband's face. She was relieved to see whatever had gone on late last night nothing showed in his craggy countenance. He must have sensed her anxious look because he turned and smiled. It highlighted the fine lines and pouches which replaced the smooth skin of his younger years. But the uncomplicated depths in his deep-set eyes seemed to be reserved for her. At times even she found it difficult to soften his dark demeanour. She put it down maturity and loved him the more for it. Her hand slipped into his. The gentle squeeze in return reassured her.

"Perhaps we mistake the Squire's intention," she said brightly. "No one would take the common land. You see, it'll all be a misunderstanding."

Over her head, Thom and John exchanged an anxious look.

Cheeks red with rage, John Flowerdew listened to the snivelling confession.

"So where are my sheep now?"

Francis wrung his hands and delivered yet another apology for the failure of his fence building.

"Most are returned, Master. The others are..." his voice faltered and the words dwindled away.

"Go on, man. Are... are where? Roasting atop someone's hearth, eaten by foxes, sitting in some thief's sheep pen? God's truth, you are an incompetent fool and I thought only your nephew was afflicted. It's clear I was wrong. And how do you explain my best tup sprawled on my step with its throat cut? Eh, answer me that."

Incensed, John hovered in front of the cowering man making fists of his hands as if tempted by an urge to hit him. He knew Francis scarcely dared raise his head to meet his eyes.

"I know nothing about that, I swear," Francis whimpered.

"No, I don't suppose you do. Well, shall I tell you what I think? I *think* you and your feeble-minded nephew sought to make a fool of me. I only have your word you carried out what I asked of you at Barwick's."

Francis swallowed nervously and his tongue flicked across his dry lips.

"You said kill the chickens, Master, so that's what we did. Why is it you ask?"

"Because sense tells me, Thom Barwick is behind this. Revenge is not a pretty thing yet it puzzles me just why he did so much damage and slaughtered my ram, for the loss of a few fowl. Are you sure you did no more mischief? What of that idiot boy? When he spoke of a woman, did he mean Mistress Barwick?"

Francis tittered, an odd sound in the still room. John's eyes pierced through him.

"Well, I'm waiting," he said.

"It was nothing, just the boy having fun, that's all."

The inkwell jumped as John's fist thudded on the desktop. Startled, Francis quivered and his face blanched the colour of parchment.

"Fun. What sort of fun?" John said through gritted teeth. "Did he harm her? Is that why Barwick put a knife in my best ram?"

"It can't be, there was but a moment..."

"I can no longer be bothered with your prattle. Get out of here. There are fences to repair, but mark my words you haven't heard the last of this. I've a good mind to raise your rent."

"No, Master, I beg you. I can hardly afford what I pay you now. There's my wife and young mouths to feed."

Francis stretched out his thin, dirt ingrained hand and John's mouth curled in distaste at the sight of it. He sniffed loudly.

"May I be excused to attend to my work?"

Dismissed by the flap of an impatient hand and grateful to escape punishment, Francis began to back away.

"Thank you, Master Flowerdew."

"Not another word. You leave me in poor humour as does Thom Barwick. I have yet to deal with him. Now be gone with you."

John spoke sharply and a fine spray of spit showered on Francis as he scuttled out of the room. When the door closed, it set the squire on a restless walk back and forth in front of the mantle shelf. He listened to the sound of the serf's feet on the drive grow fainter, but it brought him no peace. Instead his mood was black and his mind far too disturbed to rest. Disconsolate, he tossed his lank, dark hair away from his face and went in search of his boots.

He had a visit to make.

Robert Kett wasn't expecting John. In fact he would have preferred not to see his angular shape approaching him across the yard. They'd grown up together and it was a disappointment to Robert that with maturity, John developed arrogance and pomposity as his most obvious traits. It was easy to be deceived by his charm which was merely a mask for a man with few scruples. There was another reason too for Robert's discomfort, one which pained him to recall and of which he never spoke.

Their acknowledgement of one another was also complicated since they were not only neighbours, but related through marriage. Robert could never quite remember how it came about other than Alice his wife was cousin to a relative of John's. He was grateful it was distant enough to rarely be troublesome.

As he emerged from a doorway Robert brushed the flakes of lime off his moleskin jacket and adjusted his cravat. In his fifties, tall and broad shouldered, with fair hair, his was a gentle face and his sandy colouring promoted a rich crop of freckles which gave it a youthful look. As he offered his hand to his visitor, gentility didn't allow his countenance to show any expression other than a smile of welcome.

"John, what a surprise, what brings you here?"

"My apologies, Robert, I know I should have made enquiries as to whether it was convenient. I can call another time if it's not."

"Not at all, if you can give me a moment to finish checking my stores of animal feed, I shall give you my entire attention," Robert said, ducking back into the small shed.

"Animals, exactly why I'm here," John murmured, a pale smile on his thin face. "Sheep to be precise, I suppose yours are penned in?" His narrowed eyelids obscured the look of slyness which permanently lurked in his dark eyes.

Robert emerged from the shed again.

"Indeed, very securely, had to, why do you ask?"

"And you have no problem with your fencing?" his visitor persisted. The repetitive flick of his riding crop on the soft leather of his bootleg sent a soft hollow sound into the air.

"None at all, cost a pretty penny or two, mind you. But I have good men and strong wood. Have you had trouble?" Robert replied.

"My sheep managed to break out during the night, some are still missing. I just wondered if you may have gained a few extra."

"Most unlikely since I checked my flocks this morning, the fences were all intact then," Robert said, already feeling irritated by the other's continual questioning.

"There's one other thing. I've heard there's disquiet from some of the peasants about losing access to the so called common land, although why it should be free to them is a mystery to me. They need to be taught a lesson, what say you?" His loud laugh lacked humour and sounded hollow as it bounced off the stone buildings around them.

"What are you suggesting, John?" Robert said. "Surely the less fortunate deserve our concern for their needs at times."

He noticed how quickly the other changed his manner as soon as he realised they shared different views. It wasn't the first time they'd opposed each another over one thing or another. John slid his eyes away and gazed into the distance as he replied.

"Idle gossip, I'm sure. So, excellent wool prices I hear. If the demand continues we should do well, don't you think?"

"Indeed, although by all accounts, anyone with a guinea or two is turning to sheep rearing. We should be careful the market stays sharp. Now if you will excuse me, if there's nothing else, I really should attend to other matters," Robert said, with contrived politeness.

"Ah, yes, when you have as many acres as I do the work is never done. Good day to you, Robert." The nod was curt and the wave of the crop menaced. With him gone, the atmosphere lifted. When he'd tried to explain to Alice, Robert likened it to the feel of a storm. Not the loud rumbles of noisy clouds, but the oppressive stifle which pained the head. She'd laughed and told him she wasn't surprised, not with the bad feeling which persisted between them.

He pondered on John's words as he went to his stables. In reflective mood, he stroked the neck of his bay hunter. He'd given it no thought when, some years ago, he himself received a fine for enclosing a few acres. Now he was more thoughtful and wondered about the effect his fencing would have on those who depended on the free land. Not by nature a greedy man, he didn't like the discomfort he felt at being responsible for other's hardship.

A tanner by trade he worked hard, but on his father's death a not inconsiderable amount of land and property passed to him and his elder brother, William which eased their lives as gentlemen farmers. On the other hand, his wealth wasn't limitless. His estate took upkeep and seemed to cost more in taxes every year. Then there were the demands of his children and Alice, who seemed to spend money without thought. Only yesterday, she had presented him with a large bill for her spring wardrobe.

"She doesn't understand at all, does she? Eh, old boy," he said to the horse, a wry smile on his face.

The horse curled his lip as if in agreement. Resolved to speak with some of the locals when next he went into the village, he decided to walk his fences again, in case John's experience be repeated with his flock. Replacing broken wood was not a task he needed at present. Little did he realise, the very pastures he trod would soon be part of a land war more costly than all the fences and hedges in Christendom.

− 3 −

By the beginning of March the hard winter released its hold and permitted the sun to bless the land with increased warmth. Normally those who worked the land would be giving thanks for the growth of new grass and soil kind enough to germinate young seedlings. Instead, brows dark with discontent they hung out of their doors to complain or gathered by the market cross in huddles.

Day after day another joined the growing numbers. They stood in the weak sun and stamped their feet to restore the blood. Their rough clothes were hardly able to keep out the east wind which tugged at their clumsy jerkins and turned their breath into icy particles. Thom Barwick was one who made it his business to be there.

"So what's to be done, Thom," John Moulder called, out of breath from his haste. "Have we come to a decision yet?"

Thom shook his head. Like the others anxiety darkened his eyes and etched worry lines on his face. Hands in his pockets he hunched against the cold as he stood with his friend on the edge of the crowd.

"What we do know is Squire Green over at Wylby has enclosed land there which has met with no favour and there is unrest in Attleborough too, so we're not alone," he said.

"If we don't do something soon, we shall starve, that's all I know," Richard Mayhew called out.

There was a general murmur of agreement went round the group.

"I can't grow a thing, John Flowerdew robs us of every inch of the land for his own," another shouted. "With nowhere to go for firewood, we can't have a fire and we freeze come the night."

"It's not only Flowerdew, I see Squire Kett has put up fences too and the one they call Foster along the valley," a young man offered.

"The stink of sheep is the nearest I get to taking home a decent meal," grumbled a tall thick-set, bearded man at the back. "I vote we do something and soon."

Discontent made even the most placid fretful and a louder, more urgent noise issued from their throats. It was a dangerous sound.

"Aye, Will, I know, I know," Thom said his hands spread in a gesture of calm.

John moved closer to Thom and spoke softly. "There will be trouble, ugly at that, if we don't have a plan of some sorts. I can't say for sure, but some of these may take matters into their own hands."

Not easily placated, Will Medler nudged the man standing next to him and roared.

"When I meet Flowerdew, I'll cut off that which makes him a man, what do you say to that, eh, my friend and then I'll stuff it and one of his sheep up his..."

Raucous laughter greeted his remark so loud that it all but smothered Thom's words of disapproval.

"Enough of that, if you please, Will. Have you forgotten women are present?"

The few wives standing to one side looked at one another and sniggered. One was brave enough to call out.

"Good man, Will, no need to spare our sensibilities. I'll ram his seed bags along with it and not those you plant in the earth either."

Again the laughter was noisy and appreciative. Dismayed by the turn of conversation Thom shook his head and leant towards John.

"This will do no good, we must think clearly, if we become a rabble who will listen?"

Thoughtful, John said. "Perhaps we should have a meeting elsewhere. Pick only those we can trust to attend. Nothing will come of standing here day after day."

"The best suggestion I've heard yet," Thom said relief lightening his features. "My barn is as good as anywhere, far enough out of the village not to arouse suspicion. We'll choose no more than six, and meet in three days time."

He cleared his throat, and waved his hand for attention. Well thought of by those present each hushed another. Only the woman continued to gossip. Hot-headed as usual, Will, turned, and shouted.

"Hush your meddling tongues, Thom wants to speak."

"Thank you, Will," Thom said prepared to humour the big man. "It is clear our squires intend to rob us of our land. We may only be peasants, but if they have their way we shall be driven into the city to beg for our food. If we are to succeed and get back what is ours we must be organised. John has suggested we ask a few of you to attend a meeting. Those we choose will act as spokesmen for you all and you must be prepared to voice good ideas, be calm, and if it becomes necessary ready to lead. Who would be interested?"

Thom spoke with ease. In response to his words, arms waved like pennants on sailing ships caught in the breeze.

"I was afraid of that," John murmured.

Unruffled, Thom said. "Thank you. It does my heart good to see so many of you in favour. We will let you know who has been chosen. It is important nothing of this gets out. Remember a word spoken in the wrong place could be our undoing. Now back to your homes before others become suspicious,"

Amongst quiet mutterings and nods of agreement the group dispersed and the market place returned to its usual midday torpor.

"They think well of you, Thom," John said. "I wish I had your confidence."

Pink coloured Thom's cheeks and he shrugged away the compliment. John was a good friend, one whose quietly spoken wisdom was much valued. He glanced sideways at him concerned at the hollow-cheeked profile. He knew John too would have little spare food.

They walked the track together although their paths would divide a short way ahead. The hedges showed fresh green ready to start the cycle of growth again and perched on a naked black thorn branch a Mistle thrush warbled its melodious fluting song.

Thom frowned. "The storm-cock speaks of rain. I should have turned the earth ready to be planted, except I have none to work. What's left in the barn will barely provide a few turnips between us. My beasts will soon break out of their pen for want of fresh grass. Richard was right. Soon we shall have nothing left to eat."

"Sible does her best with dried beans and hog meat she salted, but we shall need to ration it before long. I suppose there's always the goat." John meant his remark to sound jocular, but neither of them could muster a smile. "At least we are all agreed the fences must come down."

The toe of his boot lifted a flint on the path, and it spun into the hawthorn. Thom held the collar of his jerkin close to his neck as the chill air raced up the track with a flurry of dead leaves and bent stalks.

"Aye, but first things first, like I said we must be properly organised and that means a meeting."

They'd reached the fork in the track and stood close, backs to the wind. "So who do we choose?" he asked.

"Will Medler for one," John said.

Uncertain Thom hesitated. "Is that wise? The man's too hasty with his temper."

"Will is better with us than against. He's built like an ox and he'll not go down without a fight. Trust me, it's the right decision."

"So be it, that's one. What about the brothers, Richard and Matthew Mayhew. Solid, good men, the pair of them," Thom said.

"I agree. Then there's Giles son of Rupert, he'll keep us steady. Handy with a stave too by all accounts," John said.

His grin made Thom feel uneasy.

"We want no blood spilt over this."

"Nor shall there be if we do things right."

"There we have it, we shall call ourselves the Council of Wymondham except we need two more," Thom said thoughtfully. "We must decide before we both freeze in our boots."

He rubbed his hands together and looked up at the Mares Tails which streaked the pale blue backcloth above their heads.

"The weather still blights us with this wind."

John tightened the front of his sheepskin jerkin and pulled a face.

"It's what all the trouble's about, damn sheep, yet it keeps me cosy warm. Shall we ask Edmund and Arthur? They talk good sense. What do you think?"

Thom nodded. "Good enough, you'll see to it, John?"

"Leave it to me, three days from now."

With Thom and John, the group made eight. Gathered in Thom's barn they talked through the night. Martha carried bowls of soup, black jacks of ale and the last of her homemade elderflower cordial to keep them all fortified. The soup was weak, a few lentils and a handful of peas was all she could spare, but they relished it grateful for something to take the nip of hunger from their bellies.

"So we're agreed. No violence. This must be peaceful at all cost. Edmund, you live in the centre of the village so you are best placed to keep your ears open. Those who work for John Flowerdew, like Francis Smith, may be grateful for his favour if they give him news of our plans. The same goes for Robert Kett too," Thom said.

Edmund nodded. His youthful, ruddy complexion pale from the lateness of the hour, he looked heavy-eyed. His solemn face showed he understood his responsibility. With a loud yawn, Will stretched his thick arms and said.

"How many teams do we make?"

His question was greeted by exasperated sighs.

"Did you not listen, Will?" Giles said his impatience obvious. "There are forty of us in this hamlet, twenty two men. Four are too old to be useful, which leaves two men apiece for the six of you. Working in small groups will draw less attention. Thom and John will be responsible for overall command. Is that clear now?"

"And all we have to do is pull down the hedges. Nothing more," Will said always hopeful of a squabble.

"Yes." John said. "You keep your fists to yourself, Will. This is no time for a fight. Remember we go out at night. Destroy every fence we find and then leave. We must act not brawl. Is that understood?"

"A pity," Will said, disappointed. "Master Flowerdew has much to answer for."

Next to him, Giles cuffed him gently on the arm. "You heard what John said."

A short, wiry man, who answered to the name of Arthur, gathered up his coat and his longbow. He nodded towards the window slit where the incoming light threw a pink hued bar on the dark stone wall beside him.

"I'm away to my bed. I've a cow and the goats to milk. Though why I worry I don't know they'll all be for slaughter before long. What use are they to a land-less labourer? Besides I've nothing left to feed them with."

Thom threw his arm across Arthur's shoulders.

"You will manage, I know you will. When the fences come down, our well to do neighbours will find we mean business. Be patient for awhile longer."

Arthur managed a smile, but Thom's words did nothing to improve the heavy crease of anxiety which fought for space on his lined forehead. He ran his hand through greying hair and pulled on his woollen hat.

"I hope you're right," he murmured.

"We'll walk with you," the Mayhew brothers said.

It was a signal for them all. They left the barn quietly and Thom said.

"Remember, now that Edmund's cousin has sent word that the men of Attleborough are to tear up fences there, we make no move until we hear how things go for them."

With their companions gone John stood with Thom outside his door.

"Have you and John Flowerdew settled your differences yet? It's said he blames you for a dead tup," he enquired. "He's looking for payment by all accounts."

The grin on Thom's face was a rare sight. "I hear that too, but he needs to prove it first."

"Somebody broke down his hedges at the same time. I saw that serf of his, Francis, repairing them when I passed a few days back," John continued.

Thom's expression admitted nothing. "Perhaps the wind shook them down. Time I sought my bed. Perchance, you should do the same."

For a moment he thought of telling John about the attack on Martha, but she'd begged him to speak to no one. Too ashamed, she'd said...If anyone asked, a fox took the chickens...He'd agreed, for now at least.

She didn't stir when he slipped into the inner room. He pushed his pallet nearer hers and snuggled close, but his mind was restless. Every night, darkness conjured up images he preferred to forget and he was grateful when slivers of daylight pierced their way between loose rags in the window slits.

− 4 −

Hampton Court Palace

Edward Seymour, Duke of Somerset stood at the casement window and gazed out across the extensive gardens. In his hand the sheet of paper quivered in response to the nervous twitch of his fingers. Whenever he was sufficiently annoyed he always twitched. His limbs trembled and the tic under his left eye jigged under the flesh.

Philip, a court advisor who'd carried the missive to him stood uncertain by the door. His every muscle tense, he was ready to flee when Seymour progressed from simple anger to uncontrolled rage. Those who witnessed his outbursts remarked how much worse they'd become since Seymour accepted his most recent appointment, leader of the Regency Council and Lord Protector of the boy king, Edward.

The Ante room to the Great Hall served as Seymour's receiving room for all state matters. Rich mahogany panels, inlaid gold, hand-turned furniture and expensive, embroidered Turkish rugs were a few of the embellishments he chose to equip his surroundings. He saw it as only natural as befitted the king's chief advisor.

Seymour was a man obsessed. Disorder incensed him, neatness was a compulsion. Six gardeners at work on the Maze held his attention. There would be instant punishment should they fail to complete the angles of the dark yew hedging to meet his exacting instructions. It seemed satisfactory but even this failed to improve his mood.

He turned and held the letter out with a loud rustle.

"So who are these people again? And where in God's name is this place, Attleborough?"

Agitated the young man made a guttural sound in his throat and gave a noisy cough.

"It's in the county of Norfolk, my lord. The people protest and say land is being stolen from them, land they say belongs to them."

"And does it?" Seymour said.

"So I believe, my lord. Of sort."

"Of sort, of sort, what kind of answer is that? Either it belongs to them or it doesn't."

"Its common land, their families have worked it for generations."

An expression of distaste crossed Seymour's face.

"I assume it's the peasants who complain again. Tell them they must sort out their own muddles."

He tossed the letter onto the soft, green leather which bound his desk and stroked down the ruffled edge of ermine on his cuff which turned back on itself.

"My lord, a few years ago, you decreed that these people had rights to the land."

Seymour uttered a snort of impatience.

"Did I? I don't remember," and hesitating searched for recall. "Well, yes, I may have pledged my support for the poor commons once. Indeed on occasion I will admit to a moment or two of sympathy for them. But pity is not a way to rule the land. Besides since then the Privy Council made changes to the law. Don't these people read?"

"They are written in Latin, my lord, few can," the advisor murmured.

"So is that my fault too? Enough, you bore me. That will be all."

"If I may just say..."

"What now?"

"It's just that I believe they have taken to destroying the fences and caused considerable damage. Some have been caught."

"Well, in that case they shall be hung."

Amazed at his courage, the advisor persisted. "They ask the King for leniency."

Seymour glared at him from behind the desk and tugged his beard with bony fingers. The other hand reached for the irritated muscle under his eye.

"Something must be done," he muttered.

"They will be very grateful, my lord."

Seymour's roar rattled the window glass.

"Buffoon," he shrieked. "I'm talking about this damned tic of mine not those dull brained peasants you witter about. His Majesty is a child, just turned nine, what would he know about such things? He plays with toys, reads books and learns to pluck the lute. Do you think I should disturb him about such a trifle?"

"As you wish, my lord," the advisor said. Conscious his bladder muscles threatened he replaced his velvet beret set with an elegant swatch of emu feathers and bowed low.

"What do they call you?" Seymour enquired with vague interest in his voice. Still bent double, the man said. "Philip, my lord,"

"Ha, not related to that infidel in Spain, I hope," Seymour said, tartly.

"No, my lord, I know no one in that country."

Back at the window, Seymour raised his hand and flicked his fingers to dismiss. Head down Philip continued to back out of the room, grateful the sweat on his brow couldn't be seen.

Chapter 4

After he'd gone, Seymour ripped the missive into small pieces, tossed it out of the window and watched it float in creamy tatters to the path below. One sliver travelled further than the rest settling on the head of a granite statue. The moment the paper landed one of the gardeners ran forward and picked up the pieces. From where he stooped he couldn't possibly see the stray fragment which adorned the stone hair.

"You've missed a piece," Seymour snapped. He scowled, slammed the window and flicked the catch back in place.

Bewildered, the gardener continued to grovel and Seymour smirked with malice.

Once out of the room it was more than Philip dare to run, but he was very tempted. He walked speedily past the long line of royalty and nobles in their heavy frames. Depicted in oils and watercolours, they glowered down from the burnished wood panels in the Long Gallery. His attention caught by a youthful portrait of the late king, when he was almost bowled over by two young boys. They rounded the corner in front of him shrieking with laughter at some private escapade whilst throwing a ball to each other.

Philip stiffened at the sight of them and flattened himself against the wood to let them pass. One, dark of hair with olive skin tones, stopped. The other, with paler features, his high brow topped by a whirl of red curls, smiled politely and broke into a skip which carried him down the room. Gold thread shot through the material of his doublet reflected light from the wall sconces. A black velvet beret clung precariously to his exuberant hair. It bounced wildly as he ran and ruby darts flashed from a brooch pinned to it.

The dark-haired boy lingered in front of Philip.

"You must take off your hat and bow to His Majesty," he piped, in a squeaky voice.

"Yes, I'm sorry,"

"No matter," the boy said with an airy wave of his hand. "Eddie, wait for me," he called as he raced after his companion.

At the back of the palace a man loitered in a corner partially obscured by shadows. He could have easily been mistaken for a vagrant, but there were few about to notice him. Philip saw him and hurried in his direction. The man stepped out from his hiding place, an expectant look on his drawn face. When Philip shook his head, the expression changed to disappointment.

"Is there bad news, Master Philip? What did his lordship say?"

Philip rested a consoling hand on the others arm.

"I'm sorry, Elias, I did my best. My lord Seymour would have none of it. I pressed the point. At personal risk, I might add, yet he offered no help."

The man, a cousin of Will Medler, sighed heavily. Short and stocky, only his wild hair bore any resemblance to his kin.

"It took me four days to walk from Attleborough, but I came with hope. Now I must return with nothing to offer those who are to be dealt with harshly. They did what they did because we shall all starve otherwise." His words trickled away, lost in what sounded like a sob of despair. Pity in his eyes, Philip patted the man's hand.

"I've been moved by your story. Perhaps if I could find Lord Seymour in a better state of mind, I could approach him again. There is no way to speak to the king but through him."

"It will be too late. My brother is one who's been caught. They arrested him and accused him of being a vagabond. In a few days he is to be punished with a hundred strokes of the birch. Another awaits sentence, but I fear he will face burning for his part. A few fences, that's all, is it such a crime when our children already go hungry?"

"You must understand I hold no power other than to approach those who hold office in His Majesty's court, I'm sorry," Philip said sadly, whilst anxiously glancing around. He'd already spent too much time talking and feared they might soon be noticed. "It wouldn't look well if I'm found talking to you, I must go."

Elias nodded. "I must leave too if I'm to be on the road back before dusk. Thank you for what you have done," he said.

He gathered his tattered wool coat closer, his head sunk into the collar for obscurity.

"God go with you, my friend," Philip said, he did not look back until he was about to enter the palace. There he paused and looked over his shoulder. There was no one to be seen in any direction.

Wymondham

When word first reached Wymondham of events at nearby Attleborough there was jubilation. They heard that all the fences belonging to Squire Jacob Green were ripped from the ground and the men responsible safely back in their homes by sunrise. The morning dew barely began to wither on the grass when the friends, Will, Arthur, Richard and Mathew Mayhew together with Edmund and Giles gathered outside *The Tavern,* a brick and thatch hostelry in the market place. Only Thom and John were missing.

"What did I tell you?" Will said, a broad smile disturbing his facial hair, streaked both silver and black in equal amounts. "All went well and this is only the start. Soon it will be our turn."

"As soon as the others get here, I say we raise a cup of Mistress Dale's fine ale to our friends in Attleborough," Edmund suggested.

"Here they come now," Giles said, as Thom and John approached.

Richard Mayhew frowned. "You'd think with such good news, they'd look happier. They don't share a smile between them."

Will greeted Thom and John with a grin.

"So what ails you two this morning? We're mighty parched waiting for you."

The serious expressions of the latecomers didn't alter.

"There's no cause to celebrate," John said, quietly.

The mood changed and concern replaced good humour.

"So, tell us. What's happened?" Giles said, his words softly spoken.

"Some of the men in Attleborough have been arrested on the orders of Squire Green. It was his fences. Somehow he knew. Four were pulled from their beds and taken away."

"There must have been an informer," Thom interrupted. "They worked late in the night and saw no one, so I heard."

Will muttered an oath and the skin of his bunched fist strained white over his large knuckles.

"If I could get my hands on that Devil's spawn, I'd twist his tongue out slowly, inch by inch. He'd be sorry he ever opened his mouth. Do they know who?"

"Too soon to tell," John replied.

The Mayhew brothers exchanged nervous glances, anxious to know, yet both afraid to ask. Arthur saved them the trouble.

"What will happen to them now?"

"The Squire called them rebels. As such they won't be treated kindly you can be sure of that," Thom said, dull eyed and despondent.

"We heard there is a letter to be sent to the king, asking him to pardon them," John said. "I don't know, it's not clear, but it means we do nothing for now at least."

"Agreed," Richard Mayhew said quickly, relief tempering his voice.

Murmurs of "Aye," went up as the others agreed and much subdued they wandered off, their faces heavy with thought.

A small heap of wrinkled, grey bean pods looked lost in the centre of the table. Martha had just finished counting them when Thom arrived home. Wan faced, she managed a tight lipped smile when he slipped his arms around her waist.

"That's all that's left. Good job we have no young mouths to feed."

Her bitter-sweet remark wasn't lost on her husband.

"For once that makes sense," he said gruffly, his head bowed into her shoulder.

Bright again, her husky laugh cheered him.

"We'll manage. There are plenty of lentils, enough rye for me to bake bread and if you could find a rabbit or a crow, we'd feast like kings."

Able to bear her own pain, but not that of Thom's, she returned the hug. Gently she stroked his hair, its colour faded with age. He straightened and touched her cheek in exchange. She watched him reach for his knife, run a finger along the blade and then put his boots back on.

"Where are you going?" She asked the question, but feared the answer.

"The knife, it needs sharpening," he said.

"Is that all?"

"Don't worry, it's all agreed. We'll not be touching the fences yet awhile. We must wait and see what happens at Attleborough. There were no objections."

"That's alright then," she said, relieved. "We still have some cider. I'll fetch you cup for when you come back."

He was gone longer than she expected. When she saw his hands, her first thought was that he'd cut himself on the newly honed knife. But there was too much blood. Dark, rich coloured, clotted, splashed on his jerkin and more on the front of his boots.

"What's happened?" she asked, alarmed.

For a moment he seemed not to hear her. He looked at his hands bemused and with a shake of his head, plunged them into the pail of cold water. It coloured and frothed, slopping scarlet from side to side.

"Thom, tell me. Where did all that blood come from?"

"One of the oxen, it had to be done. There's no food left for three of them. I kept putting it off."

She felt the hot rush of tears and couldn't check them. "But you love those beasts."

Her nose ran too making her snuffle. He forgot his own grief and embraced her, holding her tight so she felt safe.

"Love won't feed us," he said. "We have meat. I'll let it hang. Have you salt left?"

She sniffed loudly and scrubbed her hand across her wet cheeks.

"There's salt, yes, but only a little."

She pushed her heavy hair away from her face and looked bereft.

"Perhaps we could share the meat. John Moulder struggles as we all do, but he has little ones. He'll not turn his nose up at a side of beef," Thom said, trying not to meet her eyes for fear she saw his watered too.

Later she heard him. He moaned in his sleep and restless turned from one side to the other. It was just like him to make light of the loss of the ox. Inside where she couldn't see, she knew there'd be grief. His pride rested in his beasts, he must have been desperate.

Fearful for his safety she hadn't encouraged the plans being made to rid the land of the enclosures nor realised how quickly they would suffer when the fences went up. She sat with her knees drawn up to her chin and watched his troubled face. It wasn't the first time she silently cursed the likes of Squire Green, John Flowerdew, Robert Kett and the rest of the gentry who robbed them of their rights without thought of how they might exist.

Those who sent them to bed with hunger griping their bellies whilst they stuffed their own, she wished into Hell and vowed from then on she'd stand beside Thom wherever the fight took him.

She had no idea what part she might play or even if Thom would allow it. The thought amused her and she smiled in the darkness. Reaching for his hand she held it tightly until his mumblings stopped and his mind drifted into a deeper place where the dreams no longer disturbed him.

Shrunken and thick the porridge hardly covered the bottom of the bowl. Thom poked it several times with the end of his wooden spoon as if that would improve its appearance. Martha looked on, her nut-brown eyes filled with dismay.

"I can find a little more milk."

"I'll manage," he said.

He was preoccupied with an image in his mind which wouldn't leave him. The beast didn't make a sound when he led it away from the others. It looked at him with soft eyes, dark depths of trust. Practised with the knife, it was over quickly.He winced visibly as he remembered. Martha spoke twice before her words registered with him.

"You're still fretting about the ox," she said. It was a statement more than a question.

"Aye, he was a fine animal. Having three was good fortune, most only have one. I've my father to thank for that."

She didn't stop to think.

"You have two left to plough," she said.

He looked at her, surprised.

"Plough what? Have you forgotten so soon? There's no land left for that."

Last spring everything was ordered, one ox always on loan to his neighbours to make a team. Between them they tilled the land, drilled seed and planted while exchanging good natured banter as they did so. How quickly things changed, he thought.

"There's work to be done." He pushed the empty dish toward her. "Thank you, that was good."

She smiled at his lie then remembered.

"The ox?" she asked.

He nodded and went to the door. His stout leather boots were well worn. The edge of one was in need of new stitches, but he never parted with them long enough for Martha to repair it. The ox hide came to mind for a new pair.

"I've made it hard for myself," he said. "I should have skinned him whilst he was warm, but somehow, I owed him time and I had no heart for it."

The rigid line of his mouth told her how troubled he was. She reached across and laid her hand over his, small and frail compared to the heavy boned paw his made. He raised it to his lips and then with a wry smile tugged on the boots.

Beyond the cattle pen on the start of a slope and away from the other oxen, the slaughtered animal lay where it'd fallen. One leg was doubled under it, the others jutted out from the massive body in the macabre stance of death. Its shaggy hair concealed the even slash of skin across its neck, the massive blood loss evident in the dark liquid lake around its head.

Thom chastised himself for the sudden sorrow he felt. When it came to the need to kill animals he was a hard man, experienced and practical. Somehow the ox was different. When he got closer he saw the damaged front leg, flesh taken to the bone. Foxes or wild dogs, it could have been either. He knew they would return so he must set to work.

Nothing would be wasted. With the carcase skinned, the hide would go in the barn to be cured, another warm covering for the mattress in winter and maybe enough for boots too. The meat would be portioned and he could picture Martha's pleasure when he gave her the bones. She'd boil them up for stock, taking the marrow and storing it to spread on a crust of bread.

Engrossed in his labours he didn't notice her standing at a distance until he stopped to straighten his back.

"Is there anything I can do?" she called. "I see you have watchers."

She pointed to the two birds just arrived on the top rail of the animal pen. Settled in a fluff of feathers the magpie's chatted noisily, button-bright eyes fixed on the gore spread on the ground.

"You could move closer, talk to me," he said, pleased at her presence.

Grateful as she was for the meat she never enjoyed the butchering. The sight of copious amounts of blood made her feel faint and she preferred to keep her distance. Reluctantly she took a few steps nearer.

"I've been thinking," she said. "These hedges."

Concentrating on cutting out the offal, he laid the huge liver and generous kidneys carefully aside.

"I told you, we must wait. The news from Attleborough isn't encouraging. We must be careful," he said.

He shook the sweat clear off his forehead and worked on. She watched for some minutes and then said quietly.

"When you went out that night and came back late, was it you who broke down Flowerdew's fences?"

His laugh expressed relief. He never did like concealing anything from her.

"Strange that," he said, wiping the knife blade on a handful of dock leaves. "I did pull down a few and let his sheep out. It was revenge for the chicken's, that's all. Never did I think what he'd done would mean such hardship for us all. One after another they enclose the land. They're all doing it now, that's why we must stop it. But at the time..." he shrugged.

"What of the dead sheep? I know, you see, Sible told me."

"It was no match for what they did to you. But I was angry. I think I saw Flowerdew when I slit its throat," he said, still intent on the carcase. As he plunged his knife into the beast it laid bare baubles of yellow fat and a shine of membrane in the flaccid belly. "Why do you ask?" he said, chopping and slicing through the animal's viscera. When his hand emerged holding the heart and lungs, she closed her eyes.

"I'd like to help, that's all."

"It's no job for a woman," he said.

"Women often follow their men."

"In times of war maybe. There must be no battles. They must be made to listen in peace," he said. She knew there was no point arguing with him. Some of the rich fat dangled from his fingers. He held it up to show her.

"There's plenty of good soap with this lot. Can you bring a bowl to carry some of it back to the house?"

Hearing steps Martha looked towards the track. "It looks like we have a visitor," she said and shielded her eyes against the light to look beyond his shoulder. He turned to follow the direction she indicated

"Good morning Giles, how goes things for you?" she called.

"Well, thank you. I came to give you both the news from Attleborough." His eyes were drawn to the body of the ox. "Things are getting bad, I see. My wife wants to save the goats, I've told her we'll manage whilst we can but our larder is almost empty."

Thom searched among the meat and sliced through the flesh again.

"Take this with you when you go. There's more than enough to share," he said, lifting up a large piece of flank.

Giles took it from him eagerly.

"You're very generous, I thank you both. It'll be good to taste red meat again. Ellen will be grateful too, she tires of duck and fish, when I can find them, that is."

"Is she well?" Martha said, her arms held out for Thom to balance a joint.

"Thank you, yes. Worried like the rest of us. It's not a good time to be with child..."

"When is she due?" Martha asked, concerned but never envious, despite her own inability to conceive.

Giles pondered for a moment. "Sometime in the autumn, I think," he said, with a self-conscious smile at his own vagueness.

"Come to the house, we can talk better there," Thom said.

"Thom, we should move all the meat, the sun's high now, it'll soon turn too rancid to use. I've salting and pickling to do. We can't afford to waste any," Martha said, anxiously.

Between the three of them and making two trips, they managed to carry the beef back and Martha disappeared to the barn to stretch out the skin. Thom pulled a stool forward.

"Rest your legs, I'll fetch us a drink. It's thirsty work, cutting up that beast."

With two horn beakers filled to the brim and the ale jug on the table, Thom said.

"So, what's the news?"

"Not the best I could bring," Giles said grim faced. "A friend of Will's arrived from Attleborough an hour or so ago. There was no trial. Sentence was passed with the men given no chance to speak for themselves. Three are in the stocks, the other flogged. It's a bad business."

As he tipped his head back to drink, Giles's shoulder length hair swung away from his face. It was then Thom saw the scar. Puckered and uneven it ran from behind his ear just avoiding his eye and disappeared somewhere on the scalp. Surprised he'd never noticed before, he decided against enquiring. Instead he offered the jug across the table before topping up his own beaker. Giles saw the direction of Thom's look. He shook his hair back again and touched the scar.

"This," he said, "It was a present from John Flowerdew's father. When I was a child there were apples and we were hungry. He came at me with a pitchfork."

Stirred by a breeze which came from the roof, the fire flared briefly. Whatever Martha had in the iron pot above it came to life and burbled. Urged out of his musings by the sound, Thom spoke, ending a thoughtful silence.

"Did they not intend to approach the king?"

"They tried. A letter was taken, but it seems it was not well received at the palace. It's obvious there is no support for our cause there."

Thom shrugged. "It's hard to know the truth. There are some who say the king is in sympathy with our troubles, others who tell of the Lord Protector's concern. It seems we have no choice but to act, so we must raise as many as we can to stand with us. There is strength in numbers. I'm sure when the king gets to hear how badly we fare, he'll listen to our plight," he said.

Giles nodded. Neither of the men looked convinced.

— 6 —

Hampton Court Palace

Their looks were not dissimilar. Edward, the older Seymour had more grey threads running through his russet coloured beard and in the hair visible from under his midnight-black velvet cap.

His eyes too differed from his sibling's being colder, harder and a darker shade of blue. Both had fair skins heavily mottled by gingery freckles and the same thin frame which carried no excess of flesh.

Slumped back in his chair, Thomas nonchalantly raised his legs and settled his boot clad feet on the desk top. With a stony expression and lips pursed, his brother swept them away with an impatient hand.

"I'll thank you to keep them where they belong, on the floor."

"Touchy, touchy, Ned. They'll do no harm. Feel them for yourself, the softest, finest deerskin. Such quality don't you think?" Thomas mused, with one foot extended.

"How many times must I remind you, you call me Edward in the palace," his brother said, using his sleeve to rub imaginary marks off the green leather.

"So dear brother, what is it you want with me? I can't imagine you summoned me to discuss footwear," Thomas said, his hand on the symbol of office strung round his neck. Thomas had recently been made Lord High Admiral of England and was rather fond of the heavy gold necklace adorned with quail egg-sized rubies and large iridescent freshwater pearls, which he wore at every opportunity. When feeling ill at ease he would trace one of the gems with his finger. This he did now, the only sign of his inner agitation.

Edward turned and looked out of the window, his eyes following the course of the Thames and the barges on it. Not for him unsteady nerves, more a controlling of anger at yet more of his brother's indiscretions.

"It saddens me, Thomas, that despite the many honours which have been bestowed upon you, you still persist in outrageous behaviour and I fear I can no longer protect you."

"Come sir, such hasty words. Is this about that strumpet, Lord Cecil's daughter? Has she complained? I can assure you she invited me to her chamber, don't worry, I was planning to be rid. Her looks don't make up for such disappointment under the sheets," Thomas said, insolence in his lazy smile.

Edward rubbed a hand across his brow and sighed.

"I wish it were that simple. No, Thomas, it's not just a wench this time."

"So what troubles you?"

"Our late king left you in greatly improved circumstances financially and at his wish you have been raised to the peerage. Baron Seymour of Sudely, a fine title is it not? As if that were not enough, you have been appointed High Admiral too."

Indignant, it took Thomas less than a moment to haul himself upright in his chair.

"For God sake, get to the point, brother. What am I supposed to have done this time?" he interrupted.

Seated at his desk again Seymour set his elbows on its top, hands together, the tips of his fingers meeting in a turret. Resting his chin on them he looked hard at Thomas. He wasn't in fact seeing his brother, but gathering thoughts which he found distasteful. Their shared and not unhappy childhood at Wolf Hall counted for something and he still felt a blood-tie not easy to break. For a moment his fondness for Thomas threatened to overwhelm him and he was tempted to change his mind. He focussed on his brother who he saw slouched in the chair again with the arrogant expression back on his face. Damn the man, Seymour thought, nothing was more important than his own future and he couldn't allow a morsel of compassion to threaten it.

"It was my hope I could always rely on you. In fact I had thought to send you to East Anglia. The peasants need a firm hand."

Thomas shuddered and rolled his eyes upward.

"I trust you've changed your mind. I should perish in that cold and moribund place. For God's sake find me something with more excitement."

"You have never been satisfied have you, Thomas. It troubles you Henry chose me to be guardian of the boy until he comes of age. You hanker for the position of Protector, don't you?"

The good humour faded on Thomas's face. Tense in the chair, his hands clasped round the arms gripped the wood tightly so his knuckles strained under the pale skin.

"I can't deny I should have liked to be chosen."

"That's very obvious. Every dastardly thing you do undermines my role. Not content with that, you repeatedly press yourself on the Princess Elizabeth, to the extent she comes to me to complain and now you openly suggest a ridiculous liaison between our boy king and Jane Grey." Seymour thumped his hand loudly on the desk to underline his words.

A sickly grey pallor seeped into Thomas's face as he listened to his brother's rant. Unwilling to relent, Edward continued. "I could perhaps overlook all this," he said quickly before Thomas had time to gather his words together. "However, your last acts of disloyalty are unforgivable. Your ambitious scheming has taken you a step too far."

Thomas shrunk visibly when he expelled a large breath of air. His sibling pressed on. Pacing the floor, hands behind his back, Seymour said.

"It is your duty as Lord High Admiral to rid us of the nefarious activities of certain pirates. It has come to my ears you have done quite the opposite. Whilst my back was turned you have entered into some sort of relationship, hoping, I suppose, when the time is right for those blackhearts to support you. So now it is known that my brother, despite his high nautical rank encourages piracy. As if that isn't enough word reached me only yesterday, you scheme some treasonous plot to kidnap the young king. Have you lost all your senses?"

Spite replaced any pity Edward might have shown. As far as he was concerned the worst was over. He'd placed the sword deep in Thomas's chest, now all he had to do was to feel for the heart.

"So where's all your bravado now, little brother?" he snarled, the skin drawn tight on either side of his hawkish nose.

In a search of saliva to moisten his dry mouth, Thomas gulped several times. When he spoke he croaked out the words in an attempt to deny.

"I can explain. Whoever your spy is he should be put to the stake. There is no truth..."

"No sir, it is you who shall be punished," Edward said. He strode to the door and flung it open. "Guards."

Thomas whimpered. A strange sound from a grown man and Edward revelled in the fear which distorted his brother's face. In one clumsy move Thomas threw himself at the other's feet and clutched at his black hose. All the while he snivelled like a spoilt child.

"Ned, I beg you. This can't be right, I'm your brother. I'll do anything, anything you command. For God's sake, show mercy. What is it you want me to do?"

"Do? Why brother, it's too late for all that," Edward said.

Behind him two shadows in the doorway moved forward.

"Take Baron Sudley to the Tower to await trial for treason," Edward instructed. "No, wait. There is one thing, you can do, Thomas."

Terrified, Thomas tried to shake his arms free from the guards. "Yes, anything."

"Remember to call me Edward."

Thomas tried to laugh, but it was the babbling noise of hysteria. As he was dragged out of the room he screwed his head round to catch a glimpse of Edward.

"Brother," he called. "You are making a mistake and after my trial, what of me then?"

The quill dipped into the ink and Edward signed a sheet of paper with careful attention. Searching for the wax for his seal, he barely looked up. He impressed the seal and leant back as if to admire it.

"Then, well then, dear Thomas, we will meet again for your appointment at the Executioner's block. You see this is your warrant. Take him away," he said with a dismissive wave of his hand.

He flinched at the screams which vibrated on the panelled walls of the corridor then frowned and crossed the room to shut the door. He did so hate it when people didn't bother to close doors behind them.

– 7 –

Seated at his desk Seymour fiddled with his pen and considered his brother's demise. The quill had been poised over a document for some time, but he was distracted by other thoughts. Possibly, he'd been a little hasty, he thought. Despite his desire to be rid of him, his brother's beheading had not encouraged his good humour. It hadn't even been a clean job which reminded him, he'd still to take the executioner to task for needing to strike Thomas's neck twice before his head rolled free.

He scribbled an illegible signature on the bottom of the paper and pushed it away with an impatient hand. The tap on the door was a welcome diversion.

"Come," he called, his shoulders squared to make himself look more dignified.

Philip entered quietly careful to close the door behind him. The Lord Protector missed nothing. Even a door left a fraction ajar would cause him to shout at the unfortunate responsible before they'd taken a step into the room.

"Not more rubbish to read, I hope," Seymour said, his gaze fixed on the pile of papers under Philip's arm.

"I'm sorry, my lord, I'm afraid so. There are urgent matters of state to attend to."

"Sit down, sit down."

The interruption lacked interest to him as did most court matters, Seymour waved a limp hand toward a chair. There was silence whilst he sorted his quills into a straight line and turned the inkwell stand several ways before he was satisfied with its position. Then he leaned back in his chair and stared at Philip.

He thought how smart the boy looked dressed in his official outfit. Where until recently his doublet had been plain and somewhat drab he now wore a more lavish tunic in deep plum embroidered with the Royal insignia. Even the ermine collar was new. Only a wisp of fur, he'd instructed the royal dressmaker, just enough to indicate a modicum of importance.

"So how does it feel to be my private secretary? I hope you're pleased with your new position."

As he studied the young face Seymour's eyes glittered. With their hooded lids they could be likened to the wary, brittle gaze of an eagle. Flustered, Philip leapt up from the chair in order to bow.

"Yes, indeed my Lord Seymour, I am most grateful," he said.

"How grateful, Philip?" Seymour asked

"So grateful, my lord, that I shall consult no other but you in all state matters, however trivial."

"And I owe you..." Seymour murmured.

Philip completed the sentence immediately. "My total allegiance, my lord," he intoned.

"Good, good." Seymour said, his lips relaxed just enough to reflect the mere hint of a smile.

His suggestion to the king that Philip should be elevated in rank deeply satisfied him. It was also very crafty. But then no one could teach him anything about craftiness that he didn't already know.

"Come, bring your chair and sit beside me," he said. "We shall go through these tedious papers together."

When he watched Philip move, he recalled how impressed he'd been when, a few weeks back, the boy refused to give in over some plea or other. It was something about uncouth yokels somewhere in Norfolk and their hedges, if he remembered correctly. He'd thought at the time how a lesser spirited man would have fled long before Philip did. Such courage could be misused, he reasoned, so better harnessed in the court's favour.

There was, however, another reason. Seymour found himself somewhat attracted to the boy. It pleased him to have him close. Since all matters regarding the Privy Council were referred to Seymour as the King's advisor, it took little more than a minute for a royal nod of the red headed curls in his direction and the appointment was confirmed.

Philip seated himself and Seymour inhaled a pleasant aroma. The air was scented with sweet-smelling flowers, roses, he thought. He breathed deeply again, yes, roses indeed. He rested on hand on the other's thigh with a light touch.

"That's a most pleasant perfume you wear, Philip," he said.

Discomforted by the older man's intense scrutiny, Philip sat rigid. He felt the heat rise in his cheeks, but dare not move. Unusual for Seymour, he permitted himself a chuckle and said.

"What a pretty boy you are, but I do believe you blush just like a coquette, am I..."

The door flew open with such speed Seymour barely had time to snatch his hand away.

"Ah, there you are, Uncle Edward." The young king raced into the room. "I've been looking everywhere for you."

Flushed with exertion the king kept careful hold of his book, but carelessly flung his tennis racket onto the timbered floor. Both men stood and bowed deeply to their monarch. With exaggerated politeness the king stood in front of Philip and held out his hand. "And you are?"

"Philip de Montfort, Sire."

"Do I know you? I've seen you before, I think."

"Yes Sire. We passed in the Long Gallery a few weeks ago."

The boy beamed. "There I knew I was right. I never forget a face, do I, Uncle?" he said delighted with his success.

"No, Majesty. You are remarkably clever."

"Yes, I am, aren't I? What are you both doing?"

"Matters of State, Sire," Seymour said.

"Good, then I shall stay. I must learn what is expected of me."

"As you wish, Majesty," Seymour said through gritted teeth.

"Bring me my chair please, Philip."

In a room over burdened by chairs Philip looked puzzled.

"His Majesty means that one," Seymour said and pointed out a shape draped with a large cloth of purple velvet encrusted in beads and heavily worked in gold. He nudged Philip. "It covers the chair," he hissed.

Unprepared for the weight of solid wood, Philip staggered when he lifted the chair. Uncertain where to place it he dithered with his burden. The king giggled, but Seymour watched with dark brows heavy over his eyes. He hurried forward to remove the cloth and folded it carefully.

"Here will do," he said out of the corner of his mouth. "As you can see Majesty, Philip is new to such things, but he will learn."

The king laid his book on the desk and clambered up to take his seat. He looked thin and fragile, dwarfed by the dark oak with its intricate carving on the back and arms. His skinny black-clad legs dangled and his feet were some way off the floor.

"Now fetch the dais." Seymour pointed out a small wooden platform. He fingered his ornate gold chain of office with agitated twitches. "Under His Majesty's feet," he instructed in loud whisper.

Beneath his tangled bright curls, the king looked on amused. He hooked his cape into a more comfortable position and said.

"Right, now I'm ready. You may begin."

Philip took his seat again and gave a sideways glance at the royal book. Impressed in gold-leaf on the white, embossed leather the title wasn't difficult to see. The king was reading the New Book of Common Prayer.

"You may borrow it if you wish," the king said. "I thought I should read it, but I'm finding it a bore now."

"If I may say, your Grace, Archbishop Cranmer was most insistent you should finish it. He waits on your approval," Seymour said.

The king pulled an unattractive face.

"Yes very well, Uncle, but not now. Tell me, what you have there." He waved his hand at documents scattered on the desk where Seymour had riffled through them.

"The usual, Sire. Letters of demand, begging letters, some asking for your royal attendance at this and that, others pleading your intervention in matters of court, loyal allegiance, that sort of thing."

"Are *we* interested in any of them?"

Seymour shook his head. "No, Your Highness, *we* are not. You need not be troubled. Philip and I will deal with them."

Fearful it would be seen Philip turned his smile into a hasty cough. He knew that dealing with them, as far as the Lord Protector was concerned, meant tearing them all up and throwing the bits wherever his mood took him. One piece of paper wafted off the desk and floated down on to the carpet's thick pile.

"Pass that to me, I wish to look at it," the boy commanded.

Landing closest to Philip he had little choice, but to obey the demand.

"Thank you," the king said and studied the letter. "It seems people are displeased with the new prayer book. What exactly is a rebellion, Uncle?"

"Sire, some of the common people get angry about things they don't understand. It happens all the time," Seymour said.

"That's not at all clear to me, Uncle please explain it."

Only a tightened jaw and a deferential nod revealed Seymour's irritation.

"Of course, Sire. What I meant referred to the endless demands the court receives from the poorly educated. It might be of a religious nature, pertaining to lack of work perhaps or their perceived loss of farming land, that sort of thing."

Philip saw the opportunity to petition the King directly, but if he spoke out he might jeopardize his own future, yet sensitive to the troubles in his home county left him with a dilemma. It only took a moment for him to decide. Keeping his face averted from Seymour, he spoke to the young king.

"Sire, if I might interrupt. There has been the same recently in Norfolk, not about prayer books, but concerning large flocks of sheep and the people's land being enclosed. Now they face considerable hardship. I myself have kin there and it worries them greatly."

The angry hiss from behind assured Philip, Seymour was not best pleased. The enormity of what he'd done sent a cold shiver down his spine. It was too late now, it was said. An animated look brightened the king's serious features and he clapped his hands.

"Do you hear that, Uncle? Sheep, now that's interesting. I find the life of all animals most fascinating, Philip. You must tell me more. First of all, what sort of sheep are they?"

"I'm sorry I don't know, Your Highness. I could find out," Philip said, his tone apologetic.

The king looked thoughtful and chose to ignore Seymour's contemptuous snort.

"Lincoln Long Horn, would you think or perhaps Clun Forest, never mind, no matter. I shall look in my books. Continue please."

Philip made it brief especially as once the talk of sheep changed to arguments about hedges and he saw the king yawn. Still he avoided Seymour's eyes and concluded. "The men in Attleborough await their punishment, Sire, it seems somewhat unfair."

"Perhaps I should pardon them?" the king said as he picked at a thread on his doublet. "What do you think, Uncle?"

"It won't be necessary Your Grace. You may leave it all to me. There will be no need to speak of this matter again," Seymour said, with a curt edge to his voice and a look of triumph directed at Philip.

"Very well," the king said and jumped out of the chair. "I must go now. I expect my dinner is ready."

When the door closed the air in the room seemed disturbed by the hasty departure. It took a minute for it to settle again. The two men left turned to face one another. Philip waited. It wasn't his place to speak first. Seymour ran one finger along the edge of his desk. It was a slow and precise move.

"I shall overlook your meddling this time. It is fortunate for you that my mind is overly burdened by events at the Tower yesterday. But don't ever make that mistake again. Do you understand, Philip?"

The menace he intended was unmistakable.

– 8 –

Wymondham
June 1549

Only Will was absent from the Council meeting in Thom's yard. Over the last few days, mid-summers generous warmth offered them all a reason to shed their coarse linen shirts in favour of lighter tunics. As they waited apathy reflected itself in the despondent slope of their shoulders and the idle way they lazed, but it was not by choice they appeared so indolent.

It was difficult to get used to doing nothing apart from their daily efforts to find food. Landless labourers, as they heard themselves called, needed to adjust to their reduced circumstances. And being without work bought with it guilt and worse.

At the risk of being caught and punished they hunted every day. Arrows found them a rabbit or a bird, traps caught small vermin and patience rewarded them with a fish, whilst their womenfolk searched the countryside for fruit, nuts and handfuls of edible wild greens. All the while they watched helpless as the sheep flocks grew larger and hedges higher.

Frustrated and angry, they argued amongst themselves and waited for the call to bring an end to the situation. They hoped Will's expected arrival would give them the news they wanted.

"So who is this man Will knows?" Edmund said.

Thom paid close attention to the last of the reed which he threaded in one end on his new eel trap.

"Elias, he's Will's cousin. He offered to take a letter to the palace. His friend serves the king and there was hope if he heard of our plight, he might offer a pardon to those in Attleborough before they were sentenced," he said, turning the trap to admire his work.

"Which didn't happen at the time," Giles reminded. "Since then Philip sent word to Elias that things may have changed. Will is hoping to find out, which is why we all sit here and wait."

"Or sleep," Thom said and pointed to the two brothers, Richard and Matthew. Both rested their backs against the side of the barn. Heads on chests they snored loudly. Mischief relieved boredom, but even the handful of grit John showered on them failed to wake them.

It was Giles who first saw the tall, shadowed shape on the track. "Here's Will now," he said. "See how he grins. Perhaps he brings good news."

"Difficult to see anything under all that hair," Thom remarked dryly, sorting through the dried reed to start another trap.

Will's stride carried him across the yard. His boots were turned grey with dust and sweat trapped speckles of dirt in his curly hair and in his unruly beard. He sat down and wound his long legs awkwardly beneath him.

"So what's the news," John asked eagerly.

Thirst and a dry throat made Will swallow hard. The others looked on impatiently as they waited for him to speak.

"Fair dries you out, a walk to Attleborough and back in this heat. I can't tell you anything until I've had a drink," the big man croaked.

Thom pulled out a flask from his pocket and passed it to him.

"Don't take it all," he warned. "The ale's all but finished and unless I find some barley, they'll be no more."

Unperturbed Will's swallow was large as befitted his size and the others watched in silence as he took a long draught from the flask.

"That's better," he said, unabashed by the noisy belch which followed. "Elias says Philip managed to speak to the king in person. He seemed sympathetic, so he said and since then it's been announced the king has pardoned all who have torn down hedges."

Their rowdy cheer woke both the Mayhew brothers with a start. They blinked in the sun and struggled to gather their wits.

"So that means he must support us and considers the enclosures are illegal, thank the good Lord for that," John said. "Our land will be returned to us."

"Amen," murmured Thom. He concentrated on his work so the others wouldn't see the hot rush of tears. Only Edmund looked troubled.

"You're sure that's what he said, Will? We've seen no pardons yet."

He was fond of the burly man, but sometimes wondered if his hearing was as hasty as his manner. It wouldn't do to get things wrong, he thought, in view of the punishments already taken place. Dismayed by Edmund's doubts the others groaned.

"We must be sure," he said.

Giles interrupted swiftly, defending Edmund who he respected as wise and steady.

"Edmund's right. There must be no mistake, Will. This Philip, is he reliable?"

Both dogged by nature and weary from his journey, Will just nodded.

"That's good enough for me," Thom said and got to his feet. "I must go and tell Martha."

Amidst a chorus of agreement, the others prepared for their walk home.

"When shall we take down the hedges around here?" Richard asked, afraid he'd missed something whilst he slept.

"The weekend after next is the Fair and the Feast of Thomas. What better time than that," John replied.

With more meat pies crimped and ready to bake, Martha counted those already cooked. Finger raised, she slowly moved it along the rows.

"Two dozen, Thom and another tray still to cook. Will that be enough, do you think? I had so little to put in them. Last year there was food to spare," she shrugged and busied herself with a cleaning rag.

"They look well enough, wife, should I try one?" he replied.

She tapped his hand as it hovered over the pastry tray and laughed. Disappointed, he spat noisily on to the worn toe of his boot and polished it vigorously.

A piece of beef on the spit dripped juices into the flames and mingled with the aroma of wood smoke and spices. The air in the room gave off a tainted odour, but they were used to it and it didn't trouble them. Annoyed by stray wisps of hair which escaped from under her cap, Martha tucked them back with a hasty jab of her fingers. Despite her good humour she looked anxious.

"I worry," she said. "One day we shall be discovered. The law is clear. No one should be celebrating for all he was a holy man."

His laugh derisive, Thom said.

"Is it not enough our church is ruined. Since most of the stone is taken our prayers are free to float in the wind, thanks to the Abbot's conniving ways. The seventh day of this month marks a Feast day. Our Sainted Thomas Becket deserves to be remembered and toast him we will."

She grimaced at his scorn.

"We should take care that's all," she said. She reached for fresh horse-corn in the ark and sniffed the coarse crust. "What I'd give for a nicer loaf instead of this dark excuse for one."

"One day I'll grow fine wheat again I promise. You fret too much, wife," he said and tweaked her apron string as she passed.

"Yes, maybe I do," she said, wistful.

"Have we any ale to take?"

"You'll find what's left in the barn," she said, bent over the spit.

She laid the solid joint of meat in the largest earthenware dish she possessed and covered it with straw. With the last batch of pies almost ready she took off her apron and wiped her wet brow with it. When Thom returned, not only did he have a flagon of ale but Arthur's wife, Mary-Ann, who clung to him in a distraught state.

"Look who I found coming up the track," he said, grateful to push her towards his wife.

Mary-Ann collapsed into Martha's arms. It was pitiful to see her tears which continued for several minutes. Impossible to speak over them, Martha led her to a stool and sat her down.

"There, Mary-Ann, whatever's happened?" she asked.

Reassured by her gentle touch the older woman rested her head against Martha's chest. The tears were slow to stop and her sobs interrupted her effort to speak. Neither Martha nor Thom could understand one word of her hysterical jabber. Then Mary-Ann hiccoughed a few times.

"It's Arthur," she said. "They've taken him... away...he..."

Her scarlet cheeks and stray white hair caught fresh tears and she found a rag of blue cotton in her pocket to scrub them away. Thom hesitated, tears were women's business and he was tempted to leave them alone. But he was curious too.

"Come, Mary-Ann, be calm, tell us what's happened to Arthur. Who was it took him away?"

"It was Master Flowerdew's men. They took him to Norwich. Now he's locked up in the prison. Filthy place they say it is with nought, but the company of rats." She shuddered as another noisy sob escaped.

"What have they put him in prison for? What did Arthur do?" Martha said with quiet encouragement.

"Master Flowerdew's chickens, they were out on the road. He rounded them up for fear they were lost. It was only one and a small one at that, he didn't think it would be missed, chickens, well, they go anywhere they have a mind to."

"So he stole one of Flowerdew's chickens?" Thom said with some relief, not that it wasn't a serious offence but all the same.

Subdued, Mary-Ann wriggled her bulk on the stool and the wood gave a protesting squeak.

"We are that hungry, what else was he to do? The little 'uns need meat and besides the vegetables have all gone bad. He's been half out of his mind with worry."

Martha squeezed her hand and received a grateful smile.

"These are hard times, I know," she said. "So what do you think will happen now?"

"There'll be a trial," Thom lowered his voice so as not to threaten.

"No," Mary-Ann said, tearful again. "They said there was another reason so there'll be no trial. They found Arthur in a field where he wasn't meant to be. He'd climbed over a hedge, you see. Trespass was what they called it. He had the chicken up his tunic when they stopped him. He's to be flogged in the morning and then the hot-irons. He'll be so ashamed."

She covered her face with her hands and rocked back and forth. When she started to wail Thom excused himself and left Martha to comfort her.

"We're on our way to the Fair, we'll walk you home," she said, when Mary-Ann was composed again.

"The Fair," Mary-Ann whispered. "I'd forgotten."

July 1549

For many the Feast day of Thomas Becket on the sixth day of July would be well remembered as the place where their fight for justice began. But when Martha and Thom arrived laden with her roast meat and savoury pies, she looked forward to no more than a few hours of celebration.

They were fortunate to still have somewhere to hold their fair. Forbidden as it was, all would commemorate a man who'd passed into sainthood, the feast drew folk from other villages too who wished to honour him on the ragged plot on the edge of Wymondham.

Being so close to the river the grass was a sponge for most of the year and poor land was of no interest to its owner, Squire Flowerdew. He knew enough about sheep not to risk his animals with serious hoof rot let alone anything else which could mean inferior meat. A dirty fleece fetched less money too, all good enough reasons not to fence it. As long as he received a flagon or two of ale he was also prepared to overlook the Day of Beckett who he regarded as a miserable little traitor. As Flowerdew watched the preparations from a bedroom window, he made a note it was time to ask for an increase of ale before the next fair.

Makeshift stalls stretched across the rectangle of coarse meadow. Activity was everywhere. Men made last minute adjustments to woodwork whilst the women decorated tables with flowers and remnants of bright material. On what would have been a tranquil afternoon, the air resounded with the squeals and shrieks of excited children. Unable to overcome them sluggish air curled round their voices and carried them to all corners of the meadow.

"I see that wretch Francis is here," Thom muttered with a sideways glance. "Sent by Flowerdew, I don't doubt."

"See how he loiters. The man makes me shiver," Martha said.

She folded her arms round her waist as if to hold in the fear she still carried when she thought about the attack in the barn. Behind her Thom, his face set in a dark frown, carried a skep filled with meat, pies and ale. He headed towards John and Sible who waited behind one of the make-shift tables to receive the food. Under it, their three smallest children played with a ball.

Sible's baked bread, buns and bottles of cordial took little space on the square of linen and there was room to spare for Martha's contribution.

"Good day to you both, are you well?" Thom said.

The two women unpacked the skep whilst Thom set the flagon on the grass and joined John.

"We must thank the Almighty for good weather. Who knows if there'll be a fair next year, no one has food enough as it is." He sniffed the air and looked at Martha's dish of beef. "That smells good," he said.

"The ox," Thom said. "I wish we could have offered more. Are the Council here?"

"Giles will be late. His wife is uncomfortable with the child she carries. She tires easily."

Drawn by the sound of boisterous laughter and obvious high spirits Thom and John left their wives to gossip and wandered over to a group of men gathered by the ale flasks. Old George Parker, still grinding flour despite his palsied hands was playing Strip the Willow on his pipe. A melancholy tune often lost in the noise made by the drinkers, he seemed content to play it over and over again.

Empty flagons rolled on the grass as did some of the villagers. Their inebriation set their companions giggling whilst those still on their feet staggered unsteadily to refill their beakers.

"Fie Silas, shame on you, your mother will take a willow stripling to you when she sees you," Thom said when a youth fell against him and clasped him for support. The lad's stupid smile never left his face as he slid down the length of Thom and collapsed in a heap on the grass.

"What's he been drinking?" John asked.

"Mead mostly and very good it is," the village blacksmith said. He tipped the flagon upside down and a tiny trickle dribbled out onto the grass. He cast the flagon away with a snort of disgust.

"The ale's better," another said. "What's left of it."

A man from the village hurried across to Thom and John. Older and more sober than most he looked anxious as he grasped Thom's sleeve and pulled him to one side.

"Seems all people can talk about here is the land enclosures. When are we going to get a chance to pull up the fences about here? That's what I want to know."

"The Council are to hold a meeting at the end of the fair. It'll be decided then," Thom replied.

"Too late for that," someone said from the back of the crowd. "Some have left already. They've got tired of waiting."

The good humour faded from Thom and John's faces as if the sun suddenly vanished without trace. It was replaced with worried looks and heavy frowns.

"Not in the daylight surely," John said. "They're fools, whoever they are."

"Who are they and where have they gone?" Thom asked with growing unease.

"Let me see, four went I think," the man said. "There was an argument about our blessed Saint Thomas and things got a bit heated. Then one of them mentioned old Squire Hobart over Hingham way would get angry if he knew the real purpose of our fair. Ralph here, mentioned Hobart's land was now fenced. Well, that set them off again and they stormed off that way."

"They've gone to Hingham then. Were they sober?" John asked.

The man shrugged. "That's all I know," he said and wandered off.

"We should go after them," Thom said. He looked back to where they left Martha and Sible, but there was no sight of either of them. "I don't see the womenfolk."

"We're better spending time looking for them than chasing fools. We don't even know when they left here." John said. "I want no part of it if they get arrested."

Several times they thought they caught sight of their wives, but when they got closer they were wrong. Confused, Thom pushed his hat back and scratched his head.

"How many years have I been wed yet still can't recognise my wife among all these females," he said, wryly.

"Isn't that them?" John said. He craned his head over the crowd in front. "Look there, coming across the grass."

"Odd, they must have been off somewhere."

A girl passed with a tray of honey coated fruit. Thom helped himself to a piece and licked the sweetness from his fingers with noisy relish. Martha and Sible were happy to wander and stop for a chat on the way so they made slow progress towards them. Slender and pretty in their best cotton gowns they were a handsome pair. Martha's hair flamed gold lights in the sunshine and Sible's unrestrained dark curls tumbled about her shoulders.

Thom and John scowled with impatience and by the time they arrived at their side, were both peeved.

"What kept you, woman?" John rebuked his wife.

Martha shook her head. "Don't scold her, it was my fault. I was fretting about poor Mary-Ann. Just wanted to make sure she was alright. Sible said she'd keep me company."

"And was she...alright?" Thom said, short with her.

"She's still very upset. What with Arthur in the stocks and being branded. He's carrying a T burnt on his ear so she told us," Sible said in a small voice.

There was silence at the thought. Seeing Thom still looked displeased, Martha linked her arm through his.

"And what's put you in such a bad mind, husband?"

"I'm sorry, not you two. It's what we've just heard. Some have gone from here to tear up hedges," he said. "They weren't supposed to do that. John and I must look for them before it ends in a fight," he muttered.

"Who do the fences belong to?" Martha asked.

"Squire Hobart at Hingham so they say," John replied. "Maybe we should see you both home and then Thom and I will go after them. What do you think, Thom?"

Thom nodded. "I shan't go to my bed until I know what's what," he growled.

Martha and Sible exchanged glances.

"You'll both be safe, won't you?" Sible said.

A smile filtered through Thom's serious expression.

"Don't you worry, there's no one in the village I wouldn't stand up to apart from Will Medler that is, and I've seen him not a moment past. Rosie's made him take a turn round the maypole. Can you imagine, Will dancing?"

"Stands for no nonsense, does Rosie and she such a little scrap of a thing," Martha said, laughter lightening their mood as the four of them left the meadow.

Just as the shadows lurked in corners ready to overtake the light, Thom and John set off. When they passed the water meadow it was quiet again. Some, more thoughtful than others, would return in the morning to clear up all traces of the festivities.

Side by side the two men followed the twisted track to Hingham. Dusk gathered pace and had they not known the path of old it would have been easy to lose their way. As it was they needed to stop to light their rush torch.

On a bend they heard them before they set eyes on them. A mixture of shouts, jeers and noisy laughter fell on the flinty path and vibrated back again. Thom and John paused to wait for the dark shapes to fall under the light from their flames so they could identify them.

"By all that's Holy, how many are they?" John said.

"I thought it was said there were only four of them," Thom murmured. He looked calm but gripped his torch with a firmer hand.

"There must be a score or more. Where did they all come from?" John whispered.

In the yellowy glow hawthorn hedging gave way to the ebullient group whose voices trailed into silence when they saw the two men. They were all armed. Some carried thick staves others held pitchforks as well as their longbows.

The aura about them was humour, but it lacked good nature. Instead it was edged with hostility. Thom knew the line between such emotions was easily broken and endeavoured to keep a placid expression on his face. Even so his eyebrows were raised when he recognised the two men who led the group.

"I should have guessed," he murmured.

Jack and Humfrey Moore kept a slaughtering pit and butcher's shop. Easy to provoke and fond of a fight they swaggered toward Thom and John, their staves held like swords in fists as hard as iron.

"Take care, Thom, you know what they're like," John said quietly.

Jack, the eldest by a year and usually the spokesman stopped and grinned at the two men. Neither did more in return than to acknowledge him with curt nods. Jack's wide smile didn't shift, whilst the flicker of the flame accentuated the cast in one eye. Noticing leaves and twigs tangled in his jerkin, he picked them off and dropped them slowly one by one in front of Thom and John.

"You don't look too pleased, Thom. Don't want to be taking Squire Hobart's property home now do we?" he said, his thin lips twisted into an insolent sneer and the words hissed through broken teeth.

His brother tossed his greasy dark hair away from his eyes and giggled. It was a nervous sound. His skin held a shine of sweat and beads of it rested on the thin fluff above his upper lip.

"You ought to be pleased, Thom, we did a good job tonight, didn't we, lads?" he said looking round at his companions for support.

There was noisy agreement from those gathered round with "Ayes," and nods of heads to confirm his statement.

"Was that wise? You were told we'd give the signal." Thom said.

Jack gave a raucous laugh. "Wait for you and starve, do you mean?"

Sensing the tension, John interrupted. "You've come from Hingham then?"

"So what of Squire Hobart, did you meet him?" Thom asked, careful to keep his voice even.

"He gave us no bother," Jack laughed. "He locked himself in. Never came near us. No one did and every fence is ripped down. We burnt some of it too, he'll not be using it again," he said.

Thom and John turned and saw a pale orange haze across the meadows. Relieved it was no more than that Thom relaxed.

"We'll walk with you back to the village."

"Not so quick, we haven't finished yet," Jack said. "There's more to be done before we look for our beds."

Thom kept his hands in his pockets, fingernails dug into both palms. He knew he must control his temper. "So what do you intend now?" he said softly.

"Master Flowerdew's place at Hethersett is next. We're going there now," someone said.

Again nods and murmurs signified that was indeed the plan.

"It's late, there's no need for more tonight. Tomorrow we can plan." Thom ventured.

John whispered a warning. "Take care they do not attack us."

"Don't stand in our way, Barwick," Jack said, his hand slipping to the glint of steel tucked in his belt. "Talking gets us nowhere. Action's what we need. Come on men, there's work to be done."

John took a step closer to the two butchers. "That's not fair, Thom's been..."

In a sudden move, Jack grasped the neck of his jerkin almost lifting him off the ground.

"Nothing's fair, John Moulder, nothing at all. Is it fair our wives weep for the worry of it and our childer go hungry? I'd say that was very unfair. Wouldn't you? Now let us pass."

Raising his voice, Humfrey spoke. "I heard tell of someone seen pulling up Flowerdew's hedges not so very long ago. In the middle of the night, they said. Who might have done that, I wonder?"

Eyes narrowed he looked hard at Thom and his loud snigger encouraged others to laugh too.

"Now can we go about our business before I'm tempted to name him, eh, Barwick?"

"Why's he staring at you?" John whispered.

Thom shrugged and stood to one side. With little choice John did the same.

"Let them go," Thom growled. "When they've gone through the village, we'll follow."

Torches held high the group swept past. Thom and John followed quietly behind them. Even when they lost sight of them, loud voices and outbursts of laughter guided them well enough.

Bent over a trap, Francis struggled to drag out a large brown rat. The rodent's vile yellow incisors snapped dangerously near his fingers. Francis kept a careful eye on Flowerdew's house where lights still burnt until finally he grasped the rat by its tail and pulled it out. About to dispatch it with a blow to the back of the neck he paused.

Its feet paddling the air, the rat dangled. Its futile squeals spoke of its discomfort. For a moment Francis wondered if he'd imagined faint voices and the sound of feet on the drive. He strained to listen above the rat's vocal protest. When he heard them again coming nearer, he knew it wasn't a trick of his ears. No time for niceties, he dashed the creature's head on a flint and crept further into the thicket of laurels.

Through gaps in the leaves he watched the group of men pass. Some carried heavy sticks and others waved long-handled forks or hoes, the ends of them reflecting a dull glint when torchlight fell on them. He saw that the butcher brothers led the way and flinched. His memory was still sharp at what had happened when they discovered him stealing a string of sausages. Jack administered him a mighty blow with a leg of mutton which sent him sprawling on the ground. His brother followed with repeated kicks until he yelled for mercy. Scowling at the thought he tried to see who else he could recognise, but he was not in the best position and too scared of giving himself away.

He was so sure they were about to knock on the front door, he turned his gaze expectantly. But they didn't. Instead a little short of it they fell silent and turned left. He knew then their intention. They could only be heading for the pastures and he guessed that meant the fences. He watched them until the bob of torch flames disappeared into the darkness.

With every intention of returning, he left the rat beside the blood smeared flint and scrambled out from behind the laurel. A dash took him across the drive where he delivered a hammer-burst of blows on the solid oak door.

Francis jigged on the step with impatience. By the time it took for the door to be opened he guessed Squire Flowerdew wasn't in the habit of receiving visitors in the hours of darkness. Finally a chink of light revealed a small portion of something white and an eye.

"Yes, who is it?"

"It's me, Master Flowerdew, Francis."

He was gratified when the door opened more fully. In his nightshirt and fleecy nightcap, John scowled at him.

"For God's sake, man. Have you any idea of the lateness of the hour. This had better be important."

"There are men from the village on your land, I've just seen them," Francis said. He waved his arm in a wild gesture towards the darkened fields. "You should go quickly. I think they mean to tear up your fences."

His head bent forward, John fixed his eyes closely on Francis. Then he sniffed the air and looked about.

"What sort of story is this? Have you been imbibing too much ale? Who are these men, you speak of? I don't see anyone."

In his excitement, Francis raised his voice. "That's because they're spread across the meadows. They had sticks, knives, all sorts. You must hurry, Master Flowerdew. Before it's too late."

"Shush, damn you, before you wake my wife," John hissed as he cast an anxious glance behind him. "Are you absolutely sure about this?"

For a moment, Francis thought he wouldn't be believed and wished he'd minded his own business. It wouldn't be the first time his master accused him of lying. On the other hand the notion he might be rewarded made him more determined.

"Why else would I be here at this time of the night?" he said with a confidence he didn't feel. "Please, Master Flowerdew, we're wasting time. You'll have no fences left."

"You don't seriously expect me to caper down there wearing only my night attire?" He paused and drew himself a little more upright. "It is not yet common knowledge and I trust you to keep it to yourself, but I'm about to receive a knighthood. Eh, what do you think of that? Not only was I chosen as Cromwell's enforcer, but I'm a king's man and His Majesty has been gracious enough to recognise my loyal services to the crown. Soon you will be addressing me as Lord Flowerdew. Tell me, do lords run around in such articles?"

His hand held out a bunch of striped flannel and his pomp made Francis want to laugh, but matters were too grave for that.

"Master, my Lord, I really think you will regret not taking my word but..."

"Alright, alright, wait there," John said crossly and closed the door abruptly.

Francis shuffled his feet and shivered. His thin jerkin offered him no warmth and he rubbed his hands together as the night chill grew more intense. He cursed he didn't possess anything warmer.

Just when he felt his toes turn numb the door opened again. John stepped out trim and elegant in a smart brown velvet edged jacket and immaculate cream breeches. He carried an ebony cane in one hand and his beaver hat in the other. He lashed the cane in the air with imagined ferocity and said.

"There, you just wait and see what they make of this. A few strokes across their silly faces and I'll have them on the run. You see if I don't."

"Aye, Master," Francis said doubtfully.

They walked abreast across the first meadow. Apart from the occasional bleat of sheep and the sound of a distant owl nothing seemed disturbed. Gradually John slowed his step and fell behind. Francis suspected he'd already decided advancing from the rear was infinitely safer than being in the lead.

"You go ahead," John called. "We must catch these brigands. They can't go about thinking they can do what they please." He stopped and turned his head from side to side. "What's that noise?"

"Sheep?" Francis suggested.

"You're a bigger fool than I thought. Are you suggesting I don't know the noise a sheep makes? I meant the crackling noise." Then he sniffed. "By God, I smell smoke."

Green wood lacks the comfortable smell of dried wood when it burns and in a moment both men caught the acrid smoke in their throats and mopped their eyes. When they looked, a large stack of hedging was on fire. Hungry for oxygen, flames curled in on themselves and forced their energy skywards whilst the faint crackle became a roar.

In disbelief, John clutched Francis by his neck and he shook him hard.

"Why didn't you fetch me sooner?" he screeched. "These are madmen destroying my property. The fault is yours. You've neglected your duty."

Francis's eyes rolled and his scrawny frame bounced under John's grip.

"Begging your pardon, Master Flowerdew, it was you who delayed by not believing me," he gibbered.

"Don't argue, go and stop them at once," John said, striking his boot with the cane to emphasise his instructions.

A nervous titter trembled on Francis's lips. "I think it would come better from you, Master. They won't listen to me."

In fury, John struck out at him with the cane. Francis heard the whine of it and ducked just in time.

"You're useless. Useless," John screamed. "My land's burning and my sheep are scattered. I'll be ruined and all you do is stand there and whine." As if released on a spring he ran in the direction of the fire. Over his shoulder he called to Francis.

"Follow me, I may need you."

Feeling obliged to follow, Francis trotted across the grass at a slower pace. He could see shapes appearing in the dark and in moments John was surrounded by men. Relieved to see they appeared quiet he sidled nearer. Hands spread in a gesture of calm, John was speaking.

"I must ask you to all go home. I'm a reasonable man, if you leave now there will be no punishments. If you have a grievance, choose a spokesman and tomorrow we can sit down and talk about it."

Francis was taken aback. Gone was John's uncontrolled anger. Instead he appeared almost benevolent and pleasant. Emboldened, Francis moved closer, but he was careful to avoid Jack Moore and his brother who he spied standing at the front. All eyes were on the squire, no one appeared to notice him.

"Have you broken down every enclosure? Are all the animals gone?"John asked.

"No, some over the way are still grazing. We didn't get to all the hedges. Never knew how much land you have," someone called from the crowd with a hint of sarcasm.

"Come now, only a modest amount, I can assure you," replied John with a faint smile, but the darkness masked the hard glitter of his eyes. A voice spoke from somewhere in the group.

"We should finish the job, that's why we came."

Francis tried to see who'd spoken, but the flickering light cast strange shadows and no face was clear. John's smile vanished. Agitated he said quickly.

"I promise a carcase to be shared amongst you if you leave now. It's very fine mutton, I assure you."

"Is that all? You offer one measly carcase to go round all of us. Listen to that will you. I reckon there'll be a cutlet each."

Laughter rippled round the group. "That's very handsome of you, squire, but you're going to have to do better than that," Jack said.

"Very well, I'll give you two then."

"Still not enough," another shouted.

John's features tightened and his fingers grasped the cane in a firmer hold.

"Three and that's my last offer," he said, no trace of good humour left in his voice.

Jack looked at Humfrey and nodded.

"Agreed," he called out. "And we choose the beasts. We don't want none of your scrawny ewes on their last legs."

There was a murmur of agreement and Francis looked sideways at John. He knew the signs well enough. Any minute the squire would fiddle with the scar on his cheek and Francis sent a silent prayer upward for that to be the end of the bargaining. As if in answer, he felt drops of rain strike his face. But undaunted by the drizzle which spoiled his smart outfit, John still had more to say.

"Before you leave, you might like to think on this. Over yonder side of that tree is my neighbour's estate. Master Kett keeps sheep too, many on common land. His enclosures make mine look of no consequence. You might care to make a visit there. You will find he builds very big hedges. Of course if such a thing as size daunts you, I should understand." Immediately he could see indecision and hastily added. "Perhaps I could make it worth your while. Shall we say a silver shilling when the work is done?"

Francis gasped at the suggestion and marvelled at John's cunning. He thought it a masterly stroke. Even in the poor light he could see a look of triumph on the squire's face. Few spoke openly of the feud which persisted between the two men, but any chance to oppose Robert Kett would give great satisfaction to the other, he was sure of that.

Hunched in their thin clothes the men pondered. Tired of their wretched state, challenge and money were a powerful lure. Jack beckoned his companions to stand closer and spoke to them in a low voice. Francis could not hear what was said, but by nods and mutters, the idea seemed favourable.

"A shilling you say and the meat? Very well, we'll go to Kett's," Jack said.

John nodded. "As long as you do no more damage here, I'll keep my word."

Behind him the dampened wood hissed and smouldered, but it no longer interested the men responsible for the fire. Excited at the prospect of more hedges to demolish they gathered up their weapons and prepared to march off.

Well out of sight, Thom and John looked on. Hidden by a clump of young sycamores they'd managed to get close. In full leaf the trees provided good cover and voices carried well to where they stood.

"Perhaps the rain will put them off," John whispered as heavier raindrops pounded the foliage around them.

"I doubt it," Thom said grimly.

"Then we should go and warn, Master Kett before they attack. This isn't the way to go about things. Its madness," John said, his eyes fixed on the men.

Unable to light their torches for fear of discovery they slid into the darkness and headed for Robert Kett's manor house, Walsham Hall.

As Thom and John approached the rambling thatched house a horse-drawn carriage rattled past. They shrank back into the shadows until it reached the end of the drive before they moved. Late as the hour was, Robert Kett opened his door more readily than John Flowerdew. He stifled a yawn as he greeted them.

"It's rather an odd time for you to be visiting, gentlemen. Forgive me if I appear sleepy, I was on my way to my bed. Entertaining is all very well, but guests are often tardy when it comes to leaving."

"If it wasn't urgent." Thom said.

"Of course, do come in. I see its still raining," Robert said, looking down at the pools of water on the step.

Thom shook his head. "We don't have time and nor do you. You are due more visitors very shortly."

"Not tonight surely?"

Surprised, Robert took a step back and looked up to the timepiece on the wall which showed the hour was almost midnight.

"It's true," John assured, glancing back over his shoulder. "We came as fast as we could."

Puzzled, Robert smiled pleasantly. Thom and John were no strangers to him, solid men he always thought.

"Gentlemen, you intrigue me. What is this all about?"

"They are some coming from the village, ready to tear down your hedges," Thom said.

"I don't understand. Who are these people?"

"You'll see soon enough," John offered in a low voice.

Both men thought Kett worthy of their respect. As mild mannered as Flowerdew was offensive, Robert never flaunted his status as gentry or his considerable wealth. Wymondham citizens were mindful of his support of the church and his frequent donations to those in need. Equally generous his brother, William was a prominent member of Wymondham Abbey until Flowerdew and others demolished part of it.

"Be careful, Master Kett, you'll find Master Flowerday is behind some of this mischief, 'twas his idea to send them to you. They've already torn down his fences and he got them all fired up, even offered them money. We can't stay to tell you more, but they're not in a good mood," Thom warned.

A flicker of dark emotion briefly shaded Robert's eyes, but his reply was surprisingly genial.

"I'm grateful to you both. I've heard there are complaints from those in the village over lost land and it concerns me. I'm sure if I speak to them they will leave peaceably."

"For your sake, I hope so," John murmured.

Shaking the rain from his head, Thom said. "I'm sorry, we can't be seen here. Make no mistake they're intent in ripping up your hedges so choose your words with care. There's none of us wants to lose our common fields and there'll be trouble unless someone listens to us. Your sorts making profit off our loss is more than most can understand, but that doesn't mean we're all lawless men."

"All we ask is for our pasture land to be restored to us," John murmured.

"They're coming, I can hear them," Thom said.

All three turned to look as the first of the torches flickered in the drive. With a gentle hand Robert pushed the two men off the step. "Go that way," he said, indicating a gate set in the yew hedge close to the house. "And hurry."

In less than a moment, Thom and John disappeared.

68

The men straggled across the drive and came to a ragged stop in front of Robert. As before the first to speak was Jack.

"It seems you might be expecting us, Master Kett, I wonder how that was. Still no matter it saves us dragging you from your bed. A nice bed is it, warm and comfortable? And do you get into it with a full belly? What would it be, a nice plump sheep roasted over your spit perhaps. Because you see, Master Kett, most of us would be willing to crouch at your door and suck the bones you so willingly toss away. How did the meat taste? Moist and sweet, I'll wager. It should since the beast has been grazing our grass, hasn't it, friends?"

A murmur of voices suddenly swelled into noisy cheers and claps and Robert's first words were lost. Jack raised his hands.

"Enough now, let's hear Master Kett make his excuses."

At first it seemed Jack's appeal wasn't heeded either. No longer dispirited his companions chants and rowdy laughter took awhile to subside. Robert tried again. Confronted by such a lawless crowd didn't appeal, but he refused to be intimidated. Hopeful they'd lose interest so he tried to appear affable.

"Good evening to you all. It is time we talked."

"What's the use of that? All you lot do is talk," someone grumbled.

"Aye," said another. "We want action."

"Hush your voices, let him be heard," Jack said.

"You heard my brother," Humfrey yelled. "Let the man speak."

"We weren't made to wait before we went to work on Flowerdew's hedges," a voice from the back bellowed.

Robert wondered how John Flowerdew had faired with this fractious bunch.

"Thank you," he said politely. "I can't pretend I hadn't hoped to improve my fortunes when I bought sheep. But I've given it some thought and my heart isn't made of stone. It seems common land is being taken in all parts of the country. It can't be right when your land is stolen from you and your houses pulled down. Those who act on behalf of the crown have much to answer for," he said firmly.

Such an unexpected reply surprised the crowd. They turned to one another and an eyebrow or two were raised.

"Aye, he's right there."

"And what about our monasteries, they've all been took too. Our parish churches have been sacked on the orders of the king. Us God-fearing folk have nothing left to call our own," a man shouted. "Do you wonder we steal and beg? And what happens then when we get caught, we rot in prison or take a trip to the gallows. What sort of future is that?"

An elderly man waved his hand in the air. Quietly spoken, he said.

"Only last week, my cousin in Maidstone got thrown into prison. They called him a vagabond and him once an elder in the Priory. He was forced onto the streets with not a groat to his name when they took his glebe land."

"I know of a church turned into a sheep-fold. What do you think of that, Master Kett?"

Humfrey appeared from behind his brother and waved his torch close to Robert's face as they all waited for his reply.

"I say it is all wrong. I say it should stop and stop now."

The hiss of breath from the onlookers was one of approval and Robert knew then he had them on his side. He knew what he intended to do was right. It was a curse having a conscience. It had got him into trouble more than once. He believed in God and felt deeply ashamed when he listened to those who championed the continuing hatred for religion, be it Protestant or Catholic.

He'd kept his thoughts to himself and grieved in private. But this was different. This was something he could do something about. Why should he have to account for being on the wrong side of an agrarian war when he stood before the Almighty? For a moment he thought about giving them a few lines from *Utopia* that Thomas More had been moved to write when he witnessed the dire situation of the poor commons. Somehow he mused it would be lost on the company in front of him and changed his mind.

"Come on, Kett, what are you waiting for. What are you going to do? Give us our land back?" He smiled.

"I was with my thoughts," he said.

"They won't do much to feed us," someone guffawed.

A soft swishing sound of silk in the hall behind him told him Alice lingered there and the fragrance of lilies enveloped his senses.

"Robert?"

He turned and looked into the hallway. "Go back to bed, my dear. I shan't be long."

"What's happened? Why are all those men out there?"

"It's nothing serious, I promise, my love. Please do as I ask. You'll catch cold standing there."

"Very well," she said and stretched her arms in a posture of one recently woken.

He waited until her gentle footfall faded on the stairs and then taking his jacket from the hall-stand, he stepped out. He pulled the door shut behind him and nodded. "Right, gentlemen, shall we go?"

Jack eyed him suspiciously. "Go, go where?"

"To my meadows, of course, I wish to strike the first blow to the hedges. We shall take them all down every last one. Did you do the same to Master Flowerdew's?"

"Not all. We stopped when he told us to come here." Jack replied.

Robert's features didn't alter and his voice stayed level. Inside he seethed. This time John had gone a step too far. Not a malicious man, Robert was slow to rouse, but not totally unforgiving if circumstances led him to anger. Still pleasant, he said.

"Good. So then we shall march to his land and finish the job."

At first silence greeted his remark. Should a bird have flown past, its wing beat would have deafened them. They stood looking at one another digesting Robert's words. Many thought they'd misheard him. Suddenly Jack sprinted across the drive and joined Robert on the step. He waved his hat and shouted.

"Did you all hear that? Now it's out in the open. No more sneaking about like weasels in the night. We all know he's a gentleman who keeps his word. Three cheers for Master Kett."

Over a wall in the vegetable garden, Thom and John smiled at each other in relief. Less sure of what it all meant, Francis sneaked away from behind a tree to retrieve his rat for the pot. In an upstairs window which overlooked the drive a curtain trembled. Held back by a slender hand, the face it revealed looked puzzled. Alice pressed closer to the glass. When she saw her husband walked freely and deep in conversation with the men leading the group, she relaxed.

The hollow in her feather mattress was still warm when she snuggled back into it.

Hampton Court Palace

Rested on the horizontal strut that supported a burnished oak refractory table, Seymour's feet fidgeted. Clad in black satin slippers, they twisted this way and that whilst he stifled an impatient snort. The meeting of the Privy Council dragged on and got more tedious as time passed.

Charles Tyler had been speaking for best part of an hour. Seventy three years of age, he seemed unable to recall matters on the agenda, instead he rambled in all directions. Unable to stand it any longer Seymour thumped the table. Such a heavy blow sent the glass goblets skittering across the highly polished wood. Mead in the jug slurped back and forth resembling a wind-struck wave and papers shivered of their own accord.

"Have I said something wrong, my lord?" Charles said, his dishevelled yellowing wig askew on his head.

"Have you said anything right, I ask myself," Seymour snapped. "Do you remember the purpose of this meeting, Charles?

The bewildered man rustled through his fistful of papers. Some floated away to the floor, others appeared empty sheets. Then he seized on one and beamed at Seymour.

"Ah, I thought so, the problem of mice in the palace kitchens. No, that's not right. Was it about your dissatisfaction with the court seamstress, no, that can't be correct either. I've got it, something about land, my lord? Yes, that's right, I have it here."

Round the table, some exchanged glances others blew their noses on a fine handkerchief to conceal their smiles.

"Poor chap's past it," George Shelbourne whispered.

"Charles, I grow weary of your uninspiring drivel, I'd thank you to sit down," Seymour said, spite embellishing his statement. "Could someone else please remind us what we are primarily here to discuss. George, you look lively, pray tell us if you please."

His request was met by an ingratiating smile from a raffish looking young man who got to his feet. He gave a precise bow and hooked his thumbs into the waistband of his white breeches.

"Thank you, my lord Seymour. It seems, gentlemen, the matter of land enclosures is getting out of hand. There is a tumult of displeasure. Peasants in Somerset, Lincoln, Essex and I believe Kent have now been joined by aggravating behaviour from Norfolk no less. By all accounts it's a peaceable, uninteresting county, but now it becomes very vocal and the people rage openly."

As Seymour listened he tapped his manicured nails impatiently on the table.

"Indeed George, most succinct, does anyone else care to add to this?"

Seated at the end of the table, William Page raised his hand.

"I've heard Wiltshire and Oxfordshire have a revolt on their hands too."

A disgruntled frown rested on Seymour's brow and he toyed with the seal on his ring. George cleared his throat.

"Perhaps my lord, if there was recompense paid to those who whine so, wouldn't that speed up a solution?"

Palest pink flushed Seymour's face and turned darker as it reached his high cheek bones.

"George, until now I have never considered you a half-wit. You are suggesting we pay these lower classes money? Whose, may I ask?"

This time it was George's face which coloured.

"From the Privy Purse perhaps, it...it was just a thought, my lord."

A solitary snigger from John Dudley echoed the contempt which already etched lines on Seymour's face. The others looked down at their papers. Seymour sighed heavily.

"I tire of the whole business. A year ago I ordered a royal commission to make enquiries. A report concerning enclosures, in which counties and the names of anyone owning over two thousand sheep was what I expected. At that time I believe others might too have had thoughts of some sort of monetary award. Still I wait to receive this information and the money has been spent on other things, as well you know. No, George, recompense is out of the question."

The nod was polite. "Very good, my lord Seymour," he replied.

Gratified he'd put George in his place, Seymour sensed unease and glanced round the table. No one looked directly at him, but it was obvious by their expressions some hoped for something more positive. He sighed again.

"Very well, send out some of the Knights. Tell them to speak to the Squires and report back. But leave Norfolk to me. So gentlemen, if there is nothing else to discuss, I suggest we call an end to the meeting. John, you're next to him, kindly poke Charles in the ribs. Wake him up for God's sake and accompany him to his quarters. I shall need to give serious thought to his continuing usefulness on the Council," he said tartly.

Philip conducted a minute search over his clothes. He was looking for a hair, a thread or a loose button, anything out of place which might come to Seymour's attention. Summoned by a message to attend the chamber, he wanted to give no cause for him to lose patience.

The hand written note hadn't indicated why he'd been sent for, but if it wasn't affairs of the Council, he suspected it would be concerning Norfolk. Coming from the garden he could hear childish voices. His window was small like his room, but by angling himself against the frame he could just see some lawn and part of the tennis court. Rain had persisted for almost a week, but this morning blue skies and warmth dried out the grass and cast a more cheerful light.

Philip looked out, and saw the young king with two companions. They carried tennis rackets and talked animatedly as they strolled towards the court. The poor weather always affected the king. Unable to sport himself outside he rambled about the palace bored and petulant. Philip could see by the cheerful smile and ready laugh the boy's mood was as bright as the reflected light from the gold embroidery on his outfit. Philip prayed it might be so with his uncle too.

He found Seymour ensconced in a chair a towel draped over him and his feet in a bowl of water. His eyes closed, his head rested on a cushion and his hair was draped with a hot flannel. The immature fingers of the boy behind him worked hard to probe and knead the flesh on his shoulders. Beside the chair a bowl of water waited to refresh the flannel. It gave off sweet-scented floral steams of lavender and rose which drifted towards Philip. Seymour raised the corner of the cloth in order to see him.

"Sit down, Philip, we shall be finished shortly," he said.

The ministrations carried on for a few more minutes until Seymour sat up abruptly. He tossed the flannel onto the floor and said. "That'll be enough for today. You may go."

"Yes, my lord," the boy said, giving an impressive bow.

Seymour never took his eyes of the lad until he'd emptied the bowl out of the window and collected the towels up. When he'd left the room, Seymour expressed an appreciative breath. Philip waited patiently for what might come next. It wasn't what he expected. A pale smile played on Seymour's lips as he said.

"What neat haunches that boy has. A pert bottom too. Did you notice that, Philip?"

"No my lord, I can't say I did."

"A pity, in a few years he will be a fine looking boy, very fine. Are you married, Philip?"

"Not yet my lord," he replied.

"My wife Anne is a good woman, but like all wives, not always understanding of a man's needs. When you take a wife, Philip, beware of such things," Seymour said, the usual hard edge to his voice absent.

Philip felt the warmth in his cheek and felt sure Seymour must notice his embarrassment. He had no idea exactly what Seymour meant, but suspected it a matter of delicacy.

"Indeed, my lord," he replied, hoping his words would end the conversation.

"Would you like a drop of Malmsey, Philip?" Seymour asked, reaching for his decanter. "I find it most soothing when the brain is fevered."

Philip shook his head, wondering why anyone should be fevered in a room which struck him as very cold despite the improved weather.

"Not for me, thank you, my lord."

Glass in hand, Seymour relaxed back in his chair.

"This is all very pleasant, but not the reason I sent for you. The Privy Council met this morning. Once again we've been called upon to restore peace with the malcontents in rural parts of the country." He paused and sipped from his glass with slow satisfaction. "I'm not unsympathetic towards the dispossessed poor, but when I've tried to help my attempts are thwarted. Estates are no longer feudal and the process of change ever advances. The way I see it, it is understandable landowners seek to increase profits wherever they can. Over the years my Acts have been ignored and frankly I'm dispirited by it all. Now it seems we shall shortly have a land war on our hands. What I find most disturbing is Norfolk seems to lead the way in this rebellious behaviour."

He looked into the glass of tawny liquid with eyes hardened by experience and fell silent. Unsure whether Seymour expected him to speak, Philip sought for something pertinent to say. He might have known misdeeds in Norfolk would draw him into a dialogue with the Lord Protector.

"I am not sure how..."

"Don't interrupt me, I have more to say on the matter," Seymour said curtly. "Parliament has sought measures which would surely deter those who don't care to work. Nor has it encouraged the poor. Poverty is now declared a crime, but it seems neither the lash nor the gallows are sufficient. How many times must I tell you our monarch is just an infant when it comes to matters concerning the state? Yet a short while ago you took it upon yourself to speak to the king, against my wishes, if you remember. Edward's head is only full of his own deeds. He plays ball games, goes hawking and learns music. What else might you expect from one so young? Since you appear to support the cause the rebels make so much noise about, I assume you know some of these troublemakers. I'm ordering you to put an end to this disorder immediately."

Privately, Philip thought despite his youth, the king seemed to have a good grasp of the politics of the day, but his own distress overwhelmed him. He leapt to his feet.

"But my lord, the good people of Norfolk are..."

With one hand raised to silence him, Seymour's eyes were glazed like shiny pebbles. In precise tones he said.

"Perhaps these good people as you call them will be prepared to visit you in the Tower should you fail. You'll be glad to see them. They tell me the hours pass slowly with only rats and mice for company."

– 10 –

Wymondham

John's meadows lay undisturbed when they returned to them. There was no sign of him or Francis, but in the distance contented sheep grazed at will. The men set about the remaining hedges in more order this time. Satisfied they'd uprooted all of them they gathered round Robert. He'd thought carefully as to what course to follow from there. The villager's uncoordinated behaviour worried him. It was obvious, he decided, they must be directed if they were to bring about change and restore their livelihood.

"I propose we hold a meeting at my home," he told them. "There we'll discuss how we proceed. Are you all in favour of that?"

"That sounds fair," Jack said. "Does everyone agree?"

There was no dissent and the men drifted away. Relieved, Robert called his hound who'd somehow managed to sneak onto the fields and they too turned for home. The dog was well trained and ignored the ambling flocks.

Pale fingers of light from the east stole amongst the night clouds when they all finally arrived at their dwellings. For the dissenters from the village it had been a long night and one which saw the agrarian revolution whisper through the flatlands of Norfolk.

Thom, John, Jack and his brother with six others arrived at Robert's house. One behind the other they filed in the back door. Boots discarded, they stuffed their caps in their pockets. No one was late. For many it was the first time inside a manor house. They waited uneasily and looked about with obvious discomfort. Only Jack Moore and his brother seemed at home as with an air of disdain they followed Robert into his drawing room.

On their entrance, a man rose out of a deep armchair. Whilst older and stouter than Robert there was a distinct resemblance. Even the lock of heavy fair hair falling across speedwell-blue eyes was the same. His clothes marked him as a man both of good taste and wealth and he carried his maturity well.

The pride in Robert's eyes was unmistakable as his brother, William came towards him. Seven years his senior, he'd always been his guide in all business matters. True like Robert, William had inherited extensive land and property from their father, but he'd used it well. His interests were diverse, being both a grazier and an authority on fine materials, the only mercer within miles of Norwich, which Robert often recounted to friends with obvious respect.

Yet, despite all this, Robert thought how self-effacing and modest his brother remained, a true example of a Christian man. He put an affectionate hand on William's arm and said.

"Gentlemen, some of you might know my brother, William. He knows how anxious I am to stand by you as you seek justice and has travelled from the other side of Wymondham to help us."

"Good day to you all," William said as he moved from one to the next to shake each man by the hand.

Lavish was the only word to describe the size of the room, it could encompass all the villagers owned and more. Both the high ceiling and elegant furnishings left the visitors in awe of such splendour and bemused by its extravagance.

"I'm not sure we have enough seats," Robert said.

He knew most would rather stand than take a seat on such gracious furniture, but determined to make them feel comfortable he fretted just the same. No one moved apart from Jack.

"My legs could do with a rest," he declared and threw himself down on a finely carved balloon chair upholstered in heavy gold brocade. With a foolish smile Humfrey perched with deliberate force on a second of them. Thom and John exchanged awkward looks, but Robert took no notice. It was Alice when she entered the room with a tray of drinks who winced. Her husband relieved her of the tray with a smile.

"Ah thank you, my dear. Let me see, we have mead, and cider, please take one."

As Alice left the room she gave another agonised look at her husband, but busy offering the tray round he failed to see it.

"John, Thom, take a drink or my wife will feel less than useful," he urged.

Tension eased, others stepped forward and took the proffered refreshments.

"So we should begin," Robert said. "As you can see only a certain number of you have been asked to attend this meeting. Otherwise I fear too many might cause delay, differing opinions, that sort of thing. Thom will report back to our small council and Jack will speak to the rest."

His self-importance intact, Jack slouched in the chair intent on his glass of mead. Robert was not the only one who found his manner disconcerting however, they also recognised he could be a dangerous opponent if not curbed in some way. When the noise Jack made as he quaffed his drink stopped, Robert continued.

"I took it upon myself to ask William to make some enquiries. Perhaps dear brother, you might tell us what you found out."

William stepped forward and produced a piece of paper from his pocket. They could all see it was covered in scribbled figures. As gently spoken as his brother, he cleared his throat and said.

"I'm fortunate to have good friends who were able to help me. Rural affairs have suffered misery for a long time, too long in fact. I've been provided with figures which greatly disturb Robert and I. Protector Somerset ordered a count of all land throughout the country which has been repossessed by unfair means. It would seem he is much in favour of this continuing. The figure I have here is in excess of thirty six thousand acres."

A growl of anger cut across his words and one man called out.

"That man is our enemy. He should be treated as we are, hung and cut about for his contempt of our ways. He and others like him think only of profit whilst we starve. But if it's war he wants, we're ready aren't we, lads."

Discomforted, the men fidgeted and several muttered in agreement. Robert held up a hand to silence them.

"War is not the way to go, my friends, nothing is achieved by bloodshed. We must think quietly, act peaceably and pray good will prevail."

Humfrey Moore leapt to his feet.

"It's alright for you. You lot got your land and money to go with it," he said, a morose expression on his face. "I say we should fight."

Robert shook his head. "I'm sorry, Humfrey, I don't think so. What use is it if you leave behind widows and fatherless children? Who will look after them, I ask you?"

"My brother's right. We must be seen to be reasonable men. Only then will people listen to us and see what their greed has done," William remarked.

"So tell me this, Master Kett, just why would you wish to help us? Nobody's taken your land or likely will. You could put back your fences tomorrow if you wished. I can't see what it has to do with you," Jack said.

The Kett brothers exchanged a glance. Jack was right, it wasn't their struggle. Yet, perhaps it was their good fortune which made them more aware of those with so much less. For a moment the room fell silent.

Until now Thom had said little. Now he nodded gratefully at the Ketts.

"What the Masters tell us makes sense. Why else would these good men be prepared to help us if it's not to do right by us? For once I agree with you, Jack. Country gentlemen like them have no need for such squabbles. Think about it before you make matters worse."

"Well, what say you all? Will you let my brother help you or do you want discord between one another which will achieve nothing? You must decide," William said his arm round Robert's shoulders.

The men came together in a circle of muted discussion although Jack and his brother remained isolated on the other side of the room. They both glowered and then with bad grace drew into the huddle. Thom and John looked on. There was no need for them to join in, they'd made their decision.

For once Jack kept quiet and it was a white haired man more senior than the rest and strong of voice who spoke for them all.

"We're agreed, Master Kett. We should be grateful if you'd help us. If we are to win we need a wise head such as yours to lead us. As things are we sneak about under cover of darkness with no proper plan and no order in what we do," the man said. "Take us with you and we shan't let you down, I give you my word."

With a shrug he fell back amongst the others, a faint smile easing the careworn lines on his face.

"In that case, I'm ready," Robert said with an expression of humility. "If you will allow it, I am honoured to be your friend and your captain. No one should face this struggle unaided and I shall not rest until the men who live in rest and pleasures are made to see how wrongfully they behave. Be warned it will not be easy and there will be danger. We must hope Almighty God stands with us in this affair."

"Amen," William murmured.

Later when the three of them ate supper, Alice picked at her food. Her wan face looked composed, but Robert didn't miss the red rims to her eyes nor the distant look she had in them. He stretched out a hand and patted hers.

"Is something troubling you, dearest?"

He saw her lip quiver and the effort she made to keep her tears contained.

"I just cannot understand why you feel you must offer to help."

"My dear, they're our people whose wretched existence you cannot begin to imagine," he said and cupped her hand in his.

"He's right, Alice," William offered his support readily.

When Robert followed it with, "For pity's sake we are Christians, what else can we do?" and raised her pale hand to his lips, she burst into tears and rushed out of the room.

Will looked far from his ebullient self and his steps were slow as he climbed the incline and came toward Thom. He carried the bad news like a heavy load and each step was an effort.

"I'll be with you in a minute," Thom called, working the pump hard to fill the pail.

It was easier to slaughter the second ox. He could look at the remnants of his butchering without any emotion this time. The blood and detritus left on the ground were hard to move so he hurled water over it and sent scarlet droplets racing off the stones. They joined together in a red line which gathered speed on the slope. He watched it part the grass and sink without trace.

Alone in the pen the ox bellowed. It was a forlorn sound. As he heard it Thom thanked the Lord for Robert Kett and his promise to help them bring an end to their situation. Perhaps then he could spare his last beast.

One elbow propped on the gate, Will waited for him, his head rested in the hollow of his palm. Rays of the late July sun fell on his hair and lightened the iron grey streaks which now outnumbered the black. Dust rimmed his eyes, lodged in the creases of his face and turned his skin grey. He raised a gloomy face as Thom reached him.

"You look all in, my friend," Thom said.

"Elias of Attleborough sent for me. He's had word from Philip and it's not good. Lord Seymour is an enemy of our cause. Philip's been instructed to speak to us and persuade all who destroy the fences to stop at once."

"Maybe it's just a threat." Thom said. "I hear the Protector is fond of such things."

Will shook his head. "Matters are grave for Philip. He is promised a stay in the Tower should he not succeed," he said, his eyes dark pits of sorrow.

Anxious to comfort his friend, Thom could hardly reach to throw an arm about Will's shoulders. He made do with touch on his arm. "Come to the house, there'll just be the two of us. Martha's out visiting."

He stopped by the pump to wash his hands before Will joined him. As a youth, awkward with his height, Will stooped. As he shambled beside Thom, the burden of age and despondency thrust him even further forward.

"But what's to happen now?" he said, not looking up from the ground in front of him. "Master Kett tells us we should be ready to move in two days time. Once we march to Norwich and word reaches the palace, they will know Philip has failed. What should I tell Elias?"

Anxiety made him twist his cap in repeated movements as he followed Thom into the common room. Some thick, rough cut bread and a small piece of cheese on a wooden platter with a small jug were set on the table for Thom's dinner. Thom shared out the ale between two beakers and pushed the food towards Will.

"Have half with me," he offered.

Will emptied the beaker in one mouthful, but waved the bread away. Thom lifted a corner of it and pulled out the square of cracked cheese which he munched thoughtfully.

"Can you speak to Elias? He should take a message back to Philip" he said.

Wills' face brightened. "I can go to Attleborough again tomorrow. Why, do you have an idea?"

"Of sorts, is Elias to be trusted?"

"He's family. My second cousin on my father's side, of course he can be trusted."

Reaching for the jug Will peered hopefully into it and turned it until a dribble slithered from the earthenware lip.

"Sorry, Martha rations it these days," Thom apologised. "Philip must be told. Our plans are made, there's nothing can stop them now. If your cousin is a sympathiser to our troubles, he should leave the court. Whatever happens, he's not safe. Should he wish to join us, I'm sure Master Kett would be happy to welcome another by his side."

Will's look was one of amazement. "You suggest he should give up his position and run the risk of losing his head?"

Thom shrugged. "It seems to me that could happen anyway, if Lord Seymour means what he says. I think your cousin faces grave danger unless he flees whilst he can."

"Oh, I don't know, I'm not sure...it's..."

Confused, Will's brow wrinkled as he grappled with Thom's words. He knew his friend's concern for his cousin was genuine, but he felt uneasy just the same.

"It's only a suggestion," Thom said. "The best I can offer. It's up to you, I have a hog to feed before Martha gets back and Rosie will wonder where you are. Have you told her we leave for Norwich the day after tomorrow?"

"Not exactly, have you told Martha?" Will's face was laced with guilt and his laugh awkward.

He drained the beaker and wiped his mouth on his sleeve. Thom he saw he too showed the strains of their harsh conditions. His rough beard had more silver in it than the hair on his head. They were both getting too old for marches, he thought. He shook his head and his laugh sounded self-conscious.

"I intend to tell her tonight," he said. "Though I don't dare to think what she'll say."

"Best I break the news to Rosie," Will said, as he hauled his heavy frame from the chair.

Thom knew his wife. She might want him to think she was absorbed as she pulled leaves from a tough stem of kale. But he knew otherwise. Her face was expressive and he could tell something troubled her. He guessed it was to do with his announcement.

"I should have told you sooner," he said.

"Yes, you should."

"I wanted too, but I couldn't find the right moment. There wasn't much time, it's only just been arranged."

"Long enough," she said her eyes still on the vegetable. "It was Sible who told me. You leave tomorrow?"

"Aye, that's right."

The water hissed in the pan and she tossed the handful of greens into the boiling water.

"Then I shall come with you."

"No, Martha, you can't. It's not for women. This is men's business."

"But you promised," she said, stabbing the point of her knife into the fibrous stem.

"No I didn't. Come here, woman," he said, his knee extended.

He sensed her reluctance. Slow to anger she showed formidable strength of mind when she wanted to. It was one of the reasons he loved her so much. With a dignified step she came round the table. Her perch was tentative at first but not comfortable. He pulled her onto his lap more firmly. It brought her nearer too so he could smell her musky scent over-laced with one or two drops of the precious lavender water she made.

"Is it Master Kett, who leads you?" she said.

He nodded. "I never thought we'd be so fortunate. He's well learned and a fine man, they both are, Robert and his brother. William keeps him company, but it's Robert who will deliver us if anyone can. He's given his word to take us into Norwich and speak for us. He said we'd suffered enough and now was the time to end our misery. So you see we're in good hands."

"Why can't I go with you? Plenty of women follow their men. I could cook, sew buttons and tend to any who fall sick, anything."

She gave him a fulsome smile, but he saw the sadness in her eyes. Arms round her to hold her close he ran his hands over her thighs.

"There is one thing, you could do," he said, mischief behind his grin.

Hopeful, she said. "Yes, what would that be?"

"I'll show you," he said. He stood up, took her hand and led her into the inner room.

Through the window they could see the numbers who gathered outside the house. There were men of all ages, women who carried bundles on their backs and small children who romped without any idea why they were there. The Kett brothers were astonished. They'd seen the first arrive before dawn now they overflowed off the drive and into the meadow. Flattened against the glass, Robert craned to see more.

"I don't see the end. They're stretched beyond the turn in the drive and still they come," he said. "One, two, three, four." At two hundred, he gave up counting.

"The more the better, then we can be sure we'll be heard," William reassured.

"The word spread fast, some I don't even recognise. There's Will, see how he stands above the others. That must be Elias of Attleborough with another beside him and our trusty Council are with us too."

"Who *is* that man? He wears an outfit too fine for our purpose although he seeks to hide it under an extravagant cloak," William asked. "See him speaking to Elias."

Robert shrugged. "No matter, another for our cause is welcome. Come 'tis time we joined them, brother."

As he turned to the door, William's hand restrained him. "Before we leave," he said. "This bad blood between you and John Flowerdew, you have never once spoken about it. All I know is he carries a fearsome scar on his face. Surely my soft-hearted brother wasn't responsible for it."

"Not as soft as you think," Robert replied in a low voice. "It'll do another day. We mustn't keep our friends waiting." He loosened William's grip and stepped out into the hall.

Alice stood with a babe on her hip, four more children with solemn faces looked on. They were a cluster of innocence with lips which quivered and tear-bright eyes ready to bid their father farewell.

Alice struggled to keep a smile on her face. Pale and composed, only reddened eyes and charcoal coloured smudges under them revealed her anguish.

"Children, kiss your Papa. Dicken, you may go first," she said softly.

Robert bent so he could be reached and a tousled haired boy, the eldest of the children and little more than the age of the monarch stepped forward and offered his hand. A solemn look robbed him of his usual childish expression and he spoke in a grave voice.

"Goodbye, Father."

"Well done Dicken, you are being very brave. You set a good example as I knew you would," his father said, accepting the shy brush of lips.

One after another he received their dutiful endearments. For May, an angelic- faced little girl of two, it was too much. Blonde curls bouncing, she ran sobbing to Robert throwing her chubby arms round his legs. Small hands gripped his breeches and her father needed to prise her from them.

"Dearest child, I shan't be gone long and I have your Uncle William to look after me," he gently chided.

Moved by the family scene, it was William who blew his nose and sniffed several times.

"How fortunate you are to have such a family," he murmured. "I fear my life remains empty for want of a wife and little ones. Now I think it almost too late."

"Dear William, I don't believe it is ever too late for a gentleman," Alice said. Demure at all times her cheeks took on a sudden blush of pink at her boldness. The baby grizzled and sucked hard on its silver teething ring.

William laughed. "I trust it might be so," he said as he opened the front door. Robert took a deep breath and embraced his wife. He inhaled the essence of her perfume, lilies, a hint of musk and a notion of cedar wood.

"Take care, dearest Alice. I shall delay no longer than is necessary, you have my word."

"I love you," she whispered. "God be with you both. I shall pray every night for your safe return. We shall be fine, won't we, children?"

Her bright words came easily, but the look in her eyes told differently. On the step William stepped out first. Robert turned for a final wave, but the hall was empty.

When the Kett brothers appeared an expectant murmur travelled through the crowd as wind would catch ears of wheat. Robert spoke to them from the step.

"It does my heart good to see so many of you. We have fine weather to be grateful for," he said, appreciative of the sun's warmth and the tranquil clouds trapped in a bed of blue. He saw some strain to catch his words and raised his voice. "Remember this march is a protest nothing more. We act peaceably at all times. We must make it known that without access to land we can neither farm, gather wood or graze our animals. All we ask is what is ours be returned to us."

They voiced their agreement as one and William smoothed his well-cut, fine woollen jacket and murmured.

"I see they come with their weapons."

Indeed every man carried a long bow, but to them it would be unthinkable to go anywhere without it. Some added a heavy stick too or a hoe they once used on the soil.

"Let us pray there will be no need to use them," Robert replied quietly.

Thom and John appeared from the crowd. Both carried their bows and satchels slung over their shoulders. Like all the peasants they wore breeches, shirts of rough linen and crudely made sheepskin jerkins. Their smiles radiated excitement and their eyes sparkled with anticipation.

"Good day to you, Masters," Thom said, "Would you think so many would wish to walk with us? When they heard your good selves would risk all for our cause there was no stopping them as you can see."

High-spirited and already growing restless the marchers jostled one another and the drive echoed with good natured banter and jocular remarks. As more arrived to join them, Robert looked on with surprised delight as the numbers continued to grow.

"There'll be more too, as we journey. They promise to join us. We sent word they should wait for us on the Common." John said enthusiastically.

"Then there must be no more delay," Robert said. "Are you ready, William? If we are to reach Norwich by nightfall, we must leave. Let us trust the Almighty steps beside us."

The column wove their way back along the drive and out onto the Norwich road. No one took the decision to lead. Some immediately slipped behind. Others passed them and walked at the front. Good natured, affable and united they struck out at a good pace.

In their midst, Robert and William walked with Thom and John. Interested in his new friends, William chatted happily to them. Thoughtful, Robert fell silent. It astonished him how in a few days, his quiet life had changed. The faces of his distressed wife and children were clear in his mind as every step he took carried him further from them. He began to think he hadn't organised a march, but in truth was in command of an army.

At first the thought troubled him, but as Wymondham fell behind them, his respect grew for those who walked alongside him. He'd never seen many of them before nor they him. In what to him appeared a brief moment they'd given him their allegiance in the belief he would win the fight for them and it humbled him. A sense of purpose strengthened his stride and his doubts lessened.

"I've decided when we stop on the Common, I shall address them all. What do you think, William? Would you think it a good idea?" he said.

"Indeed, as long as you know what to say," his brother teased.

"I shall practice as we walk," Robert said, returning an affectionate smile.

The mass of marchers was forever shifting and moving into different positions so the ranks continually changed. Robert saw Will and Elias just ahead and beside them the stranger he'd noticed from his window earlier, who wore a heavy fur-trimmed black cloak, the collar high round his face. Methinks, he'll expire in the heat before long Robert thought and suppressed a smile.

When he drew alongside Will he said. "Will, you must introduce me to your young friend. Is he from around these parts? I don't remember seeing him before."

"Not my friend, Master Kett. It's Elias who knows him. I'm surprised you haven't met him. They call him Philip de Montfort. He was an aide to

The Protector, Lord Seymour. It was Philip who did what he could for us at court. Lord Seymour it seems is no friend in our troubles and now Philip joins us in fear of his life so Elias says."

Robert listened intently. "Indeed, indeed. Then I must speak with him. We are grateful for all his trouble," he said. "Thank you, Will."

Will grunted his pleasure and with long strides slipped away into the crowd. When Robert looked again Elias and Philip had vanished too. He tried to pick them out, but it was impossible.

Resolving to speak to Philip later, Robert returned to his mental task of preparing his speech.

After a brisk start it soon became obvious the pace couldn't be maintained.

Thom looked around and saw that many were older men less suited to walking any distance. It seemed natural the quickest would drop their speed in favour of those more used to a quiet amble. Still the numbers grew. They waited by the road side, hurried from a door, clambered over a hedge or ran from a field, more and more villagers joined along the way. Look back, look forward, it made no difference. The column marched on. But in the heat some appeared weakened and with the Common in sight Thom urged them on. Managing to push his way back to Robert, he said.

"Master Kett, it is fortunate we stop. Already many seem to tire. We should allow those less able to rest."

"By God, Thom you're right, I'm sorry. Too many thoughts," Robert said. "See the position of the sun, it's past noon already. There will be many weary and yet they don't complain. Send word to the front to turn off the road at the start of the Common. They can rest there."

Thom lay on the grass and looked up through spaces left between the oak's summer foliage. He watched froths of white cloud lazing in the blue sky. He knew Martha would see them too, it somehow comforted him. She'd stood at the door as he left. The last sight of her sweet face showed admiration mingled with sorrow, but he knew she'd shed no tears, at least not until he was out of sight.

What he'd give for a bowl of her cold pottage. He knew of no other who could make soup as she did. Her recipes were secret handed down by her mother. He'd seen her hunt for hours for wild sorrel or garlic and horseradish root or wade into the river to reach the watercress beds.

The chunks of dry bread and over-ripe cheese in his bag made a poor substitute. Will and John sat close to him. Behind them he saw the Mayhew's, Jack and his brother and the others that came from Wymondham. Only Giles was missing both he and his wife mourning their still-born child. Thom's gaze moved on. Robert Kett was engrossed in earnest conversation with Philip de Montfort. His heavy cloak thrown open Thom could see the fine quality of Philip's doublet and the sheer silk hose he wore. Despite the relaxed atmosphere, he thought the man looked flushed and ill-at ease.

Most of the walkers sought out the shade and many sprawled out with their eyes closed too weary to eat. Thom washed his food down with a mouthful of ale and was about to doze when someone shook his shoulder gently. Leaning close, John said.

"Master Kett is about to speak."

Robert got their attention with a wooden spoon which he used to hit a metal pot with vigour. The noise echoed across the grass and women hurried to silence the children.

"I should like to speak to you all. Please come closer and listen because the next time we stop we must prepare to enter the city," he called out.

He moved nearer to the trunk of the oak where the ground was raised. Hands clasped behind his back he addressed the crowd.

"Whilst you rested, I have attempted to count your numbers. It seems there are over a thousand of you. Such magnificent support humbles me. I have told some of you already I'm willing to be both your captain and friend in order to force the Government to listen to you, for you have suffered too long. You are my neighbours and I feel your misery. I pray for victory, but I'm willing to sacrifice my life for you, so highly do I hold your cause. My friends, when we reach the outskirts of Norwich we will have a struggle ahead of us. I cannot tell you the outcome, but I promise I shall lead you through it. Here's to reform of the Church and the State. For God and the King..." Robert shouted, punching the air with his fist.

It was impossible to miss the passion in his voice and without prompting the assembled crowd broke into a loud roar. Amazed at his brother's performance, William grinned and slapped Robert on the back several times.

Thom waited quietly until the tumult died down and then strode across the few feet which separated him from the Kett's. The crowd fell silent again. He said something to Robert who nodded in return. Thom pointed up to the mature branches of the oak and his voice gathered strength.

"Master Kett, this oak of England is truly a majestic tree, but you who stand beneath it are no less noble. All of us offer you our allegiance, I swear on this, Kett's Oak."

Mutual respect exchanged and when the cheers subsided, the column formed again. With renewed hope in their steps they turned north for Norwich.

– 11 –

Norwich
July 9th 1549

Sensitive nostrils were a burden, Thomas Codde thought as he crossed the market place at Mancroft. He walked with as much speed as he could without losing his dignity. As Mayor of Norwich, dignity was important to him.

Even when he held his breath so as not to inhale it made little difference. The stench of rotting vegetables under foot and the smell of an accumulation of horse droppings wedged in the cobbles, still managed to penetrate his nose. In his official position he regularly declared the state of the market an outrage. Nobody paid any attention and the foetid smell persisted.

A rotund figure with a florid, heavily whiskered face, his haste caused the heavy gold chain of office round his neck to bump alarmingly on his breastbone. He also knew by his sudden uneven gait it was likely one shoe or the other had collected a parcel of manure.

He muttered under his breath as he crossed the road and hurried along Gentlemen's Walk towards the castle. There was another more urgent reason why he had no time to waste. And that was in response to news he'd just received. Only a few minutes earlier a messenger hammered on his door at the Town Hall. Red-faced and out of breath the man imparted to him that a large crowd of noisy men were seen advancing towards one of the city gates.

At the end of the Walk the castle steps rose steeply in front of Codde. He scrambled up them and reached the top agitated and in a sweat. Through the vestibule and under the great entrance he turned into the Grand Hall. There was an air of inactivity which irritated him. Not bothering to knock he threw open the door where the garrison was quartered. He counted six slumbering men before he raised his voice and shouted.

"You miserable bunch of toad-slime, look alive. Hurry, I have need of you."

Startled by the appearance of their mayor the men groped for their breeches and jackets and threw them on in bewildered haste.

"That man," Codde said to one who looked more alert than the others. "Go quickly, fetch the Sheriff. Tell him to meet us by St. Stephen's Gate. The rest of you follow me."

Like a thread of silver braid the Yare appeared as the marchers approached Cringleford. The sight of it raised a cheer although it was a hoarse sound because lungs had no breath to spare after such an arduous walk.

Every mile they covered revealed acres of pasture and water meadows enclosed to confine huge flocks of sheep. It was a disconcerting sight. Behind the column a big sky was darkening to Prussian blue. Reduced to half its size the sun laced it with colours of pink, orange and amber as it waited to slip below the horizon. In the cooling air the men were grateful to be rid of the wearisome heat.

In order to cross the river on the narrow bridge, the marchers needed to reduce the width of their ranks and steady themselves on a rotten rail. They tramped in ones and twos, their weapons held tight. The last, a tattered group of elderly men finally arrived on the opposite bank to stand with their younger companions. Those who drove the carts loaded with stores and equipment had no choice but to lash their horses and urge them into the river in order to cross.

Robert gripped the rail with caution and raised his hand in order to silence the column before he addressed them.

"Our march is nearing its end and I commend you all for your strength of purpose which has brought us this far. Ahead are the city walls of Norwich. It is within our grasp. Hold up your heads and firm your step so they should see we have intent. Well done to you all."

Privately he knew it was quite possible some would have fallen and even died on the journey. There was no time for regret and he straightened his shoulders determined to lead by example.

When they approached the city gate he held up his hand to stop. He knew they would be expected. Very few would have missed the lone horseman a short distance back who after a curious look, wheeled his horse around to disappear back inside the city walls at a fast pace. Robert beckoned Thom.

"I had hoped we should arrive unannounced but no matter. We'll stop here. Tell them all to wait with patience please, Thom."

With the instruction given the men laid down their bows and sat wherever they could. Womenfolk who'd piggy-backed children for miles set them down with a grimace, glad to ease aching limbs and rub weary bones. Few had energy to speak to their neighbours, but tired as they were their inflamed eyes held an expectant glow now they'd reached Norwich. Some needed to help each other over the last few miles. They supported bent bodies with willing, dirt-ingrained hands whilst their own sweat washed the ground in front of them.

With his brother and Philip and Thom, Robert approached the gate. Perched in a tree the other side of the flint and stone wall, several dozen rooks watched them. At the last moment they rose as one filling the sky in a noisy black drape.

"I hope that's not an omen," Thom said, more to himself than the others.

The city gate swung open in front of them and a tableau waited under the archway.

"Looks like we are to be welcomed," William said drily. He nodded his head at the halberdiers in a group behind two men. One on foot and the other on horseback, they were both dressed in the clothes and regalia of authority. The soldiers wore iron helmets, red and white jerkins, breeches and long boots and each carried a halberd. Thom blinked at the ferocious-looking axe and heavy iron point on each of the weapons. As he gripped his longbow he couldn't help thinking how frail it seemed in comparison.

"I didn't think it would be long," Robert said, his smile mustered with effort. "It seems we have the Mayor and the Sheriff with their guards to greet us."

Codde pulled at his coat and straightened the links of his mayoral chain. He walked slowly, exercising suitable pomp and his precious dignity until he faced the small group who waited for him.

"Good day to you gentlemen. Thomas Codde, Mayor of Norwich," he said, his pudgy finger deliberately touching the jewel resting on his chest "And this is the High Sheriff Sir Edmund Wyndham of Felbrigg. How can we help you?" He craned his neck to see past Robert and his face fell. He waved a bejewelled hand towards the marchers and said. "Are these people all with you?"

"They march with us, yes," Robert replied.

There were many more than Codde imagined and unsure of their intent he gnawed his lip apprehensively. Seated on a grey stallion the Sheriff presented a more arrogant figure. His eyes flickered over the four more carefully and then he leant down to address Philip.

"Haven't I seen you before?"

His cloak held close to his face Philip shook his head and dropped his voice.

"You are not familiar to me, sir."

"Really, no matter, it'll come to me," the Sheriff murmured. "I should have thought good manners would allow you to introduce yourselves, wouldn't you, Mayor Codde?"

"Yes, indeed," Codde simpered.

Anxious not to appear hostile, Robert assumed a mild expression.

"My apologies, I'm Robert Kett and this is my brother, William of Wymondham. Thom Barwick and Jeremiah Hall are friends who travel with us."

Robert's quick thinking to invent name to conceal Philip's identity made the others gasp. If the Sheriff heard it, his expression didn't change.

"And what business do you have in Norwich?" Codde asked.

"We wish to enter the city and make our complaints known," Robert said pleasantly.

"Complaints, what sort of complaints might you have. It seems to me you bring something akin to a rabble with you, Master Kett," the Sheriff said swiftly.

"On the contrary sir, these are decent, hardworking men, who are now displaced by the stealth of wealthy landowners," Robert said smoothly. "They come to ask that the intolerable oppression by landlords be ended. The common pastures belonging to their fathers and their fathers before them have been taken away. These pastures have become enclosed and they are shut out from them. Because of this they suffer unjustly. All we ask for is the land to be returned to them for they cannot continue to eat herbs and roots. We say that the King must attend the complaints of his subjects. That is why we are here."

"Well said brother," William said admiringly.

Codde seemed nonplussed and Wyndham showed contempt in his steely gaze. Feeling more confident, Robert continued.

"I'm sure the king will lend us a sympathetic ear. We have been told he too disapproves of these enclosures and will pardon all who tear them down."

"If that's the case, it's the first I've heard of it," the Sheriff said tightly.

He scowled whilst his horse fidgeted and the halberdiers shifted their lances and tightened their hold. Codde's mouth gaped open whilst he searched frantically for words. Robert hoped he hadn't gone too far. He was anxious to unite citizens and peasants, not alienate them. An altercation must be avoided at all costs, he thought, if they were to succeed in their mission.

Despite John's efforts to calm them, the crowd became restless as if they sensed all was not well. The slow hum of their voices grew louder as they pressed on towards the gate. Codde squeaked in alarm and took a hasty step back.

Sheriff Wyndham lost patience. Spurring his horse, he galloped toward the marchers. He stood up in his stirrups and screamed at the top of his voice.

"Get back. Get back, all of you. You're nothing, but a bunch of rebels. Vagrants the lot of you, do you hear me? Norwich has no room for the likes of you. Go back to your homes in the mud and slurry where you belong."

As he realised he must try to be reasonable, his tone changed. "Leave this place now and I give you my assurance you will not be punished."

There was a great roar and the advance party watched open mouthed as the sky darkened with missiles. Rotten cabbages, stinking dead fish, flabby turnips and all manner of objects flew towards the Sheriff. Most missed their mark, but when a clutch of bad eggs broke on him dribbling foul slime down his brocade doublet he turned his horse and bolted inside the city.

Even the halberdiers grinned, but Codde looked embarrassed. In a fury the Sheriff reined his horse beside him.

"I hold you responsible for this," he snarled, pointing to his soiled clothing.

Codde searched in his pocket, pulled out a fine lawn handkerchief and held it to his nose.

"I'm so sorry, I'm not good with odours," he said, moving quickly back.

"The palace shall hear of this," the Sheriff ranted. "I can promise you, you will all be sorry."

With that he kicked his mount and departed at considerable speed towards the castle. Foreboding made him quick in thought. He must bid someone to ride to London to seek help before the city along with its notables felt the anger of such an unruly mob, but who should it be?

He recognised the man who dismounted on the castle forecourt ahead of him, if he remembered correctly not one blest with great intelligence, he would do nicely.

"Master Pynchyn isn't it? A word if I may."

In matters which required courage Mayor Codde didn't shine. The sheer numbers of peasants alarmed him. He knew that with only a few halberdiers they could do little should such a great number of men choose to become aggressive. Gratified that after pelting the Sheriff they'd settled down again and talked quietly to one another, he felt his heartbeat return to normal. He was however faced with a very big problem, one he knew he must deal with immediately. Taking a deep breath he fixed a generous smile on his face and said.

"Well, gentlemen, I can only apologise for the Sheriff's rather disappointing behaviour. That was no welcome and I can assure you, Norwich is capable of being extremely gracious to its visitors. I would of course, offer more comfortable surroundings in which to discuss this matter but there are rather too many of you to accommodate."

His high-pitched laugh accompanied his raised hand which he flapped in the direction of the waiting crowd.

"Thank you for your understanding, Mayor," Robert said pleasantly, equally anxious to avoid hostility. "All we ask is to be allowed into the city so we may rest and find ourselves a little food. Once that is so and we are all comfortable, we can put forth our grievances. Isn't that right, my friends?"

Careful to include them all Robert nodded to his companions. Codde rubbed his forehead and looked nervous.

"Ah, there you have me. You see perhaps we could accommodate the four of you but as for the others with you, I must ask you to tell them to disperse as quickly as possible."

Up to now merely an observer, William stepped forward.

"I don't think you quite understand, Mayor Codde, what my brother means, is we *all* travel together."

Cold fingers of fear tweaked Codde's gut. Things were not going to be as easy as he hoped. Perhaps he'd underestimated the odd band of men. He knew the two Kett men were educated and of good standing. Their manner, voices and clothing left no doubt in his mind. The one called Thom, he could see came from peasant stock, perhaps a spokesman for them he thought. As for the guarded, uneasy young man wearing if he wasn't much mistaken, court clothing, he begged deeper consideration. Codde decided it would have to wait. He needed a new approach to the present problem. He strived to appear relaxed.

"We are all worldly men, Master Kett, I'm sure we can resolve things in a peaceable manner. Eaton Wood is close by. Perhaps if you care to set up camp there, I could arrange to have a beast slaughtered. A fine meal of roasted beef, now wouldn't that satisfy grumbling stomachs?"

Sensing an opportunity, Robert contrived to look downcast.

"We really had hoped to enter Norwich. I'm not sure..."

"Two beasts then," Codde said eagerly.

William shook his head.

"Like my brother said, the men hoped..."

"What if I send four casks of ale *and* the two beasts?"

It was Thom's turn.

"Begging your pardon, Masters' Kett there are a lot of mouths to feed and the men have no money to buy anything."

Growing impatient Codde fidgeted with his chain. He calculated somewhere there must be a point of satisfaction.

"Oh very well, you make your case, gentlemen. Two bullocks, a sheep, four casks of ale and that's my final offer."

It had all gone very well he thought and felt a glow of pleasure at his bargaining skills.

"You are more than generous," Robert said, delighted he'd secured victual in plenty for the cause. "Thom, be so kind as to take the march to Eaton Wood. We need to catch the last of the light. We three will follow to make sure no one is left behind. Mayor Codde, it's been a pleasure meeting you. Your generosity is much appreciated. We shall be in good spirits come the morning when we meet again."

That was what he was afraid of, Codde reflected as he took Robert's out stretched hand.

"Good evening, Master Kett," he said with a pale smile and a polite bow.

Wind drifted through the trees and carried the sound of voices along with the smell of smoke from burning timber and roasting meat. Somewhere a fox expressed indignation at the night time disturbance. Those who heard it over the chatter and laughter knew, enticed by the aromas it would draw nearer. Some would see sport in using it for target practice if it did so.

A regular feed with fallen wood meant the fire burnt with fiery enthusiasm. On a make-shift spit the remains of animal carcasses dripped lethargic globules of fat. Well accustomed to such surroundings, Eaton Wood's solid trunks and leafy branches offered no threat to the men camped there. Rolled in whatever might keep them warm, good food and ale hastened sleep for many. Their snores laced the conversations of others whilst those still awake lazed contentedly.

"Would you look at us, brother," Robert said his shirt grimy and sweat-stained. Under his nose and on his chin his skin shone with meat juices and grease. "Who'd have thought we who are such pillars of Norfolk society would be sharing our beds with such as these," he said with a satisfied laugh.

William looked no better. Dirt streaked his hands and face whilst small fragments of crisp beef skin clung to his jacket. He gnawed the last strips of meat from a bone and tossed it toward the fire. Thoughtful, Robert looked on as he picked his teeth with a sliver of wood.

"When you look at them, you realise how fortunate we've been. Our dear father worked hard. Thanks to him we have prospered," William said.

"These are good men, all peasants true and I think of them and their grievances so highly I should gladly suffer for them," Robert said quietly.

A look of concern crossed William's face.

"Pray it doesn't come to that, brother."

Throwing his arm round his shoulders, Robert grinned, "You worry too much, William."

"Perhaps, so what plans do you have for the morrow?"

"I think it best we only spend one night here. This is too far south from the heart of Norwich. Tomorrow I intend to advance to Mousehold Heights. The land is high and the woods will afford us protection, besides there are excellent views over the city. As that pompous mayor is unlikely to allow us through Norwich we shall not reach there in the day. We shall need to approach from the north side of the city, cross the Wensum at Hailsdon and then stop overnight at Drayton. What think you?"

William smiled attempting to conceal a yawn as he did so.

"You lead and I follow, as will all. But you frown as you speak. What troubles you?"

Robert sighed deeply. "Sometimes I fear we shall have trouble keeping the men in check. We must always remain on the side of the law. I will not have anarchy nor be responsible for poor behaviour. So yes, I have some worries. Now we must sleep. Tomorrow may not be an easy day."

But mindful of his brother's trepidation, Robert asked for divine protection in his prayers, just to be sure.

A group sat together close by. Four of them were dozing, the fifth, Thom, rested his back upright against the broad trunk of an elm. Alert and watchful, his was the first turn of the night. Nothing had been agreed nor even discussed at any length, but it seemed only natural that Thom, John, Will, Elias and Philip would be shadows of the Kett brothers. Thinking some on the march would seek prominence and possibly aspire to being a leader Thom knew Robert and William might need protection. Such was his regard for the Kett's, it was the least he could offer and he knew the others stood by him.

Judging by the silence around him, he thought most were settled for the night. Philip was restless and fidgeted in his sleep. Thom wondered if he dreamt of being hunted down by Seymour's men. He noticed in repose, the boy's lost wary look was eased from his face. He also saw his fancy clothes were not so different in condition from his own. Spoiled by splashes of mud, food eaten in haste and with a tear or two, the lad no longer stood out.

Knees clasped, Thom stared into the fire. The flames made shapes in the dark. For a moment he thought he saw Martha. Her long hair swirled about her face, but then the wood crumbled in a shower of sparks and another image took its place. This time he saw hands holding swords and fiery scarlet particles like drops of blood which flew from them. Too real for his comfort he hastily covered his eyes and waited for the picture to change again.

When the moon crossed the sky he gave John's shoulder a gentle shake. When he was sure he was awake, Thom gratefully laid his head on a pillow of leaves and slept.

With a last anxious look at the table, for fear she'd forgotten something the serving girl returned to the kitchen where she fussed about the food and checked sufficient bread and meat were cut. She wiped the lip of the beer jugs again in case of drips and waited until summoned into the Grand Hall by those who came for breakfast.

The sudden noisy jangle of a bell told her it was time. She took the first of the platters, tapped on the door and entered the room. The men expected were seated. Summoned in haste Codde and the Sheriff's guests were influential citizens, amongst them two bankers, a Recorder and a builder of note who talked quietly to one another. Presiding at the head of the table sat the Sheriff with Codde on his right hand.

At the far end wealthy wool merchants, the Appleyard brothers appeared thoughtful. They had much on their mind, not least their relationship with Robert Kett. They knew it was the reason they'd been called to the castle, it was only a question of how the matter would be approached and by whom. Their pale eyes appraised each in turn seated at the table and in quiet discussion decided it would likely be the Sheriff. All they had to do was be patient.

Of the visitors the youngest of the bankers, Robert Chase, Under Lord Treasurer of the Privy Coffers served the king at the palace, but had his estates in Norfolk. He had a presence which set him apart from the others. Darkly handsome, his prowess with ladies was matched only by his skill with money. Charm oozed from him like juices escaping from the slabs of rare beef he was about to eat.

"Fine smells coming from the kitchen," he remarked as he stretched back from the table in order to look at the girl's figure as she moved round the room.

Recorder Sir Thomas Gawdy and wealthy banker Roger Woodhouse, exchanged glances. Both older and severe of countenance it was obvious they had little time for the dashing Chase. Only the builder, Sir David Melloe permitted himself a tight smile at Chase's impudence.

"God's blood man, you've not been called here to remark on cooking smells," the Sheriff said testily.

Chase ignored the remark and caught the eye of the girl as she passed. His suggestive leer was noticed this time by Codde. He made a point of showing his displeasure by clearing his throat several times.

"Robert, if we could have your attention."

"I apologise, Codde." Chase said. His boyish smile revealed a dimpled chin and attractive crinkling of the fine lines close to his eyes. "You know what a weakness I have for the turn of an ankle. So exactly what is the reason you've called us here?"

He impaled his sizable steak on a fork and waved it expectantly at Codde. Waiting until the ale was poured and the girl left the room, the Sheriff banged the table with his beaker.

"Mayor Codde, none of us have time to spare so perhaps you would explain."

Codde dabbed his mouth on his sleeve and told of the events when "a monstrous rabble of common men," as he called them, arrived seeking entry to the city. "Many hundreds, so I suggested they encamp themselves in Eaton Woods for the night."

"Sensible idea, Mayor," Roger Chase said, wiping his greasy fingers on the corner of his cloak.

"A mere thought on my part, it was nothing, I assure you."

Codde's modesty elicited a smile from all apart from the Sheriff. He sucked his teeth with noisy relish and frowned. "I would have suggested the same myself," he muttered.

Codde bristled. "Only you couldn't, could you my Lord Sheriff? You were too busy."

The Sheriff swiftly interrupted. "Thank you, Mayor, there is no need to recount the appalling treatment I received at the hands of such thick-witted rogues."

Immediately attentive, Chase said. "And what was that, may I enquire."

Unable to resist, Codde couldn't prevent a snigger. The Sheriff silenced him with a glare and addressed the room.

"We must have a plan of action to deal with these men which is why you have been called upon," he said. "I have sent Edmund Pynchyn to Hampton Court to deliver a message. Norwich cannot deal with this alone. We need support from the government. However, someone must ride to Eaton Woods before the march comes any nearer. Talk to the leaders, make them see sense, offer them a free pardon, anything so they disperse."

"Have we a volunteer?" Codde asked, draining an ale jug into his beaker.

Woodhouse raised his hand. "I shall go immediately," he said and stood up. His offer was not entirely of good intent for the city. He'd long craved a knighthood and the king's gratitude in a time of crisis might afford him such an honour. It was not an opportunity to be missed.

"Thank you, Woodhouse, most grateful," Codde said. "I would go myself, but I really can't be spared."

He chose to ignore the Sheriff's derisive snort. Gawdy played with a remnant of fat left on his platter and shifted uneasily in his chair.

"I fear I'm unable to offer assistance," he said in a nervous voice. "My wife is expecting a child. Her condition leaves her exhausted and troubled with nerves. I promised I should return to her the moment our business is concluded here."

Irritated, the Sheriff waved his hand. "Very well, you better leave now. Woodhouse, you should not waste any more time. You're a personable man, I'm sure they will warm to you once you explain things. You understand, like Codde here I would go myself," he said quickly. "But I think having already spoken to them a fresh voice might have more effect."

The image of the fastidious Sheriff dishevelled and egg-smeared was too much for Codde. He tittered again and hurriedly changed it to a cough. With a dark look the Sheriff ignored him and called down the table to the Appleyard brothers who listened yet said nothing.

"Gentlemen, you may wonder why I felt you should be here this morning. It seems it is your brother-in-law, Robert Kett who leads this so called up-rising. How do you feel about that?"

"What is there to feel?" one replied with quiet authority. "Our connections to him are purely through marriage and you know well we are the king's men. You can rest assured our sons are ready to pick up arms against Kett should the need arise."

"Good, good. I knew we could count on you," the Sheriff said with a satisfied smile. "Well, I think that's all."

Roger Woodhouse took his time. He changed his clothes and ordered a fresh horse from his stables. Whilst he was readying himself, he sent his servant Edgerley to load a cart with food and barrels of beer. They were a treat for the rebels, a gesture he was sure they would respond to. Then he rode ahead leaving Edgerley to coax the idle carthorses. Both fat as butter, his was slow progress.

By the time Woodhouse reached Eaton it was later than he intended and search as he did there was no sign of a camp. To be sure he listened intently. Somewhere amongst the columns of trunks, a cock pheasant coughed, a raucous clattering noise and he thought he heard the occasional grunts of a wild boar nearby.

Neither bothered him, but he checked the number of arrows in his fox fur quiver just the same. He guided his mount through the sunlit glades and on a turn in the wood he came across the remains of a fire and obvious signs of recent activity. Dismounting he held his hand over the embers and felt their warmth.

He could only guess the direction the marchers on foot would have taken, but he knew they couldn't be far ahead. To reach the city, he reasoned, they would need to cross the river and the Wensum was close. Such great numbers would move slowly so he wasn't concerned he'd missed them. He'd find them soon enough.

Turning his horse round he allowed it to trot at its own pace. From time to time horse dung confirmed he was travelling in the right direction. Low in the saddle he relaxed to enjoy the warmth, a restful balm after the gloomy confines of the castle. With a precise step the horse picked its way on the thin boards of the river bridge. He trusted the beast implicitly and didn't bother to open his eyes.

He was to regret it. A brief yelp was all he had time for before he was plunged into darkness. Not only was the material enveloping him damp, but also very smelly. He thought for a minute he would suffocate. His attempt to struggle was useless. Rough hands grabbed him and he felt himself falling. A hard landing forced all the breath from him and he offered no resistance when he felt the coarse hemp tear the flesh of his wrists.

When his assailants were satisfied he was firmly bound the odorous blanket was lifted away from his face. The three men who looked down at him appeared not only unfriendly, but exceedingly filthy too. Then Woodhouse realised he must have been taken by some of the rebels. Angry with himself for being caught off-guard, he swore loudly.

"By the saints, do you realise who I am? You swag-bellied oafs, set me free this instant."

Woodhouse was hauled to his feet and a man with a conspicuous squint leaned close to his face. Woodhouse recoiled and gathered a quantity of phlegm in his mouth which he spat at the pock-marked features.

"Why, you fat-kidney of a Codpiece," the man exclaimed. Seizing the corner of the banker's velvet lined cape he cleaned his face on it.

"Get away from me," Woodhouse screeched wildly. "Come near me again and I'll puke on you."

The other two men exchanged glances.

"Perhaps we should take him to Master Kett," one of them said nervously.

"I've a better idea than that," Squint-eye said with a malicious smile. "Take off his clothes and throw him in the ditch. It'll save someone else the trouble."

The other rebels looked uncomfortable at the idea. "I'll not do it," one said.

"It's Master Kett who must decide," the other repeated.

Squint-eye nodded. "Pity," he said and pulled a length of chain from his pocket. "Just to be sure," he said, looping it around the captive's ankles.

To his chagrin, Woodhouse found himself dragged from the riverbank into a copse of trees.

"My horse, where's my horse," he yelled.

"The beast took off in fright. You'll be on foot now just like the rest of us," one man growled close to his ear.

"Miserable hedge-pigs," Woodhouse muttered. He cocked his head trying to catch any sound of Edgerley travelling behind, but all he heard were their own footsteps on the mat of woodland leaves.

As he passed the rows of men he was astounded at the numbers. He hadn't doubted Codde when he had said there were over a thousand, but it seemed to him there were many more than that. Most watched silently, some cursed and a few spat at him. Shackled and tied Woodhouse could only shuffle behind his captors whilst Squint-eye strode ahead. The other two dragged their prisoner as best they could through the bracken and bramble bushes and he felt the spiteful thorns rip through his hose tearing lumps of flesh as they did so.

Just as he thought he would fall with exhaustion the undergrowth parted and he found himself in a clearing facing a small group of men. To his relief he saw at least three of them appeared to be of a different ilk to his captors. The fair haired two must be the Kett brothers he decided but the third kept his identity concealed by his cloak.

He knew of the Kett's as an old Norfolk family and even their unshaven and soiled appearance didn't hide their obvious difference to the peasants around them. He felt freedom a breath away. Confident of his release when they knew who he was, he fixed them with a regal look.

"My lord's," he said.

Limited by his bonds his bow was a strange affair, but he didn't think such a gracious greeting would go amiss. Robert gave a negative gesture with his hand.

"Master, will do, thank you. I'm Robert Kett, my brother, William and this is..." Robert hesitated. Nonplussed by Philip's sudden disappearance, "and these are my friends whose cause I support."

Anxious for his name to be known, Woodhouse said with haste.

"May I introduce myself? I'm Roger Woodhouse, banker of the city."

Robert Kett turned to the man with a squint and said. "And how do they call you?"

"Roland of Thornham, Master Kett," he replied.

"So Roland of Thornham, why have you made this person a prisoner?"

"We found him following us, Master. He had been for some time."

Anger replaced grace as Woodhouse said. "These foot-lickers of yours have treated me like a villain. I can assure you, I came with good intentions. In fact I'm expecting my servant to arrive any moment with supplies as a gift from the court. The king will not be pleased when he hears I have been treated so shabbily. Do you lead these men, Master Kett?"

"I have that honour, yes, and I must apologise for your poor welcome. It was not on my orders I can assure you." Robert said politely. "William and I are anxious to help these men get back their land. Every corner they considered theirs is lost to them by unlawful enclosures. We are here to ask for His Majesty's benevolence in this grievous matter. Perhaps Roland, you would be good enough to take the shackles off so our visitor is more comfortable."

Roland bent down and released the chains bound round their prisoner's boots. Dismayed by the newly made scuffs on the hide Woodhouse was about to complain but decided not to. Instead he wriggled his shoulders emphatically.

"Have you forgotten, my wrists are still bound?"

He turned round and flapped his hands.

"Later perhaps," Robert said quietly.

His ankles stiff Woodhouse shuffled sideways and half-sat, half-fell on the ground. It was obvious to him the peasants would soon be moving. Wherever he looked they made preparations. Possessions went back into shoulder bags, abandoned clothing picked up and the smouldering fire stamped out.

Since his chains were removed he'd been left alone. He fumed at the indignity. Through narrowed eyes he amused himself looking for any sign of a female form, a skirt, a girlish laugh, anything to indicate a woman in their midst. He thought he saw one, but she looked grey-haired and elderly.

Intent on his task he missed the snap of twigs somewhere close by. When he saw Robert almost beside him he started.

"By my sword, you're light on your feet, Master Kett."

Robert smiled. "It pays to be," he said drily. "Forgive us for neglecting you but we need to move with speed if we are to reach Drayton before dark."

Anxious not to travel with them and seeing his chance of any honour fast disappearing, Woodhouse changed his approach.

"Surely there is no need for me to go with you. I'm no threat to you and if you would untie this wretched rope, I can easily explain my presence here."

He made a show of discomfort when he moved his hands. Robert ignored it.

"That won't be necessary. Your servant, Edgerley has explained to us and I must thank you for such fine supplies. I must also apologise for the rough treatment you received. Edgerley watched from the trees ready to help you it seems."

"If you have harmed my man," Woodhouse retorted.

"On the contrary he is marching with us. Let me help you up, you can talk as we walk," Robert said, supporting a dejected Woodhouse as he got to his feet.

Not insensitive by nature, Robert felt some sympathy for the man. He and William had discussed at some length the unexpected arrival of their prisoner. It hadn't been part of the plan. It had been William who'd urged that it might be useful to keep Woodhouse with them. Since no one could say how the protest might end he would be a sort of insurance if needed, he'd suggested.

Much of the column passed before they joined it. With bad grace Woodhouse tramped with them toward Drayton. When he'd choked back his anger sufficiently, he appealed to Robert again.

"Master Kett, you are a well educated man. Surely you must realise, things could go very badly for you when it's found you have taken me a prisoner. I can assure you I simply came here in good faith to tell you how foolhardy it is for you to persist in this madness."

"No, sir, it is not madness. Have you any idea how these people suffer? Since land enclosures, most have been reduced to terrible levels of poverty, forced to beg or become vagrants. The remainder struggle to provide for their families whilst those like me who live in comfort grow fatter and richer at their expense."

It was an eloquent plea and inwardly Woodhouse decided Robert deserved more than a little respect, but the burning pain on his wrists and his indignity at being a prisoner sharply reminded him of his present predicament. At his persuasive best, he said.

"So as I'm a very reasonable man, what will you accept in order to abandon this protest of yours?"

Robert looked at him suspiciously.

"Who sent you to speak to me? Was it that poor frightened mayor or perhaps the good sheriff who we sent packing, although I should apologise for that except that for these peasants their condition is intolerable."

"Food, is that it? We can send food if that's they want. Let them eat well on their return journey. Just tell me what it is they need," Woodhouse urged.

Robert stopped. He knew Thom wouldn't be far away. Seeing him walk with Will, he beckoned.

"Yes, Master Kett."

"Thom, our friend here is offering to give us food."

"No one will turn that down, supplies run low. When we reach Drayton there'll be plenty of empty bellies."

Tired of what he perceived to be a silly waste of time, Woodhouse hardened his voice.

"Come now, let's not play games. You are in danger of being treated as rebels, *all* of you. Its money you want, isn't it? Forty pence, that's what I'm prepared to give you. Norwich is not a poor city. You can have it on the understanding you leave here tonight. I'll send a rider after you. He should have no trouble catching you up. What do you say to that?"

A creep of red travelled up Thom's neck and flooded his cheeks in an instant.

"I say a pox on you and all your soft-bellied spawn," he retorted.

Amused by Thom's spirit, Robert laughed and nodded.

"So, Master Kett," Woodhouse sneered. "You let a peasant make decisions for you, how disappointing."

As swiftly as it appeared the humour lighting Robert's face vanished. His eyes which rested on Woodhouse and his mocking expression glinted as if ice rested in their depths. Speaking softly, he said.

"Thom, please find Roland and tell him we have need of his chain again. So pleasant is it to have my lord's company, I should hate to lose him on the way."

Rich scents of leaf mould, damp earth and fungus permeated the air as the men settled down for the night. Slowed by heavy rain falling in jagged lines, the march to Drayton had been arduous. For early July they found the river higher than expected and more needed to swim than to wade across. Cold discomfort and sodden clothes quickly led to frayed tempers and angry exchanges. Robert couldn't recall such a change of mood since the walk began.

In the hope they'd found the driest ground, they made camp in the middle of the wood. The four carts were dragged together to provide shelter for the women and children and the horses rubbed down with any dry bracken they could find. Even the fire seemed hostile taking time to flame as if it begrudged its warmth. Both weary, Robert and Thom sat close to it whilst their clothes gave off hazy wisps of steam. Next to them, William slept soundly in a pit he'd scraped in the leaves.

Robert ran his fingers through his hair and flinched from the feel of it. Matted and irritating, doubtless it was lice which made it itch, he thought. It all added to the despondent atmosphere. He'd witnessed the first fight over food too. He lent over and touched Thom on the arm.

"Maybe I should have accepted the offer our generous lord made. Tomorrow will see us starving. Men cannot march on empty bellies, eh, Thom."

Thom's expression was vague.

"I was dreaming about Martha's boiled beef. What I wouldn't give for a steaming bowl."

"Aye," Robert said. "Alice roasts a joint of mutton. It makes me drool to think of it. She spears the meat with wild garlic and tears the spikes of rosemary on top. The fat is yellow like field flowers, crisp on the outside, soft as a woman's breast when it melts on your tongue."

Memories invoked pain and both lapsed into silence again. A sudden wind lifted tree branches and sent icy rain drops hurtling off leaves. They shivered as they landed on them. Robert hauled himself to his feet, found some dry wood sheltered by shrubs and tossed it on the fire.

"Perhaps I should check on our prisoner," he said, half-heartedly. "Yet, I don't fancy my legs will go far."

"You can be sure Roland and his friends will keep a safe watch. I don't think my lord will stray. When I last saw him he was trussed like a fowl," Thom said, patting the ground round him in search of a dry piece.

"What's happened to Philip? I haven't seen him since he vanished when Woodhouse arrived."

"He stays with Will and Elias in the middle of the march. Too frightened he'll be recognised, so Will says. He was sure he'd seen Woodhouse at the palace, that's why he disappeared so quickly."

Spreading his jerkin on the ground, Thom laid down, turning himself in circles like a dog seeking a comfortable bed. Crouched down beside his brother, Robert smiled and gently touched his hair.

"Look at him, he sleeps like an infant," he said, with an expression of deep fondness. "So tomorrow, Thom, we march to Mousehold."

There was no answer, only the gentle rasps of Thom's breathing.

– 13 –

Hampton Court

Head back and eyes closed, Edward Seymour relaxed in one of the gold chairs arranged in a semi-circle in the Music room. Only the almost imperceptible movement of his head as he moved it in time to the music indicated he was actually awake. Occasionally his lids flew open and he gazed briefly at the ceiling with its exquisite hand-painted Renaissance frescos.

It was a cheerless composition which trickled through the room. Its melancholy strains caressed the finely carved architraves and burnished wood panelling. The ambience could not have been more perfect for the recital taking place.

On a raised dais the quartet of musicians stretched their fingers as the final notes faded. Instantly upright, Seymour led the applause encouraging the small audience of invited guests with nods of approval. Instruments at rest three of the four stood and took a bow. The fourth did not.

Black satin shod feet resting on a stool to raise him up, the king waved his lute instead. Unlike his companions, his seat was modelled in the style of a throne but its size still dwarfed the slender, immature boy.

Seymour held out both hands as he hurried towards him. "Your Grace plays like an angel. An arresting performance, sire, I'm left speechless at your skill."

"Thank you, Uncle, I rather enjoyed that myself," the king replied, almost lost inside a voluminous red silk jacket. Elated by his accomplishment he wandered from the dais across to the table laden with cold meats, pastries and bowls of fruit.

About to follow him, Seymour noticed a messenger who loitered, uncertain, by the door. Changing course, he beckoned the lad forward and led him away to a quieter corner.

"State your business and be quick about it. You disturb the king's party," he said curtly.

"I'm sorry, my Lord Protector, I was told it was a matter of some importance," the youth explained. "There is a rider recently arrived from Norwich. He's been sent by the Sheriff and the Mayor and requests he must speak to you on an urgent matter."

"Tut, tut, how tiresome. Are you sure this can't wait. You can see it's inconvenient. His Majesty has guests. Where is this person?"

Cheeks blanched with apprehension, the lad shook his head.

"He waits in your apartment and insists that he speak to you immediately, my lord."

"Oh very well, but for your sake, I trust you speak the truth," Seymour said irritably and assuring himself that the king was well attended, he hurried out of the room and the messenger scuttled behind him. Through the Great Hall, Seymour turned and hurried along the maze of corridors. His cloak flew out behind him, the ermine edge like a beacon in the dim, orangery-lit passageways.

He found Edmund Pynchyn standing in his reception hall, staring up at an enormous oil painting of the late king. Painted by Holbein, it flattered Henry in his later years, some of the excesses of his rich living somewhat trimmed from his portly shape. Arms akimbo, the monarch beamed benevolently at the artist. The King Charles spaniel at his feet looked less happy. When the portrait was hung, Seymour was tempted to drape something over the dog he had hated. The scars on his shins were a clear testimony that the animal had no love for him either. Shortly after the king's death, the palace was saddened to hear of the dog's demise. The archer who shot it received a knighthood for services to the Crown. Seymour still smiled at the thought. He burst through the door, swept past the waiting visitor, turned on his heel and snapped.

"Who are you and what is it of such urgency you must disturb me?"

"I'm Edmund Pynchyn, gentlemen and master tailor of Norwich, my lord Seymour. I've ridden non-stop from Norfolk to ask for your assistance."

With a flick of fingers, Seymour dismissed the messenger who withdrew gratefully. The fingers waved again directing Pynchyn to sit. Behind his desk, Seymour picked up his quill and poised it over the inkwell.

"So what is it you want me to sign? It must be an important document if there is such haste about it. What is it you ask for? Is it a warrant perhaps? A jumped up nobleman in need of the end of a rope or have you the executioner's axe in mind?" he said.

"None of those, my lord," Pynchyn said, apologetic.

"Then what is it?" Seymour snapped.

"The poor are on the march, my lord, thousands of them. They intend to enter Norwich. If they decide to storm the city, we cannot defend it without help. I have been sent to ask you to send in troops to suppress this rising."

Seymour tapped the end of his quill on his desk and stared at him. Then fingering his beard thoughtfully, he said.

"Tell me, have you seen any of these rebels at close quarters, one in particular? Mature for one so young. Dark, most handsome, they call him Philip."

Chapter 13

Watching for any reaction, Seymour waited. Pynchyn's negative shake of the head left him disappointed.

"I'm sorry my lord. I haven't encountered any of them personally."

Impatient, Seymour tossed the quill down. He'd had people hunting Philip for days.

"No matter, so are these trouble makers inside the city walls?"

"Not yet, my lord, but close. They camp nearby."

Seymour walked to the window and stared into the darkness. In the distance a haze of lights marked the landing stage at the edge of the river. He sighed heavily. This business about enclosed land was like a flea on his back, irritating and just out of reach of his hand.

"I don't wish to belittle those in authority in your city, but it seems most inept they cannot repulse a few ignorant pig-swillers. They want an army do they? I'm not yet convinced of the need for them. I shall send someone. A herald is too important, Pursuivant Groves his underling will do. He will report back to me and then we shall see."

"But how long will that take, my lord? You are known to be most sympathetic when approached for your help. There's no one fairer."

"This, good sir, is my decision and therefore the end of the matter. Be good enough to close the door when you leave."

Pynchyn got to his feet, the sweat shiny on his brow. His only thought was the unpleasant reception he would receive on his return to Norwich with the failure of his errand.

"Very good, my lord," he said.

Unimpressed by him, Seymour watched him back out of the room, head bowed almost to his knees. He'd seen his sort before, a servile fool with less brain than a cockroach.

A thought occurred to him as he hurried back to the Music room. He grabbed the arm of a passing aide and pulled him to a standstill.

"Pray find Pursuivant Groves and tell him I wish to see him. Then take a message to the Privy Council. Find Thomas Shelbourne, tell him to draw up a law before we meet tomorrow. It's regarding the enclosures of land throughout the country. All who hold manorial rights shall in future charge a rent should they wish to allow a labourer to work the land for them. Let the common people know their place. Is that clear? Now, go with speed and make sure it is done."

His smile was thin and his eyes hard and piercing. Satisfied he would cause even more distress to the wretched life of the peasants, Seymour whistled softly as he continued down the corridor. It was short lived pleasure. The king rounded the corner. On seeing Seymour, an unattractive frown crinkled his young face. He threw his lute on the floor and kicked it in a petulant manner.

"Where did you go? You were supposed to hear me play again."

"I'm sorry, I had matters of state to attend to, Your Highness. They were important."

"Boring, boring, there's nothing more important than me," the king whined.

He continued down the corridor leaving the lute where it lay. Seymour sighed and picked up the instrument. Sometimes the burden of care the boy's father had placed on him left him feeling he carried a block of stone on his back.

Norwich
12th July 1549

Bowthorpe and the south of the city lay behind them. Ahead, a rise in the road revealed an outstanding view of the city. Below them, spread like a painter's canvas, patches of colour marked buildings. Reds, browns, greys and dingy yellows intermingled with innumerable shades of green foliage from grass, trees and hedgerows. From such a height the flint and cobble city walls resembled a bracelet girding the centre.

Washed by the pale early light the gun-metal grey stone cathedral sat in the heart of the city. Its tall spire and cloistered outlines calmed the spirits of those who gazed on it. It was Robert, William and Thom who saw it first. Robert looked back and waved his arm as a gesture of their arrival and a cheer vibrated down the dark, shuffling centipede behind them. At last their goal was reached and there could have been no finer welcome than the clearing of storm clouds and the burning orb of a dawn sunrise. To the north on their left rising steeply, a wooded escarpment afforded an even more spectacular view.

"At last, eh, Mousehold Heights," Robert smiled broadly. "This is where we shall be based until we get into the city. We shan't miss a thing going on down there and we can see any visitors before they see us. Perfect, don't you think?"

William looked dubious. "I shall share your enthusiasm, brother, when I've had a decent night's sleep. Leaves and damp earth aren't quite the same as a feather mattress." he said, rubbing the bottom of his back. "What say you, Thom?"

"Master Kett, I wouldn't know about feathers, but I shall never curse straw again."

The three turned left and led the march up the sharp incline through the trees and on to the heath. There seemed no boundary to the land. Robert dismissed the first plateau since the small shrubs offered little protection. He insisted they must select a suitable site which offered a good view, shade and would avoid the worst of wind and rain. He ignored the grumbles and led the men on. Some lingered, anxious to sit down where they stood. Others urged them on with ribald remarks and laughter. They climbed even higher when without warning, Robert stopped.

"This will be it. There, do you see the oak with its fine spread of branches. We shall deal with all business under its protection. The other trees can afford shelter when it's needed and this soft turf will make more comfortable beds. This, my friends, is our home for as long as it takes us to enter the city and make our cause known."

Whilst Thom set the men to make fires, lay out shelters and prepare an area for cooking, Robert and William made an excursion round the campsite. Morale was high again and they were greeted with nods and grins as the men worked with renewed vigour. One face regarded them with a sullen look from his position on the ground. The chain round his ankle tethered him to a stout shrub.

"Good day, Master Woodhouse. I trust you are in good health," Robert said cheerfully.

The answer came as growled oath and a fierce rattle of links.

"Perhaps I've made a mistake, should we let him go? It may do more harm than good to keep him here," William whispered as they walked past.

"He may well be of some use to us if things don't go well," Robert replied.

They walked a short way down from their position and the view became clearer. Just below, the river Wensum spun a silver thread which ran along the east side of the city. From where they stood, they faced Bishops Gate which controlled the river crossing beside Bishop's Bridge. In the grounds of the Cathedral a track led from the riverbank toward one of twelve gates which encircled the city providing it with its stoutest defences, Erpingham Gate, its sturdy twin oak doors stone vaulted and laced with heavy metal reinforcements and the pillars either side topped with cannons.

The brothers stood looking at the scene for several minutes. Robert was the first to speak.

"That will be our entry when the time comes," he said softly, pointing to the gates. "We are fortunate the water flows shallow there." He stared thoughtfully across the river. "Yes, that is where our path lies to the city."

"Or yonder possibly our escape from it," William said dryly, indicating to the west where the dales of Thorpe Morieux and Dussindale offered wide dips of green meadows with patches of gorse and bracken. They could see sheep and hear their faint voices carried on the wind. Nothing William said affected Robert's ebullient mood. Slapping his brother on the back, he said.

"I have a good feeling about this, brother. You see, these corrupt landowners will be made to rip up every illegal hedge in the land by the time we've had our say."

Tempted to urge caution, William changed his mind, but Robert knew his brother well.

"You were going to say something?"

"Nay," William said, unwilling to rob his brother's face of its wide smile.

Thom met them on their way back. He too looked enthusiastic and cheerful.

"What do you think?" he said, waving his arm towards the camp.

It was clear every man worked with a will and beyond the crudely erected shelters a fire sparked brightly, the carts were emptied and the spit already cooking an assortment of meats.

"Fine work, Thom, you coax the men well," Robert enthused.

Somewhat abashed by the praise, Thom grunted.

"And who are they?" William asked, nodding toward an ever growing crowd gathered by the perimeter of the camp.

Activated by the thought of a better life ahead, more men and women jostled in a crowd eager to join the protest. Poor in dress and with strained faces, they offered bags of vegetables, salted meat and even a rabbit or two.

"They are the homeless from the city. They ask to join us, Master Kett. They bring food and ale."

"It does my heart good to see them, but send the women home. There is no place for them in this march," Robert said firmly.

Thom frowned. "I doubt you'll shift those who've come with us from Wymondham. They see it as their place to stay with their men folk."

"They do no harm, brother and you've done well, Thom," William said, his arm about Thom's shoulder in a hug which expressed his thanks. Flushed with pleasure Thom extricated himself from the embrace. He looked awkward as he said.

"There is one other thing. I know you said we should use yonder tree for holding counsel, but you both should be more comfortable. Behind that copse is a house, Lord Surrey's, it was. But it's been empty for many a year. I've sent a party to prepare it for you. I hope I've not done wrong."

Robert was taken aback. "You surprise me, Thom. How did you know of the place?" he said.

"My aunt, father's sister, lived in Norwich. We came to visit often and my brother and I played many a game up here on the heath. We discovered it then. Mount Surrey, it's called. Lord Surrey was alive in them days, but I don't know what happened to him."

"You're a good man, Thom, we shall go and look immediately," William said. "Robert, are you coming?"

His brother didn't appear to hear him as he muttered gazing up at the stout trunk and heavy branches of by far the largest oak tree nearby.

"We need a name. The Oak of Reprieve, no. The Oak of Hope, no, that's wrong too. Reform, no, that can't be right, wait a minute, I have it. the Oak of Reformation, that's it. We shall call this tree the Oak of Reformation, a rebellious oak, if you will and all this will be called The King's Camp. How does that sound?" His eyes sparkled, and his boyish smile amused both William and Thom.

"Excellent, brother, most excellent," William said. "Now shall we go and look at what Thom's done for us."

As they emerged from a cluster of birch trees, the smiles on their faces faded. Two dozen or more men passed them struggling under the weight of objects they carried. Several had wooden furniture, some carried bedding, cooking pots, pictures, lamps and at the very back, a roll of costly looking carpet carried by two men.

Thom broke away and raced towards them, his curses audible in the clear air. Speeding their step, Robert and William followed him.

"What is this, Thom, where is this all coming from? Are the men looting?" Robert said, curtly.

"It seems, Master Kett, they took it upon themselves to remove these things from the house."

A sandy haired, thin featured man with an armful of materials spoke gruffly.

"They were there for the taking. Nobody lives in the house, what's the use of leaving it. We can make use of it in the camp."

"So what is it you have there?" William enquired.

The man shook out the bundle. Fine corded velvet, taffeta and silks tumbled onto the ground in a swathe of vibrant colours.

"They are nothing but curtains, sirrah. What possible need have of you of curtains," Robert said, coldly.

The skin pinched tight over his nostrils and tightened his lips into a thin line as he regarded the spoils. With a shrug the man picked up the heap and said. "They'll make us bedcovers. It's more than we have at the moment."

Thom wrung his hands. "Master Kett, I'm so sorry. I gave them instruction to make sure the house was fit to live in. That they steal troubles me."

"It looks badly on us, Thom. We are here to protest about our land being taken not to show others we are common thieves," Robert reminded him.

Another man, older and greyer, sidled up doing his best to conceal something behind his back.

"The place is empty and things are already broke so it weren't only us."

With barely a glance, Robert waved him away. William rested his hand on his brother's arm.

"Let them go, Robert," he said. "They have precious little else to distract them and we have no need of such things."

Ever the peacemaker, William's words seemed to soothe Robert and he walked on, ignoring the parade of Lord Surrey's possessions. Joined by John and Will, Thom and the Kett brothers walked the rooms of Mount Surrey.

The mansion was indeed in a grievous state. When their boots struck the bare boards, they spoke to them in hollow echoes and the wind whispered of the past through the broken glass.

Once the furniture must have been covered in dust sheets, but with most of it missing the sheets lay abandoned, thrown into corners. Should anyone venture to look out of the casement, shards of glass crunched underfoot and in one corner damp from water leaks curled back the flocked wallpaper. They didn't find a room which hadn't been ransacked.

"I think the men spoke the truth. There's more lost than they took away with them." William said, looking thoughtfully at marks in the dust.

"That's still no reason to steal." Robert said.

"I know brother, you're right."

Thom couldn't remember when he last felt so low. The state of the house depressed him and gloom settled over him. A hundred questions raced through his mind. Uppermost was Martha. He wondered about her managing to eke out enough to eat or if she was well or sickly. She'd promised him she'd go to her mother's, but Agatha was aged and frail and all she would do was provide company when her mind didn't wander. Who would his woman call on in a moment of trouble? It was torment for him.

He sensed Robert too was uneasy. At night round the fire when sleep eluded him, he watched him. Shoulders hunched, brow ridged with worry lines, staring far away wrapped in thought. Or thinking no one watched, hands clasped to his face to recite prayers.

When Thom did fall asleep, he slept heavily and when he stirred himself the others had gone. He found them in the breakfast room in the old house. Will who exerted all his strength on the door lock declared it solid. Robert appeared satisfied.

"John and Will, if you would fetch our prisoner, Master Woodhouse should be grateful he no longer needs to sleep under a tree. The windows are sound and there's a hearth to sleep in. The room lacks comfort, but it's dry," Robert said. "There's ample room for more to keep him company. Does our prisoner show any signs of remorse?"

Will shook his head. "He speaks only about good fellowship and offers three more cartloads of beer for his freedom, Master Kett."

"Then let him be the first to enjoy our hospitality," Robert said, dismissively.

Outside a range of outhouses looked in good order. But each was considered too small for habitation.

"That only leaves the chapel," William said and pointed to a flint and brick building attached to the end of the house. Supported by a small beam high over the door, a cross gleamed. Caught by the sun its mellow gold taxed the eye. The heavy door opened slowly and scraped over the stone step.

Robert went first. From the bright shine of day the shadowed interior confused. He blinked several times to adjust to the dim light. It smelt fusty, a combination of damp wood and cold stone. No Bible rested on the lectern and the silver was gone from the Altar but otherwise nothing appeared to have been disturbed since the day it was abandoned.

Both brother's crossed themselves, walked up the nave and gave a reverent nod. Thom, John and Will, hats in hand stood quietly by the door.

"This will do us nicely, don't you think, William?" Robert said. Even though he spoke in a low voice it still resonated from the beams overhead. For a moment his brother's gentle smile erased the lines and creases of worry which appeared to mark his face over the last few days.

"Nothing could be more suitable," he replied.

Giving instructions to John and Will to bring their few pieces of luggage to the chapel, Robert and William walked with Thom to the Oak of Reformation where they'd left some of the stronger men to erect cover as best they could.

Robert wanted it prepared as a place of assembly where they could gather to discuss affairs, but they needed protection from falling wood and poor weather. The awning was clumsy but appeared sound. Slats of wood were wedged in the lower branches and draped over them dark material provided a canopy for their safety. Late of Mount Surrey, a table and chairs added an air of officialdom and someone had even found some early heather in bloom and set it in a beaker on the table top.

"God's truth, they've done an excellent job," William said, with enthusiasm. "What say you, Robert?"

Already seated, his brother smiled gladly.

"Now we can begin our work."

Too busy to converse the only sound under the awning were the noises Robert and William made as they sucked the bones of two pheasants. Juices dripped from their fingers and they both wore moustaches of grease as they devoured their meal. Robert emptied the last of the beer into his beaker, leant back in the chair and belched loudly.

"My apologies gentlemen, but my belly rebels at such fine fare. It hardly remembers when it last received such exquisite flesh. Perfectly cooked too, where did these little beauties come from?"

He waved his hand at the skeletal remains and wiped his fingers on the bottom of his jacket.

"Some of the men left camp early this morning. They went to rip down hedges around the city. It seems they put up a score or more and a deer too, I believe." Thom said.

"You have a bird, I hope," said William, flinging the last of the bones onto the platter.

Thom nodded. "It's on the spit, I shall enjoy it later."

"I could have sworn I smelt mutton roasting," Robert said.

A flush of pink rose from Thom's neck and coloured his cheeks. "Perhaps a small sheep also came their way."

Robert gave a nonchalant wave of his hand.

"No matter," he said.

"It seems we have a visitor," William murmured.

With his elevation to herald almost within his grasp, Pursiuvant Groves walked with a purpose. He was also out of breath. Not realising how far up the heath the camp was, he'd left his horse at a hostelry in the city and walked to Mousehold Heights.

He orientated himself, straightened his tunic so the royal cipher was properly displayed and approached the tree. The Kett brothers' were already on their feet to greet him. Taken aback by the make-shift arrangements, Groves stared at them but his face remained devoid of any expression. His bow was brief, his tone formal and curt.

"The Masters' Kett of Wymondham?"

Extending his hand, Robert said. "We are indeed."

In return he received a poor effort of a handshake as Groves announced himself.

"Pursuivant Groves special envoy of His Majesty, King Edward, the sixth."

If those who greeted him expected a more friendly approach they were disappointed. Groves's brusque voice lacked both warmth and grace.

"Pray, take a seat, sir. We are pleased to welcome you to The King's Camp," Robert said pleasantly.

William pushed a chair out with his foot. With barely a glance, Groves chose a different one and sat down. Then the wind picked up the material above and disturbed it with noisy flaps. Groves looked up at it and moved again to a place close to the entrance.

"I shan't waste time, I hope to return to London by nightfall although it seems in this God-forsaken place you call Norfolk, it's unlikely," he said, as he crossed his legs and dangled a shoe. His eyes the colour of dull steel flickered over the two brothers and beneath a neatly clipped moustache his lips were as narrow as a quill nib. His pause was brief.

"The palace directed I should come here at once. The news of your arrival in Norwich has not been well received. The Duke of Somerset, my lord Seymour has asked me to find out your intent and report back to him as a matter of urgency. I stopped briefly at the castle and it seems despite their good efforts, neither Mayor Codde or the Sheriff, have been able to establish a reasonable conversation with you. In fact, I hear the good Sheriff was treated with contempt."

"Yes, we were sorry about that. It wasn't our intention."

Rudely interrupting William, Groves rapped on the table with his stick.

"It's of no consequence. From what I can see, the man is a prig and it was probably well deserved."

Both Robert and William were taken aback by the man's opinion of the sheriff, but they didn't alter their polite expressions.

"The palace considers your objection to land enclosures absurd and Lord Seymour is aggrieved by the nuisance you are making of yourselves. However, in order to resolve matters quickly, he is prepared to offer some recompense in recognition of your journey here. What do you think of that?"

Complacent, Groves leant back in his chair, arms crossed and waited for an answer.

"We think, sir, you waste your time as does my lord Seymour. What do you have in mind, a fat cow or two, perhaps some casks of beer? I wonder how many crowns might come our way from the Privy Purse. What might we be worth, eh, brother?" Robert said, with a wry smile.

William laughed loudly. Discomforted, Groves fidgeted in his chair and moistened his lips.

"Money would be no object, within reason, of course," he said calmly, although angry spots of colour darkened his cheeks. "What you can be assured of is a full pardon for you all and Lord Seymour is making arrangements for you to be visited by a man of faith. He feels most strongly you are in need of some Godliness here about. I have with me a commission to direct Robert Watson to preach to your camp. "

Handkerchief pressed to his lips to suppress a smile, William averted his gaze from Groves.

"I'm afraid you have made a wasted journey, sir," Robert said, as he got to his feet. "Do you seriously imagine these impoverished men came all this way to receive a few platitudes and a handful of paltry crowns? You are much mistaken. They are without work, without pride and without reason. Why? Because sir, they have been robbed, closed out of their land and all their grazing rights stolen from them. Land which rightfully belongs to them, by agreement if not by Deed, so they starve, their dependents starve and you and all you represent are responsible. That is why we thank you for coming and ask you to depart."

Astonished and visibly pale their visitor sat speechless. Robert glanced at William. He could see by the warmth in his brother's eyes, he'd spoken well. Groves pushed his chair back heavily leaving trails in the earth.

Holding the edge of the table, his knuckles were white. It seemed he had trouble opening his mouth, for when he spoke the words came out with a hiss.

"Very well, I shall take your response back to the palace. What I can tell you is from henceforth you and this rabble you have here," he said, gesturing a broad arc across the camp, "will now be called rebels. This camp is unlawful and should you obstruct matters in the city, punishment will be swift and harsh, I can promise you that. Just how many men do you have here?"

"About eighteen thousand and more," William murmured.

Turning sharply, Groves strode away from the table. "Well then we must prepare a quantity of stocks and prison cells to await their company," he called over his shoulder as he stepped out.

A large crowd of peasants pressed forward to form a narrow corridor through which Groves had to walk. They watched him pass in silence. When he reached the gate the jeers came together as one and sounded as if a huge storm rumbled its discontent over the camp.

Keeping close to edge of the heath four men crept in single file. From somewhere above them, faint voices and outbursts of laughter carried to them on the lower slopes. The nearer they got to the camp the more potent the air became, heavy with the smell of roasting meats and alcohol. The leader turned to the others.

"Pssst."

Those behind stopped abruptly almost walking in to one another. From under a black hat, its wide brim concealing most of his face, Mayor Codde's eyes peered out. He pointed upwards.

"There are several paths, we must be careful to choose one which doesn't reveal us too quickly. Its better we approach with caution," he whispered.

"I don't like this, I don't like it one bit," Melloe said nervously. "We are not the rebels. Just why are we skulking in the shadows when we are on official business? "

"We must keep to the plan," Codde insisted. "It's important we stay pleasant and amenable at all times. Upset these people and the city will suffer until reinforcements arrive."

"What I don't understand is how Woodhouse came to be taken prisoner in the first place," Gawdy said in a low voice. "You are quite certain of this, Chase," he asked the fourth man who squatted on a low wall.

Chase nodded vigorously.

"Absolutely," he said. "One of my household has a relation on the march. She heard it through another. It seems Woodhouse got careless and was set upon by some of the rebels. I'm assured he's held somewhere on the camp as is his servant Edgerly."

"I'd of thought the Sheriff would be with us," Gawdy remarked.

"Ah, yes. The High Sheriff excused himself. He had an engagement elsewhere," Codde said."That's why Chase kindly agreed to join us."

"Or perhaps our esteemed Sheriff remembers the last time he approached the rebels," Gawdy said. Their laughter was loud in the silence.

"Shush, shush, we'll be heard," Codde said, with an agitated flap of his arms.

Following a tortuous trail chosen by the mayor, they climbed steadily until they finally arrived on a plain of grass and scrub. The path was a short way from the body of the camp and threaded through part of the woodland which led to behind the Reformation Oak. From light thrown by the boisterous flames of one of the fires they were able to see men eating, others moving about and yet more in the background where smaller fires burned.

"There seems to be a great number of them," Gawdy said, nerves adding a quiver to his voice.

He wasn't good in the dark and wished he'd made an excuse, as he suspected the Sheriff had. Melloe sniffed appreciatively. "They eat well, for the starving that is." A hint of sarcasm in his voice wasn't lost on his companions.

"So what happens now, Codde? We can hardly present ourselves and ask them to release Woodhouse," Chase murmured.

"Quiet, I'm thinking." replied Codde.

"Perhaps we can help you with that."

The disembodied voice startled them. No one heard the men approaching. Once again Will proved that despite his height, he was lighter on his feet than many half his size. Appearing out the trees, he was followed by John and Thom.

"Look who we have here, Thom. It seems the Mayor and his friends are paying us a visit."

Codde cursed under his breath. It wasn't the way he'd hoped to arrive. By choosing a circuitous route, his intention was to search for Woodhouse rather than walk boldly into the camp. Instead being discovered lurking on the perimeter must arouse suspicion.

"Is it Master Kett you're looking for?" Thom asked.

Behind Codde, the officials shuffled their feet uneasily. Drawing himself up to look dignified, the mayor nodded.

"Perhaps you'd be good enough to take us to him. I'm not accustomed to such surroundings." He grimaced nodding his head in the direction of the campfire.

"Join us then, Mayor, you'd soon learn what it's like to live the life of a peasant," John said.

"You jest, of course?" Codde sniffed with an expression of disdain on his face. Then he remembered his intention to be pleasant and made a poor attempt to smile. He was appalled at the suggestion. With their dirt-streaked faces, matted hair and filthy clothing, the men who walked alongside were far from his usual sort of companions. In a muttered aside, he said.

"We must make the best of things. It may be we shall have to look for Master Woodhouse on another occasion."

124

Robert waited for the table to be moved and then climbed on it. About to speak to his followers, he noticed Codde in conversation with Thom. Robert held up his hands and the crowd fell quiet.

"My friends, it has been a long struggle which is not yet over. We are here because all of you want to escape from a servile life and enjoy the freedom just conditions will give you."

The men nudged each other and roared their approval. If the wind favoured them the sound would carry to the city. Waiting until it was quiet again, Robert continued.

"We have amongst us the mayor of Norwich, Master Codde, with other distinguished city notables and we welcome them. Fill your hearts with the hope of better things and ask your God to be merciful. Such great oppression must not be ignored. If our rising is successful, you will no longer be slaves. And, my friends, I intend to make it successful or die with grace should I fail."

Robert blushed. Somebody clapped and another cheered. Instantly everyone joined in and it was a tumult of noise. When he saw the shine of tears on his brother's face, Robert winked.

The applause continued. Codde looked about him and with reluctance put his hands together too. Standing either side of him, Melloe and Gawdy stood silent. Codde frowned at them and both joined in. Flushed with his success, Robert jumped from the table and made straight for Codde.

"What an unexpected pleasure, Mayor and you've brought friends. We have no quarrel with you. All are welcome at the Kings Camp. Come, sit at the table. Take a cup of mead with us."

Will was sent to bring extra chairs and refreshments and Robert escorted Codde and his company to the Reformation Oak. Perched on the edge of his seat, Codde glanced round.

"This is very nice," he said doubtfully.

"So what brings you to see us?" William asked pleasantly.

Codde thought quickly. "We wanted to make sure you have all you need."

Neither brother was deceived by the apparent friendly manner which Codde displayed, but it was a game they were both prepared to play for the time being.

"You seem to have made yourselves very comfortable," Chase said, in a sarcastic voice. Robert ignored his rudeness and refilled the beakers.

"Indeed, sir, it suits us well although we must be thankful it's summer. Not so cosy, methinks, when the winter winds blow," William said.

Those round the table smiled politely. Contemplating the mead, Codde said. "And have you had any other visitors?"

His attempt to sound casual made his question appear even more pointed. Robert exchanged a glance with William, and said.

"By that, do you mean His Majesty's envoy, Pursuivant Groves? If so, yes. We had the pleasure of seeing him only yesterday."

"The meeting went well, I hope?" Codde said, anxiety creeping into his voice.

"Not as well as he hoped." William replied. A smile twitched at his mouth when he saw the disappointment on Codde's face.

With a large swallow of his drink, the mayor lapsed into silence. Melloe spoke instead.

"I heard talk of a preacher coming from the city. Perhaps that's just what these people need. There has been much turbulence in matters of the church of late. Many have lost their way. A rousing sermon will do them good. Show them penitence is the way to God."

"On the contrary, my lord, I believe they think the Almighty has deserted them in their troubles," Robert said quietly.

To discuss religion was dangerous. Gawdy said quickly. "Is there anything you need? Have you enough food? We can easily provide anything you are short of?"

"Thank you, but we have sufficient. The men are in high spirits." Robert turned to Codde. "However, we intend to form a proper council and we wondered if you as mayor would sit with us. If you wish there is room for another of your choosing. That way our discussions will be balanced including the views of all. We should ask you to attend the camp daily. There is much to keep in order. Since we arrived here I'm told our numbers have grown to 20,000, all hungry and disinherited men. I shall do my best to keep control but there are bound to be problems. What say you?"

No one missed the look of alarm which momentarily crossed Codde's face. He in turn, had only one thought. Much as he didn't relish consorting with rebels, he must at all cost keep these people out of the city. Norwich was very vulnerable until the troops arrived he decided he had no option but to remain on friendly terms.

As if he could read Codde's mind, Robert nodded expectantly. "Well, Mayor, will you accept a place?"

Without any consultation with his companions, Codde smiled weakly. "Of course, Master Kett, it will be an honour."

Later, bathed by the placid light of a thousand stars adrift in a benevolent ebony sea, the brother's sat together. They'd climbed to a higher mound to look down on the city. Within its walls there was still movement. Torch flames guided the late wanderers and those who attended to business at all hours of the night. There were torches too that identified the two sentries who stood either side of Bishop's Gate. Each armed with a halberd they leant against the walls with casual disregard of their duty. Near them at Dungeon Tower another guard, but this time the halberdier used the base of the fortification as a back rest. His head lolled on his chest and his weapon lay adrift on the grass.

"Look there, brother. How pleasant it is to see how attentive the king's soldier's are to their responsibilities. Doubtless they'll fall asleep before long," William said wryly.

"I see one has already." Robert pointed out a dozing soldier. "I trust it'll be so when the time comes for us to knock on the city door. Did you see the mayor's face when I invited him to attend our meetings?"

"I did and I don't think he's best pleased. Just what sport is it the man plays with us?"

"One I doubt he can win and he knows it," Robert replied softly.

– 16 –

20th July 1549

The preacher carried his badge of office in his hand and therefore needed no introduction. A warm wind whipped up the hem of his gold embroidered black mantle and ruffled his surplice. Twice he needed to hold his hand to his clerical cap to prevent it whirling away.

Known by many who lived in the city, they fell back to allow him through. Some made the sign of the Cross on their breast. Others wearing hats hastily removed them and muttered "Father," as he passed them. Unable to match his long stride, Mayor Codde lagged some distance behind.

Robert looked up from the parchment he was writing on and seeing the visitors, laid down his quill and rolled up the sheet.

"We've been expecting you," he said, stepping out from under the oak tree.

The preacher smiled and put his bible down on the table.

"Master Kett? God's blessing on you, my son. I'm Robert Watson, of St. Martin's in Norwich, and I've been asked to visit and say prayers for you and your people. You have a great following, I see. Is there some place I may use to talk to them?"

Having stumbled over a grassy tussock, a flustered Codde caught up. "Good morrow to you both," he said, his forehead shiny with sweat. Behind him was a middle aged man. Despite the heat, his fur-trimmed robe and ornate doublet were the trappings of an elected councillor of the city, a high office which was evident in his aloof manner and dignified bearing. He cleared his throat which reminded Codde, he'd forgotten to introduce him.

"Master Kett, may I present my esteemed friend, Alderman Thomas Aldrich. He has kindly made himself available as a representative of the city council to sit with me at this table of yours when we discuss the matters that have brought you here."

Robert looked delighted. "It's a pleasure to meet you Alderman Aldrich. If you could excuse me for a few moments, I must direct our good clergyman to an appropriate place on the camp where he may hold a service. Do take a seat, gentlemen."

Seeing William passing, Robert beckoned him over.

"This good cleric is here to hold a service, William, perhaps you could see to it."

"I shan't speak for long," Watson assured. "Do you have any sick or infirm, I should like to give them God's special blessings."

"There are several I'm afraid. The walk was long and many elderly found it very tiring. We also have some who suffer sickness, a griping of the belly and bowels. Despite many warnings it seems they found a water pool and drank from it. It was brackish water and has done them no good," William said, as he and the clergyman moved away.

"So shall we start, Mayor?" Robert offered chairs and when joined by Thom, John Moulder and Will the meeting began. A jug of ale passed round the table. By the time William returned voices were raised.

"As I explained when last we met, we shall deal with administration problems under this tree and it will also be a court of justice. You can be assured I shall deal firmly with any who behave badly or bring the camp into disrepute," Robert insisted.

Aldrich looked disdainful and muttered aside to Codde which was easily overheard.

"This illegal camp is already disreputable."

Robert was disappointed. He'd hoped for better than a hostile Alderman who was already making clear that he was against their presence at Norwich. He turned and addressed Codde.

"Perhaps you'd care to confirm to the good alderman here, we intend there to be no trouble. Since we arrived you have allowed the men to pass freely in and out of the city. Has there been an outbreak of crime?"

Codde wriggled on his chair. "No, certainly there is nothing to report. All has been most peaceable."

"Is this true?" Aldrich said, one eyebrow lifted in an exaggerated arc. "You have given permission for these rebels to visit the city without hindrance? Is that wise?"

A pink flush of discomfort coloured Codde's cheeks. "Master Kett gave me his assurance, it seemed best not to aggravate the situation, if we are to keep the peace."

"I take exception to you calling us rebels, Master Aldrich." Robert murmured.

"You can take it any way you wish, Master Kett, and you, Codde, are a fool," Aldrich hissed.

It was a long and at times heated meeting. Robert knew Codde had been easily persuaded to be tolerant. Alderman Aldrich was not. His impatience with Codde for not being firmer with the rebels was obvious and he made repeated references to it.

Frequently the alderman referred to the protest as one 'made up of nothing but a rabble,' or 'a rebellion offering grave insults to the king made by greedy peasants,' and 'rebels deserving to be flogged.' Elbows on the table, he toyed with a vulgar looking gold ring whilst Codde, agitated and blustering, sought to calm things.

Chapter 16

"What the Alderman means is, we are sure you will see sense and disperse quietly before people gain the wrong impression of you."

"That's not what I meant at all, Codde. Kindly don't interfere. Kett here knows no good can come of these protests of theirs. Land enclosures will remain, you can be sure of that."

They all knew the mayor held more power and authority than the alderman and it suited them to maintain good relations with him. Unlike Codde, the alderman was unafraid of the huge numbers of protesters and seemed confident that they would never dare enter the city carrying arms.

"By the way, Master Kett, I hear you hold one of ours, Master Woodhouse. What has become of him?"

Codde choked and dribbled ale down his tunic. It was a minor distraction. Aldrich drummed his fingers impatiently. "Well?"

Unruffled, Robert nodded. "I can assure you he's quite safe and enjoys a degree of comfort. He might be useful to us and will remain here for now."

"Fie, Master Kett, hardly lawful, is it?" Aldrich admonished.

"Lawful, now that's an interesting word. Enclosing land, depriving people of their means of survival, *that's* unlawful, wouldn't you say, Alderman Aldrich?" Robert replied.

A noisy snort was heard and Aldrich glowered at Codde who smirked at the riposte. From under the table Robert pulled out the rolled up parchment.

"This gentlemen, is a statement of 'Requests and Demands,' which I intend to send to the king. Perhaps you would like to hear what I have written so far.

Firstly, we want the enclosures stopped, we want fair rents and we wish our common fishing rights restored, both in the rivers and the sea.

We ask for the appointment of residents clergymen in all the towns and villages particularly to preach and instruct our children in Godly ways."

Out of the corner of his eye Robert saw Codde and Aldrich exchange glances, but at the far end of the table, William, Thom and the others nodded in agreement.

"And we want free elections so we might appoint our own commissioners to enforce the laws. Now this is most important," Robert said, his finger stabbed on the words. "All bond men must be made free, for God made all men free.

Aldrich pushed his chair abruptly away from the table and made to leave.

"Before you go I should be grateful if you both would put your mark on this document," Robert said curtly.

"I most certainly will not," Aldrich stormed. "I can't speak for you, Codde, but these demands are outrageous."

Codde hurried to him. "A word, if I may." He drew Aldrich to one side, but his words were audible nonetheless.

"Think carefully about this. We must be seen to assist in this matter before we have an ugly rebellion on our hands. I fear, Alderman Aldrich, you are perhaps too hasty. I shall sign, I recommend you do too."

Taking the proffered quill, Codde scratched a hasty signature. Handing it to the alderman, he nodded emphatic encouragement.

"Very well, but I don't approve," the alderman said. Bad tempered he scrawled a mark on the paper. Throwing the quill back on the table, he stalked away from the tree. Codde scrambled after him. He turned, shrugged his shoulders and gave an awkward smile, but Aldrich didn't look back. "Until tomorrow then, Mayor Codde," Robert called.

"Possibly, possibly," Codde squeaked, hurrying to catch his companion

Hampton Court

Droplets of water were caught by light as they fell. They looked as if the man watching them had tossed a handful of diamonds into the fountain. Relaxed by the gentle sound of the water rising and falling, Seymour gazed beyond the formal garden to the river in the distance.

He'd just seen the king depart on the royal barge to attend a ceremony at Dulwich. The craft flying the royal standard and more than a dozen pennants travelled slowly up water the stiff breeze bolstering the flags firm and upright. When it was lost to sight on a bend in the river, Seymour turned to walk back to the palace. Thoughtful he plucked at the lavender hedge, crushed the mauve spears and let the perfume drift past his nose.

Having run down the length of the lawn, the messenger slowed his step so as to approach with more decorum. Seymour sighed heavily his reverie disturbed, he tossed the bruised flowers onto the path. With jaw set and eyes wary, he waited until the messenger recovered sufficiently to speak coherently.

"My lord, a messenger by the name of Nicholas Sotherton has just arrived from Norfolk. He brings a document and an urgent missive from the mayor of Norwich concerning the rebellion. He waits for you in your chambers."

Dismissing the messenger with instructions to find a bed for the night, Seymour ripped the seal from Mayor Codde's roll of vellum.

Martineau House,
Martineau Lane,
Norwich,
In the County of Norfolk

The Fourteenth Day of July
in the Year of Our Lord 1549

Duke of Somerset, Earl of Hertford, Viscount Beauchamp of Hache,
Earl Marshall, Lord Protector of England, Edward Seymour KG

My lord, I write to you with some urgency regarding the insurgents presently encamped on Mousehold Heights, whose numbers are now grown to above twenty thousand men.

Believing the enclosures of land are unlawful their complaints are many and whilst I strive to appease them, it becomes increasingly difficult.

They are convinced His Royal Majesty supports them under your guidance as his chief advisor and is therefore prepared to overlook their rebellious activities without protest or censure. The document brought to you this day contains their 'Requests' which number twenty nine. It is a full statement of their grievances, in the form of prayers, agreed by all the poor commons.

I beg you, my lord, to see fit to issue a reply which will satisfy them. Otherwise I fear we shall not contain them for much longer and our city will not survive in the face of an assault.

I remain your humble and most obedient servant,
Thomas Codde Esquire, Mayor.

"Simpleton," Seymour snarled and threw the missive on his desk. He turned his attention to the second roll which was of cheap parchment and broke the simple wax seal. Unrolling it he smoothed it out and read the 'Requests' penned by Robert Kett. One carefully shaped nail directed him along the lines whilst his features assumed a look of spite.

From his open window the sound of girlish laughter floated in from the garden. Two ladies of the court strolled in the late afternoon warmth, amusing themselves with newly learned tattle. One impatient stride took Seymour to the glass. He snatched at the clasp to close the window sharply and read out aloud, *"that all bond men may be made free, for God made all free with His precious blood shedding..."*

It was the last prayer on the page. By God, he thought, does this man ever think that his conduct is rebellion or his purpose disloyal, and he wished he and the rest of the rebels would creep back into the hedgerows from whence they came.

His frustration was tempered by a small sense of caution. His importance as Lord Protector meant he must tread with care. He'd seen for himself how quickly fortunes turned. The executioner at the Tower could attest to that. A pang of regret for his lost brother was fleeting, but the grim thought left him uneasy.

For a moment he wondered if he should consult others in the Privy Chamber about the mayor's plea then decided against it. He was after all the highest ranking of the king's advisors and would be best served by making his own decisions.

Rumbles in his belly reminded him he needed a morsel to eat and a glass of mead. He decided to ponder the problem of Norwich whilst he dined. A slice or two of roasted swan and some rare beef would assist his thinking, he decided.

Chapter 17

Seymour stifled a groan. He refused to think he'd overeaten and summoned his scribe. Armed with his vellums and quills the scribe waited at the door. Seymour flicked a lethargic finger indicating a chair next to his desk.

"Take down these words and make sure my missive is given to the royal herald for conveyance to Norfolk."

He slouched in his chair and grimaced as another passage of painful gas sought to escape his gut. His fingers placed in the shape of a steeple, he mentally composed.

"Address it to Mayor Codde and include the other dignitaries of the council of Norwich, whatever their names are."

The nib of the quill scratched its way laboriously across the sheet of vellum. Seymour writhed to get comfortable and sighed at the time it took.

"Are you ready?"

With a nod the scribe quickly dipped the quill in the ink and Seymour dictated.

'Sirs, on behalf of His Royal Majesty, I, the Duke of Somerset, Lord Protector of England hereby do instruct you to inform the leaders of the unlawful rebellion presently camped outside the city of Norwich that a meeting will be held in the autumn. I give them my assurance something will be done to address their grievances at that time. Meanwhile, His Majesty, being ever gracious, has promised a pardon if now they will disperse quietly, and return to their homes.'

"How does that sound? Read it back to me."

As the scribe took a breath, Seymour held up his hand.

"Don't bother. It's all too tedious. Let me have it."

His signature almost an illegible scrawl he pushed the vellum back across the desk.

"Make sure it has my seal affixed and see York Herald leaves with it immediately."

"It's very late, my lord," the scribe ventured to comment.

"So let him ride through the night," Seymour snapped. "Now leave me and find the apothecary. I need him here at once."

He lifted his buttocks and strained to pass wind. Nothing moved and he held his stomach, his fingers kneading to diminish the pain.

"Don't just stand there. Hurry, fool," he screamed at the unfortunate scribe.

Seymour, obsessed with his gripes didn't notice the apothecary arrive dressed in his nightclothes. He carried his medicine box and a jar of leeches.

"I'm told you are indisposed, my lord. What troubles you?"

With a loud groan, Seymour muttered an oath and threw himself forward in his chair.

"My lord, I cannot begin to understand what ails you unless you can tell me exactly what is wrong," the elderly physician said patiently.

Seymour spoke awkwardly, his voice muffled by his head resting on the desk.

"I've been poisoned, that's what's happened. Doubtless those who plague me to sort out the poor commons and their ills are responsible."

"Perhaps if I could examine you."

"Examine. What use is that? I may be dying and you waste time chattering like a woman. You can see my distress. You should know what to do."

With a violent squirm, Seymour expelled a long, explosive bout of wind. His sigh coincided with a look of peace on his face.

"I have treated myself," he said brightly. "Your services are not required. You may go now."

The apothecary bowed and with some relief absented himself from the room. Seymour stretched to be sure the pain was gone and wandered to his mirror. Fondling his thick beard he leant closer to the glass. He hoped he was mistaken, but his fingers found stripes of grey which mingled with the russet.

He scowled, lifted the glass from its hook and turned it round. In the morning, he decided, he would enquire into the credentials of the apothecary. He was far from impressed by the man's obvious lack of ability. In his court men didn't squander skills, they worked for them. By tonight's performance the medical man appeared little more than a charlatan in his opinion.

Sweat darkened the front of Thom's jerkin and more dripped steadily from his forehead. He sat away from the camp perched on a grassy mound on the heath facing the city. Behind him, arched high over the rocks and coarse-tufted grass, a row of wild buddleia nodded long purple-washed heads in the sunlight. With his legs out in front of him he wriggled to find comfort. Another stone poked its way through the seat of his breeches and he shifted yet again.

His view of the gates and the tower were clear but beyond the spire of the cathedral, the buildings were embraced by a fine haze. Parched by the scorching heat, the sky above appeared bleached. In better times he'd have given thanks for such perfect weather at the start of harvest time.

But it was all gone, a memory just like his beloved Martha and his home. Instead he'd just spent several hours in preparation for battle. Robert's instructions were clear and the marchers were organised into military units, squadrons of one hundred at a time.

It hadn't been easy. Even with the help of Will, John and some other hand- picked, trusted men, the first task had been to separate the young from the those they deemed to be too old or frail to fight. Angry at their exclusion, quarrels broke out and it had taken every ounce of Thom's diplomacy to ease the situation. Finally the task was completed and he'd slipped away to spend a few moments alone so he could regain his patience.

"Can I join you or do you seek solitude?"

Leaning on his longbow, John watched him from a few paces away. Thom patted the drought parched ground beside him.

"Find a seat if you can although this accursed ground offers little in the way of comfort," he said, flicking another pebble out of its cradle of sandy loam. "How does it go in the camp?"

"York Herald has just left and none too pleased by the look of him." John said, brushing dust off his stained breeches before sitting down.

"Robert was right to send him away, how many more royal pardons are we to expect? It achieves nothing, we have achieved nothing. All this must not be wasted," Thom said, gesturing to the mass of men they could see who wandered about the camp.

"So it comes to this. We make ready for war." John's heavy sigh echoed his own feelings and Thom laid a gentle hand on his friend's arm.

"We shall win or die for the cause. It comes to nothing more than that," he said quietly.

"The Lord Protector has promised to hold a meeting in the autumn. Do you think it's true?" John asked.

"Pah, you believe that, John, do you? Have you noticed there are changes? The mayor's smile becomes more wooden, his assurances given less willingly and in the camp the men no longer walk with their shoulders squared. They become dispirited. Hunger levels all men, my friend. And boredom makes for evil company. No, Robert is right. We must take action and soon." Thom got to his feet. "Come," he said, offering a hand to pull his companion up. "We must return and prepare ourselves."

Few ever saw Robert lose control. Even William was astonished at the anger which presently consumed him. Even as a child, he remembered his brother had the same sweetness of temper, the same sincerity and goodness of heart. Honourable intentions seemed to course stronger through his veins than his life juices. If anyone was guilty of being impatient and intolerant, William knew the blame lay with him.

"How dare they, they are nothing but dogs with forked tongues," Robert raged. "It is not my purpose to start a civil war or seek victory tainted by hatred and spite. Don't they understand that?"

He strode back and forth under the oak. His blue eyes smouldered like pits of acid and he was so incensed that from his mouth a froth of spittle gathered on his lips.

"Brother, be calm, all is not lost. I've sent out requisitions for cattle, grain and arms. There are letters on their way to our wealthier friends asking for guns and money too. Warrants have gone out to the local government, telling them we are the king's friends. It will all come, you see, we have many out there who support us and will help," William said with firm conviction.

Nervously Thom and John hovered by the table under the awning. Still Robert paced in a rage and appeared not to notice them.

"What's happened, Master," Thom asked William quietly.

"It seems York Herald took it upon himself to speak to the camp before he left. He announced the king's pardon for all of them if they went back to their homes. The men have lost faith so any offer sounded well to them."

"We sat atop the hill, we didn't know."

"I'm surprised you didn't hear the cheer which went up. When they heard his words, every man threw his cap in the air and shouted God save the king. " William said grimly. "It was a bad thing to do especially now when we are short of rations and the men are hungry."

"Kings and princes only pardon wicked persons, those who have sinned.

Chapter 18

We are not those people," Robert announced, thumping the table to underline his words. "We have only done what is the duty of a loyal subject."

"What happened then?" Thom asked, feeling sure there must be more for Robert to be so angered.

"Very dignified was my brother, he simply escorted York Herald off the camp. The herald then called on the sword-bearer of Norwich to arrest Robert. It was a foolish thing to do. There were only six of them and more than twenty thousand at Robert's back. When it was clear Robert was under threat our men would have none of it. York Herald needed protection on his way back to the city." William smiled but there was no trace of pleasure in his eyes.

Thom was the first to notice a small boy half hidden by the awning with an apprehensive look on his face. He beckoned to him.

"Yes, boy, what is it?"

The urchin sidled forward. "Please, sir, I bring a message from Harold of Walsham."

Robert's frown vanished when he caught sight of the boy's fair-hair. He reminded him of his own Dicken and he held out his hand.

"Come forward, lad, what have you to tell us," he said with a kindly smile.

"Master Harold says to tell you, he was coming out of the city with supplies and he saw the mayor giving orders for all the gates to be made fast. Seems the herald insisted, proper angry he was so Master said. That's what I was to tell you, Master Kett."

With a smile Robert felt in his pocket and found a silver coin. "You did well, here take this." The boy received the coin with a solemn look only daring to grin as he ran from the awning.

"Sweet child," Robert murmured as he watched the boy race across the camp, his prize held aloft.

Thom and John remained silent, William stood deep in thought.

When Robert clapped his hand it startled them all. His mood changed he appeared calm again.

"We must get busy," he said. "Our weapons must be sorted and inspected. I see most of the men carry longbows, several pitchforks too I daresay, but we'll need more. Can I leave it to you, Thom? Go round the camp and see exactly what arms we do have. William, did you say you had sent out requisitions? Good, then we must hope many will send the guns we urgently need."

"Master Kett, a word if I may?"

The man who spoke, intimidated just by his appearance. Tall and square shouldered, a sword hung from his belt and he held his longbow with broad-knuckled grip. His face was hidden by a tangle of long hair which fell to well below his collar. The only features visible were his mouth and a pair of dark, penetrating eyes. The timbre of his voice sounded familiar, yet they were all puzzled.

"Do I know you?" Robert said, trying to place the man.

"Philip, Master Kett. Philip de Montfort, although I hope few would recognise me now."

Robert's relief was plain to see and he immediately pulled up a chair.

"Sit, Philip. Where have you been?"

"Forgive me. I hid about the camp until I was sure I wouldn't be recognised. Lord Seymour has a long memory and I've no wish to be sent to the tower. There is something you should know. I overheard a conversation that I think is important."

"I understand, so what is it you have to tell me?"

"Somewhere in the crowd a man called Edgerley, servant to Master Woodhouse, carries arms and plans to release him when the moment is right."

"Does he indeed? William, make sure our prisoner is secure, we don't want him to taste freedom just yet. Thank you, Philip, stay close, we shall have need of you," Robert said. A fleeting smile of gratitude relieved his sombre face.

Later when he and his brother did a round of the camp, the sun was on fire in a bowl of leaden blue. It lingered just above the horizon whilst an apathetic wind barely stirred the grasses and leaves.

"It's still unseasonably warm," William commented.

"And yet there is a chill," Robert said quietly. "I feel our fortunes are about to change."

– 19 –

29th July 1549

News arrived a little before dawn. The look-outs stationed near the top of the Heights saw cannon appear on the castle turrets and watched as halberdiers dragged more onto the tranquil water meadows. They positioned them along the top of the bank which sloped to the river below.

Thom led Robert and William up to the look-out. There was no mistake, during the night the City Father's had called the city to arms. From where they stood they could see the soldiers in groups, armed with halberds and longbows and others who held flails and lances.

"How many do you think?" Robert asked.

"At a rough count, I'd say more than a hundred," Thom replied.

Dungeon Tower looked formidable. Since the monks abandoned it the garrison used it for quarters and widened the arrow slits to accommodate pistols. Three storey high, the brick and stone bastion had a flint core now fortified by thick wooden props.

Robert and William stared at it in silence for a long time. They scanned the walls of the Tower over and over until Robert suddenly shouted.

"I've got it. There, do you see. Down there, look by the gate at Bishop's Bridge they haven't bothered to guard it. That, gentlemen, is the weak spot and we shall turn it to our advantage. That's where our front line will be. Once we are past there we take the city through the Erpingham Gate."

He pointed to the cobble and brick arches of the bridge which spanned the green murk of the river.

"Well spotted, brother, they have archers in every position but not beside the bridge," William said. "Do you agree, Thom, such an oversight could favour us."

Thom nodded, but his face reflected concern. He couldn't help a feeling of dismay. The prospect of battle was not what he'd hoped for at the start of the march.

"It seems you've decided the time for talking has passed," was his sober response.

"No Thom, we should not be so hasty. It is the city who's chosen to meet us with force. Take John and go as my envoys. Find Mayor Codde and ask him to surrender. Tell him to come to the camp so we can discuss terms. I shall give him until dusk to lay down his weapons. Warn him too of our intent to raise fire on his precious city if he chooses to ignore us," Robert instructed.

141

Taken back by Robert's calm demeanour, Thom wondered if he truly wished to avoid confrontation or whether he saw, as perhaps the mayor did, the inevitability of war as the only outcome. Either way he was puzzled, but he went in search of John just the same.

Word quickly spread round the camp and with it an air of expectation. Fighting is a primeval instinct and easy to stir. The men of Norfolk were no exception. All over the camp excitement was palpable. Lust for action stirred each of them with little thought for the consequences. As he walked through the camp, Robert could see it in their eyes and smell it in their sweat and it was infectious.

"It's what we came for, eh, brother?" William grinned. "I see no other way, but to fight for our beliefs. For almost eighty years, government has prattled and laws been passed. Still our country cousins are made fools of. When harvests fail are these high and mighty men moved by those who become paupers. Wealth in their coffers is all they care about. I'm proud of you, Robert, and so are these men. Watch their faces as you move among them."

"Enough, it may not come to fighting. You are too bloodthirsty, brother. I never wanted to take them into danger," Robert said, his smile reluctant. "The mayor's not a fool, he'll come to us I'm sure."

Wherever they looked men worked on their weapons cleaning and polishing. Arrows were held up and carefully examined to check the iron heads for damage. Caught by the sun, silvery metal blinked as if they exchanged silent messages with one another across the men's heads.

Tines of the pitchforks were honed on flint until their tips were needle sharp. Robert nodded his approval when the men displayed them with pride. Those deemed too old or frail to fight sat apart with the few women making wicks. Sheep's wool gathered from the hedges, patiently rolled between calloused palms and then dipped in wax ready for the hand cannons.

It wasn't a task many of the men enjoyed for it signalled they were past their prime. Such menial work was a bitter reminder of advanced age. Robert thanked them just the same and the smiles on aged faces were tinged with regret. A dozen half naked boys sat in a circle working with foul mud. Squatting beside them, both brothers' watched them dunk a handful in bowls of water then skilfully mould them into balls. Set in the sun to dry each were impressive and effective missiles. William arched an eyebrow at Robert.

"Resourceful, wouldn't you say?"

He studied the position of the sun anxiously.

"We should go back to the oak. If Thom has managed to dissuade the mayor from calling out his soldiers, he may well have returned."

"How have we fared with the requisitions you sent out? Has anything arrived?"

William pulled a face. "I think you may be disappointed. Fresh meat has arrived. Several pigs, some bullocks and a cart load of grain and other victual too. Some have sent money. But few weapons, I'm afraid. We shall need more."

Robert's non-committal grunt signalled the end of the conversation as they arrived at the awning. The only occupiers were two hogs who rooted in the earth at the base of the tree. Robert's boot sent them on their way and with loud squeals of complaint they scuttled off through the camp. When Thom and John returned the droop of their shoulders and sombre faces conveyed little optimism, but Robert stayed hopeful.

"So how did you find Mayor Codde and York Herald? Are they amenable to calling an end to this bad feeling? Will they open the gates so we may go into the city without fear?" he asked.

"I'm sorry, Master Kett. York Herald wouldn't see us and the mayor says to tell you the rising is unlawful and we are not permitted to enter the city."

Despondency threw a pall over them all and Robert pondered.

"I thought we had an understanding. Codde makes no sense, if he won't open the gates to us"

"Then he has made a declaration of war," William murmured.

John spoke up. "Master Kett, we have no choice. We are an organised army now. Armies need feeding and if we don't have safe passage to and from the city we shall soon starve."

To collect his thoughts, Robert looked up at the sky as if the answer lay in the froth of white clouds overhead. The others waited unwilling to disturb his reflections. Around them the camp went on as usual unaware of their leader's fight with his conscience.

"Perhaps we should turn back," John ventured.

Tension crafted taut lines on Robert's face. He sat down at the table and looked carefully at his three anxious companions.

"Well, brother. What is it to be?" William said.

"William, you know me better than anyone. I stand on the side of the law and I never intended blood to be shed when I decided to lead these peasants. However, John's right about us starving, we have no choice. We shall move tonight. It's fortunate for us the moon is thin. But be sure to tell the men to darken their faces just the same."

His heavy sigh told of his reluctance. William rested a hand on his shoulder.

"You know it is a good decision. We should be equal in all things. That's why we are here. The Almighty will prevail and these good men will return home no longer denied their birthright."

Robert gave a thin smile. "Wise words, brother, I only hope you are right."

God fearing people seek out their Deity in difficult times. It was the same on Mousehold Heights in the remaining hours before the first shot was fired. Thom and John took themselves away from the camp and climbed high until they reached a tranquil place where few went except rabbits.

The two men sat in quiet contemplation. Thom ached for Martha, John for Sible and in mumbled prayers both asked they should live to see them again, that they could return as freemen and that there be an end to inequality.

Robert and William sought out the chapel. Sorrowful lines etched themselves on Robert's tired face as images of Alice and his children came to him. With his eyes closed they seemed so real he thought for a moment the Lord had sent them to him. If he leant forward he was sure he could touch them but when he did, his hand trailed through nothing. His lips moved in a soundless request for the Almighty's protection for all those he cared about.

On his knees beside him at the Altar rail, his brother brushed away a hasty tear. Without a family of his own he begged for God's compassion and His understanding of their struggle.

Prayers said the brother's rose and embraced. Neither of them had need of words.

As the final hours of daylight faded, the rebels marshalled on the grassy plateau which overlooked Bishop's Gate. Those he'd hand-picked because of their ability with shot Thom sent to stand beside the only hand cannon they had. No one was permitted to light a torch or to speak. Country dwellers were used to both seeing and moving about in the dark.

The scene below them was very different. It seemed every flare in the city was ignited to illuminate the unhurried activity of the soldiers. Armed with their longbows, Thom with the Kett brother's surveyed the scene.

"Do you see, there are less of them than this morning," he whispered.

Certainly the number of soldiers had been reduced. No more than six could be seen near the Tower and they counted perhaps fifty on the meadow itself.

"That means the City father's are either over confident or very stupid," William said.

Robert's lowered voice held a warning.

"Be very careful. Don't underestimate their fire power. Is everybody ready?"

Thom nodded. "John stands with the cannon. Elias, Will and Philip lead the bowmen. They wait for the signal."

"Then, my friends 'tis time and God help us all."

A single wave sent men to crouch beside the hand cannon. Robert counted under his breath. On reaching *five*, he shouted. "Fire the gun," and covered his ears.

The shot was random and without purpose. With not enough powder and poor skill most of it merely nicked the flints of Dungeon Tower and scuffed up lumps of dusty grass. Robert waved his hand and shouted to the gunners.

"Aim for the gates. It's the gates we need brought down."

Shot from the opposite bank appeared equally misdirected. It thudded into the ground well over the heads of the rebels and did no damage. Their own cannon suddenly fell silent, it wasn't clear why, but Thom was ready.

"Bowmen," he yelled.

They notched their arrows with confidence and no shortage of skill. Like a shoal of silver minnows, the shafts flew high in the air with a keening whine. It soon became obvious the smaller band of archers returning fire from the city side felt the pressure. Many of their arrows fell short and sank harmlessly into the Wensum.

William grinned. "This is more like it, eh, brother?"

Robert steadied his bow. "We're not inside the city walls yet. Just pray to God they don't open fire with those," he said and pointed up to the huge cannons darkly outlined above the castle walls.

Thom kept up constant fire. Sweat leaked from his pores. It ran down his cheeks and left white tracks through mud he'd smeared on his face. For him it was a desperate fight. Calling on all his strength he sent each arrow with intent to its target. Every time he heard the *thwack* of iron on flesh from somewhere behind him he flinched, wondering if John, Will, Philip and his other friends had been struck. They were good bowmen and he sought reassurance from that.

His nostrils flared under the assault of the acrid smell of gunpowder and sweat mingled with the sweetish odour of blood and he concentrated hard on his targets. A sudden tug on his buff jerkin had him spin round. A few inches away a small boy fixed dark eyes on him. He'd been running and his ribs jerked rapidly under his stretched skin.

"What is it, lad. You shouldn't be here. Have you been hurt?"

Solemn faced, the youngster didn't answer. Instead his small hand grasped the arrow hanging from his thigh and yanked it out. He handed it to Thom and reached for a second near his foot. Each left behind a spindly flow of blood which crept down his leg. Shocked by these actions, Thom searched for words. The boy spoke before him.

"Here you are, master, you may need them. Send them back to the city from me."

His thin face crinkled into a sweet smile and then he disappeared into the darkness. There was no time for Thom to react when there was a sudden cheer from around him. He blinked away a hazy mesh of sweat from his eyes and the saw the cause of the rebels delight. The halberdiers left on the meadow by the Tower were in retreat. They scrambled over one another and raced to climb the wall. Some with injuries simply sank into corners of shadow.

It was the moment they waited for. Robert's order was clear and decisive.

"Take to the river. Every man able, take to the river."

He watched Thom lead them in galloping strides down the paths and into the Wensum. They swam, paddled and clove their way across the turgid water ignoring floating waste and the bloated bodies of animals. They faced no opposition and when they emerged on the other side, a quick shake of their sodden garments and they set off in pursuit of any hapless soldier who made the mistake of stopping.

Then the men scrabbled like monkeys up the walls and vanished over the top. Slowly with a loud creak first one and then the second of the solid doors of The Erpingham Gate began to open. Robert and William watched as lit by upright unwavering torches, the first sight of the city emerged.

"Come brother, 'tis time we went, the city is ours," Robert said with a bold smile.

Thom saw them both approach and waved his bow high. His smile was less triumph and more pure emotion.

"Welcome to Norwich," he said, his voice thick as he felt the tears well. He wished Martha could see them. He fancied the pale gleam in Robert's eye was more a tear than a trick of the light. William too made a point of fiddling with his bow rather than lift his head. Then Robert cleared his throat and said.

"So what of the wounded, Thom, have we lost many men?"

"They are nearly all flesh wounds. I've left John and Will tending to them. Will stopped an arrow too. It caught his shoulder, tickled him like a louse, so he said. As for our dead, four I think."

A flicker of sorrow leached the pleasure out of Robert's face and he shook his head.

"Brave men, they died for the cause, there is nothing better than that," he said softly. "Now we must go forward. We..."

His words were cut short by an erratic burst of gunfire. It came from behind the city wall and sent them diving to the ground. The shot rattled past them and was embedded in the ground behind Robert.

"Is anybody hit?" he muttered.

"Not me," William said. "Thom?"

"No, but who the devil are they?"

All three raised their heads in a cautious move in time to see two men in uniform about to disappear inside the city. Muskets in hand they paused and looked back before they broke into a run. Then Robert recognised who'd confronted them. Charles Appleyard's two sons, his own nephews had turned their guns on him. As Thom helped him to his feet, he swore softly. "By the Devil's hand..."

"They were too quick for me. Did you recognise them, brother?" William asked, busy brushing off his clothes.

Robert shook his head. "No," he said.

The knowledge of who they were shook him. Whatever he felt he knew he must stay calm so he struggled to keep his nerves under control. It was hard to believe he dandled both boys on his knee when they were little more than babes. Were they bad shots or was their poor aim deliberate? Neither thought gave him any comfort. He agonised on the answers as his brother spoke again.

"Brother, you look pale. Are you sure you don't know who fired at us?"

"I said no." Robert replied, brusque with William.

Thom looked at him curiously. He could have sworn different.

They took their first step into the city they would now call their own. The symbolic moment didn't last for long. Civic notables in the shape of the City father's formed a line to prevent them from going any farther. They were all present, Codde, Aldrich, Chase, Charles Appleyard and a little behind, York Herald. Clearly agitated, Codde stepped forward and approached with hasty steps. It wasn't clear whether he rolled his eyes out of fear or outrage. He mopped his face with a silk square and came to a standstill in front of Robert.

"This is unpardonable, Master Kett. I thought well of you, but now, now I think you no better than those rebels of yours. How dare you."

"It comes down to this, Mayor, you closed the gates on us," Robert said pleasantly.

"You have frightened the city half to death and as for the damage..." Codde complained.

York Herald gave a snort of impatience.

"What the good mayor means is, *he* has been the one frightened. Rest assured, you have caused slight irritation to the city and brought little more than annoyance to us."

"Your ordnance did no more but inspire us," William replied. "So I think that makes us even, don't you?"

All three of them could see the herald struggle with his anger.

"That's as maybe," he snapped. "But I think you forget when His Majesty hears of this it will do little to advance your cause. I shall be leaving for London shortly, there will be no hand clapping when they hear of your reckless behaviour. This uprising gets out of hand, Master Kett."

Most of the rebels raced to the market place once they were inside the city. A few lingered. Drawn by the scene they were curious and gathered round in an impatient circle. Codde shuddered and stood closer to the other notables.

Unperturbed by anything the herald might say Robert remained genial. "On the contrary, we believe the king supports our struggle. It's thought he find enclosures an abomination of the countryside as we do," he said.

A poor attempt at a smile appeared as a crack in York Herald's pinched features.

"I shouldn't be too sure of that. I fear your informants are wrong. Besides, the Duke of Somerset, my lord Seymour will hear of this long before the king does. I can tell you, *he* most certainly doesn't find favour with such uprisings. However you have one last chance. You have my word, you will all be pardoned if you disperse now and return to your homes."

From the crowd a voice shouted out. "Don't trust him. The Devil's spawn would more willingly accept a pardon from you than we will. Go with a plague on thee, quick before we flay you alive..."

The murmurs of "Aye," grew louder and more insistent.

Robert felt his brother's hand on his arm. "A word, Robert," he said. He bent close and whispered. "Have you thought we should take them as prisoners? Our purpose is not suited if Lord Seymour hears of this too quickly. I think it might be wise."

The rebels continued to mutter among themselves whilst Codde and his companions stood stony-faced. Robert knew he had little time to hesitate. "Very well, gentlemen, you leave us with little option. Those who oppose us must be considered our enemy. Thom, William, would you take these men prisoners and escort them to Mount Surrey. Master Woodhouse will be glad of the company."

It wasn't enough for the rebels who were still restless. They grumbled amongst themselves and with brandished pitchforks and sticks formed an ever closer ring around the prisoners. Fear replaced scorn on the faces of the notables and Chase was quick to speak.

"For the love of God, take me prisoner, Kett, anything to get me away from the stink of these peasants. I demand you send them away, look at them."

A man of indeterminable age, shouted. "Who are you calling stinking? Prison is too good for you. The lot of you should hang. I say get rid of the gentry, hang them all."

"*Tear out your innards first, hanging's too quick. Hang. Hang.*" The chant grew louder, the voices more abusive.

"Take their weapons and tie them up. Get them out, Thom and hurry. If we lose control who knows where it will end," Robert said anxiously.

Having just arrived, Will and John saw for themselves how badly things were going. With his height and strength, Will shouldered the crowd aside dispersing them. In a moment the notables had been pulled to safety and bound by the wrists. Codde's voice rose above the hum.

"Not so tight," he whimpered. "My skin is delicate, it's much too tight, I tell you."

York Herald was the last to be taken. Most despised, the crowd pushed nearer to him. As they did so one rebel lost his balance and fell onto the Herald. In a flash the Herald's knife sliced the air, the point of the blade catching the man. He clutched his chest and reeled back. Through his clenched fingers bright bubbles of blood poured down the back of his hand.

Shock was replaced by uproar. The injured man was hurried away whilst scuffles turned one man on another. Robert and his companions were so tightly hemmed in they were powerless to stop the fighting. Managing at last to pull his sword from its sheath, Robert held it high.

"By all that's holy, will you stop," he yelled. "For pity's sake, calm yourselves before more get hurt."

When the fury abated some sort of order was restored and York Herald was missing. For several moments, argument raged. Robert held up his hand.

"Quiet. Enough, he's gone," he said. "He could hide anywhere in the city, we shall never find him. There are other things to attend to. Will and John, take the prisoners back to the Kings Camp."

Flushed with dismay, Codde paced up and down.

"Kett, you must summon my deputy. The city must have a mayor or there will be no order. Call Augustine Steward. Tell him he must come at once," he called out in his whiney voice.

"He's right, Robert," William said. "Where does he live? I'll fetch him."

" It's the first house in Tombland opposite the Erpingham Gate," Codde said, fingers easing the bindings round his wrists.

The rebels lost interest and soon began to drift away. William caught Thom's arm. "Choose some of them before they all go. Take them to the City Chamberlain's house. I'm told there are weapons and powder stored there. Sack the house and take all you can. Robert and I must attend to matters in the city."

It was the early hours of the morning before Thom finally rested. He'd overseen the haul of muskets and sacks of gunpowder, visited the injured and checked on the prisoners. Every muscle in his body ached and the mattress stuffed with grass was no match for Martha's sweet scented linen.

But he was euphoric from the success of the day and before he fell asleep, he planned the long walk home and imagined the feel of Martha's arms about him.

Hampton Court
31st July 1549

Gentle applause drifted round the tennis court. Bored, overheated and in bad humour, Seymour clapped the loudest and called out.

"An excellent match, sire, I do believe there is no one in the land who can serve as well you. If I may say there is no one in the land who plays tennis as superbly as Your Highness."

"Thank you, Uncle. You may say whatever you wish as long as it's a compliment," the king said. The loud female titters which followed the king's wit irritated Seymour. As did the game, the warmth and the flies, in fact, everything about the day annoyed him.

The king's carrot-coloured hair made an incongruous match with his scarlet cheeks. He mopped his forehead with the towel laid out for him, threw it to the ground and stretched out his hand for a fresh one.

"Do you think you should stop now, sire?" Seymour called hopefully. "This heat is taxing for you."

"Don't be such spoilsport, Uncle, I'm having fun."

"As you wish, sire," Seymour said testily. He slid down in his chair and closed his eyes. There were days when his patience was sorely tested and this was one of them. The king's childishness reminded him of his own noisy brood. Eight of them were enough but only this morning Anne announced she was with child again. Now all he had to look forward to were months of her everlasting complaints and ill health. It perplexed him why his wife should ail so during her pregnancies when it was a simple function which women were designed for.

Matters at court were tiresome too. The rising in Exeter had grown more vocal. As if he needed another rebellion, he thought crossly. He had Cranmer to thank for this. More discontented peasants with their popish beliefs. He'd a good mind to try them all for treason. Pleased with the idea, he mused on it for several minutes.

A polite cough disturbed him and for a moment he was tempted to ignore it. Grudgingly he opened his eyes. The court messenger looked nervous.

"Yes," Seymour barked.

"Forgive me, my lord. York Herald begs an audience with you."

"What, now? Can't you see I'm busy," Seymour said flicking a casual wave at the tennis court.

"York Herald says it's urgent."

"How urgent might that be?"

"I'm sorry, my lord, I didn't ask."

"Nor should you, it's none of your business," Seymour replied tartly.

He decided since the tennis showed no sign of coming to an end he would excuse himself. Besides his legs were stiff and horsehair poking through the seat of his chair kept attacking his buttocks.

"If it pleases you, Your Grace, I must leave the match."

"Well, it doesn't please me, Uncle," the king said, thumping his racquet up and down on the net. "What matter is so important, you have to disturb me?"

"An urgent matter of State, sire," Seymour said in the most apologetic tone he could manage.

The king's scowl was unattractive. "Very well."

York Herald was astonished at how sumptuous Seymour's apartment was. Lord Protector he might be, he certainly made himself very comfortable. Having examined all the paintings, poked the swans down cushions and run his fingers through the fur rug, he limped back to his chair to examine his bruises.

He moved his hose aside and inspected his shins. His usual pallid flesh gave way to multi-shaded bruising down the length of the bones. In his haste to escape from Norwich, his sense of direction became jumbled. Each time he thought he was headed the right way he encountered more rebels roaming the streets. His blunders resulted in several falls. One slip was on the cobbles in the market place fouled with rotting vegetables He recalled the moment with a wince.

The abrasion on his cheek bone pained him and he touched it with care. It felt wet and sticky. Seeing a looking glass on the wall, he readjusted his clothing, and was about to stand up to inspect the injury when the door opened.

"I hope for your sake this is important," Seymour said, taking the seat at his desk. "What's that on your face?"

"My lord, a slight fall, a mere trifle, I can assure you," the herald hastened to explain.

Conscious of his appearance, he attempted to shield his face with his hand. Seymour stared at him from under lowered lids. He always thought York Herald a strange man. His legs were too spindly to wear hose and his eyebrows oddly too thick for the proper alignment on his face.

"Well, get on with it. I was told there was urgency so what have you to tell me?"

York Herald swallowed so hard it constricted his throat. The strangulated cough lasted several minutes. Seymour viewed the outburst with undisguised disgust. He dabbed his face with a wisp of something lacy and his eyes glittered like winter hoar on a twig. Exasperated he debated whether to summon a courtier to have the herald removed.

"My humble apologies, my lord," York Herald finally rasped, his face aglow.

"Get on with it." Seymour ordered.

"I've ridden from Norwich with disappointing news. The peasants are rising and they have gained control. The government forces were routed and the rebels loot the city."

"Is there no end to these wretches and their unpalatable demands? What were the City Father's doing, asleep were they?"

"On the contrary, my lord, it seemed they were well prepared, but the rebels are wily."

Seymour paced the floor in front of the window, stopping every so often to crane his neck. He could just see the tennis court.

"Yes, yes, so what are the mayor and the civic notables doing about it? Did they offer a pardon?"

He saw the sudden flush appear on the herald's face, and guessed immediately it wouldn't be encouraging news.

"The pardon was rejected and the mayor and civic notables taken prisoner, my lord. I myself just escaped with my life." the herald mumbled.

"Speak up, man. I didn't hear you properly."

"They are prisoners of the rebels," York said a little more loudly.

Seymour nodded. "I thought that's what you said. God's mercy, are all these people fools that they cannot hold a city from a motley band of peasants. Since clearly I can't rely on such idiots I shall have to call on those more reliable. We need to crush these rebels once and for all." His fingers strayed to his beard. "But who, who could I get to raise an army, that's the question?"

He flapped his hand to dismiss York Herald and peered across at the tennis court. To his relief he saw it was deserted. He sat down to think and tapped the desk impatiently. Who didn't he like very much? Who owed him a favour? Who could be spared and more importantly who could he trust?

Twiddling his quill, Seymour debated his options. According to his advisors the unrest at Exeter was spreading. It threatened to become a major rebellion and on their advice he'd already committed a sizeable number of men. He had so few troops left, let alone an experienced general. A slow smile spread on his face and disturbed his usual frown. He'd got it.

William Parr, The Marquis of Northampton, Earl of Essex, his own brother-in-law. From all accounts, Lord Northampton was neither a good soldier nor a statesman. However he did squeeze the coffers for his extravagant needs at every opportunity. A placement was therefore long overdue, Seymour concluded.

Reminded by his stomach dinner must soon be served, he walked down the corridor. Strips of light from the arrow slits cast oblong gold bars on the wood block flooring. In better humour he amused himself by taking ridiculously small steps to avoid them.

"Perfect, perfect."

He sniffed the air as he passed the kitchens. Such a luxury of aromas sent him at a fast walk toward the Great Hall. Almost at the door he saw the back of his brother-in-law as he stepped into the room.

At the table in a chair higher than the rest of the company the King picked through the meat with the point of his knife. Further down, Seymour struggled to release a quail bone wedged between his teeth. Helped by a long finger nail it sprang out and he tossed it across the white linen cloth. It came to rest close to a horn on the stag's head perched atop a large haunch of venison.

Opposite, Northampton wrinkled his nose in disgust. He preferred to use a finely sharpened sliver of ivory as a toothpick. He like the others feasted well. Sliced meat on the silver dishes was popular and vanished quickly as did the assorted meat pies. All that remained of a huge sturgeon was the backbone and rib cage. Its eyes, pale rimmed and vacant fixed their gaze on the ornate centre piece, a vast decoration of leaves, flowers, swansdown and the tail feathers of a peacock.

Intent in deciding whether he wanted a cut from the ham or the venison, Seymour took no notice of his nephew's petulant voice.

"Uncle, how many times must I ask you send to the kitchen for more black pudding, it seems my favourite uncle has a lust for it."

"Indeed, sire, it is most delicious," Northampton said.

Seymour glanced across the table, his eyes narrowed at the recipient of the king's affection. Favourite uncle indeed, wait until he told him about his new command. Seymour knew he'd enjoy the moment when the pale, insipid face opposite him lost its supercilious smile.

"Uncle, tell the musician not to play so loudly, I can't hear what people are saying," the king ordered.

With a disgruntled frown Seymour pointed to his ear. The man toned down his lute with suitable grace whilst Seymour decided he didn't want either meat and settled for a sausage instead.

"So, have you told Uncle William how I excelled at tennis today?" the king piped.

"Not yet, sire, but you certainly played a most superior game," Seymour said and stabbed a second sausage from the dish.

"Come and sit next to me, Uncle William and I shall tell you all about the match."

"Nothing would give me more pleasure, Your Highness."

Northampton gave a deep bow which sent the emu plume in his cap straight into a dish of sauce. Seymour smirked and decided not to mention the collection of capers gathered on the feather.

The diners included a knight, Lord Radcliffe and his lady together with two minor noblemen which made the gathering unusually small. It suited Seymour well. Not wishing to interrupt the conversation he examined an apricot whilst he waited. Finally the talk died away and he said.

"So my Lord Northampton, are you busy?"

"With this and that, why do you ask?" he replied, as he selected a bloom-blushed plum from the silver platter of fruit.

"I need you to raise an army," Seymour said calmly. He watched for his brother-in-law's reaction. He wasn't disappointed. Northampton bit down hard on the fruit and juice spurted and trickled an uneven track through the short bristles on his chin.

"Come, Seymour, you jest. I haven't ridden to war in a long while."

"No, so it seems," Seymour replied dryly. "You are one of the few experienced generals left and the army is stretched. First the rebellion in Exeter and now the rising in Norfolk, the peasants try everyone's patience. You know how important Norwich is to the realm. Or you would if you took more interest."

"That, sir, is an uncommonly rude remark. I take offence to it," Northampton said, spitting the plum stone across the table.

"Make what you will of it," Seymour shrugged. "You are needed to end the siege of Norwich and that, sir is that."

Enjoying the altercation, the king grinned. It was a sign to the other diners that they too were permitted to laugh. Plucking the strings with nervous fingers the musician hastily changed the tune to a subdued waltz. Stone faced, Seymour stared at the prim features of his brother-in-law. The king applauded.

"Well done, Uncle, now it's your turn," he said turning to Northampton.

A creep of red appeared above his uncle's ruff and quickly spread to his cheeks. His anger reflected in the brittle glint of his hazel eyes as he ignored Seymour and appealed to the king.

"Sire, I would urge you to..."

The king laughed and jumped off his chair. He snatched an apple from the table and ran to the door held open for him by a footman.

"I have no time to consider urges," he called over his shoulder. "I have more important things to do."

As one the diners rose. Heads inclined to their chests they waited to be sure the king had left the room before they sat again. Seymour refilled his glass with wine. Decanter in hand, he said pleasantly.

"So, my Lord, you're clear are you? Raise fifteen hundred men and march on Norwich as soon as you're ready. I believe Edmund, Lord Sheffield is doing little ask him to ride with you. Dithering may cost you dear. I shouldn't like you to lose your recent title, Earl of Essex, isn't it? There's many a man would gladly accept such a prestigious position."

As he scrambled to his feet, Northampton's gilt dining chair tipped dangerously back, resting on two legs. His knuckles strained white under the skin of his balled fists and he looked outraged.

"My lord may well think he has found satisfaction ordering me thus. With a word in the right quarters, he may find his role as Lord Protector is also precarious. He would do well to remember, just who is the king's favourite uncle," he said tightly.

Without a backward glance he strode from the room. The door banged the loudly behind him.

One week later Northampton left Hampton Court with well over a thousand men under his command armed with longbows, pikes, axes, maces and crossbows. Now he was actually mounted on his thoroughbred grey stallion with his breastplates polished, white ostrich plumes pristine and about his person, a knife and sword, he enjoyed a feeling of considerable importance.

Not that he'd forgiven Seymour or that it had been easy to raise an army. The majority of men he'd recruited were mercenaries from Italia. When he smelt the garlic drizzling out of their pores and the pomade they used on their hair he wanted to vomit.

Less unpleasant were the country squires he'd turned to in desperation. With their retainers, he'd just managed to reach a little short of the numbers suggested by Seymour. Riding at his side, Edmund Sheffield hummed softly to himself. Northampton sighed. He hoped it wasn't going to persist all the way to Norfolk.

He glanced over his shoulder to look beyond his knights and noblemen on horseback to the rows of white-clad men behind. He raised his sword, waved it with a flourish and called out.

"For God and the King we ride onward to Norwich, to crush the rebels and let no man fail."

His horse danced a quartet of steps as it felt the spurs before settling into a steady canter as the army turned north.

High on a turreted balcony above the west wing, Seymour watched them leave. From where he stood the column looked impressive. Above him the king's standard cracked like a whip as a firm breeze swept it upright towards the fast moving clouds. A frisson of excitement sent a shiver down his spine. It would be a pleasure, he thought, to inform the king at dinner that the insurgents in the flat, uninteresting and hellishly cold county of Norfolk would soon be dealt with.

With their excitable nature and little regard for authority the soldiers from Italia were difficult to control. Days on the road and Northampton wished dearly he hadn't been forced to choose them.

"I just hope they fight as determinedly as their tongues move," he said irritably to Edmund. "Such is their jabber, my head is sore." He pressed a gloved hand to his temple and sighed heavily.

"Take heart, my Lord, in front of us is Norwich. Can you see the spire of the cathedral and there's the castle," Edmund replied.

Seen by the look-outs posted on the battlements the city gates stood open by the time the last of the soldiers reached the walls. When he saw Northampton raise his hand, the King's Herald, Gilbert Dethick hurried to his side. Northampton looked down from his horse ready with his instructions.

"Make haste to the mayor's house. Tell him to be ready for our arrival and that I demand a comfortable place to rest."

"Aye, my Lord," Dethick jogged off across the track.

Northampton stood up in his stirrups and stretched his calves. As he did so he looked through the gates into the city.

"The last time I had the misfortune to visit Norwich, I thought it a wretched place," he said, his tone disdainful. "I have the feeling I'm not going to alter my opinion. Have you been here before, Edmund?"

The other shook his head. "No, I'm not familiar with the city."

"I would say how wise of you," retorted Northampton.

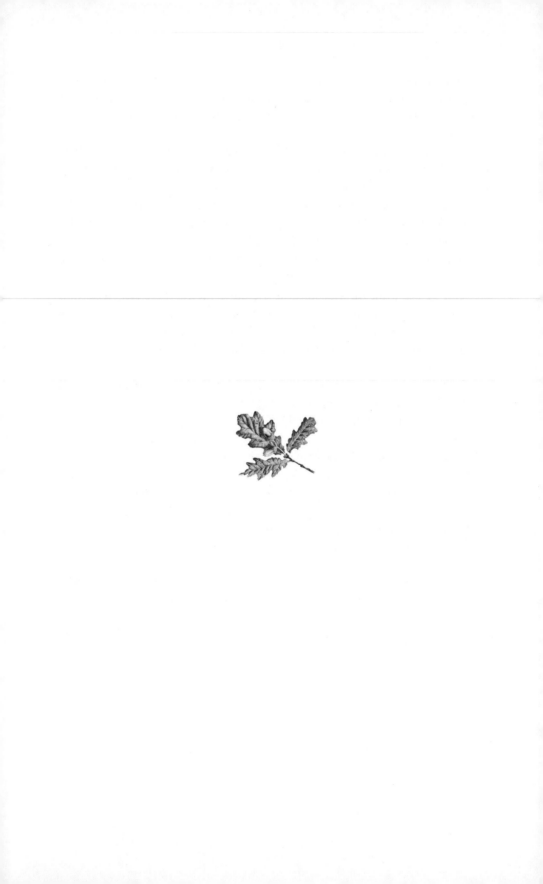

– 21 –

With the requisition for victual's signed by Augustine Steward, Thom strolled towards the Market- Place. The air was pleasant and he was in no hurry. He crossed the Haymarket where the stalls were already doing a good trade. Drawn to the baskets of herring and oysters, he felt in his pockets. They yielded nothing so he wandered on. When he reached the Market Cross it took him a moment to realise both doors of St Stephen's Gate were propped wide open.

He thought it odd. Augustine would surely have mentioned it yet he hadn't. Robert's request they remain open after the rebels took the city was quickly overruled by the deputy. They contented themselves by using the foot gates with little inconvenience.

With the sheds of corn and tanners stalls to conceal him, he hovered behind one of the buttresses and looked carefully at the men gathered under the shadow of the gate. A general astride his horse spoke with armoured knights and behind them a contingent of halberdiers stood at ease. There seemed no urgency about their manner and Thom was puzzled by their appearance.

To get back to the Heights meant using one of the foot gates and he would easily be seen. For the time being he would be forced to linger in the market. In the heat he disliked the tainted air where the smell of rot mingled with spice and herbs, but it afforded him a good hiding place.

"Tripe?" a woman said, as he stood close to her stall.

He waved her away and looked back. The dumpy figure of the deputy mayor had joined those at the gate. He judged by Augustine's rapid breaths and crimson face, he must have run from Tombland. Dethick also stood with the group. Anxious to report to the camp, Thom debated his route. The position of the sun told him it was past noon. Robert would wonder what kept him.

When he began to think he would have to risk detection and use the foot gate there was movement. Augustine's arm waved. It was a beckoning gesture of welcome and then the entire body of men started to move through the gates into the city. Taking advantage of the crush of men who crowded the pathways, Thom slipped through the gate and headed for the Heights.

The camp lazed in the afternoon sun. He found Robert and William under the oak tree. It was quiet. Only the tap-tapping of a branch on the overhead supports disturbed the peace.

"Thom, at last, what kept you? We were about to send out John and Will to track you down. Did the deputy mayor refuse to agree to more ale?" William said, filling a third cup with cider.

"No, Master Kett," Thom replied quickly. "I have news more serious than that."

"Sit and catch your breath. You look as if you have run from the city," Robert said, pulling a chair forward.

"I pretty nigh did, but no, I bring news you will want to hear. There's an army of men arrived in the city. Not all Englishmen. Most are swarthy foreigners by the look of them."

"Who leads them?" Robert asked, alert in his chair.

Thom shook his head. "A general but who I don't know. He comes with knights and noblemen in attendance and I saw a King's Herald too."

"I shall go and look for myself. Do they make camp outside the main gate?" William said. Serious faced as he rose from his seat.

"Worse than that, Augustine Steward welcomed them into the city."

"A pox on the man, I knew we shouldn't trust him," Robert said, on his feet too. "We must have a plan. Let me think. William, you must stay here and circulate the camp. We mustn't be caught off guard, tell the men to be ready. Thom, walk with me to the look-out whilst I gather my thoughts."

For awhile they climbed in silence. Thom paused to wipe the sweat from his face with his sleeve and heard Robert puff a little with exertion. A sideways glance showed Thom his companion's set jaw and the grim line of his mouth. They were the mark of a man with steely determination, but at that moment he looked every year of his age.

The fine song of a skylark above them seemed at odds with the distress he could feel emanating from the older man. The little bird dipped and rose in the speedwell blue before spiralling down to settle on gorse.

When they reached the vantage point, it all seemed peaceful enough. The Gothic spire of the cathedral dominated and beyond it a lazy sampler of patchwork green sprawled to the horizon. Below them cows and sheep grazed on the nearside water meadows. Separating the banks and overhung by clumps of straggled reed and bulrush, the unhurried river toiled its way towards the sea.

On the far side they could see six halberdiers with pikestaffs who guarded The Erpingham Gate. Robert looked up and pointed out the cannons above the vaulted walls. Thom saw they'd been turned to face the Heights as they had been in the first skirmish.

"I'd like to know what they're planning and who the general is. We must send someone to get back into the city," Robert said quietly.

"I'll go."

Chapter 21

"No, Thom, not you. You might have been noticed already. Will's too obvious, it's John who must go. But I have something I need you to do. If an attack comes it takes too long to get down from here. We should be prepared. Gather the men and lead them down to the meadow. They are to wait opposite Bishop's Gate for that's the way the army will come, I'm sure of it. Only the elderly and those too weak to fight must remain here. Go now and get them into their squadrons. When it is done, find Walter of Bungay and one to help him. I want them to guard the prisoners."

"Aye, Master Kett."

Thom picked up his bow and set off. Half way along the path back to camp he realised he was alone. When he looked back he saw Robert on his knees, hunched over with his hands clasped in prayer.

For a moment he wondered if he should wait, but decided it would look as if he intruded and besides there were things to be done. Time enough for him to pray and pray he would if they were to fight again.

Thom left the men on the riverside. They primed their weapons and flexed their bows. Confident the squadron leaders would ensure they were ready for what might come, he left them. Evening shadows bathed the Heights as he made his way back to the Reformation Oak. With most of the rebels camped below, the Kings Camp felt strangely empty. Worn and ripped laundry hung over gorse bushes or from low branches flapping dry in the breeze.

In the time they had been at the camp it had become an entity, a place of the living. Now it seemed to have lost its presence save for the old, the ailing and the women who gathered around the fire with sombre faces.

On reaching the oak he saw William and John who having checked their arrow flights were busy with gunpowder. As William measured each quantity out, John was careful to waste none as he tipped it into the bags. Robert was there too. When he saw Thom, he laid his sword to one side, tightened the belt about his waist and then buckled the sword in place.

"Are the men ready?" he asked.

Thom nodded. "I left them cleaning their weapons. So John, did you manage to get into the city without being seen?"

"Like I told Master Kett, it wasn't easy. But I managed to find an old friend of mine. It seems the General goes by the name of my Lord Northampton, Earl of Essex. I was told he dines with Steward tonight in Tombland. The soldiers camp in the market place. My friend also overheard the General instruct Steward to keep all the city gates shut. They are not to be opened for anyone. And I noticed as I came back there are only three on guard at Bishop's Gate."

"It's obvious we're not welcome in the city," William said drily.

"We'll see about that," Robert muttered as he put on his buff-jerkin. "Come 'tis time."

If there was ever a moment when Thom felt the need for God's Gospel it was then. Longbow in his hand, he said. "I'll catch you up."

Under a lattice of low branches of a nearby silver birch he fell to his knees.

− 22 −

The voice came from the opposite bank somewhere along Bishop's Gate.

"*Madre di Dio, dove siamo?* Mother of God, where are we?"

Carried across the water to the rebels the tone was clear despite the foreign language. The rebels quietened, listened and waited. Some reached for their weapons. When there was no challenge nor orders, they relaxed.

"*In nome di Dio, come faccio a saperlo?* In God's name, how do I know?"

The direction of the voices left Robert and his companions in no doubt that some of the Italia troops must have strayed into Bishop's Gate. Keeping his voice low, Thom said.

"Let's hope they've left their camp and are lost."

"Well, it's certainly not a war party, not by the sound of things. They're making too much noise. We should see them in a minute if they keep on walking this way," William muttered.

As he spoke, four men in white uniforms appeared. Across the chest of their tunic was emblazoned a large red cross. Well built although short in stature they walked unsteadily and the flames from the torches on the walls showed them clearly. Their talk was loud accompanied by laughter as a beer jug passed between them.

"Do they carry arms?" John whispered.

"None that I can see," Thom replied.

Met by the halberdiers the merriment increased. There seemed to be no language barrier when it came to alcohol. One of the guards disappeared into Dungeon Tower and re-emerged with more jugs. Before long they sat down and the roistering continued. The watchers in the shadows looked on. Robert signalled to Thom to come closer.

"A prisoner could be useful. Send some good men over there. Take them by surprise and remember no noise," he said.

Even those close to the river might be hard pressed to see four heads. The quiet ripple of the water would hide any slight noise as they passed. Certainly the carousing soldiers noticed nothing. They rolled drunkenly on the grass incapable of anything but outbursts of uncontrollable laughter.

When the four rebels appeared from the darkness, they were caught off guard. In the melee some of the mercenaries turned on the Norwich halberdiers. For several minutes, it wasn't clear who fought who.

Although outnumbered the rebels were strong, sober and ruthless. Cloaked by the shadows with one Italia taken, they disappeared back into the gloom whilst behind them two Italia lay on the ground. The remainder staggered in a disorderly pack down Bishop's Gate toward the city. Pleased with the result, Robert said. "You pick your men well, Thom. Get the prisoner back to the camp. Make sure he joins the others at Mount Surrey. And be sure to search him."

Still confused by drink the prisoner was pulled along the track. Curses in his mother tongue intruded on the usual quiet of the Heights. With most of the camp deserted the harsh clatter of his voice sent rabbits and deer racing for the protection of dense thicket.

To make sure the mercenary reached the house safely, Thom followed behind the group. In his pocket he carried the knife he'd found tucked down the fellow's breeches. He recognised an artisan's skill when he saw it. Narrow and sharply tapered, the blade was fine quality silver, but it was the beauty of the haft which stirred him. So intricate was the carved ivory that a man's thumb would be too clumsy to trace it. Embedded between the ivory were emerald and ruby stones. Each small on its own, but together an opulent swathe of brilliance which transfixed him every time he looked. Later when he showed it to the Kett brothers', it was William who thought he recognised its origins. Ivory from the east and the jewels from a place he called Mesopotamia, he told Thom. They let him keep it and it would be a present for Martha when he finally got home again.

Outside Mount Surrey the Italia soldier swore loudly again and attracted the attention of a small group of rebels. One was Walter of Bungay, a tall broad-shouldered man with large hands and rough-hewn features. Known for his unpredictable temper and poor manners, his skill with a longbow made him a fearsome opponent. Thom guessed it was the reason Robert left him to guard the prisoners. No one would escape an arrow from Walter's bow.

"What you got there?" Walter growled, needing to stoop to look at the short man. "He makes enough noise and he smells bad. Don't tell me we have to look after him as well. It's getting crowded in there," he said, with a backward jerk of his head.

"It's Master Kett's orders," Thom said curtly.

His dislike of Walter was no secret. There was something about the man which troubled him, but Thom knew this was no time for such emotion. Walter took rough hold of the Italian's jerkin and dragged him nearer for a close inspection. Too drunk to be troubled the man giggled and mouthed an obscenity. Thom saw an ugly expression on Walter's face and hastily stepped between them.

"He's a prisoner, treat him with respect."

"You toy with me, Barwick, respect. Do you mean to tell me we face an army of foreigners? If this toad is an example all we need do is blow on the lot of 'em and watch them fall over," Walter said, his lip curled in disgust.

The few rebels left in the camp who'd gathered to watch met Walter's remark with a roar of laughter and murmurs of agreement. Uneasy as he was, Thom knew he should go back to the meadow.

"I've no time to tarry here," he said. "Just do as you've been asked. Make sure he's fed and given a drink like the rest of them. If he's sober enough, Master Kett will want to speak to him when he returns."

Walter raised his hand to his head as if it were a salute, but his smirk and sloppy attitude told differently.

With Thom gone, Walter strutted back and forth, his face close to the prisoner's. Dragged under the light the man's face wore a bemused look. The ring of rebels pressed closer. Not included in the fighting force through age or infirmity they hungered for excitement. A waft of malice spiked the air and mingled with the odour of unwashed bodies and pent up anger. Walter bent down and stared at the dark features of the prisoner.

"So not so brave now, eh, soldier, what have you to say for yourself?" He punctured his words with a hard and viscous stab of his finger to the man's chest.

"*Non capisco.* I don't understand."

"Don't you back away from me, you foxy-faced foreign devil, you."

Through the miasma of alcohol the young face struggled to comprehend. Now feeling fear any maturity fell away and left nothing more than the face of a youth. Held up close, Walter's torch caught his tears which glistened at the hostility aimed at him.

"He snivels like a maiden," somebody sneered.

"Is that what you are, eh, a pretty little virgin? Perhaps under this sweet white gown..." Walter said, his hand in a claw to tug at the man's uniform.

"*Non capisco, non capisco...*"

The material slithered through Walter's fingers and dropped back into place. As it did so the prisoner looked relieved.

"Pah, you're not worth the effort," Walter said, as he gave the man a hard push which nearly took him off his feet. "You foreigners make me puke."

With a supreme effort, the prisoner spat. A glob of yellow phlegm flew at Walter's face and slid down his cheeks. For a moment there was silence. Then someone in the group retched, a noise which seemed to galvanise Walter. Fierce colour raged under the pallor of his skin and he trembled with fury. His close set eyes fired like tinder suddenly ablaze.

"Take the dog away before I throttle him," he croaked.

His hand scrabbled at his face to wipe it clean then with a change of thought he leant forward and used the man's tunic like a cleaning swab. Several of the rebels stepped forward and eager hands grasped the prisoner's arms.

"Where shall we take him? Is he to go in the house with the others?" one of them asked.

All eyes focussed on Walter. The crimson colour was gone replaced by pale skin stretched taut over his high cheek bones. As he shook his head his unruly barley coloured hair swirled on his shoulders.

"He doesn't deserve comfort," he said, each word crisp like hoar frost underfoot. "It's too good for a rabid cur. He needs to be put out of his misery."

As he sensed the menace in Walter's words a dark stain crept up from between the mercenary's legs and spread across his breeches.

"Look the dog pisses himself," someone sniggered.

Dark eyes filled with terror the man watched as Walter walked to the rail by the door and took the length of coiled rope.

"*Clemenza, ti prego, clemenza.* Mercy, I beg you, mercy." Down on his knees, the man's whimpers were ignored.

"This will do," Walter called, from beside a thick-set elm tree. "Bring him over here."

A man they called Micah, older and more cautious than some stepped forward to speak. "What are you going to do with him?"

"It's obvious, isn't it?" another whispered.

Walter didn't answer, but threw the rope over a stout branch. Micah slunk back into the group too scared to speak again. Torches by the house threw a poor light, but it was enough to illuminate the thick hemp plait Walter put round the prisoner's neck.

"One of you, fetch me the stool," he said, nodding to a three-legged affair on the porch.

"It'll need to be taller," a rebel said.

"He's only a short-legged foreign little dwarf. He won't need much."

Nobody chose to disobey Walter or his instructions. Dragged the short distance to the tree the man gibbered with hysteria. His arms pinioned he had no choice, but to climb on the stool.

"*Madre di Dio. Pieta.Pi...*"

Walter raised his boot. A dull thud sent the stool into the air. As it landed its stumpy legs and frame scattered in disarray and at the same time the branch groaned under the sudden unexpected weight hung from it.

With the rhythmic swing of the body the noise changed to a soft creak. Like voracious rats the rebels scuttled up to it. Hands grasped the supple leather boots and pulled them free. More tore at the clothing and raced away to try on their spoils.

A few turned their backs on the pillage, Micah was one. No one saw him slip into the shadows or watched him disappear on the path down to the meadow. His joints worn up by years of toil gave him an odd gait. Even so he managed well.

By the time he'd left to find Thom and the Kett brothers the corpse was stripped naked.

Micah was pushed from one to another. His white hair flopped over his face and his rheumy eyes filled with tears.

"Can you tell me where I might find..."

"You don't belong here, old man, go back to the Heights before you get hurt," one rebel told him.

Another laughed as in his haste, Micah slipped and almost fell.

"Look at you, lost your way, have you? That's what happens, no memory, see." The speaker screwed his finger at his temple and those close by guffawed loudly.

Humiliated and distressed Micah said. "I need to see someone, it's important. I have something to tell them. Please won't somebody help me?"

Reminded of his grandfather, a young lad armed with a cross-bow took pity.

"It's Master Kett you want, old man. It's him you have to tell."

Micah's thin, blue-veined hand grasped the lad's arm.

"Thank you, thank you. But where do I find him?"

"Follow me, I'll take you to him."

"May the blessed saints keep you safe, boy. You showed compassion and I'm grateful for that," the old fellow said.

Desperate to keep up, he tottered feebly on the uneven ground. Tussocks of grass conspired to snatch his feet from him, but he righted himself and struggled on. Close to the river's edge, the lad stopped and pointed.

"See that group there. That's Master Kett and his henchmen, they're all good men. They'll listen to you. You're brave, old man, I'll give you that," the boy said.

"Once," Micah said sadly, "But not anymore."

His chest felt tight and he clutched his hand to it as he fought to catch his breath. Thoughts of his wife flitted through his mind. He hadn't needed her to remind him he was too old to join the march, he knew it well enough. It was for their son and his children, he'd told her. Somebody had to take a stand against the land-robbers and his loss was unimportant at his age, he said.

He thought she understood, but on the last morning she'd turned her head away when he went to kiss her cheek. If he closed his eyes he could still see her soft skin criss-crossed by the web of age.

"I said, can I help you," Robert repeated.

Micah started. "Forgive me, my memories. Are you Master Kett?"

"The same," Robert said. "Shouldn't you be up there on the Heights? It's not safe here only the river stands between us and our enemies. Go back," he said as he counted his arrows.

"It's about what happened up there. I thought you should know." Micah's voice cracked in his throat and he fought to continue.

Thom laid an arm round the bowed shoulders and felt the sharp angle of his bones.

"What do they call you?"

Grateful for the support the other took a deep breath. "Micah, they call me Micah."

"And where do you come from?"

"I live the far side of Earsham, sir."

Thom laughed gently. "No sir for me, Micah, just Thom. So what is it you have to tell us?"

"The poor creature was terrified, but they hanged him just the same. You could smell his fear. It doesn't seem right, not a prisoner."

William and John stood silent and Robert stopped working on his arrow heads.

"Hanged, who's been hanged?" he said sharply, his features taut. "Thom, which prisoner is he talking about? Was it all quiet when you took the foreign soldier up there?"

Thom nodded. "Who, Micah, who did they hang?"

"Why, that foreign fellow. Italia, they said. He tried to make himself understood, begged for mercy. That he did. Even I knew what he was trying to say."

Robert's hand was rough when he grasped Micah's arm. The old man cringed.

"I'm sorry, Master. I thought you should know that's all."

"You did well, Micah," Thom said, to reassure.

Robert drew a hand across his brow. "Yes, I apologise, who gave authority for this? Who was it ordered it?"

"The man they call Walter from Bungay. It was him who put the rope round his neck." Micah said.

"When word gets out it'll be bad for us," William said.

"I know, I know, I promised no violence," Robert muttered.

Thom glanced at the opposite bank. There was still no movement, just the dark outlines of the dead soldiers. Besides them their abandoned weapons gave off a dull glint each time the torch light wavered over them.

"That decides it then. We have no time to waste. John, choose your men. I want you to get back into the city. Move with care and find any of our sympathisers to join you. We need people inside as many as we can who are able to fight. You, William, rouse the squadrons and make ready with the muskets. Thom, walk Micah to the Heights and then return here. Say nothing, is that understood? There's nothing can be done for the Italian. May the Lord have mercy on his soul. I'll deal with Walter of Bungay in good time. For now there is much to do. We will attack the city a little before dawn. Go now." He flicked his fingers at them. "And make haste."

Apprehended on their way back to the market place, the three Norwich halberdiers and the drunken Italians were marched to Tombland. They looked in a sorry state when Northampton and Augustine Steward were summoned to reprimand them. A robust dinner of roast mutton and a jug of Steward's finest wine meant both men were replete and being short of sleep somewhat querulous as well.

"Well, Master Deputy Mayor, what are we to make of this?" Northampton said testily, as he struggled to close the top buttons of his breeches.

"If you'd allow me to question them, my lord, I'm sure there is a reasonable explanation," Steward floundered.

"Reasonable eh, is that what you call it? I see nothing reasonable in your ill-run city being allowed to have so much liquor available. My troops are drunk and your soldiers no better. Make them stand back lest I die inhaling their fumes."

Steward hurried forward, a flap of his hands directing the men to move. The halberdiers had the grace to look ashamed. Not so the mercenaries who belched loudly and greeted everyone with bucolic smiles.

"Question them," Northampton barked, his finger pointed at the halberdiers.

Steward enjoyed authority and injected severity into his voice.

"Explain yourselves. My lord is not a man to make a fool off. Begin, begin."

The most sober elected himself spokesman. "We were set upon by the rebels from the Heights. I swear we never saw them coming. One of the Italia was taken prisoner. It was all over in moments."

Seated on a chair his eyes half closed Northampton appeared to be uninterested until he heard word of the rebels. At once he changed stance.

Rigid and hawk-faced he was alert in an instant.

"Are you telling me they're in the city? Why didn't you know this?" he shrieked at the hapless Steward.

"No, General," the halberdier corrected. "They are not in the city but close, just the other side of the river. Some of them must have swum across."

"What sort of mayor are you? It's all a disgrace," hissed Essex.

"I'm just the deputy mayor," Steward ventured in almost a whisper.

"So it would seem. And why isn't the real mayor here? Got himself taken prisoner, that's why."

"I apologise, my lord, I'm only..."

"Gad's tooth, you're a nincompoop, that's what you are. Left to you, 'tis likely we could have been murdered as we slept. The citizens of Norwich deserve better than this. Smarten yourself up and get out there. Strengthen the city at every gate. These scoundrels mustn't be allowed to get the upper hand. Don't just stand there. See to it man, before I take your head as a plaything."

Flustered, Steward turned to the halberdiers.

"Take the foreigners back to their camp. Then make sure their commanders know of the General's orders. Every man to defend the city, that's what you tell them."

"Then find Lord Sheffield. Say I sent you and tell him of this. He'll know what to do," Northampton said, making no attempt to cover a yawn. "I'm going to my bed. I hope for your sake, Steward, it's a comfortable one."

"Only the finest goose feathers, I can assure you, my lord," the other replied.

– 23 –

Despite his peasant status, like Thom, John was natural leader. It only took him a few moments to pick his men. Whilst the citizen's still slept, he, Will, Philip and six trusted others swam the Wensum, scaled the city walls and melted into the alleyways close to the castle. They were unopposed, but they were not unobserved.

The informant didn't linger. As a sympathiser of the king it wasn't safe, not if he fell into the hands of rebels. After a dalliance with a comely serving wench, he'd spent the night pressed up against a cattle trough for warmth. Several hens and a piglet shared the space with him. Roused by the sound of low voices, he looked over the top of the trough and saw the last of the rebels come over the wall.

At the same time on the far bank of the Wensum, the camp waited for the call to arms. Lined up in their squadrons they fidgeted and talked in low voices. The first fingers of daylight seemed tremulous in the pale sky as if they too hesitated to endorse what was to come. There was no birdsong and the wind blew chill from the river.

Sure such information would be worthy of a reward the informer was careful to remain unseen. He crawled away until it was safe to stand. Then he ran all the way to Tombland. Once he'd delivered the news he'd seen rebels in the city, he was disappointed to be pushed aside as Northampton called for his second-in- command, nobleman Edmund Sheffield.

"Ah, Sheffield, I've decided to offer the rebels a pardon. Who would you suggest as an envoy?"

"Forgive me, my lord, but isn't this rather sudden. Are we sure Kett and his rabble intend to resist us. Surely once they see your command there'll be no opposition," Sheffield said as he stood by a window looking out.

"With the rebels running around at will I have no interest in being in this city any longer than I must so appoint an envoy and be done with it," Northampton ordered.

"As you wish, my lord," Sheffield replied.

The small group made an ill-assorted collection. Led by Dethick with a trumpeter and backed by a squad of halberdiers, General Harry Sutton marched to Pockthorpe Gate north east of the city. Never comfortable at the possibility of discourse, Augustine Steward trailed some way behind.

Sutton was in a bad mood and heartily sick of the city's problems. His position as envoy decreed he should be a diplomat; after a night of scant sleep and too much mead he had no intention of being diplomatic and certainly not with a bunch of rebels. His orders to offer them a pardon didn't sit well with him and ill humour was evident on his face.

"How much further is it?" he grumbled to Dethick as they entered another cramped and evil-smelling alleyway. "I could be taking my breakfast at the Maids Head as does my Lord Northampton and Lord Sheffield had I not been forced to behave like a sewer rat looking for these miserable peasants."

"If the information is correct, General Sutton, we should find them very shortly," Dethick assured, unperturbed by his companions ill humour.

It would have been difficult to avoid the crowd that met their eyes when they emerged beside Pockthorpe Gate. When word spread the rebels were again in the city impoverished supporters left their beds and flocked to their side. John and his band now numbered nearer sixty than six. They stood defiant as Sutton strode towards them.

"You said there were no more than six or seven of them," Sutherton snapped.

"So the informant said."

"Perchance he has bad eyesight or more likely can't count. They look an ugly rabble. Make sure the soldiers are close by. We may have to leave quickly," Sutton muttered.

"You, there," he shouted, his imperious wave intended to summon John. "Step forward. I have word from my lord Northampton who offers you a most generous pardon."

With his instrument positioned to his lips the trumpeter prepared to play, a precursor before the announcement of the pardon. Usually quiet spoken, John's voice seemed to have gained a strength which carried far, drowning out the trumpeter's first notes.

"I don't recognise you, sir, although something tells me you are nothing but a lackey of Northampton. Still abed, is he?"

"Such impertinence will do you no favours, I can assure you," Sutton spluttered in anger. "My lord Northampton has been up for many hours."

"So why isn't he here in person?"

"Because, sir, he has better things to do than talk with an oaf such as yourself."

The rumble from the crowd sounded ominous. Steward who had just arrived looked aghast.

"General, is it wise to take such a tone?" he whispered. "If we anger them who knows what might happen."

Chapter 23

A look of disdain from the General shrunk Steward into nothing and he retreated.

"God save me from lily-livered fools," Sutton snarled.

Just the same he beckoned the halberdiers forward. They raised their lances and took a defensive stance. They still seemed a paltry few compared with the restless crowd who glared at them from across the square. John, Will and a rebel they called John Flotman who led the city supporters climbed the steps of the Market-Cross so they could be seen by all.

The fastidious Sutton wrinkled his nose in disgust at the sight of their matted hair and unshaven faces. Like all the rebels after weeks of rough living, they looked derelict. Philip didn't join them. His defection from the palace meant he still feared he might be recognised and be betrayed so he preferred to stand in the midst of others.

It was John who spoke. In a confident voice he said. "I speak for Master Kett, a brave man as we all know. We have no need of your pardon, sir, for we have done no wrong. We have lost what is rightfully ours. Our land has been wrongfully stolen from us."

Loud roars of approval from the rebels interrupted John. Never taking his eyes off the soldiers he held up his hand for silence.

"Master Kett is a man who upholds the law. Aye, that he does." He pointed at Sutton. "You, sirrah and your precious Northampton are nought but traitors. Isn't that so, my friends?" he said, his hand making a wide sweep of this closest to him.

"I've heard enough," Sutton snapped to his companions. "Come, I must report back to Lord Northampton. We're wasting our time here."

"Indeed, indeed," Steward said, anxiety making him extremely nervous. He was the first to start the walk back to Tombland, quickly followed by Sutton and the others. Unsure of their orders the halberdiers hung back until beckoned by Sutton. The crowd's derisory laughter followed them as they speeded their step at the turn of the wall.

"Aye, that's right," Will's voice boomed after them. "You're nothing but weak women. Run back to your masters and tell them we are ready for you. We shall fight until there is none of us left on our feet."

The three clambered down from their position amidst cheers and applause from the rebels. Flotman vanished back among the crowd, but John caught Will by the arm.

"Can you get back to Master Kett? Tell him now is the time to attack. Once Northampton gets word he'll gain the upper hand whilst our men still swim the river. Hurry, Will. We depend on you."

Will frowned. "My clothes are only just dry, why me?"

"Because long legs like yours get you across the water in half the time, that's why. God speed, my friend," John said with an affectionate hug.

The big man laughed and started back up the stone and flint wall.

Within sight of Tombland and the shadow of the castle, Sutton stopped. Used to warfare he was accustomed to quick decisions. Whilst his companions were only concerned with their safety he was thinking ahead. He selected two of the halberdiers.

"I want a man on every cannon above Bishop's Gate. See to it immediately. The river serves us well and with any luck we can pick the rebels off as they try to cross. There is no time to waste. Hurry now. Find your superiors and tell them it's General Sutton's orders."

At a quick trot the halberdiers headed for the castle. Their sloppy salutes filled him with dismay, but there was no time for reprimands.

– 24 –

5th August 1549

When word spread through the camp they were to fight foreign mercenaries, indeed men from Italia, the rebels became invigorated by their own anger. Tension was palpable and they stood with their shoulders squared and an expectant light in their eyes. Robert walked between the ranks of men. It was as he feared. They were poorly armed and he cursed his own stupidity for it. At his side Thom saw the concern on Robert's face.

"What troubles you, Master Kett?" he said quietly, when they reached the final squadron.

"Just look at what they carry. Pitchforks, balls of mud and a few have cross-bows. Why don't I see them all with their longbows?"

"There's been difficulty making arrows. We've had those unfit to fight working through the night. As soon as more are ready, I have runners to bring them to the squadron leaders. There are muskets too for some and they all carry knives."

"I hoped our supporters would send us more when the last delivery of grain and meat arrived," Robert said with a heavy sigh. "I send them with so little and yet their hearts are strong. Did you smell the stench of their sweat? It's the sign of men ready to fight to the death. I know it."

He shaded his eyes and stared up at the cannons atop the gate. Their black gape was swung towards the riverbank and Thom heard a sharp intake of breath.

"God's blood, they have a man at every one."

At first Thom had difficulty seeing anything more than the guns. Then a glint from a sun-tipped helmet showed their opponents position and he could pick them out as they stood ready beside the cannon. An icy chill ran down his backbone and he hoped Robert didn't see him shiver.

An image of Martha flashed into his mind. Her smile always warmed him and her hands soothed, it seemed so long since he saw her last. When she bid him farewell with a wave the breeze lifted her hair as it escaped from under the quaint cap she wore. He knew by the set of her face she fought to control her tears. For a moment he thought he heard music. A jig it was, Martha so loved to dance.

When the cannon ball impacted on the water, the explosive splash sent the sweet notes away and drove all thoughts of home far from his mind. As a second followed it he saw Robert's hand signal and heard his order.

"Are you ready, men? First rank into the water. Longbows take aim. Fire. Second rank, follow up."

The sky went dark as arrows pierced the soft shades of morning. Beneath it the river heaved against the bank with the weight of the hundred men who plunged into it. Pale smoke drifted past them as if a thread of flimsy gauze wavered in their midst. It was a passive response at odds with the growl of the cannons.

Thom ran to join the second line poised to jump. Within moments, Robert gave the command and he leapt off the bank. His breath caught in his throat and he struggled to find a momentum to carry him forward. Desperate to reach the far bank the men frog-kicked the surface of the river, their weapons held above their heads. Water filled their boots and plucked at their clothes doing its best to thwart their progress.

Time and again shot flew towards them and was met by the screams and howls of those whose bodies halted its passage. Thom had no time to look round. He didn't need to. Every time his hands parted the water it flowed back to him in scarlet wavelets. He flung himself against the muddy bank where others had crawled before him. Some, half dead, collided with the drowned, others he trod on as he hauled his body out of the water but he made no apology. There was no time for such niceties.

He knew he risked his life when he stretched out on the grass, but there was no strength in his legs. With huge effort he got to his knees. His hands slipped in puddles of blood, slime and fragments of tissue fell from his sodden clothes. Finally he was upright.

Hellish noises around him continued and then he realised something was different. When he glanced up the cannon sat silent. Released from the barrage of shot the rebels on the meadow surged forward with yells and shouts to encourage those who still swam for their lives. Their weapons waved in defiance, they raced past Bishop's Gate.

No gate could withstand the force of the Devil who manifested himself through the wild-eyed strength of men filled with hatred. As the axes gashed the gates apart, a hail of splintered fragments showered the grass. By the time Thom reached them, the sturdy oak resembled matchwood. With a final heft the Erpingham Gate fell open and the rebels streamed into the city.

Anxious to find his friends Thom hung back in the shadow of the leper hospital. He'd seen both Will and Philip in the water, but in the frenzy lost sight of them. At first it seemed hopeless. Men charged past him across the meadows of the Great Hospital and even trampled on fellow rebels who had fallen. Full of passion and fury their voices were strident and uncontrolled.

From where he stood Thom could see Northampton's army face to face with the rebels. The soldiers slashed and hacked with lance and boar spear.

In return the rebels thrust their pitchforks forward and snatched up halberds from the dead and dying soldiers.

In full plate the soldiers were better protected, but the tine of a well placed fork quickly extracted an eye or gouged strips of flesh from an unprotected throat. The air resounded with screams and the smell of blood.

Thom found his knife and was about to join in when he noticed a tall man with wild hair who swung his blade from side to side. He felled those he encountered as if they were tree saplings. At first Thom wasn't sure if it was Will. Then the shaggy head turned and he recognised him.

Their eyes met and Thom pointed to Will's head. It shone scarlet with edges of crimson flesh which curled in a sardonic smile from one side of his scalp to another. It looked a massive wound, but Will laughed.

"Methinks, you didn't dodge quickly enough," Thom said when he was close enough.

"My skull against your skull anytime," growled Will, with a well aimed blow at a soldier. The man staggered, cupping his hand under his armpit. Warm and viscous the blood gushed, filled his palm and splashed to the ground below. Swung with ferocity Will's flail sent the man down where he collapsed in the pool of his own blood.

Off guard for a brief moment Thom felt the sting of a blade. The sleeve of his shirt fell away in one and red beads welled and ran together down his forearm. Will despatched the attacker with a single blow to his neck. Thom ripped the sleeve from its last remaining stitches and bound his arm whilst Will fended off another soldier.

"What of Master Kett and the others?" Thom asked.

"They were safe the last time I saw them," Will replied. As fresh leakage from his wound dribbled down he wiped it to clear his eyes. "Master Kett had John taking one of the Generals as prisoner up to Mount Surrey."

There was no time for more talk. They'd pushed the soldiers back to St Martin's at Place Plain well beyond the Market-Place and the city gates at Bishop's Bridge. Drenched in blood, theirs and their comrade's, the rebels fought on as they drove the army towards Tombland.

From behind locked doors and barricaded windows, the citizen's of Norwich waited. Despite their precautions, the smell of killing permeated their homes, enough to make them retch.

Thom lost sight of Will and with no time to look for him or the others, he stabbed and slaughtered with grim intent. He like all the rebels fought for freedom and fought for his life on that summer day in early August.

Edmund, Lord Sheffield turned his horse and drove it forward at a canter. Slow to respond the beast skittered and pranced. Ears flat to its head and nostrils flared it huffed noisily. Impatient with its performance Edmund resolved to change mounts at the earliest opportunity. He'd long since lost sight of Northampton in the crush of fighting men. Now he found himself a lone figure amongst the rebel hordes outside the Cathedral gate.

Isolated and anxious, his spurs were heavy in the horse's flanks as he tried to encourage the animal in another direction.

"You stupid animal you are nothing but useful to feed my hounds. Get moving will you?" Edmund cursed and pulled hard on the bit. This time the animal threw its weight on its back legs, rose up and scrabbled the air with its hooves. Edmund would never know whether it slipped on its own urine or a patch of blood, but he lost his seat and fell heavily on the cobbles. As he landed his musket was wrenched from his hand.

Winded, there was little he could do but look up through his visor at the ring of faces which surrounded him. The rebel's expressions sent a tremor of fear through him. He couldn't remember the last time he'd seen such hostility. Dirty and bloodied they muttered among themselves as they shuffled closer. He knew he must act quickly. It was clear they didn't recognise him. When he told them who he was, he was sure he could persuade them he would be useful to them.

About to sit up he felt a boot on his shoulder which sent him back down again. It was a struggle to get his helmet off. Then he said.

"Nay, don't be hasty. I could be of value to you. I'm Edmund, Lord Sheffield, second cousin to your late King Hal. Take me as your prisoner, I shan't resist."

He offered his hands up, but nobody moved.

"Your prisoner then and eight pounds in gold to the man who takes me," Edmund pleaded.

Still laid on the cobbles he watched the ranks of legs and feet fall away with relief. He'd been sure the offer of money would work, but instead of being seized he was confronted by the sight of a short, dour-faced man who stood looking down at him. Gripped in his hand a spike-headed mace hung on its chain.

William Fulke was an artisan. No one could skin a beast as quickly as he. He could bone out a carcase in minutes. His prowess as a butcher was matched only by his woodcarving talents, his furniture sought after by many who could afford such things. He was also a stalwart rebel.

"My lord makes a pretty offer," he said softly. "But there's not one amongst us would take your money. Sit up sirrah, and take a look at these men. They come seeking justice not a rich man's handout."

With a rough hand he hauled Edmund to a sitting position.

"Then let me help you, there must be something." Edmund's terror was clear in his eyes and in the drool which slithered from his lips. "Let me up and I'll speak to Lord Northampton. I beg you," he whined.

"He wastes our time and there's fighting to be done," someone in the crowd shouted.

The remark was met with nods and sounds of agreement. Fulke swung the mace and its shadow fell on Edmund's face. It missed his head on three occasions. The fourth time Fulke used a little more vigour and the spikes flailed the skin off Edmund's face.

His screams incited those who watched. Their own wounds forgotten they stamped and cheered as they watched Edmund's mouth fall slack and heard his cries reduced to a frothy red bubble. With methodical precision, Fulke swung the mace time and time again. As it spilled out of Edmund's brain the meat looked like the jelly of pale brawn. The roars of approval grew in strength as if to keep time with each blow.

Atop Edmund's twitching body his head was no more than a pink bundle of macerated flesh and shattered bone. One eye remained intact, a dangle of fibres and eyeball which rested on the pulp. The macabre sight no longer appealed and the mace swung still. Sprawled on the cobbles Edmund was left for the crows.

No one wanted to tell Northampton about Edmund's death. In a quiet huddle Dethick, Sutton and Augustine Steward discussed the details in low voices. With iron nerves it was rare for them to feel distress, but the manner of Edmund's demise filled them all with disgust.

Sutton pressed for reassurance several times, "The halberdier was quite sure it was Edmund? By all accounts, it wasn't a pretty sight. It could have been anyone."

"There is absolutely no doubt, General. The man watched it all from behind a wall. He saw Lord Sheffield's horse unseat him." Dethick pulled out a large yellow kerchief and mopped his brow.

"Who's going to tell Lord Northampton, that's what I want to know," Steward whispered.

"Well, master Deputy Mayor are you our volunteer?" Sutton asked with a spiteful smile. "After all the city is your responsibility.

For a moment an expression of panic crossed Steward's face then he stiffened his shoulders and replied.

"I think not, my lord. Army matters are no concern of mine, 'tis you who should speak to your leader."

They expected dismay not the vitriol which hurled out of Northampton's mouth when he heard the news. There was a nervous silence as he paced the floor and raged.

"Dead, you say? There's nothing honourable about slaughter and that's what it was. Edmund was killed by nothing less than a rabble of uneducated serfs. Were there no troops close by apart from one soldier and he hiding by the sounds of it. I want him found, do you hear. He should give account of himself, nothing short of a coward if his story is true."

Sutton cleared his throat. "Lord Sheffield's body has been retrieved and the reason for his death is quite clear. There was no mistake, I'm afraid," he said.

"And now you tell me the city is fired and we are defeated," Northampton fumed and turned to reach the castle battlements to see that defeat with his own eyes. Sutton and his two companions followed more slowly. When they stepped out from the narrow doorway they were unprepared for the violent scenes in the streets below. Torched by the rebels two of the city gates and a row of houses were ablaze. Screams from those trapped mingled with the roar of fired timber. Smoke curled upwards as the flames grew and spread their orange glow deep into the leaden sky. Closer to the ground the grey air hung shroud-like as if it prepared to swaddle the corpses which littered the cobble stones.

"I knew it was folly, Seymour will answer for this," Northampton muttered. "How many men did you say we've lost?"

"I couldn't say for sure, my lord," Sutton replied in a low voice. "But those still alive are in some disarray. They have thrown down their arms and some have run from the city."

Northampton swung round to face the men. Steward squirmed under his gaze grateful he wasn't being asked the questions.

"What of my commanders, Sutton?"

"I fear many are dead, others captured by the rebels, my lord. As for the one in charge of the mercenaries, I saw him run like a rabbit."

Caught between shadow and flame the strange light illuminated the faces of the four of them. Northampton appeared to be thinking, his eyelids drooped low over his eyes and his mouth set in a hard line. His fingers strummed the stone balustrade.

"The army has failed us then? That settles it, we leave Norwich tonight," he said. "Sutton, round up those you can find. We march to Cambridge within the hour. Master Steward, have someone pack my belongings and see they are brought to the castle. I shall wait here until all is ready. Those dogs will stop at nothing. It's not safe for me to be seen on the streets."

A sudden squall blew across the turrets. It struck them hard, tugged their clothes, hurled rain into their faces and howled as it raced through the battlements. They all hurried for the stairs to escape its unexpected arrival.

The storm lasted for several hours. It soaked the bodies which lay on the stones, collected their blood and carried it between the cobbles. The burning houses were battered to a weak smouldering and in the commotion, Northampton and the remains of his army hurried away unseen.

On the lower floor of Dungeon Tower, the Kett brothers', Thom and Will took shelter from the relentless rain and recounted the day's events. Covered by Robert's cloak, Philip rested. His hand was roughly bound to cover a deep gash from the blade of a halberd. One stool remained empty waiting for John. As they talked they watched for a signal from the scouts. Sent by Robert they were to comb the city for any sign of Northampton and his army. When a torch dipped twice they breathed a sigh of relief.

Even their loved ones would have trouble recognising them. Their clothes were tattered blood-stained remnants, their faces dark with dirt and their hair wet. Robert dipped his neckerchief in a puddle of rainwater, rung it out and cleaned his knife blade.

"So, Thom, do we know how many of our good men fell today?" he asked.

"Some say a hundred, 'tis difficult to count. What say you, Will?"

Busy trying to pick fragments of flesh from the point of his lance, Will nodded,

"Aye, that number at least. And I saw Walter of Bungay with a mortal wound."

Robert crossed himself and sighed. Relieved of his post as prison guard, Walter was sent into the battle on Robert's orders. Now his dishonourable behaviour would no longer need to be addressed. It meant he died a hero, but Robert was prepared to allow him that.

"John's late. Has anyone seen him?" William said as he dried the rain off his musket.

"Some sheltered in the cathedral when the rain fell, perhaps he is with them," Thom said, hopeful yet somewhat concerned.

"We should return to the Heights, I must look to the men," Robert said. "We'll find John there, warm and dry I don't doubt," he reassured, but his confident smile didn't match the worry they all felt.

On the way back to camp the conversation was of their victory, how they would manage the city now it was theirs and of supplies which must be restocked. No one wanted to speak of John or cared to imagine what might have befallen him.

Before they reached the last incline they heard the groans of the wounded. The rain added to their misery despite planks secured into tree branches to offer some protection. They lay on sodden pallets bandaged by companions and comforted by friends. Many would die before morning, but the talk was cheery by those who tended them. A priest wandered down each row. He intoned quiet prayers and offered benediction. Too late for some, he knelt to close their eyes before he moved on.

Robert and William spoke to each man injured and those who ministered to them. The air already had a sickly-sweet odour of suppuration.

"They need fresh dressings," Robert whispered to his brother.

"I'll go into the city at first light with some of the more able. We'll bring back whatever we can find," William assured.

There was no one sitting under the oak nor could anyone say they'd seen John. Thom searched one half of the camp, Will the other, but there was no sign of him.

"Has anyone seen John, John Moulder? We search for John Moulder."

Someone stirred in a group round the fire, a thin man with a blood spotted strip of cotton tied round his head. He waved his arm.

"Aye, he fought alongside me. I saw him fall, that's all I know," he said with a shrug.

Thom and Will exchanged glances. It wasn't necessary to speak, their eyes mirrored their anguish.

Thom went alone to search for John. His entrance to the city was unhindered. Without the protection of their gates the streets looked vulnerable. Here and there a torch lent a pale flame. From the light he could see the husks of the burnt out houses. Their charred timbers spat smoke half-heartedly at him as he passed and the reek in the air was too vile to identify.

The few he saw in the market place or in the streets which bordered it were searching for loved ones as best they could in the darkness. Close to Thom a woman's sudden wail told of the discovery she had so feared. He stopped and laid a gentle hand on her arm. She raised grief-soaked eyes to acknowledge him then her thin back stooped further into a cheap shawl and she shuffled into the shadows.

Each time Thom stumbled over a corpse he applied the same reverence be it rebel or king's man. He knelt by each to close their eyes or smooth away plastered hair from a bloodied brow. He did not have a quarrel with them.

The death of his own countrymen taxed him enough, but when he discovered a young mercenary his tears spilled. Even lifeless the boy's black hair still bore a gloss like the wing of a raven caught in sunlight. His skin resembled blanched parchment and long eyelashes rested on cheeks chubby with youth. Blood from a chest wound diluted by the rain turned his white tunic to the softest blush pink. It reminded Thom of the wild rose that rambled in the hedgerow close to home.

Home and Martha, he sobbed openly for a moment at the memory before he moved on.

Just past the Cathedral there was no sign of battle. Free from the litter of corpses the cobbles were clean and softly silvered after the rain. It was then Thom saw a lone shape in a darkened niche in the wall. As he crossed the road he dreaded what he might find.

John's head fell on his chest as if he slept. One hand rested in his lap the other clutched the broken shaft of a lance. Thom could do no more than whimper as he crouched down beside the figure.

"My friend, my trusted friend." he whispered.

John always wore a simple cross carved from bone which hung on a thong of black leather. Trapped between the stained, tangled rags of his shirt it rested on the remains of the lance at the point where it disappeared into his chest.

Lifting his friend's head with care, Thom eased the thong over it. Wherever his fingers rested they came away dark and sticky. He slipped the cross into his pocket. He would clean it and give it to Sible as soon as he returned to Wymondham.

He could only wonder at the courage of a man who would attempt to pull out the lance that had taken him down. With infinite patience, Thom grasped the shaft and pulled out the rest of the lance then hurled it away and the cobbles received it with an echoing clatter of metal on stone.

The rain came again. It plastered his hair to his head and ran with his tears down his cheeks. With a deep sigh he lifted John's body onto his shoulder as once, a long time ago, he'd carried Flowerdew's ram. He showed more care to his burden this time. With slow steady tread he carried John back to the Kings Camp.

Seated under the awning, Robert addressed the rebels and made his instructions clear. Sombre faced his tone was stern so they should understand the importance of his words.

"Yesterday we took control of the city. God and justice prevailed but our battle is not over yet. Northampton and his men scuttled away in the night like the rats they are. There will be more like them so it is too early to celebrate. It seems when the army left wealthy merchants from the city joined them, but they left behind their wives and children. I intend no harm shall come to them. We must remember those we lost and strengthen our resolve for now we fight for widows too."

He paused. Thom stared over their heads as images of Sible, flashed into his mind and he wondered just how he would break the news to her.

With his voice steady, Robert continued.

"It doesn't please me to hear some of you have already behaved badly. I'm told that early this morning you have entered the city and thieved from the good citizens of Norwich. Some even complain of abuse and threats to them."

A group at the front pushed one man forward to speak for them.

"You should know why, Master Kett. These people support the king and sheltered the soldiers. What else would you expect us to do?"

"I will allow neither pillage nor bloodshed, is that understood?" Robert replied sharply.

Abashed the man stepped back and Robert continued.

"We shall take only what we need for the camp. Of course that includes mutton. You have my permission to slaughter sheep wherever you may find them. Tradesmen will be treated with respect, but should they choose not to help us they should be warned they will be regarded as our enemies. As such they will be imprisoned at Mount Surrey. Shortly my brother will call for all the squadron leaders to assemble here. You will be given lists of the stores we need. All our supplies are low, there is much to do. The rest of you will see to any repairs necessary to your equipment, make sure your weapons are in good order and generally make yourselves useful."

The men wandered away and those left under the awning sat immersed in their thoughts. Sobered by John's death each carried their share of grief and it was difficult to find purpose. Thom closed his eyes and recalled the day of the fair. He could smell the grass, hear the children's voices and feel Martha's arm linked through his. It seemed a long time ago and for a moment he wondered whether their fight for freedom was worth the dreadful price they would pay. Ashamed of his doubts he chastised himself. This was no time to waver he owed John's memory more than that. Running his hand through his silvered hair he tried to concentrate.

"Master Kett, I must be occupied. Have you a job for me?"

"Indeed I have," Robert said."We need authority in the city. I cannot run the camp and be there as well. Augustine Steward is not to be trusted. My idea is to set up a garrison in the grounds of the Cathedral. William and I have spoken about this and he will be in charge. You and I, Thom will give thought to what comes next."

"I shan't let you down, Master Kett," Thom said gratified by Robert's trust.

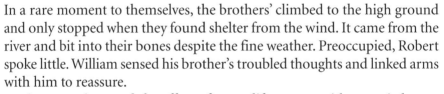

In a rare moment to themselves, the brothers' climbed to the high ground and only stopped when they found shelter from the wind. It came from the river and bit into their bones despite the fine weather. Preoccupied, Robert spoke little. William sensed his brother's troubled thoughts and linked arms with him to reassure.

Sparse rations and the effect of camp life meant neither carried extra weight and they reached the lee of the Heights with barely a misplaced breath. From where they sat they looked down on the spread of the city. They could see the usual movement in the streets and markets, but the vibrancy was missing.

It had been over a week since Northampton and his army took flight. Since the shopkeepers had boarded up their premises and gone into hiding, trade had all but stopped. Although at first the rebels heeded their leader's words and behaved honourably, it wasn't to last. Each day Robert hoped more disillusioned peasants would join the rebellion, each day he was left disappointed.

"I had such hopes, William. I felt sure after our victory word would spread and more would join us."

Lying on his back on the grass, William rested his head on his hands and gazed up at the sky. His jacket torn and with shreds of linen for a shirt, he no longer looked like the prosperous landowner he was.

"I heard there was a rising at Hingham and another at Watton. Neither succeeded it seems. We must hope for better things," he said.

Robert thumped the ground with his fist. "No, brother, we must do more than just hope. We cannot fail now. The men tire of this lack of activity so they loot and steal. Steward, the useless Deputy Mayor has vanished and disorder rages in the city when darkness falls."

Chapter 25

He fell silent and it was left to the noise of the insects to fill the vacuum. Somewhere in the long grass a cricket harmonized with another and the heavy heads of red clover bent under the weight of yellow-legged bumblebees. Eyes closed, about to doze, William dreamed of his garden. He tried to remember which flowers would be in bloom, Robert's words startled him.

"I have an idea. We should send a hundred men to Yarmouth. They will spread word of the rebellion and order the port to surrender. Those who wish to join us will seek leadership and can travel here to the camp. What think you of that?"

Robert was already on his feet as reluctant to move William stretched and slowly sat up.

"Come brother, we must call the Council together," Robert urged.

They gathered under the awning, but with two more of their number missing the empty chairs were a poignant reminder. Arthur had struggled on, but now lay with the sick. The burn on his ear never healed when infection set in. Frail and wasted he would play no further part in the rebellion. But it was John's seat which depressed them the most.

"William agrees so what do you say? Shall we march on Yarmouth?" Robert asked after he outlined his plan.

"We need new recruits and there must be many who would march with us. So I say, aye. Who will lead them?" Thom voiced as the others nodded.

"You, Thom. I find it hard to spare you but Will supports my brother in the garrison and the rest of you must aid me here at the King's Camp. Thom, pick your men and start for Yarmouth in the morning, if you will. Philip still suffers and lacks strength. We can't count on him yet awhile. Come, William, 'tis time we attended prayers and then we have details to see to."

– 26 –

Great Yarmouth was a hard day's march east of the city laying on the edge of the North Sea. No one could ever mistake it. Every milestone passed reinforced the potent odour of fish which clawed the air. As the town's shape appeared in front of them, Thom breathed a sigh of relief. Malaise seemed to have overcome them, spirits were low and they'd fallen behind despite leaving Norwich as the sun came up.

The hundred men who marched lost time on difficult terrain. Low water in the dykes left them deceptively deep and the bog itself sucked at their feet and pulled them back. They lost count of how many saltwater creeks of green sedge and dark mud they had to cross and when they reached the far side of Acle, the going was no easier.

It was a poor road, the surface pitted and worn with more stone than earth. Hardly a man who marched possessed serviceable foot wear. Months of use and several immersions in river water rotted the soles and split the sides of the boots of those who had them.

It was the fifteenth day of August and the ground was hard. Flints sharpened to knife points ripped through leather with ease and men swore at the discomfort. The weather spoiled their tempers too as they struggled with the heat. The four hand cannons being pulled along at the rear of the file shone not with polish but with human sweat as the men took turns to haul them.

They passed no one. Their only companions were the large numbers of sheep that grazed the marshland on either side of the road. Thoughts of home were strong in Thom's mind. How he would've praised God for such a day to lift his sheaves.

He wondered if he would ever reap golden grain in his own fields again. It dismayed him to pass so many deserted dwelling-places and glebe lands. Their owners left with no ground for tillage went in their hundreds to the city where they were forced to turn vagrant and beg.

Where were they now, these jobless men, their wives, fatherless children, widows? He shuddered at the thought and walked with his head down for fear others would see his distress.

The plan was to reach Yarmouth by sunset, but when they halted close to the quay a high moon shot silver shards onto the surface of the black water. It tipped the masts of the herring boats too, which rode their anchors with gentle motion on the swell.

Set between the flint and cobble walls the town gate stood ajar. Few paid attention to the scruffy, dejected men who threw their longbows and

189

muskets aside and flopped to the ground. Thom expected to see a watchman on duty so he was not surprised when several men appeared out of the shadows. He took a step towards them.

"Halt where you are and state your business," one said.

"I'm called Thom Barwick and these men and I are part of the Norfolk Rising. I speak on behalf of our leader, Master Robert Kett. Who is in charge here?" Thom said pleasantly.

"It'll be me you want, Nicholas Brownlow, Mayor of Yarmouth." The flicker of light on a wall sconce illuminated the speaker. Thom was met by a cold, blank stare from eyes which held no emotion. What could be seen of the mayor's face under a dense matt of whiskers appeared fleshy, the nose was large, the line of the mouth thin and set.

Thom smiled. "It's been a long march from Norwich. We could do with a meal and a place to lay ourselves down."

Hostility sparked from Brownlow and with an abrupt toss of his head, he said,

"Not in my town, you won't. You're not welcome here. If you choose to sleep this side of the walls, so be it. We want no trouble from those who break the law."

Indignant, Thom was quick to rouse. "No, sir, you are wrong it is you and those like you who make us seek justice. We only want back that which belongs to every commoner in the land. Or would you have us starve?"

Brownlow shrugged his heavy shoulders and turned away. One of his retinue whispered to him but the words didn't carry. Frustrated, Thom considered how best they should win favour whilst his men looked on. Before they left the Kings Camp, Robert had stressed the importance of them getting into the town. Thom knew it was imperative they did so in order to enlist more men to join the rebellion. Before he could speak again, Brownlow turned back and said in a more civil tongue.

"I'm not an uncaring man. If it's food you need, it will be brought to the gate. When you have fed and rested, I suggest you return to Norwich. There is nothing for you here."

"Then I must ask you to surrender to us," Thom said sharply.

"On whose orders do you act?" Brownlow countered.

"On the orders of Master Kett."

"I give not a fig for your Master Kett," Brownlow said with a mocking smile.

He turned abruptly and walked through the gates. As he did so he signalled to one of his companions who closed them. They all heard the clunks as bolts rattled into place and keys turned in their locks. Such finality was unexpected and in belligerent mood the rebels took up their weapons and looked expectantly at Thom.

"Be patient," he said. "Let them bring food. We shall fight better on a full belly."

Brownlow dispatched the last of the horses with a sharp slap across the rump.

"Ride hard for London, we count on you. Demand to speak to my lord Seymour and no other. Don't take the muffles off their hooves until you are well clear of here and stop for no one," he called.

In dark clothes the three riders raised their hands to acknowledge the orders. Within moments of leaving Brownlow's side they merged into the shadows. Wise to the rebel's location they chose to leave the town by a little used track. Shielded by the overhang of a merchants house, Brownlow waited, his ears attuned to any sudden noise. When he judged his messengers were safe, he headed for the Tolhouse.

Apprehension left Thom awake until a pink glow splattered the horizon. He knew delay would be costly so with quiet commands, he urged his men forward. Peppered by musket fire the town gate fell with ease. Encouraged, as they'd met with no resistance, the rebels raced on towards the town square, but it was quickly obvious that Thom had misjudged Brownlow. Armed and angry the men of Yarmouth waited for them.

Brownlow was no coward and led from the front. Well equipped with weaponry his men advanced through the narrow streets and appeared from round every corner determined to keep Yarmouth secure. Moses, Thom's second in command swore loudly as an arrow whispered past close to his head.

"Where are those who would stand on our side?" he grumbled. "Surely some Yarmouth people will come to our aid, yet I see none."

Hidden by a stack of barrels on the quay, Thom returned fire before he answered. He tried to keep the doubt out of his voice.

"Give them time."

"Methinks time is something we are short of, we are far outnumbered," Moses said grimly.

Sounds of shot carried across parkland behind the Tolhouse to a small abbey. In fear their Chapel would be looted, the monks hurried to conceal the Benedictine regalia, silver plate and themselves in under- floor chambers. Such was the build of the Priory it was no hardship to find suitable places, but the monks were terrified. Already fragile after the Act of Dissolution, their very existence was tenuous and their religious activities only continued behind doors kept firmly locked. However they had no need for concern. Thom gave clear warnings to the rebels. The monks and their possessions were to be left alone. So whilst shot and arrow assaulted the town, the faded grey stones and ageing pillars of Cauldwell Priory remained untouched.

Not so the partly built Haven at the end of the quay. A sudden roar of fire took them all by surprise. In an instant flames reduced building materials to smoulders and laid the partly built site to waste. Thom and Moses hastily sought another position.

"By all that's holy, that was close. Things don't go well, Moses, not well at all," Thom muttered as he caught sight of some of the rebels sprawled on the cobbles. He shook his head more in despair than anger. "Master Kett was wrong, we have no support here there are too many of us dead already."

"Perhaps 'tis time we left this wormy place before we all perish," Moses said, his wary eyes never still.

Musket reloaded, Thom grimaced. "Then we fail."

"Better we fail than die."

No one could be sure whose shot started the blaze, but incensed by the damage Brownlow and his men pressed forward. A thick mist suddenly appeared. It wafted across the town centre and obscured everything. Houses, boats in the harbour, even the last remnants of the Haven vanished. Bewildered, Thom strained to see through it.

"What in God's name is it? Is it sea scud?"

Moses sniffed loudly. "No sea mist ever smelt like that, burnt grass more like."

"Hay, they've set fire to haystacks, now we can't see anything. Where are the devils now?" Suddenly Brownlow's plan dawned on Thom.

"They've done it on purpose. How can we attack when we can't see?"

All around them noises changed. The sound of shots and arrows were replaced with strangled cries and curses. When for a moment the smoke faded or changed direction, Thom and Moses could see the fleeing shapes of their men as they turned and ran.

"Curses, we're lost. To Gorleston," Thom shouted at the top of his voice. "We meet at Gorleston, meet with us there."

On a sun-dried knoll outside the village a mile from Great Yarmouth, the pitiful few rebels left threw themselves down on the ground. Thom sat on an upturned wooden pail. Beside him perched on a milestone, Moses lent wearily on his longbow. Tired and despondent no one spoke. Their glazed eyes rimmed black by soot they looked at one another's sweat-streaked faces.

The water skin passed from mouth to mouth. Throats gurgled, hawked and spat foul saliva onto the grass. For some it was almost too much of an effort. Thom took his turn, mustered his strength and said.

"There are many of us missing, tell me what you know of their fate."

"We are less than twenty," Moses murmured.

"I counted ten felled in one place," someone said. "Roger Dale and his brother were taken prisoner. I saw them pass me in irons. It was before the smoke came." His voice failed and the words tailed away.

"What of the cannons?"

"They have them all," another replied. "Muskets and bows too."

Thom ran a hand over his brow.

"It's worse than I thought," he said quietly. "It's best we don't stay here long. Brownlow may still pursue us and I intend no more will die. We march back to the King's Camp."

"We march? You surely jest with us, Thom. A walk is all I can manage and a slow one at that," Moses said with a wry smile. He shook a shoe and the last remaining strips of leather crumbled and fell off.

They gathered up what was left of their weapons and trudged towards the road to Norwich. Disappointed and poor company Thom walked alone. He knew Robert Kett would be sorely disheartened when he learnt of their failure.

– 27 –

Hampton Court
17th August 1549

Bemused, Seymour struggled to absorb the information imparted to him. It wasn't often he was lost for words, but at that moment he seemed incapable of finding one. Devoid of either kindness or a desire to understand, his gaze rested on the dust-ingrained and dishevelled riders from Yarmouth. With effort he tried to keep his temper.

"You," he said, his imperious wave directed at the man he thought looked the brightest.

"Yes, my lord."

"If you waste my time, you will pay dear. Only last week I'm told Northampton and his miserable excuse for an army fled from Norwich, leaving the rebels in charge of the city. Now you beg for help for your cursed part of the county. Are these rebels so difficult to silence?" Morose, he pulled at a loose thread from his sleeve and toyed with it. "Well, are you going to answer me that?"

"Great Yarmouth is but a small town, my lord. Master Brownlow fears for its safety and that of our women and children. The rebels appear an unruly lot and seek more support for their cause."

"Very well, tell Brownlow, I shall raise another army. This scurrilous rabble of men must be silenced once and for all. Leave now and make sure you close the door," he called after them.

Irritated by the harsh feel of his ruff he wrenched it off and scratched his neck as he mulled over the news of the assault on Yarmouth. The day started well until the arrival of Brownlow's messengers. Now the uprising gave him yet another problem to deal with and the growing rebellion sorely tested his patience. They were nothing but simple peasants, it was an outrage they could bring such disorder, but who could he find to end this situation for good?

It was at times like this he missed his sister. Jane and he were always close and shared many a secret and dilemma together. Every time he looked at the young king his heart pained for his mother. She kept wise council and he grieved as much as Edward's father had when she died of childbed fever.

Feminine giggles drew him to the window. Lady Mary Fitzpatrick walked with a page on the terrace, heads close and he the cause of her laughter. Newly arrived at court, Lady Mary caught his attention the first time he noticed her. Fresh faced and with robust proportions, she refreshed his jaded eyes. He was amused by the page too and cursed at the weakness of his flesh. God's truth, how could he concentrate on matters of State with such visions? He forced himself to look away.

His eye was caught by the chess board on an occasional table. Finely crafted in jade the pieces required him to make a move. He picked up a king, deliberated and changed to a pawn. The game threatened stalemate, not so very different from the recurring problem of land enclosures.

Disgruntled and impatient, he shook the board and felt a modicum of pleasure when the pieces scattered across the floor. A knight rolled further than the rest and the name came to him. John Dudley, Earl of Warwick, this was the man he needed. Unlike the cowardly Northampton, he was a man of tenacity on a battlefield. Seymour gave a complacent smile. Without doubt, Dudley would rout the turnip-headed peasants of Norfolk. He strode to the door, scolding himself for not thinking of him sooner. His bellow bounced off the panelled walls and echoed the length of the corridor.

"Fetch the Court scribe, there is to be a proclamation."

At the knock, Seymour smoothed down his doublet and turned to face the door.

"Come."

"You sent for me, Seymour? I came as quickly as I could, 'tis a hard ride from the north and my horse threw a shoe."

The Earl of Warwick slapped his riding gloves down on the desk top with a familiarity Seymour found distasteful.

"Enough, I have no interest in how you got here, only that you are here at last," he said testily. "There is need to raise an army and you will command it."

It was no secret that at times he doubted Warwick's loyalty. Even as he looked at him he was suspicious of the man's small, close set eyes and thin lips which curled downwards into his neat, goatee beard. Seymour took a deep breath and attempted to relax. His choices were few and it wouldn't do for his animosity to show at this time.

"Well, well Seymour and who is it you have a quarrel with?" Warwick asked.

"More than a quarrel, I assure you. The rebellion in Norfolk gets out of hand. Each day its ranks are swelled by yet more common vagrants from the city. It must be crushed once and for all. You should look to London, Essex and Suffolk for your men."

Chapter 27

"But I thought not a week ago Northampton had been instructed or are the rumours I hear, true? That he ran like a woman to Cambridge," a slight hint of amusement tugged the corners of Warwick's mouth.

"Northampton is feckless. The man has neither your strength of character nor skill when faced with combat," Seymour said with scorn. "You showed your mettle on the battlefields of France. I trust *you* will not fail me and your king this time."

He could see by Warwick's cynical expression, he scarcely believed his flattery but the game continued.

"It would be an honour to serve our monarch, and your good self." Warwick said his bow little more than a servile gesture.

"Good, good. Then make all haste and put an end to this irritating land war which has raged for long enough. Remember, elevation with a title will be yours once these wretches are put in their place."

"Consider it done, Seymour, consider it done."

"How does the Duke of Northumberland sound to you?"

Warwick picked his way carefully over the fallen chess pieces. This time the smile reached both his mouth and his stony gaze.

"It sounds well, Seymour, very well."

Seymour idly picked at a tooth. "I thought it might," he said, between his fingers.

"We are ready to leave, Seymour and I think you will agree, this is an army to be proud of, thirteen thousand of them at the last count," Warwick said, his wave directed beyond the front of the palace to the assembly of soldiers preparing to march on Norwich. Both on horse and on foot it was indeed an impressive sight and Seymour's smile indicated his satisfaction.

"You've done well, Warwick, I knew you wouldn't fail us. They seem well equipped. We must just hope their ability matches their appearance."

"Indeed, Seymour. I also took the liberty of hiring 2,000 Teutons."

Seymour frowned. "Foreign hirelings, is that wise? It seems the Italia who marched with Northampton were as useless as he is."

"Not any old hirelings, Seymour. These Germans are to be feared. They call them Landsknects, all of them pike men, swordsmen and experienced gunners and their skill is matched only by their courage. They will meet us in Norwich a few days after we arrive. They cost me dear, but with their discipline and lust for fighting, I can promise you there will no mistakes this time."

"I shall look forward to hearing all the news. I wish you God speed, Warwick, or should I say, Northumberland?" Seymour chuckled. "Now make haste and get the job done."

As with Northampton, Seymour watched from the west wing as the men now led by Warwick, marched past the last of the Court buildings and vanished round a bend in the road for Cambridge. There they would increase their numbers from what was left of Northampton's men. After that three days march would see them in Norwich. It had been Seymour's idea to stop on the way for reinforcements and he congratulated himself for the thought. It also took care of that fool Northampton who sat idle. He would do well to learn from a proper warrior like Warwick, Seymour mused as he peered over the brick and stone battlement.

He didn't delay on the windswept turret. The final days of August brought with them flurries of rain from a dismal sky. Already low hung clouds seemed about to touch the heads of the soldiers.

Norwich

As the golden embers of an afternoon sun wavered on the horizon, the last of the flour from the gristmill slid to the ground. Awkward with his bandaged hand, Philip struggled to lift his sack. Will hefted his sack with ease onto his shoulders and together they carried them toward the cooking area. The incessant rain of the previous two days left a quagmire under foot despite the best attempts of the day's warmth to dry the ground.

Thom turned his horse loose and watched it pass the wagons and climb towards the higher grass. Sun-baked to a crispy brown from weeks of drought it now seemed to have assumed new energy in a matter of hours. The grass offered a lushness smelt by the beasts and over Mousehold Heights, horses foraged at will. No need then for costly feed.

Each passing week brought more women to join their men. Most were content to fetch and carry, scrub laundry and prepare food. Others offered services which Robert and his brother, preferred to ignore.

Knowing his wife's feisty spirit, Thom often wondered whether one day he'd see Martha come to find him as other wives did. He'd have liked that since their days apart had turned to weeks. But her pretty face was never among those who arrived at the camp. No man was disgruntled when the women did the cooking. The smell of fresh pan dough baked over the fire enlivened their spirits when they sniffed the air. Will rubbed his belly as they walked to the awning.

"We'll eat well tonight, fresh mutton and bread, eh, Philip?" His enthusiastic slap across Philip's shoulder brought a grimace to the other's face.

"Have you forgotten his hand?" Thom reproved.

Immediately, Will looked aghast.

"Forgive me, my friend. I sometimes forget my own strength."

His remorse was genuine and met with a ready smile from Philip, both men, unlikely, but good friends since the early days of the march.

Thom paused when he saw the Ketts under the awning. Their heads were close together and they discussed something intently. Robert's mood had been changeable since their defeat in Yarmouth and Thom knew it troubled him.

"Look yonder," he said. "Master Kett and his brother appear disquieted about something. I wonder what's happened."

"Since word reached us my lord Warwick brings an army and should arrive today, are you surprised," Philip murmured.

"Aye, that's what it must be." Thom replied, his eyes on the sheep which turned slowly on the spit.

"We'll soon know," Will said, his stride lengthening. "So, Master Kett, you look troubled? Is it, Warwick, if it is, we're ready for him and his pox-ridden army."

"I wish it were so, Will," Robert said quietly. "Thom, a neighbour of yours rode in only an hour ago. It breaks my heart to tell you this, but he has news of Martha."

"What's happened?"

"She's had an accident."

Clarity still eluded Thom despite his frantic headshake.

"Then I must go to her."

William's touch was a gentle restraint. "No Thom, I'm sorry, you don't understand. There was nothing could be done. Martha is dead."

His eyes full of pain, Robert laid a hand on Thom's arm. "She was found in the river close to King's Beck. Your neighbour thinks she must have looked for food, a fish perhaps, the watercress beds; it isn't clear. They all search for something to eat. There was a mark on her head as if she'd fallen. Although there has been little rain the river flows fast and deep there, your neighbour said. He pulled her out, but by then it was too late."

Pain exploded in Thom's chest and his vision darkened. Tight bands of metal cut into his forehead and refused to loosen. His hands scrabbled at his skin to claw them away and his legs refused to support him. He tried to speak, but his swallow failed. For a moment he thought he would choke. Then a trace of saliva filtered into his mouth, but his eyes were fixed in some distant place. They closed abruptly and then just as quickly flew wide open. It looked as if he was about to cry out, but the silence was more dreadful to those who watched. He tried to fight the tears, but they flowed just the same.

No one spoke as Robert stepped forward and guided Thom to a chair. He motioned William to fill a beaker with mead and held it out to the stricken man. Will and Philip laid an arm each about their friend's shoulders, rested them there and then with sorrow etched on their faces they withdrew.

Confused, Thom ran a hand through his hair still thick, but turned iron-grey since the start of the rebellion. He took the mead and swallowed it in one draught. Another and one more followed in quick succession. About to remark on it, William was silenced by Robert with a shake of his head.

The beaker slipped from Thom's grasp and rolled across the grass. He stared at it and saw it slowly change shape into an image of a woman's face,

Martha's face. He knew he only had to reach down to touch it and he would smell her, feel the soft texture of her skin, watch her lips curl into her impish smile, listen to her as she always sang when she cooked their food. He blinked to see her more clearly, but just as she arrived so she vanished. The horn beaker faintly striated and chipped with age lay still in front of him. A pale bubble of mead clung to one edge.

It was two hours or more before Thom, supported by Robert and William, trod an unsteady line to his mattress. The air was heavy with cooking odours and noisy from the babble of voices as the camp settled down for their food. No one noticed the two men help their companion down to his bed and cover him with a sheepskin. Thom hadn't spoken since he was told the news. He simply drank enough mead to take away the pain and to relax the contours of his face. As the Kett's turned to leave, Robert went down on one knee and whispered.

"You should eat. I'll bring just a little, the choicest pieces."

The reply was poorly given, a brief headshake was all, but Robert took it as a refusal. "Very well, I shan't press you. We salute your bravery, Thom. If you wish to leave the camp and return home, we would understand."

At first there was no response. Not a flicker of an eyelash or the quiver of a muscle on the ashen face. It was grief made more poignant by those oblivious to his loss as they roistered and caroused round the fire.

"Good night then, Thom," Robert said, about to get to his feet.

The strength in the hand which shot out to grasp his arm surprised him. Thom's eyes remained closed, but he spoke clearly.

"What is there to go home for? There is work to do until we win our fight. And by God, win it we will. Until then leave me in peace. I'm no company for anyone tonight."

A single tear forced its way onto his cheek and meandered down his face. As Robert and William walked away, Thom turned and buried his head in the crook of his arm.

24th August 1549

Delayed by a tumult of storm and rain, Warwick's army arrived at the city walls of Norwich a day late. Such were their numbers, that those who walked the end of the march were nowhere in sight. With local reinforcements they numbered between 8,000 and 14,000 men and when a little after dawn they were seen by rebel lookouts from the high ground at the Heights, a signal was sent to the camp. Those gathered under the awning exchanged glances when they saw the rag flutter.

"They're here, and it's almost a relief," Robert murmured. "Now we know what must be done. Doubtless Warwick will send in a herald to offer yet another meaningless pardon. Thom, are you sure you want to wait with us? Methinks you slept little last night."

Only his expressionless eyes betrayed Thom's lack of spirit as he nodded.

"My place is with you. Let us hear what double-tongued promises they make this time."

"As you wish. Philip, alert the squadron leaders, if you please. Tell them to make ready. We are well entrenched here, let them come to us."

Chosen as a runner, a strong young man sprinted to a standstill in front of them. Early rays from the sun forced their way through the leaf canopy and strange shaped shadows played on him as he paused to catch his breath.

"Take your time," Robert said gently.

The boy pointed up to the lookouts.

"I'm to tell you they come in their thousands. We have yet to see the full number of them."

His shoulder appeared bowed by the heavy crossbow which hung from it and his fingers played an agitated rhythm on the handle of a knife in his waistband.

"Thank you, lad, you've done well. Return to your place and keep us informed," William said.

Before Philip had time to leave the awning, word of the enemy spread fast and the rebels were already massed in ranks around the tree. The air was thick with the smell of their sweat and a dark underlying current of nervous anticipation. Robert cast his eye over them. The seriousness of the moment marked in his tense face and tightened jaw he lent towards his brother.

"I feel concern," he whispered. "Warwick will come well equipped. Do you think we have enough men?"

"We are strong in numbers if not in weapons," William said."See brother, even at this late hour more come to join us." He pointed to a group of men newly arrived who stood a little apart armed with what appeared to be crudely carved sticks. Their hunched and tattered stance seemed to cry out the hopelessness and drudgery of their situation as they looked about them.

"Artisans fallen on bad times, by the look of them, but they will fight as well as any," he added.

A shadow fell across the awning and Will appeared followed by a smaller more rotund figure in his wake.

"Master Dethick comes to speak with you, Master Kett."

The florid countenance of the King's Herald broke into a forced smile as he held out a plump hand. Behind him his escort of four halberdiers and a trumpeter waited. Surrounded by the rebels, none of them looked at ease.

"Master Kett, so we meet again. I come on behalf of the Earl of Warwick. He is most anxious to avoid any further bloodshed and therefore instructs me to proclaim pardon for all who now return to their homes. The offer comes from our gracious king himself and you can be sure he has much sympathy for your cause. How say you at such a generous offer?"

Dethick's last sentence was a little wayward of the truth. He knew full well the boy king had little or no views whatsoever on the matter since it was never discussed with him. His own ears heard fresh criticism of the Lord Protector Seymour as a weak and ineffectual man. It was common gossip in the shadowy halls of Hampton Court Palace and Dethick suspected dark plans were afoot.

However it wasn't his business and he had enough to deal with in Norwich. So he tapped his foot on the ground and waited for Robert's reply.

From under the table, Robert retrieved the sturdy set of library steps purloined from Mount Surrey and climbed them so no one would miss his words. William and Thom stood on either side of him. Philip, despite his changed appearance, had quickly vanished into the rebel crowd. He still feared being recognised by anyone from court.

"My friends, we have received another royal pardon, this time brought to us by my Lord Warwick. The good herald here tells me the king offers considerable concern about our plight. We are asked to disband and go back to our homes. What do you think?"

So contrived was Robert's politeness, few suspected anything less. As he finished speaking, shouts of "*God save King Edward*" echoed across the camp and a general mumble of good natured conversation broke out. Of late it was rare for the rebels to be so affable and it surprised the rebellion leaders.

By Dethick's smirk it seemed he thought he'd achieved success. He motioned Robert to step down and flushed with self-importance strutted up to the top step and held up his hand for silence.

Chapter 29

"I'm delighted you seem to have seen good sense. Hurry now, pack up your belongings and go home. Master Kett misleads you if you think you could ever win and you have suffered much hardship for nothing. Turn away from him and go now, you will not be harmed."

They were the wrong choice of words. As if a sudden storm sprung from nowhere so the rebel's disposition changed and as one they began to chant.

"No. No. No. No to the herald, Kett is our man."

From somewhere in the crowd a boy darted to the front, turned his back on Dethick and dropped his breeches. The sight of the small, exposed buttocks raised a roar of approval as the child jigged up and down for several seconds. Delighted by the laughter the child danced back and forth, then without warning he stiffened and fell. Little arms outstretched he embraced the earth impaled by an arrow through his heart.

Stunned into silence heads craned to see where the arrow came from. Will stepped forward from amongst the crowd. His look of outrage mirrored those who looked on.

"You young whelp. Why did you do that?"

The halberdier from Dethick's escort calmly lifted his cross-bow again. "He disrespects the king," he called back. Someone shouted "*treachery*" and bedlam broke out. Thom reached the boy first and fell on his knees by the slight body. Behind him even the herald was taken aback by the unexpected murder. He clutched Robert's arm in an effort to hold him and explain but his words were an incoherent babble amongst the shouts of outrage.

Between them, Thom and William freed the lifeless child and Thom hugging him close to his chest, carried the boy away. His look was tender as if perhaps he carried Martha. The crowd parted to let him pass and closed again in a solid rank of hostility.

"Don't blame the soldier, Master Kett," Dethick whined. "His loyalty to the Crown made him hasty. It was a stupid mistake."

Robert's reply sounded remote as though he was alone and talked to himself.

"These good people look to me and I'm responsible for them. Perchance the child's death is a sign and I should accept Warwick's promise of a pardon so there should be no more deaths. They trust me. But what have I done for them? Taken them away from their homes and all which is dear to them. I must put things right and at once."

His jacket over his arm he turned to his brother. Subdued and anxious the crowd looked on.

"You and Thom must look after things for me until I come back."

"I don't understand, brother. Where are you going?" William asked with concern.

Robert ignored the question and looked to the herald.

"Where will I find the Earl of Warwick? I must speak with him immediately under a flag of truce. I need to end the rebellion."

Delighted, Dethick looked smug.

"This is excellent news. My lord waits at St Stephen's. I shall ride ahead of you and tell him of your intent."

With a wave to his escort to follow, Dethick mounted his horse and cantered along the path to the city. Unsure what was happening, the rebels stood back to let him pass. As Robert stepped out to follow, William gripped his arm.

"Are you sure what you do is right? You gave your solemn word to our neighbours, how will they feel when they learn of your change of heart. Can we trust our enemy? I doubt it. I beg you. At least speak to them before you leave. And what about Thom, he buries a child."

"There is no time to delay. You tell Thom when he returns."

"No, brother, I have a better idea," William said, grim faced. "Let us speak to those who trusted you. See how they feel about a pardon. Perhaps they think as I do that we are being duped by Dethick, on the orders of Warwick?"

Before Robert could speak, William beckoned the rebels. Theirs were eager faces bewildered by the turn of events.

"Look in their eyes, what do you see, brother?" William murmured.

Shame flushed Robert's gaunt, weathered face. He saw trust and belief in the soul of every rebel who pressed closer to him. How could he think of giving in to Warwick? He chided himself for his muddled brain. Perhaps the death of the boy caused his doubts, that and the toll of the past weeks. He felt so fatigued and it was difficult for rational thought. Somewhere above him he heard his brother's voice. It interrupted his thoughts and he saw William on the steps ready to address the crowd.

"My friends let us have a show of hands and call Aye, if we still trust our leader. Those in favour of giving up must step forward and be counted."

There were no voices of dissent. To shouts of "we are with you and God bless our leader, Master Kett," a chant began, *Land and liberty, land and liberty.* The sound grew from a murmur to a huge roar like the sea when it's whipped by a wind so powerful it causes cliffs to part and tumble into the foam.

"Now do you believe?" William whispered as Robert dashed his eyes with his sleeve.

– 30 –

Even though the shadow of the closed gate partially obscured Warwick's face, those close couldn't miss his irritated expression. The herald was the cause of his displeasure and Dethick's constant shuffle made clear his own discomfort.

"I can't understand what delays Kett, my lord. He said he would follow me."

"And when would that be, eh? Did he mean tomorrow or in a week, perhaps? I warn you, Dethick, my patience is about to desert me."

Northampton spurred his horse and scratched his beard in thought. A young officer on horseback attempted to calm his impatient mount. Northampton gave Captain Bury an unpleasant look. It didn't go unnoticed the youthful captain seemed greatly in favour with Warwick. A cock-sure little upstart, in Northampton's estimation, he'd make sure to keep a careful eye on him.

"Perhaps I should ride to the Heights and drag the man out," he said finally. "We shall be stood here until sundown it seems for the want of a common rebel."

"That won't be necessary, I will send Captain Bury, I'm in no mind to wait any longer," Warwick said, a scowl distorting his angular face.

"So, my lord, do we have a plan?"

"No, Northampton, *we* don't. I however, do. You, Dethick, get out of my sight. Your mumblings about a truce seem to have been nothing but a waste of time."

The herald wrung his hands and rolled his eyes skywards.

"I'm so sorry, my lord. Kett assured me of his intention. It seems I was wrong."

"If you give me any more cause to think you lie, you can save your apologies for the hangman's rope," Warwick said irritably. "We delay no longer. Northampton, prepare the troops to breach the gate. I intend we take Norwich now."

No sooner had he spoken than the order was given. Pounded by shot, St. Stephen's gate fell in a shower of broken wood. The noise and vibration echoed across the city.

"We must move swiftly," Warwick urged as his horse trotted over the debris. "We'll have stirred up the rebel camp. Until they get organised they'll be as useless as a wet nurse without a babe on her tit. We must make the most of it. Captain Bury, take some men and deal with the camp. Word has it they hold prisoners. I want them freed. Tell them to join us in the city. Northampton, you make your way round and demand an entrance to all the gates. We need them open for the artillery. I don't need to tell you what to do should you meet resistance. I shall be at the Guild Hall."

He enjoyed seeing Northampton still smarting from remarks made about his failed attack on Norwich. Through gritted teeth, Northampton inclined his head. His thoughts were written across his face for all to see. The impudence of the man, speaking to him as if he were an imbecile, hadn't he fought in as many wars as Warwick? Of course he knew what to do. He fingered his sword with a thin smile and barked his instructions to his troop.

Fearful of punishment, Dethwick waited until the men began to move and then slipped away. In undignified haste he scuttled along Tombland and took refuge in the Deputy Mayor's house. No one saw him leave and after a liberal amount of the mayor's mead, he didn't care if they had.

Alarm sent people in all directions. When the soldiers marched into the city centre, peasants and nobles alike watched and wondered. Those who were loyal to the king and military waved and smiled. Supporters of the rebels hurried home and locked their doors.

Accompanied by his escort Warwick slowed his horse, turned a corner on the north side of the Market Place and trotted up Gaol Hill. He paused in front of the pillory. It was occupied by a skeletal man dressed in a ragged assortment of clothes. His grizzled head lolled against the wood, the weight of him slumped between limp wrists. At his feet remnants of rotten vegetables gave off the smell of sour curd. Two geese poked their bills through it and turned away from the slime-ridden remains. They were quickly replaced by an emaciated hound. Mange robbed it of most of its fur where scarlet skin and sores now festered. Head down and wary-eyed, it gulped down most of the waste then urinated against the wood frame before it wandered off.

With a nod at the imprisoned wretch, Warwick called to an officer behind him. "See if he still lives. If he does, kill him. We shall have need of the pillory to set an example. The rebels will soon see the King's men are resolved to be rid of them and they'll be begging for death when they know what's in store for them. Perhaps we need more pillories and a gibbet post too. When you've finished here, find a carpenter to see to it."

His brief laugh chilled all who heard it. Dismounting beside the wooden tower one end of the Guild Hall, Warwick waited. Captain Bury approached at some speed from the direction of St. Stephens. His dappled grey mare slathered at the bit as she crossed the remaining yards barely stopping before Bury sprang from her back.

"Have you good news, Captain, that bids you ride at such a fast rate? I hope it is to tell me you've released all the prisoners," Warwick said, unfastening his helmet.

The Captain's face was animated.

"Indeed, it's good news my lord and there's more. Master Woodhouse, Master Chase, York Herald and Codde the mayor are among those we have set free along with several city notables. They make their way here on foot to join us. There was such confusion when the rebels heard the gate fall, they ran like startled mice and no one had time to notice us."

"Well done, you accomplish much, Captain. It's a comfort to have you close."

Both the Captain's smile and demeanour were modest as he inclined his head to Warwick.

"Thank you, my lord."

"There is one thing. I still see nothing of the artillery," Warwick said as he dismounted.

"They are delayed, my lord, due to the foul conditions of the last two days. The cannon became bogged down. They have been waiting for the road to dry, but I've had word they are in sight of the city."

"Then I suppose we must wait," Warwick said with an irritated sigh. "Walk with me. I'm in need of refreshment." He led the way through the flint-knapped arch into the Guild Hall. "You said there was more news. What might that be?"

"On our way back we came across some rebels. They made their way from a tavern, and they weren't expecting us."

Warwick's idle gaze dropped slowly from the open timber roof above his head.

"Where are they now?"

"I have them guarded by some of my men on the other side of the Market Place."

"How many are they, Captain?"

"About fifty, I'd say, my lord."

Warwick picked an imagined speck of dirt from the back of his white kid glove.

"Hang them," he said.

Erected in haste close to the Guild Hall, the position of the gallows was important. Seated by the window in the Council rooms on the first floor, Warwick watched the spectacle. Beside him a cask of ale and a platter of rare beef kept him fed.

The hangman was busy. Barely had one body been dragged away before the hemp noose was occupied again. One after another the rebels were summarily executed. So impromptu was the event blindfolds were forgotten and the handcart slow to arrive to take the corpses away.

Hidden from view on the steps of a tannery in the shadow of the Castle, Thom and Will witnessed the hangings in disbelief. Sent by Robert to spy on the enemy they'd crept unnoticed into the city. It was the excited shouts of the crowd which drew them toward the scene. Then they saw the reason for the enthusiasm and in silence they watched the bodies jig like marionettes. Will craned his neck, his voice hoarse as he said.

"I don't see a priest. Can you see a priest? I know some of them. They're God- fearing men. No one should die without a holy man."

Thom swallowed hard as he struggled with a mixture of horror and rage.

"I doubt they had time for a prayer, so much for a promise of peace and the king's pardon."

"If you're seen up here you'll be next," an unfamiliar voice said. "Didn't you hear the proclamation? All who are caught out of doors will swing with them. Best you be gone from here. The king's my man, but I don't care to wait around."

An aged leather-worker stood at the foot of the steps. Remnants of his hair were bleached yellow, his hands and forearms stained walnut and the skin of his pouched face drawn in all directions by the acidic nature of his trade.

"Our thanks to you, old man, we were just leaving," Thom said, nudging Will who still stared mesmerised by the ghoulish sight.

"Kett's men by the looks of you," the fellow said. The blue eyes watching them were astute and the old man's gape empty of teeth when he grinned. "Don't worry, I shan't say anything."

When he'd limped his way down the track, Thom and Will slipped out of the city and hurried back to the camp.

With quiet authority, Robert and William rose from their seats under the awning. Their taut faces and grim expressions told of their reaction to Thom and Will's account of the hangings.

"Did Warwick give cause for such a swift decision?" Robert asked.

Will shook his head. "We saw none."

"They should have at least been heard, given a chance of a fair trial," William said his eyes dark with sorrow. "All has not gone well here either. The prisoners have been freed. Warwick's men caught everyone by surprise. Our guards were easily overcome and in the confusion, we lost our advantage."

Thom stared beyond the spire of the cathedral to the green meadows behind it. Hugged by skinny-trunked trees with puffs of dark foliage, a roll on the land made it dip and rise again. He tried to remember how long it was since they'd marched from Wymondham, but it blurred. The only clear thing in his mind was an image of his Martha and the feel of a hard knot in his throat when he thought of her.

"Are you with us, Thom?" Robert said gently.

Thom turned his bleak gaze away from the view. "Aye that I am, Master Kett."

"So Warwick hung our men without reason, then we are decided," Robert said, picking up his musket. "We shall tell the squadron leaders to make ready. It's time we took Norwich back, we have deaths to avenge."

William gave a wry smile. "Fie, Robert, I never thought I would hear my gentle brother speak of vengeance. This was to be a quiet rebellion, was it not?"

"Things change."

They embraced briefly and Robert intoned a short prayer asking his Maker to grant them success. Dismayed by the news of the hangings, both brothers were in pensive mood as they left camp to join the rebels who gathered to await their orders.

Assembled on the river bank and unsure of their instructions, the rebels moved uneasily. At the sight of the Kett brothers they were at once attentive, but before Robert had time to address them the sound of shot carried to them from somewhere above. As puffs of smoke drifted into the ether there were looks of alarm on the rebel's faces.

"What the devil..." William had no time to say more when Thom and Will appeared from the far side of the camp. There was no fear in their expressions only looks of elation as they raced towards them.

Thom reached them first almost too excited to speak.

"We have ordnance, Warwick's artillery is ours. It seems the driver's of the gun-carriages lost their way and walked straight into some of our men. They took the east road instead of the west. Will, you saw it all, tell Master Kett of our good fortune."

Robert's face of late so ridged with worry eased into a broad smile.

"By God, you bring good news. Tell us Will, how did it come about?"

The big man's eyes gleamed with pleasure.

"It is like Tom said. The fools took the wrong road and whilst the army in the city wait for arms, we have it all. They never even struggled, just held up their hands and hardly a shot fired. Didn't speak our language neither."

"So what have we captured?" William asked equally delighted.

"Several cannon, two wagons of musket, flint, shot and gunpowder. We can do with every bit of it," Thom replied.

"I thank our Lord for answering my prayers," Robert murmured.

A buzz of voices and smiles from the rebels told they too had something to be joyful about at last. But their zeal was short-lived. The sudden clatter of firearms from the direction of the city and a pall of smoke floating through the sunlight on the rooftops was a sharp reminder there was a battle to be won.

"Every man into the city any way you can. Scale the walls or find an open gate, take care and may the good Lord protect you," Robert shouted.

"It seems they are impatient," William said he and Robert turned their horses towards St. Benedict's Gate. No sooner were they in the city when they were met by foot soldiers. They rode hard into the fighting whilst with weapons drawn, Thom and the rebels spread out behind them.

As the Ketts approached the Maddermarket the sight froze them in their saddles. The killing was frenzied, ruthless and unstoppable. His face aghast at the scene, Robert gripped his reins with hands that trembled.

"By God, I never thought I would be witness to this."

"Will, Philip and Elias left before us, they must be here somewhere," Thom muttered, his eyes desperate to find them in the chaos. He'd lost Martha and John, surely not the others so soon.

The men battled the length of the streets, but rebel and soldier alike were hampered by the bodies of the dead and wounded. Awash in their own blood their groans and screams echoed against the flint angles and hollow walls. The smell of flesh and the buzz of flies were a dreadful combination which filled their ears and throats.

They all felt the ground vibrate behind them followed by the sound of galloping hooves. Thom turned to look over his shoulder in time to see four horsemen approaching wearing the king's uniform. Before he could use his sword he was knocked to the ground as they thundered past.

Winded, he struggled to roll out of the way as he heard the horse's returning. From his position he only saw the bellies of the beasts. When he could see again the light returned and the clashing of metal on metal finally stopped he could hear Robert's voice somewhere close.

"We are taken, Thom. It's up to you now. For God and Norfolk," he urged.

The sound of a hand striking flesh was harsh and unforgiving. Then unfamiliar voices babbled and mixed with loud curses made understanding impossible. Thom raised himself on his elbows and looked for a weapon, but his sword and pike were nowhere to be seen. Mortified he cursed and dashed away the sweat which blurred his vision. When he could see again, the Kett brothers were shackled a short distance away as the soldiers prepared to lead them behind their horses.

Bruises already darkened Robert's face and his lower lip detached from his chin rested in a puddle of gore. More blood splashed on his chest and stained the skin of his hands. Sure they were mortal wounds Thom felt terrible fear. His eyes turned to William. When he saw his left arm dangled without purpose he realised the blood was his and it was Robert who tried to staunch the blood from a huge gash to his brother's shoulder.

The ferocity of a sword strike cut through both jacket and shirt in one. Even from a distance, Thom could see the glossy gleam of William's collarbone exposed without flesh or muscle to support it.

As Thom steadied himself his hand touched something cold. When he looked he saw it rested on the alabaster face of a lad. His nut-brown eyes were fixed on the heavens, an empty stare which reminded Thom of the ox he'd slaughtered months ago. Unable to control a shudder he quickly closed the boy's eyelids. The hair on the youthful brow was stiffened with dark red clots from a ferocious wound to his skull which had exposed shards of white bone and fragments of brain.

In front of him more rebels and halberdiers fought one another. Yells, shrieks and curses mingled with the noise of steel on steel and the bloody encounter felled more than were left standing. When Thom finally managed to see across the market place, Robert and William were gone.

He retrieved his longbow and a lance which lay beside the dead boy and managed to crawl into a recess in a wall. There was little room and he was forced to crouch. The space smelt of urine and the noxious odours of battle, but his legs trembled too much to carry him far. Through his thin shirt the edges of jagged flint cut into his shoulders. It was bearable pain compared to the grief he felt for the Ketts. He'd come to look on them as brothers and now they were lost to him. Misery overwhelmed him and he felt no shame for the tears he shed.

When he finally felt calm and the street was quiet, by a cautious, roundabout route he made his way back to the King's Camp on foot. He met others also in retreat and a pathetic band they made as they supported the walking wounded dragging themselves up the slope to the camp.

Anxious hours passed as Thom kept a look-out for Will. Weak from lack of food and fatigue he almost wept again when he saw him walk towards him.

"You took your time," he said in an attempt to lighten the mood but neither could respond with more than a look of relief and a hasty hug. "What of Philip. Is he safe?"

Will shrugged. "Alive and fighting like a lunatic with blade and musket when I last saw him. I thought he'd be back by now." He frowned and looked around. "Are you on your own? Where are the Masters Kett?"

Sombre-faced, he listened carefully as Thom recounted the story of the brothers' capture. Then he shook his shaggy head and muttered under his breath. "It's bad, God help them."

Together they went to the awning where many of the unhurt, but frightened rebels waited unsure of what to do next. The Kett's chairs stood empty and askew just as they'd left them that morning. Not yet willing to announce they were taken prisoner, Thom spoke to the men.

"We are safe here," he assured. "Lookouts will watch through the night. Not one soldier will take a step on the camp without being seen. There is much to be done before you can rest. Tomorrow will come soon enough."

Glad to be given their orders, the rebels dispersed. Below them the city lay quiet at last and the city gates closed and bolted. In the camp food was made, the wounded tended to and those who had carried back some of the dead saw them buried in the evening light in a quiet corner of the Heights.

Somehow the bad news got out but few chose to speak openly of Robert and William. Already low, morale plummeted as the word passed from one to another. Where would new vigour and fresh hope come from? It was a question nobody dared ask.

The day's end brought with it a gentle wind which rustled the leaves with a comfortable sound. It tugged at the material draped from the branches and sent the pennants hanging from the long pikes into a wild dance. As a sickle moon rose above the horizon, Thom stretched his legs and shifted in his chair. He'd no heart to move and he knew Will felt the same. Not only had they lost Robert and William, but again it appeared they'd lost control of the city.

Will fiddled with a flap of skin lifted from the back of his hand by the tip of a soldier's knife. The wound didn't go deep and a crust edged the neat parting of the flesh. Will poked at it thoughtfully with his thick finger.

"Will, for God's sake, will you bind the damn thing up."

"I'm sorry," Will said. "My mind wanders."

Immediately ashamed of his short temper, Thom apologised. "No, 'tis I who am sorry," he said.

"So, have you decided what we do?"

Thom nodded. "We have little choice. Tomorrow at first light we retake the city and it is the bridges which we must make for. We divide the men into two columns. You will lead an attack on Bishop's Gate, I will go to Connisford. It is our only hope of recapturing Norwich unless you have a better plan?"

"Shouldn't you be asking me too?"

Philip lent heavily on the side-prop which supported the awning. His smile parted the grime and sweat which coated his face and all but obscured his eyes. When he moved he grimaced. Thom saw his friend held his right arm close to his chest supported by his free hand under the elbow.

"Philip it's good to see you, but your arm troubles you. Let me see it."

"It's a trifle, a mere scratch," Philip said.

He accepted help to a chair without protest. Anxious to do something, Will hovered.

"I'll fetch liniment," he offered.

Thom unwound the bloody rag wrapped roughly over the wound. As it fell away he caught his breath as a whiff of putrefaction invaded his nostrils.

"When did this happen?"

"This morning when we took Warwick's ordnance off him, I felt the sting but there was no time to trouble about it."

"It's a musket ball by the looks of it." Thom said when he peered into the depths. He held the torch closer but the flame refused to be still. "I need Will," he muttered.

A look of alarm crossed Philip's face.

"What are you going to do?"

"Get the thing out and clean up the wound. We need every man we have and you'll do no more fighting until it's treated or would you rather lose your arm?"

Philip fidgeted in the chair. When he saw Thom pass the blade of his knife through the torch flame his pale face blanched to stricken white.

Will appeared back under the awning with a flask, "A woman gave me one of her herbal concoctions. Comfrey, it heals everything so she said."

Thom waved it toward the table. "I could do with your help, but first find the biggest beaker of mead you can. Our friend here will need to drink plenty and then a strong pair of arms round his chest should do it."

When the first cut of the knife slowly slit the flesh and bit down on the bone, Philip fainted.

25th August 1549

Diminished by Warwick's haughty demeanour, the shop-keeper was ill at ease. He twisted his hands into uncomfortable patterns as Warwick continued to question him.

"State your business in the city."

"I'm a master carpenter, my lord. It's a small business, and I hardly make a living," the man whined. "A few looms for the weavers, that's all."

"So you say you overheard the rebel's conversation and you're sure they said Connisford and Bishop's Gate?"

Wizened and shabby, the fellow nodded. "Aye, my lord, clear as a lark it was. They stood at the end of one of the paths leading to the camp and spoke of their orders. I hid behind a tree and didn't move 'til they'd gone. They never caught a glimpse of me and I swear I heard every word."

Warwick called one of the knight's forward.

"Find him a shilling for his trouble," he said. Seeing a smile replace the man's quivering lip, he turned to reprove him. "If I find you have lied be sure your liver will feed my dogs before the day is out. Do you understand?"

The man nodded, pocketed the proffered coin and backed to the door. Warwick waved him away with an impatient flick of his fingers. Grateful to be dismissed the man hastily returned his hat to his head and left the room.

For several minutes there was quiet. Warwick paced by the window his expression one of deep thought. His mind sifted through the new information and decisions which must be made. Among the assembled knights and high-ranking soldiers, one man was conspicuous for his lack of uniform. Like the others, Mayor Codde dared not speak.

His internment at the Kings Camp had been beneficial for him. Loss of weight gave his face more character and his girth more structure. The marks on his wrists had all but faded, but he touched them from time to time just the same.

From the Guild Hall casements the most striking view was of the gallows. Caught by an early morning ruffle of wind the soft sway of the noose looked innocent. Warwick's eyes followed its movement. It amused him to see the ladder broken in two and abandoned at the foot of the trestle. He couldn't recall the last time he ordered so many to their death at one go.

"So they are to meet us both at Bishop's Gate and Connisford, they must still have considerable numbers if that's their intention. Is that a cause for us to worry, I wonder? What say you, Captain Bury?" he said, contemplating the citizens scuttling across the cobbles.

"On the contrary, sire. I have a company at both positions, any advance will be well resisted," the Captain replied, in a confident voice.

"Good, good," Warwick murmured.

He turned to the room and his eyes wandered over the faces of those he'd summoned at dawn. When they rested on the uneasy countenance of the mayor they grew wide with surprise.

"Mayor Codde, I see you are back with us," he said. "How was your stay with the rebels?"

Codde flinched at the weight of sarcasm in Warwick's voice. He wasn't sure if he was grateful for his recent subsistence diet particularly when his clothes hung from his frame like a limp flag. His blush conveyed his embarrassment at being picked out.

"Well enough thank you, my lord," he replied in a reluctant voice. "I believe it is you I must thank for my release."

Warwick chose to ignore Codde's mumbled gratitude instead turning to address Captain Bury. "I have in my mind the idea that we should destroy all the city bridges. I believe there are four. That way the insurgents will have a great deal of trouble gaining entry. It's no easy job swimming, weighted down with arms."

At once Codde was agitated and waved an anxious hand.

"My lord, a word, if you please," he said.

Warwick fixed him with an impatient glare and sighed loudly.

"Well, Codde, what is it?"

"I must ask that you do no such thing. With respect may I point out there was a great deal of damage when the Marquis of Northampton marched his army here. The city was sacked and then fired. If we lose our bridges too, who will finance all the repairs? It is sad to see our fine city so ravaged. I would urge you to reconsider."

The tenseness in the air was palpable. Few dared to question any of Warwick's ideas but there was so much passion in Codde's voice the others altered their opinion of him. Amazed at himself for his bravado, Codde saw the respect he'd gained and beamed with pleasure. Not so, Warwick. His chainmail gloves banged down on the arm of his chair.

"Mayor, in view of your recent captivity at the hands of the rebels, I shall overlook what I perceive to be a degree of rudeness on your part. Lord Seymour, the Duke of Somerset expects a victory. Why else would he have sent me here? And I'm not a man easily beaten. Unlike the good Northampton, I shall not turn tail and run. I had hoped that with the Masters Kett safely on their way to the Tower to stand trial, the rebels would surrender. It seems they have not learned their lesson, but by God they will.

However, I'm not an unreasonable man. Captain Bury, destroy the bridge at Whitefriars, in the meantime, I shall reconsider the other three. Does that suit you, Codde?"

The others in the room hid their smiles behind their hands when they saw Codde all but danced on the spot. "I don't know how to show you my gratitude, my lord," he bumbled.

"Then don't try," Warwick said, threading his gloves carefully onto his hands. "I shall not depart from Norwich until I deliver this city to the crown or die in the process. Codde, if you wish to thank me speak to the citizens and make them swear on the cross they will drive out every one of Kett's followers they find. Come, Bury, you and I have business to attend to. The little matter of a bridge, remember."

As they rode side by side towards the Maddermarket, the Captain said. "Forgive me, sir, but..."

Warwick groaned. "Not you too, that obsequious little mayor is enough for one day. Go on, tell me what troubles you."

" I thought you should know, we lost many in the fighting over the last two days. I believe some three hundred died. Many more were wounded. If we continue to lose men at this rate we shall struggle to continue if we're not careful."

Warwick reined in his horse and faced his Captain.

"Haven't you forgotten something? Tomorrow sees the arrival of our foreign reinforcements, the Landsknechts are already close. Most of them have travelled from Germany, but I'm told to expect some Spaniards too. Over a thousand well trained battle hungry mercenaries. Should we depart when victory is close?" he said.

With a fierce jab of his spurs, man and horse charged forward and left Captain Bury well behind. When he caught up, Warwick gave him a sly look and they both grinned.

"If this turns out as well as I anticipate, there will be honours for both of us, *my Lord* Bury," Warwick said between snorts of laughter.

Thom's idea of a double attack instead became a dreadful affray. He sat with his hands held to his brow, his face blackened by smoke, his eyes red-rimmed and sore. As he listened to Will's story when he attempted to take Bishop's Gate, he found his thoughts were on Robert Kett. What would *he* have done, he asked himself. Will's angry voice droned in the background until Thom wanted to stuff his fingers in his ears.

"Houses burn and the merchant halls are in ruin," said Will, still defensive.

"It doesn't matter, Will. We both failed."

Philip, his arm still too cumbersome to lift his sword sat looking at both despondent faces.

"All is not lost. You managed to set Connisford on fire Thom, and no men were hurt. We are still worthy to hold up our heads and Master Kett would be proud. I just wish I'd been there with you."

"Thom, we stand together, that's all that matters," said Will.

He pushed his wild hair from his face and frowned at the feel of blood and dirt which tangled in it.

"A miserable attempt to retake Norwich, if you ask me but thanks for the kind words," Thom replied wryly.

Somewhere above them on the heath birds warbled their last songs of the day. Closer, smells of roasted meat drifted toward the awning. A sign that the year was about to slide into autumn, infant acorns hung close to the leafy branches of the oaks and rowan berries darkened into vermillion clusters.

Torched by Warwick's men earlier, Whitefriar's Bridge still smouldered and smoke was clearly visible to the east of the city. Their thoughts distracted, all three men lapsed into an uneasy silence. No one noticed a lookout until a cough disturbed the reverie. Philip beckoned him to come closer.

"Have you news for us?"

The man nodded and pointed his longbow down to the city walls by St. Stephens.

"We've just seen a new company arrive. They were met at the gate by Warwick's men. The column is long and they carry arms. Foreigners they are by the look of their uniforms, but it's difficult to tell from a distance. They're like nothing we've seen before."

"Thank you, you've done well. Go back and keep watch. Report to us if you see any more activity," Thom said. "There's no telling what schemes Warwick has afoot so keep your voices low."

As he watched the man depart despair overwhelmed Thom. He was tired of the campaign and was concerned for the Kett brothers. This wasn't how it was meant to be and he wanted none of it. His mind looked to the future, but pain gripped him at the thought that Martha was no longer there to share it with him.

For the first time since the rising started he felt fearful of defeat. Yet Robert Kett had seen fit to leave him to see the fight through and he knew he couldn't fail him. Will and Philip remained silent, their expressions troubled by the uncertainty they saw on Thom's face.

A sudden thump on the table startled them both. Thom relaxed his fist as if he'd found new vigour from somewhere and straightened his back in the chair.

"You have a plan?" Philip said quietly.

"Are you going to share it with us?" Will prompted.

"We're with you whatever it is," said Philip.

Thom sensed their relief and a small smile slowly crossed his tired face.

"What would I do without you both, I wonder? Yes, I've decided. Warwick will never come here to fight us. Only a fool would attempt such a move given our position. His men would flounder if they climbed such a steep hillside and we'd pick them off like the weevils they are. So my friends, we will take the fight to him. Tomorrow before daybreak, we shall abandon the Kings Camp and move to Dussindale."

"Is it wise to risk a battle on open ground?" Philip said slowly." Some might think it folly when we are safe here."

"We are not safe, we're besieged and I fear we shall never drive Warwick out of the city," Thom said firmly. "Trust me. It's the right thing to do."

"Its madness if you ask me," Will grunted, his dismay obvious.

"Then perhaps it's as well, I didn't."

Thom's sharp reply silenced them both and he continued.

"Have every man who can hold a weapon ready as soon as there is light in the sky. Now, we eat, shall we see whether there is food left for us?"

Somewhere in the city a trumpet played a reveille. The strident notes carried over the treetops into the vales and up into the clear air above the camp. It was a confident sound and stopped them in their tracks.

– 33 –

26th August 1549

Still cloaked by a seasonal mist, the meadows of Dussindale just before dawn offered no more than the peace of undisturbed pasture. The sporadic bleat of a sheep and the soft rustle of another tawny leaf as it drifted down from the birch trees was all that could be heard.

At first it was difficult to place the sound. Windmill sails spun by the wind perhaps or the noisy hum of wild bees about to swarm. It came from the east as did the first rays of a sun about to rise on the horizon. Norfolk's landscape occasionally lent itself to undulate in gentle slopes that fall away to flat fields and Dussindale had such a lowland heath on its approaches.

Hidden by this, the rebels took time to appear from behind its gorse studded protection into the open. Then the reason for the odd noise was revealed for as the peasants poured down the valley and marched boldly onto the turf, they sang in rich bass and baritone together.

'The country gnoffes,
Hob, Dick and Rick
With clubs and clouted shoon,
Shall fill the vale, Of Dussindale.
With slaughtered bodies soon...'

Bent and twisted like an old watercourse long since dry, the column was haphazard. Led by Thom, Will and Philip all on horseback, those mounted followed first. Behind them led by Elias, came the foot-rebels carrying as many weapons as they could hold whilst females, children and horse drawn carts made up the last segment of the peasant army. They positioned themselves several ranks deep. Voices were loud and talk boisterous as they pushed forward. Thom's raised arm halted them and the work began to fortify their position.

"You all know what you must do. Time is short. Squadron leaders, take charge and God bless every man," he called.

The air snatched his words and tossed them to float and fall wherever they would. Grass, crushed underfoot, gave off a rich smell as the men set to work. Anything thought useful had been taken from the King's Camp before they set fire to it and whatever could be found was ripped up from the land. Some plucked gorse and branch and laid one on another, others fashioned traps in the earth deep enough to hold a man and the strongest dragged the carts together to make a barricade. Those skilled with short daggers cut down thorn wood and made stakes for cavalry pits. Orders were given by the squadron leaders and the birds who lived in the hedgerows took flight as the sound of rough voices disturbed their dawn rising.

Women and children were sent to hide in the bracken and the last of them had just vanished under its substantial fronds when the sound of harness echoed in the air. Faint at first it grew in intensity as Warwick's army appeared. Realising there was no time to waste, he had moved fast and it was the mail-armour clad mercenaries mounted on their chargers who led a dark centipede of soldiers in quick marching formation.

"Mother of God," Will said, his words a hiss in Thom's ear. "Methinks we will do well to save our skins."

Philip held his sword with both hands. As they slid over the haft their tremor was obvious. Thom steadied them with his own hand.

"Have courage both of you, we must stand fast, we will prevail," he said softly, not looking at either of them when he spoke. How he wished he felt as confident as he sounded.

"No, Thom, this is fool-hardy. We should have stayed at the camp, we were strong there," Philip declared.

Behind them the rebel's voices swelled from a murmuring to an agitated rumble as they watched the king's men assemble in ranks which defied anyone who tried to count them. Thom hesitated. He knew he'd made a mistake, thrown common sense to the wind and used a plan which without skill behind it was fated to be a disaster. His frown deepened but he breathed steadily, his heart refusing to accept the fear which threatened.

Dear Lord, from henceforth, grant us victory and bless the king's majesty. His prayer wavered.

With solemn attention to duty the Royal Standard bearer broke from the ranks and on his sturdy skewbald horse slowly advanced towards them to offer one last pardon. After a dozen paces across the grass Warwick's cavalry moved forward. The sun ignited the shields into fiery silver and trapped by indecision, Thom watched them, transfixed by the spectacle in front of him. He barely felt Will's tight grip on his arm or heard Philip implore him to give his orders. Instead his only desire was to stop the fierce drum which beat in his ears and run far away from the scene in front of him.

Was it a rebel's impatience or nerves, no one would ever know, but the explosive puff of a musket shot somewhere behind him penetrated his inertia. Now it was too late, fight they must.

For a brief moment the standard bearer remained upright in the saddle. Then as dignified in death as he was in life, he slowly slipped sideways and fell onto the turf. It seemed no other signal was needed.

As Warwick's cavalry charged the ground shuddered as they broke the peasant lines. The rebels turned to flee, but were cut down as they ran.

Chapter 33

Massacred they fell one upon another, their bodies piling high. Shattered bodies rained like hail onto the gore soaked ground. Those who managed to escape the halberd or the shot felt the lance impale them to the stained earth.

Behind a row of wagons, Will and a few others held out until their shot was gone and their quivers empty of arrows. A halberd in his hand, Will cautiously raised his head above the side of the wagon, but as he did so a flash of light blinded him and the explosion from a cannon ball tossed his sturdy frame up into the air as if it were a slither of wood. Stunned he lay as if dead.

It was over. By the time the sun moved into the last quarter of the sky at day's end most of the rebels were killed and the rebellion crushed, just as Warwick had promised. He swung his sword over his head and signalled that victory was complete. Lifting his visor he breathed in the rancid air and a smile of triumph barely altered his hard features as his eyes scanned the fallen and noted the few who still stood.

Will's ravaged face was barely recognisable under the layers of blood, sweat and mud as he struggled to his feet. Seepage from a shoulder wound turned his vest crimson and more blood trickled slowly through his scalp. He recalled the stab of pain he felt when a knife glanced off his collarbone and slashed through the flesh. His attacker was too close for him to use his sword and they'd struggled hand to hand before Will's height and weight got the better of the halberdier.

The blow to his head came later and he touched the wound with careful fingers, it seemed little more than damage to the flesh. Staring at the carnage around him in disbelief, he was sickened by the sight of two crows squabbling over a shred of skin and he flapped his arm at them. It was a weak gesture and the birds travelled no distance before they lurched back to the ground and waddled off like a pair of stout, black-clad monks.

"Lay down your arms and in the king's name, I will guarantee you are pardoned," Warwick shouted. He stood in his stirrups so they would all hear him, but he struggled to make his voice carry over the cries of injured horses. "See the beasts are dispatched quickly," he called to Captain Bury over his shoulder.

With no more than a sigh most of the tired rebels threw down their weapons. It was a measly pile of pitchforks, axes, longbows and the occasional sword or musket retrieved from dead soldiers in earlier skirmishes. One or two held tight to their bows, but nothing passed Warwick's steel gaze.

"Come now, I give you my personal assurance nothing will befall you. Lay down your arms, you are to be pardoned and have nothing to fear," he said with a glib smile.

Will tossed his backsword to join the heap. He still grasped his longbow, but a passing soldier wrenched it from him and he saw it join the pile. Teeth gritted he took comfort from the feel of his knife tucked tight in the waistband of his breeches.

Weakened by loss of blood he swayed on his feet. It was an effort to turn his head, but he needed to know how many of his friends still lived. He'd seen Elias and the Mayhew brothers cut down almost at the start, but there were others still unaccounted for. He blinked rapidly as he tried to clear his hazy vision, but the ground refused to stay still.

He had no idea where Thom and Philip were or even if they still lived. When he managed to cast his eyes around him he saw neither of them nor Edmund. Instead, soldiers picked their way round and across bodies filling their leather pouches with booty. When he heard the women screaming, he knew they had found them too.

"You," Captain Bury said, his boot in Will's back. "You've surrendered, remember, stir yourself and join the others."

Another time, Will's reaction would have been his fists when he felt the nudge. Instead exhausted he shambled forward obediently. Had he been shorter it would have been difficult to separate him from those already lined up. Shoulders slumped and heads low, they stood in silence one behind the other. Captain Bury and his men rounded up the last of their comrades and sent them forward. Nobody paid attention to the fearful wounds some had, it was enough if they could place one foot before the other. The man in front of Will turned his head and said to him.

"So what happens now? What will they do with us?"

Each time his lips moved saliva and blood welled through the gaps where his teeth had once been and dripped from his chin. Each time he scrubbed it away with filthy fingers.

Will looked in Warwick's direction and said.

"He says we are to be pardoned." He saw a faint look of hope cross the others' grimy face, shrugged and looked away. He too wanted to think the pardon offered would be honoured, but knew these were men whose kindness came in the shape of the hangman's rope.

Thom and Philip's fate concerned him more. With no sign of them in the ranks of those who'd surrendered he could only assume they lay amongst the dead. It was a dreadful thought. His shoulder throbbed and left him unable to concentrate. He turned for one last look as they were marched towards Magdalen Gates and the road into Norwich.

At first glance it looked as if a dark mist had stretched across the meadow until he realised it was swarms of flies which buzzed in manic circles a few inches above the feast of flesh.

– 34 –

They'd ridden hard north until the sound of ordnance faded and Norwich lay a good distance behind them. Unlike Philip, Thom was a poor rider, but crouched over the horse's neck he rode for his life. His belief he would die before the rebellion ended had became stronger with the passage of days. With Martha gone it was unimportant to him. Destiny had spoken. He would just prefer it was in a manner less inglorious than the fate which he would suffer on a ragged swathe of blood-stained grass.

With their eyes focussed on the road ahead neither Thom nor Philip spoke. When a lesser path was offered Philip chose it and Thom was happy to follow him. At times he glanced behind him in the hope Will too might have managed to escape. Each time he was disappointed for the road remained empty.

There had been no time for Thom to consider the morality of his flight. He'd never thought himself a coward, but he knew from the moment they left the Kings Camp his decision was flawed and he had led the men to their death. It was an onerous burden to him, but as he urged his mount on he decided escape was the only sensible thing he'd done that day.

When his horse encountered uneven ground the hard earth threw its gait out of kilter. Thom winced each time the lance wound to his thigh received such a jolt. Dried blood stiffened the leg of his breeches and it rubbed over the torn flesh. A smaller wound to his forearm pained him too, its throb a distraction.

There had been no time to enquire about Philip's well-being, but he judged by the dark stains on his companion's shirt and vest he was also injured. Thom gritted his teeth and urged his horse on. When it suddenly went lame, he all but fell off. Clutching on to its mane, he righted his seat with difficulty and allowed the horse to come to an uneven stop. Philip turned his horse and came back to him.

"My beast is lame, there's no time to waste you must go on without me," Thom said breathing hard from the wild gallop.

Through his mask of sweat and dirt Philip's grin belied the desperate situation they were in.

"No, my friend, we stick together. We'll outwit them yet and see them in Hades, have no doubt about that. You can ride behind me. Where are we, anyway?"

"This is not a place I know well, but I think we are close to Swannington. There should be a fork in the road just ahead," Thom said.

Just above the horizon a young moon bled a lemon glimmer onto its drape of shaded clouds. Soon darkness would rob them of any landmarks. Tired and hungry he knew neither of them would be fit to travel much further with only one horse between them. Philip voiced his concerns too. When they reached the fork he said.

"I think we should stop. What lies at Swannington?

"A cottage or two, perhaps somewhere to lay our heads if we're lucky," Thom said. "I told you I don't know these parts. What to do with the horse worries me more. He's of no use to me now."

"Turn him loose. We've no time to tarry here. Who knows who might see us? Let's just hope Swannington finds favour with our cause," Philip said with a wry smile.

They waited long enough to see the horse limp toward a copse of elm and stop to browse. Hopeful they would soon find shelter, Thom and Philip walked to spare their remaining mount. Its neck dark with sweat and flecked with spittle they knew it too was close to exhaustion.

The area had an air of unhurried ease typical of rural homesteads and no one passed them.

What was left of the daylight dwindled away and only the occasional glow from a reed lamp in a dwelling studded the darkness. Had the mare not strayed to the hedge they would have missed the shelter they sought. Philip stretched to look over the hawthorn and brambles.

"Look here. It's a barn of sorts. Methinks it will do us well and there's nothing close. We should be safe for a few hours. What think you?"

Thom joined him and nodded.

"My legs will take me no further." He clutched his jerkin closer and shivered. "The air turns cold. Tether the mare and we'll take shelter in there until we've rested."

They were grateful for the smallest beam from the moon to reveal their surroundings. Caution warned them to move with care as they pushed through a gap in the thorn and then with longbows ready they circled the immediate area around the building. As far as they could make out the barn squatted in a corner of a long meadow. There were gaps in the thatch and stones adrift from its walls and from its appearance it didn't look as if it were used often. Tilted towards it an elm's low branches swept one side at each gentle waft of air.

They had to stoop to gain entrance. Inside despite its outer neglect there were signs of its recent use. Bales of hay smelt fresh and when Thom ran his fingers through grain in one of the sacks it was still warm and moist. A hook and a fork propped in a corner looked freshly cleaned too. His instinct told him they should move on. Philip glanced across and looked puzzled.

"Thom, you frown. Will this not do?"

Chapter 34

"Well enough but something troubles me. Perhaps my mind is too fuddled. No matter, we'll be gone before anyone finds us here. I crave food but I need sleep even more," Thom said impatient now.

They shredded one of the bales and fashioned rough beds. Before they settled they did a check of their injuries. Neither had much but they satisfied themselves they were only flesh wounds. Philip insisted they should be cleaned. He found a grain scoop under sacking and went in search of water. What he brought back looked green and smelt foul, but it washed away crusted blood and they both admitted it soothed their torn flesh.

Neither of them heard her arrive. Small, scrawny and aged, she might not have been a threat to them had she not stood over them with a pitchfork. The prongs wavered, first over Thom and then close to Philip's head. Awake in an instant Thom spoke first whilst still half asleep, Philip could only give her a bleary stare.

"There is no need for you to be a feared, Mistress, we mean no harm," Thom said as he struggled upright.

"That's as maybe, but you are strangers just the same. What brings you here?" she asked the pitchfork still close.

"I'd be glad to explain if you could put down the fork. All we wanted was somewhere to lay our heads and a little food if you could spare it."

Thom's smile was meant to charm, but the countrywoman would have none of it.

"We have barely enough for a platter between ourselves and none to spare for the likes of you," she said.

Philip looked indignant despite his sleepy state.

"And what likes would those be, mistress? Our crusade is for a just cause and one which will put food back on your table and crops in your fields again."

The old woman showed no sign of pleasure at his words, but merely tightened her hold on the pitchfork and moved back to the doorway.

"So you *are* rebels, my husband said as much. Well, you've come to the wrong place. We support the king here and long may he reign. God bless him," she said.

"In that case when we've tidied your barn we shall be on our way," Thom said haste directing his movements as he gathered up the hay.

The pitchfork never wavered and Philip too sensing the urgency bent to pick up his pouch and longbow ready to leave. He tried to muffle the moan when he felt the pain sear deep in the tissue between his shoulder blades. When he straightened stiff muscles tore the wound again and he yelped.

"Can't you see he needs help, mistress and you look like a fair-minded person," Thom cajoled.

"I'm sorry 'tis too late for that. My husband rode to Norwich more than an hour ago. You should have tied your horse more securely then it wouldn't have wandered into our yard. That's what made my husband come looking. The king's men will arrive any time now."

Thom and Philip exchanged a glance and Thom lunged at the pitchfork. But the pain in his thigh slowed him and the old woman was light on her feet. Always eloquent in speech, Philip said.

"Surely a good woman like you would hold no grudge. After all we have done you no wrong other than rest in your barn. For the love of God, mistress, if you have any mercy in your soul, let us go."

She laughed then, but the sound was hollow and showed no compassion.

"Why would I do that when there might be a silver testoon come our way when the authorities arrive," she said. "So you can keep your charm for them."

When her words took the smiles from their faces, she hesitated, but then they saw resolve stiffen her back and give her new energy. From all she'd heard it was time the rebels left her city alone, what little was left of it. Some nights she'd hardly slept for the sound of cannon when the wind turned to the north. Philip fumbled in his pocket.

"I believe I may have a gold coin in here somewhere. We should be happy for you to have it for your trouble."

Avarice plundered her rheumy eyes and she shook her head.

"No, I'll not be bought by the likes of you. I told you the king is our man. Keep your money to yourself. We shall be glad to see an end to the troubles and good riddance to you all."

Feet braced she kept her position and stood defiant.

"These damn wounds, I have no strength. We must both take her," Thom murmured, but then they all heard hoof beats pound the ground and stop close by. When Captain Bury entered the barn, his amusement was obvious.

"By God, I do believe she's held them at bay with a pitchfork," he chortled. "You have a good woman here, Master Fox. She can join my army any time she wishes."

− 35 −

Hampton Court

First his hands spun the ornate globe on its ebony stand then he played with a priceless jade figurine on the desk. The king fidgeted and Seymour watched him with barely disguised impatience. When the boy stood over the chess set and wriggled the board so the pieces fell over, Seymour's hiss was audible. Not for the first time he wondered if his position as Lord Protector was worth the aggravation.

The king's eyes glittered with laughter. Hands on his slender hips his smile crinkled his fair skin and gathered his reddish freckles together.

"Uncle, why are you in such a bad humour today? You are no fun anymore. Come to the gardens with me and we shall race. I'll wager you will lose breath long before me."

"I don't doubt I shall, sire. Affairs of state give me cause to worry which may account for my mood. I had hoped to hear from the Earl of Warwick by now. It seems during the rout at Dussindale, two important rebels made their escape. He has strict orders to find them."

"And what will happen to them?" the king piped in a bored voice.

Seymour stared out of the window, eyes fixed on the distant gleam of the river.

"They have friends waiting for them in the Tower," he said. "There must be an example made."

He turned back to the room only to find he was talking to himself. The door was wide open and the king gone.

"That boy tests my patience," he muttered with a disconsolate frown as he closed the door.

His fingers loitered over the silver dish on his desk as he deliberated over which sweetmeat to pick. He bit into gingerbread, changed his mind and took a sugared almond instead. He spat out the nut when the sugar was gone and selected a preserved plum.

About to pick up another he heard footsteps in the corridor. He was at the door in three strides his cape whirling in a flurry of blue silk as he flung it open.

"Warwick," he bellowed. "Where in God's name have you been? I expected you hours ago. You have good news for me, I hope."

Warwick ran a weary hand over his brow and nodded. His hooded eyes seemed even more sunken in his gaunt face but triumph sparkled from their depths.

"My apologies, my Lord, I have only just heard from Captain Bury. He tells me he rides with all haste to bring you the two escaped rebels. Both the peasant Barwick and Philip de Montfort were found in a barn after a loyal citizen had cause for suspicion and informed Captain Bury."

"What excellent news, my dear Warwick. I knew when I chose you, you wouldn't let me down. Have a sweetmeat," Seymour said and pushed the dish across the desk.

So de Montfort lived, he thought with deep satisfaction. It would be a pleasure to meet him on such different terms. From the open window a raised voice projected its reedy volume into the room.

"Uncle, have you forgotten? I'm waiting."

The look of victory faded from Seymour's eyes and he uttered a sort of grunt. Sullen faced, he raised his eyebrows and sighed loudly.

"The boy simply doesn't understand. To him everything is a game. He expects me to run round the gardens with him whilst the gravest matters are dismissed with an airy sigh. I shall have to go, I suppose but such demands don't please me, Warwick, don't please me at all."

"I too have things to do so if you will excuse me, my lord, all I need is your orders regarding the prisoners," Warwick said his yawn concealed behind a gloved hand.

"Take them to the Tower, of course. Let them languish there for awhile and give some thought to the inconvenience they've caused. Then they will go on trial. It must seem to look as if we offer them a fair hearing. There'll be nothing of the sort, of course. In due course they will all hang for treason."

Seymour bit into a piece of candied pear and sucked it with relish. His satisfaction was obvious in his complacent expression, yet his eyes were never still. They flickered with a brittle intensity which unsettled all whose gaze they fell on. Warwick shifted his feet and waited unsure of what might come next.

"So, Warwick, is your work finished in that troublesome county?"

"No, my lord, I shall return tomorrow. The rebels who lived were promised a pardon, but I intend to punish them severely. The prisons already overflow and they don't deserve to go free."

"So you intend to disregard the terms of surrender?"

"Of course, what other way would you wish it, my lord?" Warwick replied with a faint smile.

They were interrupted by a sound not unlike small stones thrown against the casement and Seymour stormed to the window, a fiery expression on his face.

"If that's the king..." he glowered about to lift the catch.

A smile relieved his face of its peeved look when he saw that it was rain.

Chapter 35

Caught by a sudden rush of wind the drops slapped against the glass with the ferocity of lead shot. In seconds the garden took on a mystical look as the grass and trees were obscured by a heavy veil of low cloud. In the distance lightening exploded its electrical force over the river and Seymour rejoiced. Jubilant he clapped his hands and said.

"That settles it then. If the Almighty didn't hear my prayer, Thor did. No games in the garden for me, eh, Warwick? Come, we shall dine instead and you can tell me all about the salvation of the city of Norwich. It's a fine way to end the day I think. What say you?"

Warwick managed an hour of sleep before he left London for Norwich. His escort at his heels he rode hard and stopped only when it was necessary to change horses. It was almost noon when they took the last rise in the road and saw the great spire of the cathedral in front of them.

He signalled a halt and wiped the sweat from his face. The thought of the task ahead of him gave him little pleasure, for at times death sickened him, but he wouldn't consider any alternative. Nor would the city dignitaries permit one. With his arm raised to point a left turn he wheeled his horse and spurred on his mount in the direction of the Kings Camp.

A day's ride behind him, Captain Bury led his troop at a slower pace in order to stop outside Wymondham. Their orders were to identify the oak tree on the Common where Robert Kett with his brother addressed the peasants gathered at the start of the rebellion.

Early September offered a mellow day. Some weeks earlier the sun reached its zenith, but with the approach of autumn it sat lower in the sky. Close to the road gold light zigzagged through the rufous leaves of a stout oak and chased shadows down the crinkled bark. Bury stood up in his stirrups and shielded his eyes under the lip of his helmet. He looked round at the trees which bordered the open land with a copper beech in the centre. With a shake of his head he looked again at the oak on the verge.

"This must be the one," he said pointing. "I see no other like it. Are we agreed this is the tree my lord Warwick means?"

The squadron leader next to him nodded.

"I'm no expert on trees, Captain, but it seems the most likely. May I ask why we search for it?"

Bury leant forward and fondled the ear of his mount. His thin-lipped smile was brief. Then he straightened, adjusted the scarlet sash over his white jacket and said.

"We have to find it because the Earl of Warwick has plans for it that's why."

His companion looked puzzled.

"Plans, what sort of plans?"

Bury, more concerned they reach Norwich before sunset rattled his spurs, an impatient gesture which silenced the other.

"Instead of asking so many questions I suggest you rouse those idle whelps of yours," he said his head inclined towards the troops who sprawled on the grass behind them. "We march immediately to meet the Earl at the rebel's camp on Mousehold Heights."

Chastened, the young squadron leader turned his mount and shouted commands to his troops. When he turned back, the formation lined up behind him, Bury and his horse was already on the way back to the city.

— 36 —

Norwich

On the orders of Warwick, the survivors of the battle, over three hundred men were led into hastily made pens and held like cattle in the Market Place. There they were left for hours to be ridiculed and taunted by the citizens of Norwich.

Propped up in a corner Will tried to sleep, but the discomfort and noise made it impossible. His belly griped with hunger and he ached from being jostled by others. Earlier he'd made several tours in his search for his friends. Depressed by his failure to find them and supposing they were dead he drew his knees up to his chin, encircled them with his arms and rested his head. At least if he kept his eyes closed he was spared the sight of those who gloated at the rebels defeat.

For most of the morning they'd been the target for a hail of rotting vegetables and occasionally a fish or a boot so when he felt a thump on his shoulder he didn't react. He felt it again a deliberate blow and he opened his eyes. A wagon was drawn up close to the side of the pen and he faced one of Warwick's men.

Like the majority of the mercenaries the soldier was well muscled and stood wide and square shouldered. His Teutonic face showed neither concern nor mercy as he pushed Will and a few other rebels into line with an impatient hand. The other never left the haft of his broadsword. The breeze snatched wisps of blonde hair from under his helmet and pasted them across his broad cheeks. He flicked them away and each time his neck strained against the leather collar worn to protect his throat.

Will had no idea why nine of them had been singled out, but he made sure he remained at the rear. Still refusing to accept his companions were lost, he lingered deliberately and looked closely at every rebel he passed. Thom or Philip, surely one survived. It was a thought he'd clung to since their defeat.

The man at the head of the queue addressed the mercenary.

"Why do we travel like this? Where are you taking us?"

His reply was a prod in the back and a gesture to move onto the wooden step to the wagon whilst another heaved his bruised body up to follow. One after another they climbed in. The youth in front of Will limped forward and whimpered clutching his leg as he tried to raise it. One side of his breeches flapped open and revealed a horrific thigh injury. Crimson flesh gaped like a pair of pouted lips and the wound leaked odious yellow liquid which ran down his calf.

Will saw the mercenary take aim with his boot and in a stride he stood between them. He was far taller than the soldier and with his clenched fists and dark glower presented an ominous challenge.

"Foreign swag-belly," he growled. "Don't make me teach you a lesson. Can't you see the lad's hurt?"

Looking hard into the mercenary's sapphire blue eyes he saw nothing but stone in their depths. With a deliberate move he turned his back and supported the wounded rebel until he was seated on the floor of the wagon. The mercenary shrugged, but made no move to stop Will. Instead he lounged back fingering his sword.

"Very commendable," a voice said. "Now you know why you were picked. I asked for nine of the bravest and I'm not disappointed."

Warwick sat astride his horse watching with a sardonic smile. Will showed no fear as he spoke.

"We were pardoned, I don't understand. What is it we've been picked for?"

One in the wagon called "Aye, that's what I want to know," as he shuffled up to make room for Will. He squinted at Warwick. The rest of his head was swathed in a clumsy bloodstained dressing tied in a knot over his forehead leaving only one eye visible.

As he shifted in his saddle the links of Warwick's hauberk made a soft metallic rattle and the tail of his sash fluttered as the wind disturbed it. His voice mocked when he said.

"My apologies, gentlemen, I thought you would have been told. Indeed it is most remiss of us. We shall travel together to a place you will remember well, your so called King's Camp. It's not far, in fact just outside the city walls, but some of you would find the walk difficult. How many weeks were you there? Six, perhaps seven I'm told. Robert Kett and his brother sat in judgement under an oak tree, did they not? What was it called? Ah yes, The Oak of Reformation. I see some of you nod. By the time we reach there the gallows will have been built. Should you find such a short journey tedious you might pass the time deciding which of you will be the first to be hanged." He laughed, tipped his hand to his helmet and turned his horse away. "Shortly we shall meet again, I look forward to it," he called over his shoulder.

The vast crowds who traipsed up onto Mousehold Heights hadn't enjoyed such a spectacle for a long time. Whatever food or ale they could lay their hands on they brought with them. After weeks of tension, the citizens were ready to enjoy themselves. Had they been honest many would have confessed their support for the rebellion, yet when the battle was lost they sealed their lips and changed allegiance.

A flock of carrion crows wheeled around overhead or perched on the uppermost branches of the Reformation Oak. Beneath it, Warwick was ensconced in a comfortable chair to watch the executions. It seemed perhaps he favoured Will more than the others. Certainly he allowed him to watch the dismal deaths of the other eight rebels before his own. A stoic to the last, Will's face remained impassive throughout and with his hands clenched few saw the rivulets of blood which seeped out of the wounds his nails inflicted on his palms.

The youth with the leg wound was the last before Will. His violent trembling made it difficult for the attendants to lash him to the wooden hurdle and as the last leather thong made him secure he voided his bladder. The crowd cheered with delight as a dark stain pooled on the ground.

A black-garbed cleric stepped forward and stood at his head to dangle a silver cross in front of the youth's frightened face. His mediocre voice intoned the well practised words.

"My son, you have been found guilty of treason. That is you have acted unlawfully against our Sovereign King, Edward, and his Government, his Ministers and the State. You have shown no repentance nor asked for mercy. Therefore in accordance with our Law the punishment shall be death. You have been brought to this place to be hung, drawn and quartered. Have you anything to say?"

There was no reply from the youth. His lips moved at speed, but whatever he said was a silent conversation. Ashen faced he kept his eyes tightly shut and his white knuckles poked through the taut skin of his thin hands. Unable to watch any longer, Will bowed his head. He feared for the boy, yet strangely had no such concerns for himself.

It wasn't difficult for him to follow the grisly process. He had only to listen to the crowds. Soon their voices reached an exhilarated roar and when he heard the soft slapping sound of flesh on flesh he knew the youth had suffered the final obscene assault on his body. In four quarters he joined the bloody pile of tissue on the wagon which later would deliver the rebel's remains for exhibition in the Market Place.

When two mercenaries came for him, Will glanced towards the audience of nobility who sat with Warwick. Despite the knot of emotion in his gut he kept his gaze firm when he and Warwick locked eyes. Cold blue steel appraised him without emotion and Will knew there would be no reprieve. Warwick bent his head to listen to a remark by one of his companions and laughed.

Will moved his shoulders on the hurdle. He must have lost weight because sharp bumps in the wood dug into his back and he knew he was too tall for it when he felt his heels drag on the ground as they approached the gallows.

At first the noise from the crowd remained an indistinct hum. Will closed his eyes.

"My son, you have been found guilty of treason..." the cleric recited.

The words floated into Will's conscious mind, drifted there and lost themselves in the music. He and Rosie were dancing a jig to old George Parker's pipe and both the holy man and the excited voices of the spectators were an unwelcome intrusion.

He felt the rough hemp chafe his neck and tried to shake it free, but Rosie wanted to go faster. His eyes flickered open to catch sight of the laughter on her pretty face, but she spun him so quickly he couldn't focus. The spiral made him dizzy as they whirled and whirled...

− 37 −

Tower of London

The Constable of The Tower bowed low as Seymour dismounted. On a quadrangle of grass a brown bear wearing a collar and chain paid little attention to the scene. The movement of people happened too often to stir his curiosity besides when he sniffed the air no one carried food. Having raised his head he then returned to his doze.

"If I understand correctly you have come to see one of the prisoners, my lord. He is indeed fortunate you take an interest in him," the Constable said as he led the way under Traitors Gate.

"I'm not exactly interested in him it's more a matter of unsettled business. Where are you keeping him?" Seymour asked briskly.

"In the Bell Tower, my lord, with the others, both the Kett brothers and the man called Barwick," the Constable replied.

Seymour smiled. "It's very satisfying wouldn't you say, all four ringleaders who held Norwich to ransom here to enjoy His Majesty's hospitality. Is there any word when their trials begin?"

"I haven't heard, my lord."

Recent rain had pooled on the cobbles and dripped from the stained stone walls. Seymour gathered his cloak tighter to his body and side-stepped the water where he could. The air was cold here and few who passed under the Gate could resist a shiver. He wondered if that was the reason for the sudden chill which struck him or perhaps he was remembering his brother's recent end.

They left the light behind them when they started up the narrow stairs. As they climbed Seymour felt the bone-crunching cold ooze from the walls. The Constable fumbled with his torch, when a draught wrapped itself round the flame and pulled it in all directions. Shadows created macabre shapes on the grey flags and a shudder ran through Seymour as a rat emerged from them and narrowly missed his feet.

Straining his eyes to peer through the gloom on the stairway Seymour was forced to rely on the Constable's legs as a guide. With so little fresh air damp and mould added a fusty smell to the atmosphere and Seymour began to regret his decision to visit Philip.

Outside a massive iron-girded door the Constable reached for the bunch of keys on his belt, but Seymour restrained him.

"I shan't need to go into the cell. This will be close enough."

The Constable gazed at him a moment in silence then said. "As you wish, my lord," and slid back the grille.

"You understand this is a private visit," Seymour said in a low voice.

He saw the curious look cross the man's face, but he had no intention of enlightening him.

"Indeed, my lord, you can be assured of my discretion."

"Very well you may leave. I'll call when I'm finished."

The Constable turned on his heel and disappeared into the darkness. Seymour slowly approached the door. At first he only saw the spindle of light from the slit in the flints and a wall decorated with thumb-screws, bracelets, collars and pincers. When he looked down, he barely recognised the creature who sprawled on the soiled floor of the dungeon. A cloak thrown over his body hardly concealed Philip's nakedness and his feet were bloodied from lack of toenails.

It was the face which appalled him the most. He'd once thought it pretty, but now it bore the look of a spectre. Ragged locks and a tangled beard added to the wasted appearance, but it was Philip's eyes which Seymour was drawn to. They seemed to smoulder in the dark pits where they rested. No defeat registered in them, more a spirited defiance. It was a painful surprise for Seymour. How could a man in these circumstances offer such a challenge? He struggled to understand the feeling of pity which overwhelmed him when he looked at Philip. Not even his brother in the moments before his death had managed that. It was Philip who spoke first.

"Why, my lord Seymour it is really you? I never thought I would be worthy of such an esteemed visitor. Are you satisfied, my lord, with what you've seen?"

Philip croaked his words and his wry laugh was no more than a cackle torn from his parched throat. Seymour allowed his weight to slump against the door.

"I'm sorry, Philip, I would have hoped to see you looking better."

"Better, in here with maggot bread and rats for company. Surely you jest, my lord. The torture was hardly bearable, but the vermin disgust me more."

Seymour collected his thoughts and endeavoured to overcome his compassion.

"It could have been very different, Philip, you do understand that don't you? What possessed you to leave the court? I'd have looked after you?"

"I found a more worthy cause, my lord," Philip replied and licked away the drops of blood which seeped out of the cracks in his lips.

It wasn't what Seymour wanted to hear and his mettle returned. He straightened himself and his words were brusque.

Chapter 37

"It's a pity you were so stupid, now it's too late to listen to your grievances. The rebellion is over and the king is most relieved. There is nothing more to say."

"So why did you come, my lord? I thought when I saw it was you, there might be a pardon."

Seymour shook his head and said softly.

"I couldn't even if I wanted to. The country needs to understand there is no place for those who rise up against the Crown. There must be punishments, you do understand, don't you, Philip?"

Philip struggled to his knees. The cloak slipped away and Seymour winced at the raised wheals and blackberry-coloured bruising which covered Philip's flesh.

"Surely, my lord, when I explain at my trail how so many are forced to beg and steal just to feed themselves. That others have stolen their land."

"No, Philip, please don't raise your hopes. There will be no trial, not for you or the man called Barwick. The Privy Council has decided only the leaders Robert and William Kett will go in front of the judge. Not to be heard of course since you are all guilty of high treason and must take the consequences. However it's a gesture to keep the tongues still of any who misguidedly believed in your so called up-rising."

His head bowed, Philip sighed and his eyes dulled.

"So be it, I have little spirit to fight anymore but what of the good men who surrendered at Dussindale? I hear they were all granted the king's pardon," he said.

"They have all been hung. The citizens of Norwich expected it, nay, demanded it. The Earl of Warwick had no choice," Seymour said firmly.

Philip's composure vanished replaced by a look of horror. When Seymour saw it he felt a moment of sorrow. He'd always been divided in mind about how best he should manage the enclosed land issue. In weak moments he might easily confess to having some sympathy for the poor commons, but then again there was the matter of keeping law and order.

"Then let Warwick and the swag-bellies who hung them drown in their own bile," Philip snarled.

He slumped to the floor and drew the cloak over his head. Seymour waited for a moment then slammed the grille shut and called for the Constable.

"I shall make arrangements for all four prisoners to be moved to Norfolk in the next few weeks. They will be discharged out of your custody to the High Sheriff of Norwich. Meanwhile see to it de Montfort has wine with his bread when he next has a meal," he said as they travelled back down the dank stairs.

On his way to the palace he remembered he'd never answered Philip's question as to why he'd visited him. The more he thought about it, Seymour realised he didn't know himself.

– 38 –

When the halberdier pushed him, Thom fell hard against the rough stone wall. Hindered by his ankle shackle he's been unable to save himself. The sharp edges of flint tore through the flesh of his shoulder and forearm leaving cuts which bled in spurts. As he blundered out into the light he screwed up his eyes against the bright glare. The halberdier moved him on with a prod from his lance.

"Hurry up we don't want to keep the Captain waiting. Just think you're going back to the heathen land of yours. Nice that. I hear the people of Norwich like nothing more than seeing one of their own hang. And this time there will be four of you fresh for the noose."

Rough and vulgar-looking he sniggered loudly, cleared his throat and deposited a gob of phlegm on the cobbles in front of Thom, who with clenched fists did his best to step over it. Then he shuffled awkwardly under an arch and round the corner of a tower.

Two lines of halberdiers were assembled on the green and beyond them Thom could see three more prisoners already seated on horses. Each was chained to an escort who rode beside them. He and Philip had not been parted long, but it was the first time he'd seen Robert or William since their arrest.

Thom wondered how they'd fared in the terrible conditions. No better than him, he was sure, yet all survived. Time hung heavy day after day. Did they use their nails to scratch marks on the damp walls as some had done in his dungeon or strained to reach the window slit just to breathe fresh air? They must have thought of their families too. As he thought about his beloved Martha; lost in his reverie the halberdier's wrench on the chain reminded him their ordeal was not over yet.

Once they reached the grass Thom was close enough to greet his friends. They'd all been ill-treated and he knew he looked no better than them. Nonetheless he was shocked. Unable to support himself Philip lay against his mount's neck. Robert and William looked better although the conditions they'd endured left them gaunt and they appeared very frail. He noticed William's left hand appeared shrivelled and he moved his arm with awkward stiffness.

Both brothers smiled faintly when they saw him, but it didn't spread to their eyes nor alter their torn mouths and bruised faces. All were dressed in ill-fitting clothes which were torn and stained and they were without boots. Their time for conversation was short.

"I'm sorry," Thom muttered.

He looked for reproach, but there was none.

"No matter," Robert said with a resigned shrug. "William and I discussed it many times. We were both prepared to give our lives."

"And what of your trial?" Thom asked.

The halberdiers closest frowned at William's loud laughter.

"What tomfoolery that was. We were both taken to the law courts in the Star Chamber at Westminster. When we got there the Judge already wore his black square. Neither of us spoke nor did anyone speak to us. No accusation was read and we were sentenced without trial. It was as we thought. The Judge mumbled something, the Privy Councillors agreed and we were led away. We expected no less, eh, brother."

"You there, enough talking," one of the halberdier's shouted. "Captain Bury is due any moment. He will be escorting you ruffians back to Norwich."

Rough hands separated Thom from the others and he found he was at the back of the file. As they moved off he turned for a last look at the Tower. Its forbidding stone walls took on a silvery gloss as fine drizzle dampened them and he shivered. Loathe them as he did, he knew that what lay ahead made them seem almost benevolent.

The journey was unremarkable. A steady plod mile after mile, then they'd passed Wymondham and would soon reach the Common and then Norwich before dusk. After Cambridge, they encountered few people and even less homesteads. Rural Norfolk offered both solitude and peace as if the world there slowed.

Apprehensive as he was, Thom found himself nodding off with the tedium of his horse's rhythmic tread. Even the halberdiers rode in silence so when they turned the bend in the road they too were startled by the sudden commotion.

Rooks darkened the sky as they wheeled and spun in noisy circles above a tree on the verge. Thom saw it was the gnarled oak where they'd gathered before they marched on the city three months before. Only from where they halted it looked dark and distorted.

As if he relished the sight, Captain Bury stood up in his stirrups with a triumphant wave of his hand and pointed to the tree. Then he turned his horse and led them closer. Thom repressed a groan as it became obvious what hung from the branches. As he absorbed the full horror his heart pounded and he could hardly draw breath.

This was where they had all stood with the Kett brothers bonded by hope. Never did they think the oak would claim such bounty before autumn stripped its leaves. The boughs strained under the weight of bodies.

Only this was no arbour with branches laden with fruit. What had fallen already spoiled the ground in heaps of rotting bundles. The stench in the air overwhelmed all who took breath and filled them with revulsion.

Thom tried to catch the eye of his companions, but others blocked his view. Captain Bury raised his arm and the chain between Thom and his escort tightened as the halberdier moved off. Thom's heart slowed again, but he wouldn't look back.

"Not a pretty sight, eh, rebel," the halberdier beside him mocked.

When they reached the city walls he managed to exchange a glance with Robert. The grief in his eyes was pitiful to see, but like his brother his head was held high and despite the circumstances they looked a dignified pair. Not so, Philip. Thom feared for him when he saw his wan face and weak state, but the curious crowds gathered to wait for their arrival pressed close to the horses and he lost sight of him.

Thom recognised Edmund Wyndham, High Sheriff of Norfolk, who rode across the Market Place to meet them. Behind him a single body wrapped in chains swung from the gibbet on Gaol Hill. Another sat battered and slumped in the pillory close by and even more horrible a smouldering heap of faggots and debris told of a recent burning. Distressed, Thom wrenched his eyes away from what he knew was a place of slaughter for more of the rebels. So much for the pardon he thought bitterly.

Their progress to the Guild Hall was accompanied by angry shouts and jeers from those who looked on with obvious malice. Many tried to reach out to clutch at them or aimed their spit with precision as they passed. Some beat drums with a slow tattoo, others yelled obscenities. Halberdiers flourished their lances and several held Boar spears which they jabbed at the crowd to keep them back.

When they finally reached the Guild Hall, Thom breathed a sigh of relief. Even though they were to be imprisoned in the dungeons, he fancied it would be more congenial than having to face the hostile townsfolk. Wyndham waited for them in the Grand Hall on the first floor. He gave a cursory nod as they were led in their chains to stand in front of him. Philip needed support from a halberdier, but still he swayed and with a small gesture of compassion, Wyndham indicated he might have a chair.

Of medium height and build, Wyndham's high cheek bones, pinched mouth and stony look assured them of his hard demeanour. His distinctive badge of office hung from a splendid chain round his neck, the gold a match for the ornate buckles on the front of his shoes. A bony hand held a thin cane which he tapped with measured pace on the table beside him. The other held a sheet of parchment which he took a moment to consult.

"*Step forward when I say your name,*" he said. "*Master Robert Kett, Master William Kett,*

Thom Barwick, Philip de Montfort. You have all been found guilty of high treason, in that you carried arms without the king's permission and in so doing rose up against the Crown and incited others to do the same. On the instructions of the Earl of Warwick, you are to be held here until such time as you be taken to a place where you shall be hung from the neck until you are dead. The warrant is signed by Lord Edward Seymour, Lord Protector, on behalf of His Majesty, King Edward the Sixth."

Only Philip broke the eerie silence in the room. His eyes bulged in his haggard face, his teeth chattered and he began a series of loud whimpers. Thom saw the look of savage satisfaction on Wyndham's face as he signalled to one of the halberdiers. He motioned with his hand to the bowed and terrified man and said. "Take him away."

Philip was part carried and part dragged out of the room. As Thom watched he wondered if his friend would survive long enough to feel the hangman's noose around his neck.

Later in the day the sun was low in the sky and threw its beam directly onto the exquisite colours of the stained glass windows of the Assembly Room in the Guild Hall. In turn they illuminated the panelled walls and turned them into burnished timbers of the finest mahogany. Those gathered within were personal guests of Warwick and numbered civic notables, affluent city merchants and esteemed members of Norwich society.

Amongst them Thomas Codde loitered in front of the heavy laden tables and deliberated on the sweetmeats, pickled oysters, boiled capons, dried tongues and other delicacies which tempted his palate. He was also anxious to speak to Warwick who held court at one end of the room. Watching him carefully, Codde sidled nearer until his courage and a lull in conversation allowed him to attract Warwick's attention. He gave him an obsequious smile.

"I wondered if I might speak with you, my lord."

"What is it, Mayor, I cannot spare you long. Now we have the traitors here at the Guild Hall, Lord Seymour is insistent I keep him informed of the arrangements for them next week. I leave for London shortly."

"My lord, I just wanted to thank you for your excellent command. I know I speak for all the citizens of this fine city when I tell you we are most grateful to you for ending the nuisance caused by Kett and his peasant following."

Warwick sipped his spiced wine thoughtfully. "Don't be too sure this is the end of it," he said with a sage look. We should not be too complacent. Ownership of land has caused problems for years. The only answer to such up-risings is to crush them without pity. That's why Kett and the other ringleaders must be made an example of, peasants must know their place."

"Indeed," Codde murmured without moving.

Draining his wine, Warwick summoned a page who carried a ceramic flask among the guests.

"Well, was there something else?" he snapped at Codde whilst holding out his goblet to be filled.

Codde shifted uneasily. "I just wondered whether any more peasants should be punished. I recognise some who I'm sure followed Kett, who walk freely in the city."

"More? God's blood, Codde, if all the common people are done away with who will be left to work for us? Have you thought of that?"

Rebuked, Codde mumbled his reply. "No, I hadn't, my lord."

"Don't look so miserable, Codde. I'm thinking there shall be a day of festivities after the punishments have been carried out, so Norwich may celebrate their escape from rebellious men who would harm your city. Surely that will cheer you?"

Not wishing to anger Warwick further, Codde forced a smile.

"Indeed it does, my lord, thank you."

– 39 –

7th December

Winding stairs led down to the crypts of the Guild Hall. At a fork in the dim passageway the prisoners were taken separate ways. The Kett brothers were ushered to the right whilst Thom found himself pushed to the left. He heard his name and looked back.

"Thom, farewell my friend, I'll pray for you. May our end be swift and God show us his everlasting love," Robert called.

"May the Lord have mercy on our souls," Thom replied.

He raised his hand and in the gloom saw theirs lifted in return. Then moved on by a rough tug of their chains they both vanished from view. Thom knew it was likely the next time they'd be together would be on the executioner's handcart.

Behind him the slam of the door was final and the bolts rattled into place. There was no shortage of stale air, but the only light came from a torch in a sconce high in an arch of the wall outside the cell. It burnt feebly and threw a weak glimmer on the dank stone before it filtered through a small grille set at the top of the stout oak door. It was the only relief in the otherwise impenetrable blackness.

By holding out his arms Thom touched the walls on either side and tried to judge the size of his cell. Fixed to a ring set firm in the flint floor his chain allowed him to measure two strides either way. Even the cell in the Tower permitted him more freedom than this coffin-like room, he thought. He wondered how long it would take for madness to set in.

Despondent he sat down and reached for the beaker and wooden platter on the floor. The water tasted brackish and when he put the bread to his lips he could smell mould and the musky smell of a rodent. Hunger forced him to nibble a mouthful and as he chewed he pondered if there was any means of escape. Realising it was a futile thought he shuffled until his back rested against the damp wall and closed his eyes.

Thom's time in the Tower had taken its toll. Sunk in apathy, he made no effort to recall how long he'd been incarcerated in the crypt. The occasional sounds which filtered down to him from the rooms above soon lost importance as his moods swung from despair to derangement. At first he played games; pretended they'd triumphed in the rebellion and even accused the warder of his wrongful arrest. The warder just grinned and left him another bowl of slop.

He talked to Martha and dreamt of her too. They made plans for when they were together again, but he when he woke and found he was still alone in the cell, he'd blubbed like a child. As the days passed he grew more depressed and his fanciful notions stopped.

When the time came on a dismal morning in early December, he lay curled up on the floor in his usual position.

"You are summoned, Master Barwick," the warder said as he helped him to his feet.

Thom's reply was a grunt. Older than most with a kindly face the warder helped him change into a rough tunic then led him out of the cell. Thom stumbled up the spiral stone stairs in the dark and when he stepped into the courtyard behind the Guild Hall the light pained his eyes. His back was bent and his gait awkward as he shuffled behind the warder. With his hair and beard grown as one, it shrouded his pallid face so most of his features were lost apart from his lack-lustre eyes.

A small group of onlookers stood in silence as he passed. They watched with passive interest, only later would their excitement take hold. The warder led the way across the green to where men were at work putting together the woven panels which made up a hurdle. Another already completed was propped against the wall. The sight of them instilled a moment of fear in Thom. His imprisonment left him weak and he had difficulty shaking off his feebleness. Then from somewhere within him he felt the spirit he thought he'd lost and the fire returned to his eyes.

"I don't go alone then?" he said firm-voiced, his nod indicating the two hurdles. "Who else travels with me?"

"Master Robert Kett," the warder said over his shoulder. "You're both going up to the castle. You should feel honoured. The Earl of Warwick has travelled up from London especially to see you both hang," the warder said in a civil tone.

They stopped beside a gate which at that moment swung open to admit a troop of halberdiers. They were dressed in striped hose of black and fawn embroidered on the front and at the back with the royal blazon woven in gold. Each carried a halberd stave decorated with gold tassels. Filing off to the left and right, they formed two long lines extending to the corner of the green. The warder felt in his pocket and pulled out a length of yarn.

"Its orders," he said as he pulled back Thom's unwashed hair and tied it.

To be without the matted curtain was a relief and a pale smile hovered on Thom's lips. He knew it was less about his comfort and more for the benefit of the hangman but he was grateful just the same.

"Thank you," he mumbled.

The approach of winter made the air cool, but after the rancid odours in the crypt, Thom inhaled each lungful with gratitude as they waited.

"Is there anything else you want to know?" the warder asked pleasantly.

Thom was glad of the conversation it made things feel normal for a short while at least.

"You held Master William Kett and one called Philip de Montfort. Are they still here?"

The warder shook his head.

"Best you can do is pray for their souls," he said. "William Kett was hung from the west tower of Wymondham Abbey yesterday and de Montfort was burnt at the stake in the Market Place last night. I'm surprised you didn't smell it in the vaults. It was as if God himself was mightily displeased the way those faggots collapsed and roared round the poor wretch."

Thom was sure there was pity reflected in the gentle brown-eyed gaze as the warder looked at him. But there was no time for more. A halberdier holding two horses beckoned and as he did so, Thom saw Robert appear from another door. At the same time two monks stepped forward and moved to take their place one beside each hurdle. Both had a large rosary which hung from their wrist and their brown robes fluttered round their feet with each slow step.

Thom saw Robert was also bare-footed and clothed in grey sackcloth. Their eyes met for an instant and then the warder's hand guided him down onto the hurdle. The chains felt heavy across his chest and rubbed the skin of his wrists and ankles. He'd barely eaten a spoonful of thin porridge, but he tasted bile and sweat broke out on his brow. With determined effort he bit down on his lip and prayed for strength.

Tormented by the thought of William and Philip, Thom was no longer filled with detached indifference but a mix of rage and despair. When the pious face of the monk looked down on him he turned his head away. He felt the monk's hand laid on his and the cold flesh made him recoil.

"Repent and save your soul," the holy man said with zeal.

"If you were truly God's man, you would know what injustice has been served when we only sought to take back what belonged to us. Instead you try to force your popish words into my ears. I will have none of your despicable beliefs. Be gone, I have no need of you or your succour," Thom said bitterly.

The monk raised his eyebrows heavenwards and said.

"God loves us all, my son. I shall pray for your soul nonetheless."

"As you wish," Thom muttered.

Tethered to the hurdles the horses moved away followed by a procession of onlookers, officers of the army, and the escort of halberdiers. At the rear the two monks were hurriedly joined by an old priest. Dressed in black silk he carried a lighted taper in a massive silver candlestick and as they slowly moved off he could be heard chanting a doleful dirge.

One behind the other Thom and Robert began their last journey through the Market Place, up Gaol Hill and into the castle grounds. The horses were deliberately slowed so everyone could witness the spectacle. It seemed that the whole of Norwich wished to watch them pass and their eager pushes and shoves sent many into the odious puddles of putrefaction underfoot.

Spread on the hurdle, Thom's thin frame felt every jolt on the cobbles and he winced at the discomfort. At the sight of Thom and Robert, sighs were audible and sympathisers soon silenced any hostility. A faded-faced young woman managed to break through the spectators outside the Guild Hall. With red, work-roughened hands held out she ran first to Robert and then Thom. Tears streamed down her face and her words were cracked and broken.

"God bless you, sirs. You did all you could for us. One day we'll be free and 'tis you we must thank."

Sour-faced and rough with her, a halberdier dragged her away and pushed her back amongst the throng. Thom could still hear her distraught voice long after she disappeared.

The slope up to the castle was the worst. Both horses laboured under their load. Thrown from one side of the hurdle to the other, Thom felt his bones crunch on the uneven cobbles. He stared up at the sullen grey of heavy cloud. He hoped it wouldn't rain and then wondered why he was bothered.

On the level ground which was the fore-building in front of the keep, the hurdle jerked and stopped. The chains fell away and heavy hands seized him. Knowing it was useless Thom offered no resistance. Wrenched to his feet he stumbled and would have fallen had he not been tightly gripped by both arms. It was painful to move and when he tried to raise his head his neck muscles were stiff.

When he managed to straighten he looked around. There was no sign of Robert and the crowd was different. Now the assembled audience were illustrious visitors, uniformed knights, peers of the realm and other fancily dressed notables. He recognised the Sheriff and Mayor Codde amongst them. Codde seemed unable to keep still. He rocked up and down on the balls of his feet in his attempt to see over the heads of his taller companions. Every so often he mopped his brow with a voluminous spotted kerchief.

In the front row sat the Earl of Warwick, elegant in his gold-trimmed grey silk tunic, his breast heavy with elaborate insignia. Without his helmet his shoulder length granite-coloured hair merged with his neatly trimmed beard. With his hooded lids and well fleshed nose his was an autocratic face. He sat with his legs crossed, beating a tune on his knee with one hand. The movement sent out pin-points of light reflected from the rubies and opals set in the thick twists of his gold ring.

The new gallows were barely finished. Two carpenters sent the final nails into the crossbeam with a precise tapping sound and then moved silently away. Thom stared at it and saw Robert with his escort. As he mounted the steps, Robert supported himself against one of the posts. Bare-headed he appeared a small yet dignified figure. The links of chain that festooned his neck made it a grotesque collar the weight of which bowed his shoulders. Salt tears filled Thom's eyes in such a rush he was blinded, but with both arms held firm by his escorts he was unable to raise a hand to clear them.

Distorted by his blurred vision it seemed to Thom the phantom which was Robert shimmered back and forth. Somewhere close a bell tolled, a single bass note and the hangman stepped into view. Robert's nod was unmistakable and the onlookers gasped simultaneously.

The hangman indicated with his hand and bent towards his prisoner. In a swift move, Robert was hoisted by his neck his body flew upwards and dangled. He swung unhindered. Just as quickly the hangman removed the noose whilst the halberdier raised a white cloth as a signal to those below. Then he and a soldier eased the body over the battlement and guided it down to hang from the wall. One of the chains was looped over a metal ring set in the flint so Robert was suspended for all to see. His body rolled against the stone and as it did so the wind plucked his fair hair and blew it in all directions.

Thom's dismal groan went unheard in the loud clamours of appreciation. He shivered and felt ice flood his veins. One amongst the crowd pushed his way out of the throng and strolled past the keep to the castle steps. When he reached the foot of them he looked back with a smile. John Flowerdew was enjoying the moment.

He couldn't remember the day he first lusted after Alice Kett. Now he could well imagine her as the lonely widow with her children huddled to her, desperate for a father. Patience, perseverance and a little caution were all that were needed for him to take her as his mistress, he told himself. With his fingers on his scar he felt malicious pleasure when he glanced up at the body. All those years ago when Robert's billhook raked his flesh to the bone, he remembered what he'd said at him.

"One day Kett, you'll answer for this," he'd blustered through the warm blood which trickled into his mouth. "I'll have that woman, you see if I don't. Alice shall be mine. It's only a matter of time."

The same sensation he'd felt then as he'd watched Robert shrug and walk away was back in the pit of his belly as he experienced an acidic outpouring of jealousy which burnt the lining of his gut.

"Well, you're not so sure of yourself now, are you Master Kett?" Flowerdew muttered through gritted teeth as he sauntered towards the Market Place.

Thom could hear relaxed conversation from the crowd and Warwick beckoned. This time he indicated Thom should be brought nearer. Determined his shake wouldn't be seen, he stiffened his legs and shuffled forward.

"So, Barwick," Warwick said. "I thought you should see Master Kett set an example before you join him. What price your leader now, eh? I have no idea how long it will take him to die, but it will be days, I can assure you. Later he'll be tarred and left to swing until piece by piece he rots away. It will remind hasty men of the reward of rebellion. But take heart, I intend to return *you* to the citizen's of this good city to do what they will with you."

His fingers snapped crisply and a group of halberdiers appeared from the Great Hall. They struggled to carry the oblong, rust-coloured lump of oak which they set down with a loud thump. It was the quartering block. The onlookers shuffled their feet and smiled in anticipation...

– After Events –

Edward V1 (1537–1553) was crowned King in 1547 aged 9 years after the death of his father, Henry V111. He died aged 15 from tuberculosis.

Lady Jane Grey was appointed his heir, but ruled for only nine days. She was beheaded and succeeded by Edward's half sister, Mary Tudor (Bloody Mary)

What of Seymour himself? Edward Seymour (1506-1552) was appointed as Lord Protector at the time of Edward's minority. He was held responsible for the protests, rebellions and riots and was removed from power in 1549 and imprisoned in the Tower of London.

Released by Dudley after a year, he made a failed attempt to overthrow Dudley and was executed for the crime of Felony.

Edward V1 noted in his Chronicle *'The Duke of Somerset had his head cut off upon Tower Hill between eight and nine o'clock in the morning.'*

The Earl of Warwick, John Dudley (1504–1553) succeeded him. He was tried in 1553 and died on the scaffold.

The rebellion in Norfolk was to be the last great movement by English people in social revolt. Over a period of six weeks Norwich was turned into a bloodbath and in the bitter battle over 4000 people died, the losses greatest amongst the peasants.

The Oak of Reformation at Mousehold was felled to make way for a car park. Kett's Oak still stands filled with concrete, braced and supported on the old road near Heathersett between Wymondham and Norwich.

Until the eighteenth century church bells were rung in Norwich on 27th August to commemorate the city's deliverance from the rebellion. Attitudes changed and in 1949 a plaque was put up outside Norwich Castle on which is written:

'In 1549 AD Robert Kett yeoman farmer of Wymondham was executed by hanging in this castle after the defeat of the Norfolk Rebellion of which he was the leader. In 1949 AD, four hundred years later, his memorial was placed here by the citizens of Norwich in reparation and honour to a notable and courageous leader in the long struggle of the common people of England to escape from a servile life into the freedom of just conditions.'

There is also a plaque in Wymondham close to Market Street erected in 1999 to commemorate Robert Kett and his fight for justice for the common man.

"*I am ready to do whatever not only to repress, but to subdue the power of great men.*" *Robert Kett reported 1549.*

Robert Kett was no lower class peasant. He came from an old and prosperous family and owned many manors himself. All the property of Robert and William Kett was confiscated and given to the Crown. In 1558 Robert Kett's grandson was burnt as a Nonconformist heretic by order of Elizabeth 1.

– About the author –

Margaret Callow lives in a village to the north of Norwich with her family. Working for most of her life as a health professional, she has always found time to write poetry, much of which has been published.

A growing fascination for social history, particularly in the lives of working people developed and *A Rebellious Oak*, her first novel, is the result.

Margaret is currently working on her next book, also set in Norfolk.